THE LAST TIGER

Also by Anthony Lavisher

The Storm Trilogy
Whispers of a Storm
Shadows of a Storm
Vengeance of a Storm

With Jamie Wallis
Vengeance

Anthony Lavisher

The Last Tiger

[signature]

07.08.21

This edition published by Kindle Direct Publishing 2021.

Copyright © Anthony Lavisher 2021
Cover design by © Judit Pasti 2021

Anthony Lavisher has asserted his right to be identified as the author of the Work in accordance with the Copyright, Designs and Patents Act 1988.

All rights reserved. No part of this publication may be reproduced, stored in a retrieval system, or transmitted in any form or by any means without the prior written permission of the author.

Published in the United Kingdom by Kindle Direct Publishing.

ISBN 979-8-72-766491-9

All characters in this publication are fictitious and any resemblance to persons real or dead is purely coincidental or used by permission.

For Hamid.

Acknowledgements

On a trip to India in 2005 I met the most amazing man. His love and passion for his homeland was infectious, and we fast became friends. On the adventure that followed the idea for this story began to stir, and in the coming years, upon my return to that most amazing of countries, our friendship and the idea for this tale became even stronger.

I would like to thank Hamid Shah and his family for their friendship, their kindness and inspiration, and my wife Amy, for holding my hand on our adventures.

To Ken Griffiths, my friend and agent, for helping me to pursue and realise my dreams, and to Emma Hatton, Debbie Morgan and Dannii Elle, for ensuring that I did not get carried away with myself.

A special mention should go to Charlotte Rees, for her care, diligence and suggestions that were invaluable to finishing the manuscript.

Further appreciation must go to Judit Pasti for her glorious cover art, and to all of you, for continuing to journey with me on my adventures.

Here's to the next one we are about to share...

CHAPTER ONE

Fortunes

The flames leaping out of the jet's engines were raging wildly now, forcing the light aircraft to pitch and drop rapidly through the dark cloud cover as it dived towards the earth thirty thousand feet below.

What had started out as a promising day for Jon Galnia was rapidly going downhill now, and as he dug what nails he had left into the arms of the black leather seat, he struggled to keep down his lunch. Anything not belted up or stowed away flew about the luxurious cabin, crashing into seats, windows and everything that got in the way.

The jet dropped again, sending Jon's stomach back into his mouth as he choked on his own fear and ducked down into his seat to avoid the whisky glass that zipped past his head to smash on the door of the cockpit, several metres away from him. Crystal glasses were easily replaced – it was the loss of the fifteen-year-old bottle of Dalwhinnie that pissed him off. Despite his predicament, he managed to scowl at the broken screen of the large tv, from where the rich amber liquid now dripped enticingly. He had plenty of bottles in his cellar at home, but he hated to waste a good single malt.

As if to remind Jon of the immediate danger, the captain's voice broke worriedly over the klaxon that sounded its warning inside the jet.

"*We have lost both engines, Mr. Galnia,*" he apologised, his English accent trying to retain some composure. "*It is inexplicable! Our engineers checked the jet over as normal before we took off from Moscow.*"

Jon fumbled for the communications button on the seat's left console and flicked at it. "I don't want excuses as to why and how – just fucking land us safely."

"*Yes, Mr. Galnia.*"

Jon swore furiously and punched the switch off as he heard the co-pilot beginning to mutter something. He couldn't believe this was happening to him. Everything had been going so perfectly for him recently, since his lawyers had managed to get the IRS off his back. Using his father's old contacts, he had destroyed the paper-trail that led the Feds to his door and framed one of his competitors. It was amazing what a couple of million dollars could do when you wafted it under the nose of an unscrupulous lawyer; and if you could follow that up with a few threats to the families of the investigators who were getting too close to the truth, your problems just seemed to disappear.

Despite the new regime's softening on immigration, the American authorities were still paranoid about attacks on their home soil, so much so that it was embarrassingly easy to make it look like his main competitor – an Egyptian – was laundering money to help fund and set up terrorist training camps in Arizona. *All too easy*! Finger a few lesser players for being involved, and Jon's Guardian Angels had managed to kill quite a few birds with one very expensive stone.

Six months of legitimate business dealings with his electronics trading company '*Galnia Global Industries*' whilst channelling his dirty money through shell companies, had also managed to alleviate some of the heat and suspicion that was still floating around. Nobody was stupid enough to think that Jon, the only heir to the fortune and power of the notorious Giovanni Galnia was clean. It was just that nobody had been clever enough, so far, to prove anything to the contrary.

Jon was in no doubt, however, that he had got lucky this time and because of this, he had decided to turn his attentions to his Russian operations whilst he allowed his wife, Maria, to run the electronics company; carrying on with its legitimate trade from China and Taiwan.

Whilst he kept out of the heat, it was time, Jon had thought, to make some serious money out of the old Soviet Union and the business empire he had set up there over the last two decades, following his father's death.

Usually happy for things to run on the ground without him, Jon had enjoyed several months of distance governance, getting used to the taste of the Soviet streets again, finding the thrill of the game that he had not enjoyed playing stateside, the last few years.

But that extra dedication had brought with it unwanted attention, and after only a couple of months he had been forced to fly out to Moscow personally and placate those he had somehow managed to piss off without even being there.

Jon scowled as he thought about the events that had led him to this moment, and, as it appeared, his impending death. It felt like no matter what he tried to do these days, he always seemed to piss somebody off somewhere…

Sucking in a breath, he tried to calm himself, something he was never any good at. Despite his predicament, he caught himself thinking of the meeting he had been summoned to, and the woman he had met there to flesh out a deal that would placate those in the

Russian Mafia he had offended with the territory he had *acquired* over the last few years without their consent.

Licking his lips, Jon closed his eyes, still seeing her face, still smelling her perfume…

The jet shuddered again as it dropped down through the grey clouds, jolting Jon back to the present and the immediate danger that faced him. Fighting against his own fear, his anger and the G-forces at work inside the cabin, he held on to anything that could keep him in his seat and swore loudly as the jet protested again and slammed his head against the headrest.

John watched the chaos rage around him for a few moments, regaining his senses as hatches fell open before him and oxygen masks dropped from the ceiling around the cabin, twitching madly on their cords like the condemned from a gibbet.

He reached out vainly to grab at the oxygen mask spinning wildly about in the air before him. Behind him he heard a shriek as his long-serving cabin attendant Sara gave in to her fear. Straining to look over his shoulder, he could see the dark-haired Mexican, who had worked faithfully for him for eight years now, ashen-faced and struggling to stay in her seat at the rear of the jet. Their eyes met briefly through the billowing curtains, and he tried to convey his sympathy and lend her some of his own waning strength. Again, the elements flung him forward in his seat, and he grabbed hold of the oxygen mask as it hit him in the face.

Jon flicked at the communications button again. "Where are we, Robert?" Tugging down on the cords, he placed it over his mouth and nose and sucked gratefully on the air within for a few breaths.

"We are over Indian airspace, sir. Madhya Pradesh

region, in central India!"

"Can–" Jon's question was cut short as the Jet dropped several thousand feet again, buffeted and brutalised by fierce turbulence. "For fuck's sake!" he swore.

"*We have lost all outside external communications, sir,*" the pilot reported. "*I fear someone has compromised us*!"

"No shit!" Jon cursed, as he fumbled for his cellphone. Tapping in a code at the third attempt, he thumbed through his contacts, searching for Maria. Mumbling angrily to himself to distract the terror creeping into his bones, he sucked in another lungful of oxygen from the mask as he called his wife.

It appeared that the Solntsevskaya Brotherhood, the Mafioso he had pissed off in Mother-Russia, had decided to take over his interests after all, rather than having the perverse slice of the offered Galnia pie. They must have paid someone off in his ground crew at Vnukovo International to sabotage the jet, or further afield at Bahrain, when they stopped there to refuel.

If he got out of this in one piece, Jon was determined he was going to find out who had done this to him and make the bastards suffer. As he listened, almost patiently, to his wife's voice mail message, he wished that he had not agreed to 'drop' in on their interests in Taipei for her.

"…*get back to you sooner rather than later*!"

"Maria, it's me!" Jon said urgently, after the beep. "We are over central India – the jet's been compromised and we are in the shit. It seems the meeting didn't go quite as well as we were led to believe, honey."

The plane plummeted again and Jon nearly dropped the phone. "I don't know how I am going to get out of this one, but you need to get onto the Indian authorities and let them know we are going down." The realisation of what was happening suddenly hit home and Jon lost his train of thought. "I-I love you, Mari! Look after my son for me."

He locked the phone bitterly and placed it in his shirt pocket. Blue sky came suddenly racing into view through the cloud cover outside the jet's tiny windows, and bright sunlight spread throughout the cabin.

"*Brace yourselves – we are coming down fast!*" the pilot's voice ordered them, as he finally dispensed with any formalities.

Jon snapped a quick look out the window to his right, the blue sky lost in flames and trailing, thick black smoke. He caught the briefest glimpse of high, wooded hills on the horizon, before he put his head between his legs and tried to suck his dick.

Behind him, Sara Gonzales screamed. Before them, the earth reached up and plucked them from the sky.

CHAPTER TWO

Discord

Jon awoke with a gasp and shudder, reaching up through his empty lungs for the air that was absent. Shaking uncontrollably, he slowly opened his eyes and tried to blink the grogginess from them. They immediately played tricks on him and he shut them again tightly, wincing as he felt the sharp stab of pain in the back of his head.

For the briefest of moments, he found himself looking up at the tangled, twisted canopy of a forest overhead. The blue sky that should have been peering down through the branches at him was smothered by an ominous blanket of thick, curling black smoke – understandable, given what had happened. It was the fact that he was moving slowly through the terrain while laying flat on his back that confused the crap out of him. The land shifted as he slipped through his surroundings, instinctively trying to get away from the danger.

He had no recollection of what had happened following the impact. He hadn't just pretended to suck his dick; he had nearly bitten it off as the force of the impact threw him about in his seat. The noise of the land connecting with the jet had screamed through his soul, drowning out everything else, and just as he found a breath to swear, something struck him from behind and he had blacked out.

As he tried to fathom what was happening and failed

miserably, he suddenly began to feel the pressure of a firm grip on the collar of his Roberto Cavalli shirt. The silk fabric was being dragged up his aching body and he could feel his tie choking him.

Coughing up his panic, Jon opened his eyes again, straining to look back over his forehead to see what the fuck was going on, and who was ruining his bloody shirt. Fifteen hundred bucks from the designer's store in Beverly Hills, and the rest of his suit was five times that sum. Jon chuckled madly, despite himself. He had just lost a jet worth over twelve million U.S. dollars and all he was smarting about at the moment was his ruined designer suit and the loss of a fine, single malt. *The insurance company is going to love this...*

Jon saw the blurred image of a white-haired man peering worriedly down at him as the pressure on his throat lessened and the trees above him stopped moving.

"Sorry, Mr. Galnia," the pilot apologised, his pale face worried and streaked with the blood from a deep cut to his forehead. As Jon struggled to sit up, his surroundings began to spin and he lay back down again, muttering angrily.

"What happened?" Jon gasped, fighting for breath as a breeze blew more choking black smoke about them.

Robert slipped his arms under his employer's armpits and continued to drag him away from the wreck of the jet that was blazing away in the jungle, no more than a hundred feet away. The surrounding trees and undergrowth were on fire and the choking smell of kerosene hung in the air, stinging his eyes and thickening the bile already in his throat.

"I managed to crash land between two hillsides," Robert said, clearing his throat. "We lost both wings on impact and crashed through the jungle for several hundred feet."

"Where are the others?" Jon asked, unable to fully comprehend how lucky he was to still be alive.

The pilot frowned. "Sara is still unconscious... and Steven is dead!"

"Fuck it!" Jon snarled angrily.

Robert nodded his head sadly, mistaking his employer's anger for sadness at his co-pilot's loss. Jon, however, was just pissed that he was going to have to pay the man's widow a substantial amount of money if they survived this. As if this trip hadn't cost him an absolute fortune already.

"I tried to activate the *ELT* before impact," the pilot said, grimacing with the effort of dragging his employer through the jungle. "But it appears that it was also not working."

"The what?"

"The Emergency Locator Transmitter."

"*Figlio di puttana*!," Jon hissed angrily, his mind racing with a thousand accusations. "Someone doesn't want us to be found."

After a few moments, Robert laid his employer gently on the ground and slipped a satchel off his shoulder.

"Here is a medical kit, Mr. Galnia," he said, dropping it on the ground next to him. "You should see to that cut on the back of your head. I am going back for Sara and some supplies."

Without waiting for an answer, the pilot hurried back through the tangle of undergrowth. Covering his mouth and nose with the sleeve of his arm, he was soon lost in the thick curtain of billowing smoke.

"Thank you," Jon called after him. The words sounded strange coming from his mouth. He was used to apologising to his wife a lot, sure, and dishing out a bollocking, or worse, to his employees from time to time. *But offering his thanks*? The last time he had actually thanked anybody and meant it, was when his father's Will was read out by the family's solicitor.

Groaning, Jon fumbled for the satchel. Opening it, he dragged out the white medical kit and looked for some swabs to treat the back of his head with. Tearing open a packet, he began dabbing tentatively, and swore furiously as fresh pain diverted his thoughts away from his rising fury. Discarding the first swab, he opened another one, and after packing the kit away, he slung the satchel over his shoulder and tried to stand. For a time, his vision swam, and he spent many moments on his hands and knees as he fought for some strength and balance. Finally, when the undergrowth around him slowed down enough for him to grab onto something, he managed to use the slim trunk of a tall tree for support.

Breathing heavily, Jon looked back through the jungle. He couldn't see a thing now through the black smoke and covering his mouth, he turned and stumbled away. The pilot would just have to come and find him. There was no way Jon was going to hang around here to choke to death. With his vision swirling, Jon pressed the fresh swab to the back of his head and staggered away into the choking tangle of the jungle, unaware of the bright orange glow rising in intensity through the blackness behind him.

With a huge roar the jungle shook angrily, sending Jon flying through the air to land heavily on his left shoulder. A wave of heat swept over him, blasting his body and drying the sweat from his bared skin, momentarily. Reeling from the shock wave, Jon swore and rolled onto his good shoulder, scowling at his torn shirt. Reluctantly, he stared back through the jungle, shielding his eyes from the raging furnace that was once his private jet. Taking a steadying breath, Jon hauled himself up again and swayed as his senses failed him. Ignoring the words hissing in his mind, he stumbled away from the burning jungle and tried to get as far from the fire that was engulfing the undergrowth, as best his condition would allow him.

Another secondary explosion tore through the jungle behind him as he staggered away, and he fumbled with his right hand for the cellphone in his pocket. Fishing out empty cloth, he shook his head and then chuckled.

"Fucking typical!" he sighed, too weary for any real venom in his words, as he searched vainly for the missing phone.

Well that was it then! He was stuck in a jungle with no food and water, no contact to the outside world and... Jon swallowed back his realisation for a moment, before giving into it... he was probably alone now. There was no way Robert could have got back to Sara and made it out again before the jet went up. No way at all. Cursing his absent luck, Jon carried on stumbling through his surroundings, picking an uncertain path through the choked foliage and vines that seemed determined to block his path.

For a time, he wandered aimlessly, tripping over everything in his way, before his thoughts took hold of his spinning head and shouted loud enough for him to stop and listen. Groaning, Jon slumped against a strange looking tree and slid down the rough trunk with his back to the bark.

The jet's communications had been blocked, the SAT phone was lost, and the only way anyone could even know they had gone down, was the message that he had left for his wife; which in itself did little to ease his tension. By the time Maria had started looking into matters and had alerted the Indian authorities, the U.S. Embassy and anybody else who gave a shit, he would either be dead from the intense heat and humidity of the day, or dying from hypothermia from the cold of the night. And if none of that got to him, he was sure that there was no end of things in the jungle that would love to feast on his pasty flesh.

Jon swore bitterly again. It was his way of dealing with stress when he didn't have anyone else to take out his anger on. Taking several deep breaths, he remembered the calming exercises his therapist had taught him, just before he had lost his temper and fired her. To his astonishment, and despite his predicament, he started to relax and focused his mind on what things he could do to survive through this.

One! He was in India. He had never been to the country before today, but he had watched a few documentaries before.

So, w*hat did he know about India*? Well for starters, there was lots of poverty and it was the second largest growing economic power in the world (and consequently one of the largest polluting nations, too!) – a diverse range of faiths, beliefs, customs, great food, and, of course, the tigers... well, if there were any of them left now.

Jon scowled, thinking back to the reports on the news these last few months, of the media-induced frenzy that the feline disease wiping out the big cats around the globe could now be passed on to humans via their pets. Later disproven, the resulting mass-panic, stirred up by the media, had most of the planet fearing another Covid-style cleansing – one that had briefly given the mad-man in charge of the Free World even more excuse to close up his borders before he lost his presidency in a bitterly-fought election, narrowly avoiding impeachment.

Jon threw his head about in admiration. To him it sounded like it was just another excuse for the pharmaceutical companies to make billions of dollars out of a cure that wasn't really needed... this time.

Just another Millennium Bug, waiting to line the pockets of the shareholders...

Jon shook his head. None of that actually helped him much. But it gave his mind some focus and steered him away from the unaccustomed fear that was starting to kick him in the balls. *So, what else*?

Two! He was a billionaire, three, maybe four times over, thanks to his inherited empire. But none of that money was going to help him from where he was standing, sitting.

Three! Some fucker had done their very best to make sure he never reached his destination. And they had very nearly succeeded, too!

Jon offered up a swift prayer and blessed himself. Closing his eyes, he turned over the possible culprits in his mind.

Naturally, the obvious choice as the prime suspect would be those fucking double-crossing Commies he had met with, the Solntsevskaya Brotherhood. Perhaps it had been their plan all along? Let him and his Russian Empire, operating under the guise of *Volston Real Estates*, gain in power, allow them to set up their interests and build up their networks... then, when the pie was baking nicely in the oven, take them over by cutting the head off the chef and stealing the cherry. Jon could almost appreciate them and admire their cunning strategy, but after all the trouble they had gone through to set up the meeting, all of the threats and warnings beforehand to get him to come to Moscow... why not just kill him? Why go through all of that pretence with the meeting in the hotel with the woman, Anna, just to drop him out of the sky on the way home?

He had plenty of other enemies, sure he did. He'd pissed off a lot of people when he started bloodying noses, once he took over the Family from his late father. The Marchelli Family from the south-side of the city of Philadelphia had been trying to muscle in on his father's territory for decades, and had tried even harder when the young Galnia had come to power. Jon had soon put a brutal stop to that uprising. He had spent several million dollars on softening up his opposition's business partners – the seedy politicians, the counsellors and police commissioners who were reliant on their dirty money. Following a few well-orchestrated disappearances of prominent and beloved family members, the Marchellis' had finally offered him their white flag of truce.

Tempted to burn their flag, Jon wisely let them retreat; but had ordered his people to keep a close eye on their activities ever since.

Could it be them? Jon shook his head. They were ambitious, power-hungry, certainly. Who the hell in his world wasn't? But after the blood feud before, they were not stupid, could not afford another war. So, he should strike them off!

Jon laughed. It pissed him off beyond words and it would fester and eat away at him if he let it, not allowing him to think about his first priority.

Survival!

Come on, Galnia! he growled at himself. First things first! Get out of this sauna of a death trap and get to the nearest phone. Wait for the cavalry to arrive, and then get back home to your family, back home to Beverly Hills. Once he had recovered, he could think about his plans for revenge. He was in no doubt that he would have his day of reckoning, but for now, as he looked about the jungle and swore once more, he knew it would not be for some time.

The tree he rested against reminded Jon of how uncomfortable its bark was and muttering, he scrambled away, forcing himself to stand. For a moment his vision swayed again, and he spread his arms out wide to balance himself. When his surroundings snapped back into focus before him, Jon rolled the agony from his tightening neck muscles and headed in the opposite direction to the smouldering pile of millions of dollars.

He walked aimlessly for what felt like hours, but was only probably twenty or so minutes, before he had to stop and rest from exhaustion. The heat and humidity in the jungle was so intense that his body was covered in a thick sheen of sweat that did little to improve his mood, further ruined his clothes, and dripped periodically into his eyes.

All about him, the trees were alive with irritating sounds. Coloured birds swooped through the jungle, screeching warnings and flashing their long tails as they glided away from him. There were other sounds, too, and fleeting glimpses of agile, long-tailed and white-furred monkeys that leapt through the tree canopy around him and fell silent as he passed them by, watching curiously, as if to say '*What are you doing here, pale face?*'

Jon gave them the middle-finger, taking out his frustration on the nearest thing he had to a friend right now. Sighing, he sat down on a fallen tree trunk and tried to keep up with his ragged breath. Bored, the family of monkeys chattered amongst themselves and began grooming each other.

Fuck, it was hot! Wiping more sweat from his stinging eyes, Jon shaded them with one hand as he looked about his surroundings. Everywhere he looked, it was the same; a twisting, choked labyrinth of giant trees, huge bushes and plants, creeping vines and bright, pretty flowers. *The only thing missing was the dinosaurs...*

Something took a bite out of his pale flesh and he slapped his neck angrily. He would be eaten alive before he could starve to death at this rate! All about him insects foraged, and he eyed those that came near to him warily. As he glanced to his left, he saw something slither away into the undergrowth and he leapt up, cursing.

Snakes!

Jon swore again. He hated snakes more than he hated the IRS, and unlike Harrison Ford, he wouldn't have a sheet of glass in front of him if he came face to face with one of them. He hauled himself up onto the felled trunk for protection and stood, scanning his immediate surroundings. He felt a chill work its way across his skin as he spied a web between two large bushes, away to his right.

Spiders!

Those hairy bastards were right up there on his list, just below the snakes, and here he was dropped on his arse in amongst them.

Jon laughed for some time and it felt good. Anyone passing by would have thought him a madman, but to the multi-billionaire, his mirth was priceless. When his chuckles died down to a breathless snort, he wiped away the sweat-mingling tears and raked one hand through his dark hair. His hand came away even wetter than it had been before and sighing, he wiped it clean on his tattered, filthy trousers.

Cajoling himself down from his protective perch, Jon headed away from the snake, steering clear of the spider's web as he trudged forlornly and inadvertently back the way he had just come from.

After another hour of watching out for insects, snakes and anything else that could kill him, Jon was forced to stop for yet another rest and admit he was stumbling around in circles. After a while, one bit of foliage, one, tree, one fucking monkey all looked the same, and after taking his frustrations out on a bush, until his designer shoes had nearly fallen off and he couldn't breathe, he had decided to just head in one direction and not try to read the land.

By the time the jungle, if possible, had started to become even denser, thickened by young bamboo, Jon had decided to carry a huge, thick stick for protection. Anything that buzzed, hissed or moved too close to him, he vowed, would feel his wooden wrath. He had, for the first few minutes, swatted at any insect that appeared before him. But he soon found his strength waning, and without any water or food, he decided it best to conserve his anger and energy.

The terrain was getting tougher now, as it rose steadily, and after a while of sliding back down the choked slopes in his shoes, he spied the large, spade-shaped leaves of a huge plant. Frowning, he moved over to it, and then grinned. He had seen a film once, set in a jungle, where they had lived off the land... *what was it called now?* He couldn't recall the title, but in it they had drunk from the leaves as the moisture collected and spilled down the plant, from leaf to leaf.

As Jon studied the plant, he picked a suitable leaf and positioned his face underneath it, tilting it towards his open mouth. Moments later, his fraying patience was rewarded and he felt the warm, sweet taste of the moisture as it spilled intermittently down his throat. For many minutes he chose the wettest leaves on the plant and repeated the process until his neck was aching and his thirst, for now, was quenched. His head was still throbbing, however, and using another leaf, he fished two painkillers from his first aid kit and downed them as quickly as he could. The constant bird calls were grating on his nerves and everything about his predicament was pissing him off!

Jon shook his head ruefully. He was Don of his house and empire, capable of unspeakable acts... and yet, despite all that, he hated swallowing tablets, and winced like a girl. He grinned. Well, at least he would never be able to top himself by taking a pill overdose...

Not that he was going to give anyone the satisfaction. By now, whoever had sabotaged his jet would probably know that it had gone down, and they would be sitting back, sipping on champagne and spinning on whores to celebrate.

Premature! Jon thought, feeling fresh anger rise again. Calming himself, he took several long, deep breaths and at last allowed himself to think about his wife and child.

At least there he could find comfort; find the focus he would need to keep himself alive, to keep going.

He had met Maria when he was still not sure about what his dick was for. She had been the youngest daughter of the Beladetti Family, at that time, close supporters and allies to his father. For years they had played together as children, sweeping around the huge gardens of their respective homes, getting in the way when there were important meetings going on and brutal decisions being made. Jon and Maria became good friends well before they became lovers, and the transition from childhood friends to sweethearts was unexpected and, much to the annoyance of Jon's elder brother, Alessandro, very untimely.

Jon sighed, wiping the sweat from his eyes. His heart began to pound and his breath caught on the lump in his throat as he thought of his wife; tall, elegant, raven-haired and beautiful. Maria was a modern-day version of the wife of a Roman Emperor; beauty personified, powerful and his equal. She might look like a model from the front cover of Vogue, but this goddess could just as easily tear your throat out if you crossed her. Yes, she was the calm in their marriage, the one with clarity of thinking, the one who thought before she acted, but she was also the daughter of the Cosa Nostra, and her blood was still thick with its code and ruthlessness. It made her the perfect empress for the Galnia house and empire. She was the matriarch and, as far as Jon could tell, she was more feared than he was.

She was his world, his strength, his calm and without her, he would have probably ended up the same way as his brother...

Maria had blessed them with a son in the early hours of July 29th 2015. As with the rest of her pregnancy, the birth had proven just as difficult, and she had to have an emergency Cesarean. Jon smiled, feeling his throat tighten with emotion as he recalled the brightness in her eyes and the joy on her weary face, as she held her son to her breast and wept. Her bloodline, and Jon's, would live on.

Giovanni Jon Galnia Junior was a happy boy. Sure, not all boys were heir to billions of dollars and would one day inherit the Galnia Empire with all the stigma, reputation and problems that would come with it; but at the moment, his son was a care-free six-year old, who took everything in his stride with that winsome, innocent face and those great big brown eyes. And of course, not all kids had turned up at kindergarten and then prep-school with a driver and bodyguard, who remained outside, waiting for him when he finished. But Gio did not let that stop him making friends and having fun. He was just another normal child with normal friends. He liked racing around the playground, playing Star Wars and X-men with his pals, waving imaginary lightsabers at hordes of foes and beating up his mutant friends. He was happy and blissfully unaware of the problems his parents had to deal with, how terrified his mother was until he came home safely every day, and for the next few years at least, he would be spared as much of their world as his parents could shield him from.

Jon sighed and felt the lump grow in his throat. The thought of not seeing his son and wife again left an empty void inside of him, and for probably only the second time in his life, he felt scared, really scared! Not the kind of fear you felt when a deal was going down, or the Feds were at your door; but the type of fear that plucked you from your security, shredded your nerves and soiled your pants.

"God, I hope this is not your way of making me repent my sins?" Jon asked, staring up at the blue sky through the jungle's canopy, "because I haven't sinned enough yet!"

He forced a chuckle through his sob and blessed himself. Well, whatever the almighty had planned for him, Jon was sure it wasn't sitting on his backside and waiting for his summons. Rising up, Jon found his bearings again, staring through the jungle to, what any boy scout would have told him, was the north. The ground began to rise steeply there and he flicked his eyes wearily to the lower ground.

No point wasting what precious energy I have! No! For now, he should stick to the lower ground, try to find somewhere to shelter for the night and then see what tomorrow would bring. Gripping his stick, he picked a path through the dense undergrowth, eyeing every leaf, every branch, for the next insect or creature that was going to end his charmed life as he attempted to leave his headache behind.

Unfortunately for Jon, his headache stayed, weighed heavily down on him and compounded his misery, as he stumbled his way through the darkening jungle for the next couple of hours. As each step became harder, each rasping breath thundered in his head and his senses began to fail him, Jon called a halt to his misery and sat down on a boulder. Panting, he tried to wipe the sweat from his eyes and gave up. He was too tired to try, too exhausted to go on and too pissed off to bother. The sweat tingled on his lips and he licked them hungrily, ignoring the tightening rumble of hunger in his stomach.

Jon closed his eyes and shook his head; wincing as his neck reacted from the tension and his head roared in fury. Thinking back to his therapy sessions again, Jon breathed in deeply, held his breath and then released it again, slowly. Surprised by the sensation and effect it had, he repeated this exercise another three times and then sighed contentedly. It had never worked this well for him before...

When the storm raging away in his head abated for a few seconds, he heard a sound off through the tangled jungle thicket, away to his right. Cocking one ear in that direction, he listened again and heard only the continuous orchestra of insects and prattling, grating song of the birds.

And don't even get me started on the fucking monkeys...

Chiding himself, Jon tested the back of his head and groaned. The wound was very tender, the blood clotting now and his hair a mess. Scowling, he cast a disdainful look at a monkey, as it watched him from the protection of a tall tree with spiky leaves. They looked at each other for a few minutes, before the monkey got bored and started scratching his chin.

Another noise dragged his attention back to the right and Jon forgot about his problems and his audience. Again, he had to tussle with his pounding head, the local chatter and the thoughts of what had happened to him, but, after a moment, he sifted through all of that and detected the faint voices for the first time.

Jon stood up, chasing after the hope that lurched in his chest and almost exploded in maniacal cries of delight. But as he tripped and fell to his knees, he caught hold of his wits, and reined in his excitement as his cautious nature took a hold.

'*You won't live long if you aren't careful!*' his father had said to him, as Jon began to learn and understand about the world he had been born into. It had proven the most valuable thing, well apart from the money, that his father had passed onto him, and he had never forgotten that day, when his father had taken him to one side.

Sub-consciously, Jon crouched lower and strained to hear any more voices as the monkey started calling for its buddies. Glaring at the monkey, Jon picked up what looked to be a pine cone and threw it at the bloody creature. He missed by a wide mark, but the monkey must have read his intent and scampered off through the trees, screeching angrily and flicking his long tail in a salute of his own.

Jon grinned ruefully and then listened again. Nothing! Absolutely nothing! As minutes slipped by and his fears began to ease, Jon rose slowly. Easing his grip on his makeshift staff, he stretched. His mind was already playing tricks on him, teasing him with whispers of hope, prodding at his composure with tantalising promises of rescue.

Berating his caution, Jon began heading in the direction of the phantom voices and prayed that he found nothing. He would be even more pissed off if he had just passed up the chance of rescue because of a monkey and his Cosa Nostra paranoia.

After half an hour of futilely scanning the ground for signs of life as if he knew what he was actually looking for, Jon decided that he was in need of some rest. There had been no voices, only his subconscious desire and need for someone to rescue him, point him in the right direction, or lend him their cellphone. Sighing, Jon looked about for inspiration. He needed to find shelter for the night, somewhere he could stay warm and avoid any of the creatures that might come out at night and chew his head off.

He laughed, perhaps a little too loud, as he scattered some birds from their roosts and scanned the jungle around him. Here he was, worrying about what could kill him during the night, when, at any moment a hungry, dying tiger could crash through the trees and drag him off to feed on his throat. Grabbing hold of his stick, he adjusted the position of the medical kit's strap on his shoulder.

Jon had always wanted to see a tiger in the wild, not the ones you used to be able to see behind a fence or glass in a zoo, but here, in their natural habitat. But as he unknowingly turned back to the north and began heading for the higher ground, he selfishly hoped they had all died out and that he would never see a tiger again. Well, not until he was relaxing at home and watching a David Attenborough documentary on the Discovery Channel.

By the time Jon found somewhere suitable to shelter for the night, the jungle was blanketed in shadows and he was on the verge of collapse. He had no idea how long he had stumbled about, no recollection of how he got there, but as he stared into the cluster of boulders that formed a natural cleft in the rocky hillside, he was just thankful that he would be able to hide away for the night.

He was already cold. His body, once soaked with sweat, was now chilled by the rapidly cooling air. Jon shivered as he created a leafy screen around the entrance to his makeshift home by pulling off branches from nearby trees and plucking the huge leaves off the giant plants. With his teeth chattering, he struggled into the narrow cleft, probably caused by a landslide, and turned stiffly to pull the undergrowth over the entrance.

If he survived the night, which he was determined to, Jon would make for the higher ground in the morning by picking his way up the incline at a slight angle, so that he could conserve his strength and not exhaust himself too soon in the day. Shaking, he drew his knees up under his chin to hug his shins. He still couldn't believe this was happening to him and hoped that when he woke in the morning, he would be back in his four-poster bed, his wife snuggled into him and one of her long slender legs curled over him.

A noise outside made him start, jostling him from his fantasy, and he listened to the night as it began to choke the jungle in its smothering embrace. Jon tried to clear his mind, failing miserably. Despite his rising delirium and his pounding head, he was still furious. Still pissed that someone did not have the courage to face him directly, resulting in an underhand, cowardly attempt on his life. Where was their honour? Their code? The more he thought about it, the more Jon was sure it was not anyone Mafioso.

Again, the jungle drew his attention away, his skin prickling with fear as he heard something large foraging about outside, near to his hiding place. As he held his breath and tried to calm his fear, he knew, with certainty, that he would not have any strength left tomorrow for anything.

The night began to smother the day, trading one set of creatures that could kill him for those he would never see coming.

Jon cursed, knowing that it was going to be a very, very long night indeed!

CHAPTER THREE

A Friend in Need

A slow, cold dawn crept through the jungle. Gently probing the darkness to chase away the creatures of the night, it fell tentatively upon the unconscious form, slumped face down across a woman's motionless body. Unable to wake up the still forms, the faint light spread further into the darkness, stirring the plants, insects and creatures to life once again.

As his surroundings began to wake and the warmth of the rising sun began to find him, Robert Williams reached out for the safe shore of the bank, drowning before his reach in tormented dreams. With his last breath, he pulled himself from the depths of his unconsciousness.

He was cold, stiff and disorientated. Each muscle screamed as he tried to move, every inch of his skin cracked as he shifted his body to free his weight from the woman beneath him.

Choking, Robert opened his eyes, blinking the dryness from them, rubbing the dried soot from his face with the sleeve of his blackened shirt. Pain tore through him as he fought for breath, hawking and spitting away the filth that clogged his nose and filled his mouth. Falling backwards, Robert's vision cleared momentarily, and he caught a glimpse of the flight attendant, Sara Gonzales, face down on the sodden ground before him.

Moaning, Robert crawled across the scorched earth,

ribbons of daylight knifing the canopy overhead. He was not aware that his clothes were blackened and burnt, he did not register that his hair was singed like the summer straw fields, and that his shaking hands were blistered and swollen.

With panic raging through his head, Robert turned the dark-haired woman over. She was pastry pale, her once-olive skin glistening with fever. Losing his breath, the pilot picked her left arm up by the slender wrist and felt for a pulse.

He found her there, fighting against the darkness, stirring with hope, though only faintly.

"No!" Robert hissed, his blistered lips tight and full of fire. His memory, stolen away by the force of millions of dollars going up in flames, was slowly, thankfully returning, and as he tried to remain calm, he spied the bright orange, florescent jacket to his right; burnt at the edges, but still intact, unlike most of his surroundings.

He hurriedly checked Sara over, feeling her body for broken bones, checking her for any punctured ribs. Thankfully, he found none. Despite her scorched clothes and the blisters on her face, it was only the cut to her left leg that gave him concern. There was also the welt on the side of her head, from whatever had knocked her out, but he hoped she was not in any immediate danger.

Once she was wrapped up in the jacket, Robert reached for the second emergency medical kit he had retrieved from the jet along with Sara, and then, just in time, the body of his friend for nearly ten years, Steven.

The pain of his loss overcame any physical agony, and the pilot sobbed as he realized, once Sara was safe, he had not had time to go back for Steven a second time. Robert collapsed, allowing the cold ground to soothe his burns.

When the jet had crashed, the jungle wrapping itself about the cockpit's canopy with lethal intent, the window had shattered after a hundred screeching, crashing metres, a large, broken branch piercing Steven through the chest. He must have died instantly, and after having scrambled to pull his employer to safety, the pilot had gone back for his friend and Mr. Galnia's aide.

Mr. Galnia!

Despite his unanswered shouts to find him, the pilot knew his employer was safe somewhere, well beyond the explosion – that much he could remember. As Robert looked back through the misty jungle, beyond the blackened thicket, smouldering branches and leaves, hoping for a glimpse of his employer, the only thing he could see were the remains of the Galnia jet, broken and burning, some two hundred yards away.

His senses returning now, the pilot gagged on the thick, clinging black fumes of the kerosene. Had the jungle not been so damp, so verdant, Robert assumed that he would have burned to death without ever waking, and the devastation to the area would have been for miles, not just feet. Remembering himself, Robert opened the medical kit, cleansing the cut on Sara's leg with anti-bacterial wipes, before treating the wound with Savlon. After her leg was wrapped in bandages, the pilot used the tube of cream to soothe the crisp pain in his burnt hands.

Robert swallowed. His throat was as raw as the jungle about him and he was glad he had retained the wit to grab some water from the supply cupboard. As he unscrewed the nearest bottle and put it to Sara's lips, he wished, even more importantly, that he had remembered to bring his phone.

Sniffing back the irony, Robert drank sparingly,

despite his need, and knew that he had done all he could in the time he had, far more than aviation regulations would have asked him for; first and foremost, see to the safety of the passengers and crew, get out as fast as you could and leave all belongings behind. Nowadays, mobile phones were not considered possessions; they were an extension to people's hands, as necessary to them as breakfast and their morning coffee from Costa. They could not go anywhere if they did not have a phone, could not live a normal life without them.

Robert's laugh was loud and heavy. His wife always nagged him that he should take his phone with him, should at least have it switched on – but Robert was part of the old brigade, hating the damned things. A man of few words, but generally ones that actually mattered, he found he did not need a phone; if he had to call someone, he would use a payphone. Maybe even write to them.

The one blasted time...

His eyes lingered on Sara for a moment, before his sluggish thoughts caught up with them and he scrambled to her side, feeling guilty as he fished through the pockets of her trousers.

Robert held his breath, drawing out a slim smart phone from a back pocket, and for a brief moment, wondered if his awe and surprise was akin to what Arthur had felt like, as he drew forth the sword from the stone.

Chuckling, Robert heard his wife's voice again, trying to drag him back from the past, get him to tear his attention away from the pages of his beloved books in his study for a few moments.

The broken screen lit up as he pressed the button on top of it. Sure, he was a dinosaur, but he had two children, well two adults now, and he had seen them do it enough times before they had both left home.

Shit! Robert snarled, dredging up the bitter temperament of his employer. The phone still had charge, but it needed a pin code to unlock it.

Robert reached out a hand and brushed dank tendrils of hair from Sara's face. She looked a lot like his daughter and his heart ached with the thought that he might not get to see his family again.

"Come on, lovely," he whispered, stroking her beautiful face.

It was then that Sara stopped breathing.

The shock and circumstances of Jon's predicament had settled deep into his bones that night. With only his anger to keep him warm, he spent his hours jerking away from anything that made a noise, trying not to scream as something scuttled by him, or crawled near his face.

Sleep, if that's what you could call it, was impossible, as his mind kept him awake more than the jungle did. Every single thing that moved either sang, screeched, hissed, slithered, chattered or growled and was sat outside his hideout, waiting and ready to chew his balls off.

"*Well they mostly come at night, mostly!*"

Jon had chuckled away deliriously to himself for a time. Stereotypically, most people expected that his favourite film was The Godfather or Scarface, or perhaps that show, The Sopranos, but they were wrong...

As the night screeched away and a deep chill settled into his bones, Jon's headache returned and he hid his agony away in the clammy palms of his hands. Forgetting his therapy sessions, his anger festered away as he wished he had remained stateside, cursing the day his ambitions had dragged him to Russia for a spanking.

Every waking hour stretched into what felt like days, and just as the sharp rocks were beginning to feel like soft pillows and he was about to fall asleep, the edges of the darkness began to lighten, the grey ever-so-slowly turning to white gold.

Bleary-eyed, Jon tried to move, but his body was stiff from the cold. Snarling, he gritted his teeth to stop them chattering as the night shift changed and the dawn watch began greeting the day. The jungle came alive again, clamouring to be heard, shrieking and chattering in celebration.

It did little to improve Jon's mood.

Kicking aside his makeshift screen, Jon shielded his eyes and fell out into the morning, waving his stick to scare off any foes, pretending not to notice the huge spider he had shared a bed with last night as he went back for his medical kit. With his heart lurching in his chest, Jon swept a gaze about his surroundings. He swore again when he could not see a rescue team picking their way up the slope towards him, all smiles and waves, carrying a bottle of champagne and some caviar for him.

No! Lord have pity, he was alone. He had only the trees for company, the plants that were on steroids, the beautiful birds and of course not forgetting those fucking monkeys.

Craning his neck, Jon could see the slivers of blue above the tall trees, but he could not feel the sun's warmth as the shadow of a monkey leapt from branch to branch above him. Pain tore through the wound on the back of his head and his vision began to spin. Moaning, he stumbled back down the slope, grasping at the rough, jagged trunks of the trees, stabbing at the ground with his stick, fighting to keep upright on his $1000 shoes as his heart began to race and his chest began to tighten.

"Oh, no you don't! I'm not ready yet," Jon hissed, as he reached the jungle floor and began heading into the deepening thicket, keeping the rocky incline to his left. He needed to find something to drink, needed to risk something to eat if he was going to have any hope of reaching higher ground and get out of this shit-hole. As he blundered on his way, his stomach cramping, he laughed.

It had not even been a day, yet, and here he was thinking the worst, trying to fight off the feeling that this was it, that his luck had finally ran out.

Feeding off his anger, Jon focussed on his unsure footing and each step that took him on, closer, closer towards whoever had dropped him on his arse in this country, and their payback he would soon come to cash in.

On Jon stumbled, his Cavalli shoes slipping and sliding beneath him, as the terrain began to drop further away and he found himself clinging to boulders and vines to stay upright. At one point, a huge, dark grey lizard scuttled away from him and Jon's high curses cut through the thicket, startling birds and sending the monkeys in the branches above him, leaping for cover.

Sweat streamed down his body and his clothes were torn and ruined. Muttering, Jon tried to focus on his wife and his son, but his feverish body, the pain in his head and the chill clinging to his glistening skin, stole them away from him.

"Don't leave me," Jon pleaded, as an image of his wife, tall, elegant and smiling, faded away in the streaming sun.

Jon shook his head. He needed water, and fast, but his leaf trick wasn't working yet as the sun had not stoked up the embers of the furious day, and the berries he had found on a bush a while back had looked at him challengingly... "*Do you feel lucky, punk?*"

Jon didn't feel lucky – in fact, if he admitted it to himself, he had never felt more vulnerable. All his life he had never wanted for anything, had taken everything for granted and anything that was given to him, offering little, if nothing in return.

Right now, he would give away his entire fortune, just for a bottle of water and a plate of Cacio e Pepe.

Licking his dry lips with an even dryer tongue, Jon pressed on. The jungle loomed large before him, a tangled maze of vine, trees, rocks and plants, lit up occasionally by a flash of colour. Until the summons from the Solntsevskaya Brotherhood, everything had been going well, so well that he and Maria were actually enjoying life again, loving the other's company for a change. With the Feds not on heat anymore and eager for his leg, the map of Jon's interests around the world were beginning to look like the board game Risk, and the game was turning in his favour. All of his operations and companies were producing vast amounts of money for the Galnia house, and with some careful management through his shell companies and his abrupt way of dealing with any employees that got too greedy, he had taken to his father's work with relish, weeding out the unnecessary and fashioning the remaining companies into very profitable businesses.

Jon snorted, wincing as fresh pain tore through the back of his head. The irony of being stuck in a country, where there was the potential to invest and make lots of money was not lost on him. At the moment, he had nothing to bargain with, not even his phone. Just his trusty stick...

His swirling gaze drifted to the silver band on his left hand and he smiled. He might have nothing right now, but being here, alone and scrabbling around for his life, he started to appreciate that he actually had everything he needed back at home, high in the hills off Coldwater Canyon Drive.

And failing that, he had his wallet, his Gold Amex and his anger.

Clenching his bruised and thorn-torn fists about his stick, Jon set off, invigorated with his new found energy and purpose. High in the branches before him, a family of the long-tailed bastards watched him, their curious heads bobbing and their wide eyes intent on him. Their tails flicked and they studied him silently as he passed below them. Looking up, Jon spied a mother, clutching a babe to her breast.

Waving with his middle finger, Jon hurried on, a grin spreading across his face. He had survived two attempts on his life, one gunshot wound to the shoulder and the attentions of the U.S. Government. He could get through this, he would, he knew it.

Blessing himself, he kissed the silver wedding band on his left hand and topped a rise, gasping for the breath that was becoming harder to find in the rising heat.

"That was quick," Jon chuckled, looking up to the heavens. Below him, through the jungle, the land fell away down the slopes of a gorge, down through the trees and rocks to a snaking, glistening, glorious diamond sparkle of a twisting creek.

Robert Williams fell back from Sara Gonzalez, his arms aching, the sweat streaming down his face to sting the burns on his cheeks. Panting, he gathered his composure and pulled the woman's blouse back over her chest and buttoned it up to protect her dignity.

Puffing the relief from his cheeks, Robert thanked his medical training as he wrapped Sara tight in the fluorescent jacket to keep her warm again.

She was alive... for now.

Not aware of his own exhaustion, Robert tried to stand. Slowly, he staggered to his feet, his surroundings spinning wildly about him, then snapping to a halt before his raw eyes to reveal the jungle ahead. It was still early morning and his watch told him that it was 6:45am in Moscow, which, if his memory served him well, meant that in central India, it was probably about ten the same morning.

Dragging a hand through his stiff hair, matted with filth, Robert could see that the land here was fairly even, with no hard terrain to carry Sara through. He looked west, though he did not know it, keeping the wreck of the jet to his left. The path through the jungle there looked kinder. Looking back to Sara, he knew that he needed to get her to somewhere sheltered, somewhere close to the jet, but away from the stench of the carnage. No doubt the Indian aviation authorities were aware that the jet had gone down, were already assembling a rescue team to scour the area for survivors. They needed to stay close, but not too close.

Well, that's if they can locate us. Robert shook his head, trying to lose the worry that they might not be found at all. Someone had done their very best to make sure they couldn't be located, should anyone survive the crash... but was that all the precautions they had taken?

So much for the easy pay packet! Life, it seemed, had a funny way of throwing a spanner at you when you least expected it.

Robert had grown up in St. Athan, in South Wales. His father had been a pilot instructor at the airbase there, staying on to help oversee the maintenance of aircraft after operations were shifted from the base in 1955. Although he had been thirteen when they finally moved from Wales in 1970, growing up around the RAF had given him a love for aircraft that had made him want to follow in his father's footsteps, and would one day lead him to become a commercial pilot. He had been steered towards a safer career and prospects by his mother, after his father had died from a heart-attack whilst playing golf at a charity day for retired servicemen.

Qualifying with one of the highest grades and reputations, he flew transatlantic flights for British Airways and United Airlines for almost twenty-five years, where one day, seven years ago, Mr. Galnia was a passenger in First Class, flying from LAX to London Heathrow.

To this day, his employer would swear to him that it was the smoothest landing he had ever experienced, and unbeknownst to Robert, even now, Jon had been stressed at the time with the Calvante fall-out. He was in the market for an experienced pilot after the last one had been approached by the Feds to become a mole.

Apparently, Jon had liked the calming sound of Robert's voice so much, that he had asked to see the pilot after the flight. Over a glass of scotch, Jon had offered him a job as his personal pilot. The timing could not have been more perfect. Disillusioned with the corporate demands and the looming thought of retirement, Robert decided that in his latter years he needed to ensure his two children (one was at Oxford, studying political history) had some security in this insecure world.

Robert snapped back to the present, wincing wryly. If his wife Janine could see him now, she would deal him that "*I told you* so," look of hers, though they had all profited from the notorious Jon Galnia's wealth, as had his late father's charity.

Despite the reputation of his employer and the dealings he might have heard on the hundreds of flights he had captained for the Galnia Family, Robert was happy with the decisions he had made, even if his reputation had been stained irrevocably with his former colleagues and peers…

Although he was reluctant to leave Sara unattended, Robert knew they needed more supplies, and he stumbled back towards the wreckage to try and salvage anything he could use to keep them alive until they were rescued – extra supplies, food, more water, and enough material to make a fire, should they need to spend another cold night in the jungle. He had been with the scouts growing up, and had learnt many things with them that, until this day, he never thought he would need to use to stay alive.

Making a slow, careful search of the debris and wreckage, Robert stayed as far away from the burning carcass of the jet as he could. Over the next hour, he returned to Sara's side several times, bringing back extra food supplies, one bottle of water, a blanket and some of the wreckage, that he hoped to be able to use to build a shelter. He would still need to move them away to safety from the jet, to try and find somewhere where the air was cleaner, and he drew in several breaths, as he thought about the reserves of strength he would need to tap into over the coming hours.

Finding his first strength, Robert knelt beside Sara, slowly hauling her up in his arms. She moaned, stirring in his protective embrace, then fell silent again. Robert watched her fearfully for a time, thankful for the shallow rise and fall in her breast. Swaying, the captain steadied himself, ignoring the sweat that ran down his face, dragging fresh agony from his burns.

Sweeping a final look towards the jet, and towards his friend, Robert headed away from them to the west. A family of Gray Langur monkeys leapt through the trees ahead of him and he was glad of the company.

Jon's eagerness and rising delirium to get to the water guided him down the treacherous slope, far too quickly. Picking a course through the maze of tangled trees, rocks and undergrowth, he slipped and slid his way down, his stick steadying him and his free hand grasping for each trunk of the tall, mutant trees.

Something buzzed about his head, and panicking, Jon held onto a gnarled trunk, swatting at the unseen predator with his stick. He missed, as the large insect circled behind him. Diving in for the kill, it sank something into the flesh at the nape of his neck.

Pain tore through Jon's neck, and swearing, he slapped at the fire there. For a brief second, he stared at his stick, his eyes flicking to the trunk he had just let go of.

"Ah, sh–"

Roberto Cavalli slipped from underneath him and Jon fell onto his back, the force dragging the breath from his curses as his momentum threw him down the gorge. Almost immediately his stick was torn from him by nature's grasping hands and with a dull crunch his senses were dazed as his head glanced against a tree. Disorientated, the landscape somersaulted past him in fleeting, spiralling images of colour.

For an eternity Jon fell, his body battered and twisted as he crashed into what felt like every single obstruction on the steep slope. Pain tore through his left shoulder as he grabbed for an exposed root of a tree to slow his descent, but tumbled on, leaving a deep, muddy burn in the palm of his hand.

Jon panicked. An insect had succeeded, where many had failed. He could not breathe, could not focus on his surroundings long enough to halt his death fall.

Well, that was until a huge trunk loomed large before his eyes and filled his vision with darkness.

CHAPTER FOUR

Here, kitty, kitty...

Maria Galnia slipped from her black dress, hoping the warmth of the California sun streaming through the open window would wake her up. It was mid-morning now and she was drained after a busy night of fundraising in downtown Beverly Hills for the local school. The ornate mirror above her dresser reminded her that she was not getting any younger, and resisting the need to spirit away a strand of white from her raven black hair, she sat on the huge bed, rubbing the sleep and mascara from her eyes.

Placing one stocking-clad foot over the other leg's knee, she massaged the memory of the high heels from her sole, surprised that her hips and thighs did not tighten in protest. All that Pilates was paying off, it seemed.

Hiding her face away in the tangled dark tresses that tumbled about her shoulders, she thought back to the previous night and the smile she had had to paint on her face, brighter than the scarlet stick on her lips. An attentive smile here or laugh there to the husbands, the numerous dignitaries and failed celebrities present, or a gentle touch to their arm or elbow never failed for Maria. It went a long way with some of the wives, too – though she was not really into that kind of thing. In one night, with one dress, she had probably helped to fill the school board's coffers for at least another two years.

Maria smiled. It would be a few more years before Gio would be joining the school, but with Jon away and a little extra time on her hands, it didn't hurt to start laying out some fresh networks. Her tiny whirlwind was in his last semester at Greenwood Prep, in North Hollywood, before he moved on to his next private school, San Fernando Valley. Maria had always wanted Gio to move to Bridges Academy to start his Grade 7, and she had certainly made an impression on the principal last night.

Licking the ambition from her lips, Maria turned her attention to her headache and chided herself for the champagne she had not been able to resist. *When will I ever learn?*

In the early hours, Jon's *Consigliere,* his adviser, Paolo Romano Junior, and her protection for the night, had spirited her home to Villa de Valdez, back through the high, iron gates and past the men guarding them. Maria drifted away for a time and could only recall the clear sky that night, scattered with stars. After that, well, all she could remember was checking in on Gio... she had woken up beside him, early the following morning, when he began stroking her face.

Falling back into the embrace of the bed, she dragged the silk sheets about her, thinking of Gio, of how he had incessantly wanted to tell her everything about his dream; of how he had been fighting dinosaurs with his friend, Harry. Chuckling, Maria shook her head, fending off the well of sadness filling her heart.

He was growing up so fast, *too fast!* She didn't want her little man to grow up – she didn't want him to have to be exposed to their life, their *real* life, before he could actually learn to enjoy and appreciate his own.

I never had that chance... Maria thought, sadly.

Fortunately, for the sake of her hangover, Gio's nanny Louisa had taken matters upon herself to get the young

Galnia washed, fed and into his school clothes. Maria normally insisted that she do that, have breakfast with her son and see him off, along with his bodyguards, to school, but today she couldn't even manage that.

Muttering, Maria stretched herself free from the sheets, arching her back and rolling the tension from her shoulders. Stifling a yawn, she looked over at the bedside table, seeing her private phone laying forgotten there. Crawling on her knees and elbows to it, she rolled onto her back and unlocked the screen, surprised when she saw that she had a voicemail from Jon. Thumbing open the voicemail, she slipped the phone under her tangled hair and fell back into the comfort of her pillows.

In her line of work, in the life that she led, she had many phones; her phone for her public face, the phone for the shadows and a third phone, this phone, the one that only Jon had the number to. *But he never left her a voicemail!*

As Jon's voice filled her ear, her heart began to race over her crawling skin. Shocked, she sat up in bed. Flinging her feet to the wooden floor she fought for breath as she stumbled over to the window and stared dumbly out at the day. As Jon's strangely calm message ended, Maria collapsed to her knees and screamed, staring in disbelief out of the window to the grounds, lost to a sprinkler that glistened like a Roman candle in the brilliant sun.

Worry, fear, accusations and recriminations, all kinds of thoughts kept Maria on her knees, as she tried to gain control of her emotions and thought about what she would tell their son, how she would tell him, if the worst had happened.

She had argued at length with her husband when Jon had been summoned to Russia, to meet with representatives of the Solntsevskaya Brotherhood. Their reputation for negotiating was not a good one, and Maria believed it was too dangerous to allow Jon to go himself – he should have sent one of his men in Moscow to the meeting, Aleksi Cardov or Maksim Lebedev. Both men were trusted former associates of his father, who had faithfully served the Galnia interests for many years.

Jon, however, did what he always did, listened intently, nodding his agreement, pretending that he was considering what she was saying, before ignoring every word she had wasted to go and do what he wanted to do, anyhow.

Drawing in a calming breath, Maria wiped the fear from her eyes and opened up Google, stabbing with shaking nails as she searched for the American Embassies in India.

For a moment, she stared down at the screen, fading in the bright sunshine. Finding the number she needed, Maria paused, regained her composure, and then dialled.

Pain before his confusion. Agony before his curses.

Jon lifted his pounding head weakly, his eyes filled with blood from the fresh wound to his forehead that now complemented the injury to the back of his skull. For a time, he lay where he was, tangled in the terrain, his body twisted about a jagged boulder with the steep, choked incline looming mockingly above him.

Fearful he had broken something other than his pride, Jon lay there, unsure of where and who he was. His skin glistened, his body trembled, and his vision swam as the morning carried on around him.

From somewhere deep, he finally dragged up the

courage to move, his breath ragged as he rolled onto his front. Fingers of pain lanced through his side, stabbing at his ribs like a heavy-handed pianist.

Wiping the blood away, Jon stared ahead at the creek, meandering gently through the gorge before him. To most, the sight would have filled the soul with its beauty, but to Jon it was just another excuse to realise that he was sinking deeper into the pile of shit he had landed upon. Sunlight filled his view, the sky above blue and clear, a sure sign that it was going to be another furnace of a day. Birds sang mockingly and insects buzzed – though no longer keen for his flesh. As he pushed himself up onto his knees, Jon could see that his trousers were torn, his knees grazed and already black with bruises.

Fighting against his pain, Jon crawled on his ruined knees towards the creek, the gentle, musical song of the glistening water calling to him seductively. Another week and the water would be gone, dried up by the sun. Another few hours and there would be a corpse here, dressed in ragged, ruined designer clothes.

Crawling through the flowers and plants filling the bed of the gorge, Jon reached the creek, plunging his face into the cold, clear, crisp waters. It was the most wonderful thing he had ever tasted; even better than the bottle of Armand de Brignac champagne the mayor of Beverly Hills had given to him for his forty-fifth birthday. Coughing up bile, he drank as much as he could, pulling his aching carcass into the shallows to cool his wounds and refresh his irritation.

Sitting in the creek, Jon allowed his thoughts to wander, much like his senses. The heady scents of his surroundings overwhelmed him, chasing off the lingering stench from the fumes of his jet that still burned away in his nose. Bees droned about him as they foraged for nectar, and butterflies danced in the sunlight. As Jon threw water into his eyes to clear away more blood, he spied a beautiful butterfly to his right, sweeping in elegant, silent arcs, its long tail forked like a swallow's.

He watched the butterfly for quite some time, not realising that he had forgotten his injuries for a while, had not even thought about his predicament. It was the most relaxed he had been for many a year, and it had not cost him any money.

Who needs a therapist? Jon thought, his mind taking over again.

Realising, somewhat reluctantly, that he could not sit there forever watching the wildlife, Jon forced himself onto his knees, back into the arms of his pain. Washing his muddy hands in the cool waters, he fought against the stinging pain from the angry burn on his right palm. Rising up, Jon swept a spinning look about his surroundings again, clamping a hand over his injured side. The gorge he had fallen down on his quest for water had killed any chance he had of reaching higher ground now. There was more hope across the creek, however, as the land spread away from him for quite some distance, before reaching up into the blue again to strangle his hopes.

Muttering a prayer, Jon waded across the clear waters, searching for a path, one that could at least afford him a route through the jungle. Further up the creek, Jon spied the sleek, squat mammal drinking from the water. It eyed him with red, malevolent eyes for a time, before darting off back under the shade and thicket of a huge tree.

Shivering, Jon hugged himself, as the chill of the water began to bite. Throwing a look in the other direction, it was then that he saw the tiger.

Jon blinked, shaking the sun from his eyes. On the cusp of the jungle, beyond the creek, past the rocks and boulders, he could see the beast, laying in the shade, watching him with huge orbs of liquid amber.

Jon closed his eyes, fighting against his emotions, his rising fear, his pain and delirium. Over the drumming of his heart, he dared to look again, relaxing as he realised he was losing his mind. It wasn't a tiger, how could it be? It was just the sunlight, splitting the shadows with burning blades of light, playing tricks on his tattered composure.

The tiger blinked, opening its huge mouth to reveal its boredom and the teeth that would soon tear the flesh from his skinny carcass. Despite the fear threatening to strangle the last breath from his lungs, Jon couldn't help but stare when he should have been running in the opposite direction. *A tiger?*

He ignored his own caustic sarcasm and trusted what he was seeing, despite having just done several rounds with a trunk of a tree and coming off second best.

It *was* a tiger! Jon took a step back slowly, his shoes keen for the water again. As far as the news would have you believe, backed up by the experts they had dragged out daily until the story had become *old* news and forced you to find another channel, the *Feline Flu* epidemic, as the media was calling it, had decimated the world's big cat population.

All across the globe, scientists had raced to find a cure, a vaccination that would save the wild lions, tigers, leopards, all the cats that were being found dead, choking to death on a virus that liquefied their intestines and gave them a painful, agonising release from the persecution of the human race.

With the shadow of Covid-19 still haunting mankind

– despite the majority of people reverting to selfish type and forgetting all they had learned about themselves during the globe's year-long lockdown – the jaded world took notice as they thought about someone else for a change.

Jon had always found that he loved animals more than most of the humans he had met in his life, and he had been devastated by the news when it first came to light, back in the spring of 2021. As it began to transpire that this virus needed to be taken just as seriously as Coronavirus, that domestic cats and those great cats in captivity were also being affected, the planet sat up quickly for once, taking note of the race for survival, forgetting about their differences and wars for a time. Well, for a little while, at least...

Some months later, as the cats began to die in people's back yards, and Jon's own cat, Capone, started showing wasting symptoms, the scientists found a cure quicker than they had for Covid-19, and it was the Holy Grail for those still lucky enough to be around.

Madre Natura, it seemed, had been thwarted again, and Jon had lined up personally in a patient line to buy the dwindling supplies of medication that would save his beloved cat. It was the best $10,000 he had spent on an animal, as Capone was back hunting birds in the grounds of his estate within a month.

And that, one expert had suggested on Fox News, though later vilified by his peers, had been where the problem had started. A virulent strain of H5N8, otherwise known as *Bird Flu*, it hadn't started in some lab in China, it had been passed on to the feline world through the very prey they hunted. Nature had not been exclusive with her victims, and all the cats had suffered across the globe. It made perfect sense to Jon, but then what did he know?

Fine for the millions, billions of domestic cats around the globe, as a cull would probably do the world a favour – but the wild cats, the big cats? For many, especially the tiger and snow leopard, already fucked over by man, after months of one not being reported seen anywhere in the countries they inhabited, it was feared that both species of great cat had been dragged into the history books by someone else's fickle finger of fate. The lions had fared slightly better, because of their numbers, the prey they ate and the restrictions quickly put into place in their reserves…

Jon sniffed back his disdain, then froze as the huge head turned curiously in his direction, a fan of white whiskers, as thick as his fingers, twitching his way. Back home, some dumb shits had even kept tigers as pets, seeking attention and a slot on some obscure cable channel. Jon hated that. Those magnificent beasts were not pets for the rich, the famous, or the deranged; they were God's own gifts to the world and before the man upstairs had intervened, mankind had been doing its best to wipe them out.

"Listen to you," Jon said. He was no *Madre Teresa*, more *Signor Capone*, and here he was passing down judgement on other people.

So far, the tiger had decided it wasn't hungry, and Jon slowly backed deeper into the creek, marvelling at the breathless beauty, the miracle before him. For a time, he forgot his head wounds, did not feel the cracks in his ribs, was not aware of the blood running down his face – he just stared at the tiger.

With another yawn, the big cat lowered its huge head onto even bigger paws and closed its eyes – though the pricked ears still turned towards any sound. The tiger's powerful striped flanks, a beautiful tapestry of flame and shadow rose and fell with each breath. Jon swallowed hard, his throat raw again, the sun slow-roasting his pale skin.

Maria is not going to believe this! Jon thought, then swore when he realised that without his phone she would *never* believe him, either. No one would.

His body filled with determination suddenly, a desire to find a phone and get on to the scientists to let them know that there was a tiger still alive. As Jon stepped back again, he hesitated, wondering suddenly if the tiger would be better off left alone.

His thoughts distracted, it was then Jon stumbled on a rock and the tiger was up on its powerful haunches, its fangs bared and its anger rumbling through its body in warning before he could draw breath.

Jon panicked, turning to flee, then heard a mewl of pain, almost like Capone at the back door, when he hadn't been allowed back into the house for a week after clawing the Italian leather on their imported sofa.

Turning reluctantly, slowly, as if expecting to be devoured, Jon was surprised to see that the tiger had collapsed, pulling one of its hind legs on the snare that had just saved his life. Blessing himself, Jon stared through the rising sun, his fear dissolving to anger, then refreshing with hope when he realised someone had been trying to catch an animal... *A Ranger? Scientists? Poachers?*

Jon shrugged at his own thoughts. Well whoever it was, they had bagged more than they bargained for, had probably just earned themselves a small fortune... Jon paused, chuckled, then shook his head. If he survived, that would bring far too much attention his way. But it did tell him that he had not dropped from the sky into a jungle where he would not be found. *Someone had been here before.*

The tiger struggled again, then lay back down weakly, leaving Jon to wonder how long the poor beast had been here. Rallying himself, he stooped down, his shaking fingers finding a stone large enough to defend himself with. Eyeing the big cat, he slipped through the creek, closer, but far enough away from the tiger's reach.

All was quiet now, but for the thunder in Jon's head and chest. A tree behind the tiger shook, as the great cat shied away, baring its fear and pain in warning.

"Hey now, puss," Jon called, then laughed. *Idiot!* He could see the blood about the tiger's back right, no, back left paw, where the wire and the cat's desire for freedom had bit deep over what could have been many days.

Delving for courage, Jon stepped closer, stopping as he was sure he heard the faint, mechanical *whirr* of a camera, or something. Hesitating, he scanned the jungle beyond, but with the sun filling the gorge now, he couldn't see anything. Shaking his head and doubts away he moved to the right of the tiger, ignoring its curling lips and mouth full of daggers, as it recoiled, growling in fear.

Gripping his rock, Jon felt a bit like David as he came within several feet of the beast, dwarfed by the sheer size of the cat. Sure, he had seen the tigers in San Diego Zoo before, had been left breathless by them, as they lounged in the sun, sleeping and waiting to be fed – but nothing could prepare him for the emotions, the sheer magnificence of seeing a tiger in its natural habitat.

In that one moment, Jon bore the weight of mankind on his shoulders and the guilt for those who had taken these beasts to the brink of extinction, allowing them to fall foul of nature's wrath. Their shame took him to the thicket, beyond the growls of the tiger, past the huge tail that swatted the air angrily in warning.

With one eye on the tiger, Jon followed the snare into the jungle, finding the tree it was tethered to. He swore when he realised the snare was made from steel wire, thought again about the damage it must have done to the tiger.

He found the clamp binding the snare to the tall tree and slowly began to unscrew the steel carabiner. Jon hesitated, looking at the huge cat that had quietened down and was watching him through the screen of undergrowth with unblinking, curious eyes.

If I let it go, it will eat me... Jon thought suddenly. He looked back at the tiger, who flicked its tail impatiently.

Cussing, Jon finished unscrewing the device and gave the tiger some slack on the wire snare. His heart froze as he dropped it and slowly reached for his rock.

For a time, the tiger just stared at Jon, sizing him up. "Go on then, scat," Jon hissed, his voice strained, choked by his fear. "You're free, go."

Jon waved his arms and the cat leapt up. As it did, it began to realise that it might be free and it backed slowly away. The tiger took several steps, but finally its trapped paw stepped from the loosening snare.

For a brief second it eyed Jon again, licking its lips hungrily.

"Don't even think about it, Tony," Jon warned, raising the rock in his hand. He yelled again, throwing the rock towards the tiger.

With a blink that could have almost conveyed hurt and confusion, the tiger turned and bounded away down the gorge from view in two powerful strides.

Jon stared into the sun for a time, trying to calm himself, amazed at what he had just done. He collapsed into the arms of his laughter, a rich, deep peal of delirium and joy. A while ago, he had felt like he was going to die – now, at this moment, he knew that he had never felt more alive.

Drawing his battered knees up under his chin, Jon buried his head in them and rocked backwards and forward, his body heaving, his composure breaking down into wracking sobs. As the realisation of what had just happened overcame him, Jon fell back to the ground, staring dazedly up at the tall tree trunks towering above him, up at the sunlight breaking the canopy in golden ribbons.

The trees began to swirl, framing his darkening vision in silver as events overpowered him and Jon Galnia fell into the arms of his rising exhaustion.

Jon did not see, sometime later, the shadow that slipped across the rocks towards him.

He did not feel the hands that reached out to grab him.

CHAPTER FIVE

Hope

Robert Williams snapped awake, gasping for breath. With shaking elbows propped on his drawn knees, he blinked away his troubled dreams and searched for Sara Gonzales. She was still beside him, her serene face covered in a feverish sheen of glistening sweat.

Robert rolled across the rough ground to her side and was thankful for the shallow rise and fall of her breast. Emptying his lungs with relief, Robert kneaded the pain from his temple with the palms of his trembling hands and attempted to clear his vision.

Finding shelter beneath the branches of the largest tree he had ever seen, a tree whose leaves fanned out in a brilliant explosion of nature, Robert had ensured they were protected from the elements by the wreckage he had salvaged to make a shelter. Building a small fire to keep them alive through the cold night, he had ensured Sara was wrapped in the blanket, before settling down beside her. He had fallen quickly into his exhaustion, only to be pulled back regularly through the night by the screeches, the piercing calls and the almost electronic chatter of the jungle, that did its level best to keep him awake.

Not one to struggle with sleep, generally, Robert fell through the long night, nodding off to sleep and starting awake as he shuffled his dreams and worries together, not certain at times of which was which.

A cold, grey light probed the lower jungle now,

suggesting that dawn had arrived, though not in force. Strangely quiet, his surroundings remained still, no breeze to stir the thicket, no calls to spoil his solace.

We will need more water today, Robert thought, ignoring the growl of hunger from his stomach and his desire to finish off the sandwiches he had started and the last of the water. He flicked a look towards Sara, whose need was greater than his, and shook his head sadly. *We will need more than that...*

After several minutes, Robert rallied the strength he needed to rise and search their immediate surroundings, keeping their makeshift camp and the flight attendant's still form within view. One turn wrong, one momentary lapse and he might never find her again.

The jungle offered the captain little hope. No oasis to satiate his thirst, no magical path to lead him to safety. There was only nature's endless labyrinth before him and he cursed himself, wishing he had spent more of his time on the ground than in the air.

After several minutes, Robert gave up, trudging back across the forgiving ground towards his charge, gathering fallen greenery as he went. They would need a second fire, to act as a signal to anyone searching for them, as he would not be able to rely on the jet for much longer. The smouldering wreckage was a mile to his left now, still smarting angrily from the sabotage, still underlining how *lucky* they were to be alive.

Fighting against his grief, trying to remain strong, Robert hurried back to Sara's side and knelt beside her again. Reaching out a hand, he caressed her cheek.

"Come on Sara," he whispered, noting the desperation edging his words. "I need you. Come back to me."

She did not stir, did not respond to him, and stifling a sob, Robert took her left hand between his clammy palms and squeezed them gently.

"Help is coming, lovely," he whispered. "We'll just sit here for a time and recover our strength. It will be alright, we have survived the worst of it!"

Help did not come.

For a long while Robert sat at Sara's side, watching the golden light fill the jungle, listening to the life that stirred their surroundings and the hissing flames from the signal fire. As the shadows slipped away and the animals, the birds, the insects and the reptiles returned, so did the heat. It was a cleansing warmth at first, quickly restoring some hope and vigour to Robert's bones, before draining his enthusiasm and sapping his strength long before he had even attempted to try and find some water.

Sara remained in the grip of worry for Robert, thrashing occasionally, muttering the odd word in Spanish that Robert could not understand. Frustrated at the shackles that kept him by her side, irritated with the absent courage he would need to leave her there and go foraging, Robert spent his time cursing his predicament.

Did Hannibal Barca turn back when his epic journey across the Pyrenees was on the cusp of utter disaster? When all about him seemed lost, did Alfred of Wessex lose his faith? Robert shook his head ruefully. The greatest names throughout history, his beloved history, had made the hard decisions, had not given up, despite the odds, and here he was, the day after the crash, ready to do that very thing, preparing to use his own lack of courage as an excuse to wait for someone else to save the day.

"How much more inspiration do I need?" Robert berated himself, rising.

Studying history helped him to escape from the present and to learn from the past, to understand the great civilisations and of how the world had been shaped and forged into the broken sword it was today. Mankind was still making the same mistakes of their forbearers, never learning from the past, not listening to the ghosts of those who had left their tales for other ages in verse and prose and recount.

Clenching his fists tightly, his mind swirling with whispers of the tales that inspired him, the characters, now lost to the mists of the past, who he found more affinity with than most people he had met in his own life... well, with a couple of rare exceptions.

"I'll be back soon," he promised Sara, looking down at her, underlining his words with a firm nod of his head.

It was then, for the first time, that Robert detected the distant, rasping thunder of the approaching helicopter.

Reining in his excitement, of which he shared with Sara repeatedly, Robert listened intently, watching the blue skies and the plume of trailing smoke above the jungle for a glimpse of their rescuers. With his heart racing, any doubts he harboured, any worry he had, slipped from his aching body, stealing away the taut pain from the burns to his face and hands.

The helicopter flashed low over them for the briefest of glimpses, a black shadow that left its roar behind, moments after it had passed. Mesmerised, Robert watched the trees swirl madly above him in a frenzied dance, closed his eyes as he felt the force from the helicopter's rotors cool and dry his face.

A bit of an aviation anorak, he couldn't be sure what type of helicopter it was and at this moment, he did not really care...

Smiling gleefully, Robert looked down at Sara. Her hair was blowing madly about her face, their surroundings full of fallen leaves, caught up in the arms of their rescuers wake.

Moments after, Robert's hopes began to fail as the helicopter slipped away into silence and the jungle's inhabitants returned to their daily routines. The hollow quiet pressed down upon the pilot and he tussled with his fears, resisting the urge to race after the helicopter.

Surely they had seen the smoke from the wreckage, traced the scar across the land?

An hour slipped away, taking Robert's hopes with them. The rescue team would need to find a safe landing zone somewhere, of course, then pick their way across the jungle to the crash site. Heaven knows how far that might be, how long that could take.

All thoughts of rescue were forgotten as Sara began to whimper and thrash. Kneeling beside her, Robert held her down gently, whispering soft words of assurance.

"Sara, help is here," he hushed her. "Hold on, just a little longer."

When she was calm again, Robert rose up, shielding his eyes against the brightness, staring towards the wreckage for signs of life. On a fallen, rotted trunk, some distance away, a large lizard lounged in the sun, warming its bright green body. A huge eye bulged and swirled as it watched Robert rise, eyeing him warily.

"We'll be out of your way soon," Robert grinned, feeling his hopes rally.

Another hour dragged across Robert's nerves, clawing at his fraying composure as no help arrived. Just as he was beginning to believe that he had been hallucinating, dreaming up his rescuers, he spied the shadows shifting in the sunlight.

Squinting, Robert shielded his eyes, eyes that widened as he picked out the detail of a man. His breath caught on the joy in his throat and his heart quickened with excitement as a second, and then a third rescuer appeared out of the hazy gloom.

The signal fire worked!

Robert cupped his hands about his mouth and roared out a call for help, a high, strangled cry that sent the lizard scuttling for cover and the monkeys nearby, away with their anger, high into the canopy overhead. Robert waved madly as his calls echoed several times away to silence, and the rescuers' heads snapped in his direction. Robert would recall later, though at the time his mind was full of glee, that he must have leapt several feet off the ground as he punched the air happily.

"We are saved, Sara, we are rescued," Robert cried out, his face no longer aching from his burns, only his relief. He did not even think about his employer at that moment.

There were six in the rescue party and three of them hurried away from the wreckage, picking their way up the rising ground towards the man before them. As they neared, Robert fought back his tears, tussled with the grief that swept through his body.

"Are we glad to see you," Robert called out, smiling broadly as the nearest rescuer came close.

Tall, lean and fresh-faced, the man raised his gloved hand in greeting, hurrying past the fallen tree towards them.

"What the hell happened?" the man asked, his cropped head turning, as his dark eyes fell upon Sara's still form.

Robert followed his gaze, returning his attention

quickly back. It was then that he studied the man closely, sensed his first doubts rise to the surface in warning.

The man's face was covered in a thick, dark beard, the darkest thing on his body. Pale faced, his mouth split into an affable broad smile, his eyes gleaming in the sun. His brown hair was cropped, his ears large and the left full of studs and what looked to be an earpiece. Clothed in grey trousers, the man wore dark, hard boots and what looked to Robert be a dark green tactical vest. His bare, muscular arms bore several tattoos, and a thick strap cut diagonally across his chest, though Robert could not see what for.

"Are you ok, sir?" the man asked again. Robert nodded, his eyes flicking beyond to the man and woman stood several metres behind, both equally dressed. The woman, who wore a wide-brimmed khaki hat, turned to look back down towards the wreckage and it was then that Robert saw the rifle, slung over her back.

The first man spoke again, though Robert did not hear what he said, as he was beginning to panic. *None of his rescuers were Indian*.

"Sorry," Robert stammered. "I am just in shock, that is all. We thought we would die out here, before help arrived."

The man nodded, offering a sympathetic smile. "You sure picked a hell of a hole to drop in to. What happened, man? Where are you from? How many people were onboard?"

The man had what sounded like an Australian or Kiwi accent. Robert panicked inside, and his fear may have flashed in his eyes as the man tensed slightly.

"We lost one engine," Robert explained, trying to think, trying to remain calm. "I brought her down as best I could, but w-we lost our co-pilot – and Sara's badly injured. Can you help her, please?"

The man nodded, apparently satisfied. Running a hand through his beard, he looked behind, waving forward the second man. Bald-headed, this man was even bigger, his huge arms flexing as he dragged a pack off one broad shoulder and hurried towards them.

"Is there anyone else?" the Australian asked, dragging Robert's attention back as the second man knelt beside Sara.

Robert Williams' heart threatened to make a run for it, as if something was inside his chest, and his eyes darted about worriedly. *Were they looking for Mr. Galnia? Why did that woman have a rifle?*

"Just the three of us," Robert lied, hoping that his words were more convincing than they sounded. "We were heading to Taiwan to pick up some clients."

Sara began to thrash and the large man tried to calm her down. When Robert finally looked back from his concern, the lean man stepped close, slamming the butt of a rifle into his face.

The man watched the white-haired pilot crumple before him, before turning to the woman.

"Get on the horn to them," the New-Zealander snarled, shouldering his weapon. "Find out who the hell they are and who else was with them."

CHAPTER SIX

Ramifications

First Secretary Aasim Rana was already on the telephone to the Minister of Health when his aide, Samira, knocked on the door to his office and entered without waiting for permission. Frowning over his steel-rimmed spectacles, the First Secretary sent her his displeasure as he nodded his head to the voice in his ear.

"I understand, sir," he answered, waving his aide to him with a sharp cut of his free hand. The voice on the other end of the line droned on as Rana watched the young woman hurry to his desk. Leaning across, she passed him a note, then stepped respectfully back two paces, hiding her face from his irritation.

Unfurling the note on his desk with thin fingers, Rana's eyes narrowed as he struggled to read the words on the paper that were lost to the blistering day outside the window behind him. Ignoring a question from the Minister of Health, he looked up at his aide, forcing her to look to him with the weight of his stare as he covered the mouthpiece with his hand.

"He is on the phone now?" Rana whispered, raising his voice to be heard mid-question, above the rattling drone of the air conditioning.

Samira nodded. "Yes, First Secretary. He insisted it was very urgent."

Licking his lips thoughtfully, Rana motioned for her to remain a moment, as he turned his attention back to the impatience in his ear.

"Forgive me, Minister," Rana said hastily. "I must attend to an urgent matter. Be assured that when it arrives, I will ensure your proposal gets the full attention and time with the Prime Minister that it deserves." He paused, nodding his head. "Yes, yes, thank you. Blessings on your day, too."

Rana slammed the phone down, pushing his spectacles back up his narrow nose. Sighing, he fixed his dark eyes on his aide.

"Give me a few moments, Samira," the First Secretary said, sighing heavily, "then put the ambassador through. Oh, and can you bring me some coffee, please?"

Samira dealt him one of her youthful, flashing smiles to hide her relief, then hurried for the door across the dark green carpet.

She had replaced the redoubtable Heera, who had served him so well these last few years before her retirement, and in the three months she had been with him, Samira had breathed fresh life into his office, and into his otherwise stressful existence. Rana watched her leave, marvelling at the way the sun gleamed in her thick, midnight-black hair. He shook his head reproachfully. He should not allow it, but she was starting to get under his skin, itching him back to life in a way that he thought never to experience again, though it was tempered by his growing irritation with her.

A traditionalist, Rana was finding it hard to ignore that Samira had clearly been westernised as so many girls were these days, preferring a skirted suit and blouse to the Sari and Chunni. He had fought tirelessly with his own two daughters over the last few years, as they, too, were seduced by the lure of western fashion and materialism, and he was not sure if it was a fight he wanted to lose again.

Rana felt his heart begin to race as his thoughts began to stir, stolen away from an older man's wants to the matter at hand.

What did the American Embassy want?

The internal comms on his phone lit up and Samira's honeyed voice echoed above the air-con. "First Secretary, I have Thomas Miller, from the American Embassy here in Delhi, for you."

"Thank you, Samira, put him through," Rana responded. Picking up the receiver, he waited for the echo to cut off, before pressing the flashing red light on the console.

"Mr. Miller, this is Secretary Rana," Aasim said.

"*Secretary Rana, sorry for the impromptu call,*" a soft, American accent responded in his ear. "*I am Thomas Miller, the United States Federal Aviation Attaché here at our New Delhi Embassy.*"

The First Secretary felt the room cool another ten degrees. "What can I do for you, Mr. Miller?"

"*Earlier today, we received a call from one of our citizens, back home in the U.S. She had received a voicemail from her husband yesterday, a business man, that said his jet had lost its engines and was going down over central India,*" the measured voice responded. "*I was hoping to liaise with you, as we have heard no reports of a jet crashing.*"

Rana sat forward in his chair, barely able to find the words forming in his throat. "I fully understand your concern, Mr. Miller. I can assure you, as you can probably tell from my shock, that we have had no reports of such a crash, either. Be certain that I will look into this matter immediately with the Ministry of Civil Aviation and report back to you with my findings."

"*That would be much appreciated, sir,*" came the due response and Rana smiled as Samira returned with a cup of coffee for him. "*Naturally, we will need to work closely with you on this matter, as I will have to report back to The White House as soon as I can clarify what has happened to one of our citizens.*"

"Of course, of course," Rana spluttered, allowing his eyes to trace the curves of Samira's hips as she departed again. "Have your secretary contact my office with the details of the flight, and in the meantime, I will look into this matter with the utmost urgency."

"*I appreciate it, First Secretary,*" Mr. Miller said. "*Your aide has my number and I will await your call. Thank you for your time.*"

The Ambassador was gone before Aasim could respond and he glowered at the phone, before slamming it back down. *Nobody took the time, these days.*

Alone now, Rana could allow his fears to overcome him. Sipping at the over-boiled coffee, he juggled the plates, suddenly beginning to spin above his head. The Gods, surely, were not trying to intervene now? *Surely not?*

Instead of calling Samira, the First Secretary unlocked the left drawer of his desk with the brass key he had in his shirt pocket. Suddenly sweating, he reached for the back of the drawer and pulled forth the burner phone that was hidden behind the diary and stationery.

Unlocking the Nokia, he thumbed down to the third contact on the phone and dialled his man at the Civil Aviation Authority. He needed to check the credibility of this story and, more urgently, he needed to confirm that if it had, where this jet had crashed and why he had not already been informed about it.

This was not going to be the day, Rana snarled silently

as the call started to connect. *They had come too far for the fates to intervene now.*

Samira Jethwani looked up from her desk as the First Secretary hurried from his office. Dressed in a suit, one size too big for his sharp shoulders, the small man hurried over to her, his briefcase clutched tightly in his right hand. Samira frowned before she could hide her concern. Aasim Rana had buckled under the weight of pressure on him and the Prime Minister in the last few months since she had joined. Thin-faced anyway, his cheeks were deeply hollowed by sleepless nights and deeper glasses of brandy, and his thick dark hair was now streaked with streams of silver. As he stopped before her, the First Secretary searched for a calming breath, giving Samira time to notice how his dark complexion had paled somewhat since the call from the American Embassy.

"Cancel my appointments for this afternoon, Samira," he said, turning to leave.

"But, First Secretary," Samira cried, halting him in mid-step. "You have a meeting with *NDTV* at 3pm. They will not take kindly to another cancellation."

"They can take it however they want," came the spitting response, and before Samira could recover from her shock to protest, Aasim Rana was gone, his haste and anger crashing after him.

Samira looked down at the diary, open on her desk, her hazel eyes widening with worry as she stared at the 3pm entry there. There were already far too many shadows stretching over the Lok Sabha, and she was determined that her burgeoning career would not be swept away by the coming storm.

Eager to distract her concerns, Samira headed for the

First Secretary's office to clear up the shattered cup she had heard Rana break, moments before he had left.

Aasim Rana dabbed his forehead with his handkerchief, staring up through his sunglasses at the clear sky, watching in wonderment as a solitary *Cheel* wheeled silently above him. He marvelled as he tracked the beautiful Raptor through its cloudless kingdom, of how it had somehow managed to find some air in the still heat of the heavy day.

On the ground, the midday heat and distant traffic roared in his ears, stirring the embers of a furious headache, his temples already taught with tension. Feeling he was starting to slip into paranoia, Aasim dragged himself back to the Black Kite, watching as it slipped away towards India Gate and the tourists that braved the furious sun for their photo opportunities.

The First Secretary sighed, turning his attention to the shade of *The Canopy*. The beautiful Cupola with its domed canopy, at this time was a tranquil oasis, surrounded on its island by four lawned pathways, a short walk east of the tourists gathering about India Gate. Aasim knew they would be here soon, braving the traffic with their tour guides, heading towards him to spoil his solace.

A trolley rattled behind him and Aasim turned, seeing that a young man was already positioning himself underneath the shade of a tree, ready for the influx of pale flesh that would be craving his cold water and ice cream. The man smiled broadly in his direction and waved.

Nodding his head, certain he would not be recognised here at this time of the day, Aasim reached for his newspaper and fanned his face with the *Times of India*, ignoring glimpses of yet another stark headline. Delhi at this time of the year was always hot, but events, so carefully planned, so thoughtfully orchestrated, were beginning to stiffen with cold uncertainty.

Could that one telephone call ruin everything?

Jostling the thoughts swirling about his head, Rana sat down on the lower step of the simple, yet beautiful monument that had once held a statue of the *Rex Imperator*, George V. Some years ago, the statue had been moved, and since that time the pedestal had remained empty. In 1981 the Indian Parliament had raised the popular idea in the Sansad Bhavan, the parliament house, to commission a statue of Mahatma Ghandi to be placed on the empty pedestal.

Aasim watched two sparrows bicker in the hedgerow for a time, then turned his thoughts to the empty pedestal. The ghostly image of a statue shimmered in the heat for a moment and the First Secretary smiled wanly.

He and Prime Minister Nehru were about to raise the suggestion of the statue again in Parliament, only this time, with their party *Bharatiya Janata* holding the majority, the idea would become more than just populist fancy – a fact realised by Rana, who had already had a statue commissioned. The public and tourists would be overjoyed by the news that the Father of Democracy would forever watch over the distant monument to the fallen.

Aasim sighed. A few positive headlines would certainly ease their turmoil for a few days...

Any thoughts of the political storm that rumbled across the papers each day were dispelled as the First Secretary spied the tall, lean man hurrying through the haze towards him along the western pathway. As if sensing Aasim wanted to be alone, the sparrows took their debate over towards the ice cream seller, who threw them some crumbs from his lunch tray.

"Apologies," the bald-headed man offered, fighting for his breath. He hurried to join Rana under the shade, his pale blue shirt stained under the armpits. "The traffic on Mathura Road was terrible; a truck lost a wheel and overturned. It will take me many hours to get home."

Aasim waved away the man's discomfort, feeling himself prickle with irritation. "Well, I will try to keep this short for you, Hasit," he hissed, leaning close, feeling his shirt drag across his skin like wet parchment. "Why have I not been informed of the crash in Madhya Pradesh?"

Hasit blinked the fear from his eyes. "A crash, First Secretary? No! I can assure you, there has been no such thing."

Rana grabbed the man's left wrist, digging his overlong nails into the flesh. "Then explain why I had a call from the American embassy this morning? A woman received a message from her husband – his jet was going down over Madhya."

Hasit recoiled. "We have been monitoring all no-fly zones, as you requested. My team have been in place for two weeks now, despite the Union's outrage. As soon as it is done, things will return to normal – all records will be erased, all traces removed."

Rana let go of the shaking wrist, his mind reeling. Since the Feline Flu outbreak, the Indian Government had imposed strict no-fly zones over all of their National Parks, as the forlorn race to save the tigers there began. International attention was fixed very firmly on India for many months, though it waned as the weeks slipped by and the reports of sightings became less frequent. As the number of big cats found dead decreased, the media's attention turned elsewhere, returning to political matters around the globe.

Shaking his head, Rana held up a hand in apology. He fixed his man with a narrow stare. "You are certain? There was no plane?"

"I will double-check, First Secretary," Hasit blurted. "But I would have been notified – this is such an important week... only one aircraft has entered the region and you–"

Rana glared Hasit into silence. "I want to hear from you within the hour. They will make contact soon, Hasit, and I must report to the Prime Minister before the Americans start to lose patience."

Hasit rose, nodding his sweating brow rapidly. "Of course, of course!" He turned to hurry away, then hesitated as he sent a promise over one shoulder. "I will look into the matter of this jet for you, sir. It is most perplexing."

Aasim Rana waved the man away and sent a look towards the ice cream seller. The man was sleeping with his back to the cart, a newspaper over his face.

There was a time, some years ago, when his life had been that simple...

Shaking his head, the First Secretary watched as Hasit was swallowed up by the shimmering horizon.

If the Americans started to dig further, it would become more than just *perplexing*. There was much more at stake than recovering the corpses of a few foreign citizens, it was the very foundations of Democracy at risk should events happening in Madhya Pradesh become publicly known.

Aasim Rana rose, stretching his aching back, stamping the heavy tension from his legs. Fishing in a pocket for his phone, he flipped it open and called for his driver, parked nearby on the Shahjahan Road.

There was no time to waste. He needed to get back to Raisina Hill. He needed to speak to the Prime Minister.

CHAPTER SEVEN

A Friend Indeed

Jon fell through a dream – not the kind of dream where you land in a soft, king-sized bed, with a bottle of Dom chilling on ice and two long legs wrapped about your waist, neither of them belonging to your wife. No, not that one, the one where you are pushed, falling, falling swiftly away from safety into nothingness.

Each time Jon was about to hit the bottom of the unseen pit he snapped awake, only to be dragged back into his unconsciousness and the voices that whispered at him from the shadows.

Amidst the cacophony, the roar of those who had shared his life with him so far, Gio's incessant excitement piped loudest, chatting about everything and nothing, as Jon came in from a long day.

Papa, papa! We destroyed the Death Star, but Vader escaped. Will you help me catch him? Will you?

Maria's voice came next, as she argued with him and displayed her ability to convey a thousand different emotions in one warning word.

Jon!

A honey-sweet, heavily accented Russian voice whispered mockingly at him next and Jon moaned in torment as he thought about the woman he had met with in Moscow, saw her tongue lick the taste of the whisky from those painted lips, all over again.

It pleases him...

71

"I bet it fucking does," Jon snarled, thrashing and moaning.

Jon did not feel the hands that pushed him back down onto the rickety bed, was not aware of the concern that wiped a damp cloth gently across his sweating brow.

Come hai potuto, fratello? Sei assetato di potere?

The shadows wrapped unseeing arms tightly about him as a gunshot sang out to him from the past, echoing loudly. Jon panicked, struggling to escape his fate as he slammed back into the darkness.

Jon lurched awake, clutching at his chest, fighting for the breath that would not come. His surroundings, not much brighter than his nightmare, span before him and he collapsed back, exhausted, as his heart raced and his eyes rolled in his head.

His head lolling, Jon found a breath and drank deeply, fighting against the nausea filling his throat. Above him, smoky rafters danced seductively in a flickering light and his nose, once clogged with kerosene, was now filled with incense – he knew that, as Maria had gotten into all that crap, a few years back. Even the cat was pissed off with the smell of the house these days.

Growling, though it came out as a groan, Jon fought against his body's desire for rest. The sight of the wooden rafters and the wattling roof above him was suddenly filled by the concerned shadows of a face, a dark, wizened face lit up by bright eyes and teeth that were framed by a comforting smile.

"Where am I?" Jon slurred. His throat was dry and he felt like he had been sampling his own Russian product.

The shadows smiled at him and said something that Jon could not hear, or understand. The face brightened and an eager head nodded to enforce further unheard words.

Confused, Jon shook his head, regretting it as his vision blurred and the pain in his body cried out for attention.

"Phone, I need a phone."

The smiling face shook from side to side as if it understood and as Jon fell back into his dreams, he had the feeling that his troubles were only just beginning.

The only other time in her life that Sara Gonzales had awoken to utter confusion was the day after the operation that had saved her life. Since the day of the car accident, she had grasped her second chance of actually living her life with both hands. Shaken from her faith, but not torn from it, each new day on the path God had shown to her, every breath she drew was a bonus. Sara had taken her second chance with both hands, travelling the world, seeing new things, sharing new adventures.

Not bad for a bright, yet tempestuous girl from Cananea, Mexico, who had grown up not really knowing her father, and had spent her days getting into more mischief than she could handle as she tried to care for her ailing mother and four siblings.

To Sara, that life seemed to belong to someone else now, a jigsaw of fading memories that she could never piece together, could not fully complete.

She would never forget that day in the hospital, however, some eight years ago now, when she had slipped from her three-week coma into a room full of bright lights and blurred, concerned faces.

Dazed and confused, Sara blinked awake, her senses struggling to catch up as her cold, numb body began to register its pain. Shaking, she raised her head, struggling to keep it upright as she tasted the dry cloth in her mouth.

Sara began to choke on her panic, gagging and moaning as she fought to control her fear. Her vision cleared as she struggled to sit up from the camp bed she was resting on, and as her muscles screamed and fresh pain knifed through her right leg, she was dragged back down by her wrists, zip-tied to the bed's frame.

Panting, she fought to calm her fear, failing to steady her erratic breathing.

Where am I?

Unable to register her predicament, Sara closed her eyes, grimacing as the pain in her head started to overcome her. Try as she might, she could not recall a thing. All she knew was that she had been on an international flight with Jon Galnia, flying out of...?

Puffing out her worry, Sara turned her attention to the left, away from the stiff agony on the right side of her head, and tried to take in her surroundings. As her sight adjusted to the interior of the tent, she became aware of just how hot she was. Her clothes were soddened and the tent was heavy and humid.

It was then that she realised she was not alone, that Robert Williams was also gagged and tied up, his arms wrapped behind the tall central pole of the canvas prison they were being held in.

Sara thrashed as she kicked herself upright and pain shot down through her injured leg. Forgetting her own predicament, she swore through her gag, as the sweat on her arms frosted over with worry.

Robert was a mess. His scorched head was down, resting on one shoulder, and the dried blood on his face was redder than his patchwork maze of burns.

"Rob," Sara growled through her gag.

The pilot did not respond, though he continued to snore fitfully, his chest rising and falling steadily. Sighing with relief, Sara looked about the tent. Apart from two metal-framed camp beds and the empty table and chair just beyond Robert, there was nothing, nobody else.

Where was Steven Gaines? Where was Mr. Galnia?

Her mind was starting to work now, the embers of her spirit beginning to glower. Although she could not remember the events of the last few days, *something* had clearly happened. Dark thoughts surfaced momentarily, thoughts about her employer and the potential danger she had accepted when she had decided to take the Galnia dollar.

Had her employer's luck finally run out? Had she abused her second chance?

Her wild hair danced as she shook her head in denial – immediately regretting it, as fresh agony spun her senses for a moment. Calming herself, Sara tried to relax her body, eyeing the ties that bound her to the bed. The plastic bonds were pulled tight and she could see the red marks from where they had cut into her wrists.

Tugging furiously away from her rising panic, she sat up on the side of the bed, wincing as the thing creaked and groaned in protest. Throwing her caution at the sunlight spilling through the canvas door, she dragged herself and the bed across the rough ground towards Robert.

Her heart roared in her head as she came near, not hearing the steel-framed bed scrape across a stone, not realising that there were distant voices, once engaged in debate and now ominously silent.

Using her tongue that was so dry it felt like it belonged to somebody else, she tried to force the gag from her mouth. The cloth... that was actually Robert's tie, she realised, did not move as it was bound far too tightly.

A shadow fell across the entrance and Sara froze in panic as the canvas door was thrown aside, parted by the searching metal barrel of a rifle.

Sara blinked the purple hues from her sight as a woman filled her view.

"And where do you think you are going?" the woman enquired, her voice filled with curiosity.

Before Sara could respond, the woman, her identity hidden by the sun, stepped aside as a larger man stepped into the tent. He carried a bottle of water in one hand and stepped forward, kneeling slowly before his captive.

"Hey, calm down," the man soothed, studying the terrified face before him. "You were knocked out after the crash – you are suffering from blood loss and severe concussion."

Sara recoiled as the man forced her to sit back down on the bed and reached behind to untie her gag.

Gasping for air, Sara swallowed her words as the man unscrewed the bottle of water and held it towards her.

Hiding her fear, Sara nodded her thanks and drank thirstily from the offered bottle. The man held it to her lips for some time, then pulled it back as the water began to spill down her chin.

"That's enough, for now," the man stated. He stood up, stepping back alongside the woman.

"Who are you people?" Sara gasped. "Why are we tied up like this?"

The woman looked to the tall man questioningly. She had the deepest red hair Sara had ever seen. Neatly plaited, it reached down to the small of her back. Short and slender, she was dressed in green combat trousers and a matching vest, her slim waist belted tightly, bearing two large pouches. When the man did not reply, the woman looked back at their *guests*, watching them both with emerald eyes. She had one of those faces you couldn't read, but there was more than enough to hold your attention there in the full lips and freckles that some super models would kill to have.

The man folded his arms across his chest and Sara could see the tattoo on his right forearm; a skull with a dagger pierced through it, though the hilt appeared to be a fern leaf.

"*Quid Pro Quo*, miss," the man said, his accent soft, yet harsh at the same time. He flicked his eyebrows meaningfully. "First, who are you?"

Sara's heart raced as she tried to grasp onto her response. He had a strong face, the type of face she would have found to her liking, had the circumstances been different. She glanced about the tent, flicking a look to the woman, towards Robert, towards freedom, and then back to the man when he clicked his fingers impatiently in front of her face.

"Help us to help you."

Sara's brown eyes flashed angrily, though she hoped it looked like frustration. "I cannot! I don't know where I am, how I came to be here. Why I am tied up like this?"

The woman placed a gentle hand on the man's arm as the flight attendant began to sob, her fear and confusion overcoming her.

"She is still concussed," the woman whispered, soothing his rising anger. "If you hadn't hit the pilot so hard..."

The man winced, drawing in a calming breath as he unclenched a fist. Sighing, he looked back to the woman, tied to the bed before him.

"Get some rest," he said, gently. "You are confused. I can't blame you, after what you have been through." He turned to leave, then stopped, looking back over one muscular shoulder. "We'll bring you some food later. In the meantime, gather your wits as I will want some answers to my questions *next* time."

The man stalked from the tent and his companion stood for a time, watching, as the flight attendant fell back deeper into her despair. Wincing, the woman shook her head sadly and followed her captain out into the sunlight.

Sara stopped sobbing after they had been gone no more than a minute. Dragging in her composure, she sat up again, shaking free from her distress. As terrified as she was, she had only broken down to buy her thoughts some more time. Anyone who could learn to speak and walk again after a near-fatal accident had nothing to fear anymore from the unknown. It was just another challenge to face, another test of her faith.

They would be back later, he would be back, and he would want answers. If Sara was going to get through this, if she was going to find out what was going on, if she was going to get answers of her own, she would need to give them something.

Steeling herself, Sara Gonzales fell back onto the bed and cleared her mind. When the man returned, she would have his answers.

When he came back, she would be ready for him.

"So, what do you think?" the woman asked, as she joined the man back at the table and put her hat back on. He was hunched forward, palms pressed downwards, pouring his attention and frustration over the map of the region again, diverting his anxiety there.

Sam Brooks studiously ignored her question, just one of his many traits that got under her skin and clawed at her patience. Sighing, she stared out across the lagoon, at the best office she had ever attended a meeting in.

It was the heart of the day and the sun, some 45°c, was becoming intolerable. Double that for the humidity and it felt as if you had just got out of a bath, fully clothed in combats. Fidgeting with discomfort, she wanted nothing more than to get the hell out of the heat as soon as possible.

Pulling her sunglasses from her breast pocket, she put the shades on, staring at the surroundings that were now their base of operations. The waters of the lagoon shimmered in the sun, a diamond pool that glistened grey under her *UV* protection. The ground before the water was sandy, cracked and dry from the Indian summer's wrath; crying out for the monsoon season that was just six weeks away.

The jungle surrounding the lagoon writhed in the heat and before her the woman could see a solitary cloud, nestling below the summit of what she had identified earlier as *Vulture Point*. A cry drew her attention back to the water's edge, just beyond the large expanse of ground where they had been able to set down the helicopter and pitch four tents. A large *Dhole* still bickered with some of its pack, as they fought over the scraps from the carcass of what would have once been, probably, a deer or perhaps an Indian gazelle.

Insects buzzed about the kill, darting in amongst the wild dogs for a share of their lunch, and for a time the woman forgot why she was actually there. Across the water, flocks of white birds drifted lazily together, sharing the day's news, debating what and where they should feed next. She couldn't tell what they were from where she was, but she would guess they were probably *Red-throated Loon*.

Another species she could tick off her list. The one moment of joy she had found since they had approached the target area and spotted the crashed jet.

"Lisa," Sam muttered, dragging her attention back, as he traced the map of the region with a thoughtful finger. Eyeing the scar on the side of his head, she waited patiently, ignoring the static hissing from the radio on the table beside the map.

"The latest *ping* came from one of our cameras in Sector 4," Sam said, fixing her with the briefest of looks, "the same camera we had success from before we were deployed."

Lisa ran a hand over her forehead, wiping away a bead of sweat. "The terrain looks heavy going. It will take them a day's tabbing to reach it, and God only knows how long to get back."

Sam rolled the tension from his broad neck then diverted his thoughts by cracking his knuckles. "Uh huh!"

Lisa looked away, wincing at the sound of his popping knuckles. *She hated that sound!* She had never liked it growing up when her brother did it, even more so when he started to do it in her ear to make her jump. The day she left home to go to university Lisa had breathed a long, hard sigh of relief. Matt was still a jerk, even now...

Sam's concern at finding the crashed jet had not been helped by the conversation on the scrambled phone with their employers. They were reminded, in no uncertain terms, that they were working to a deadline and that there had to be no loose ends, *nothing* that could compromise what they were trying to do.

Lisa swallowed, glancing back to the tent where the two survivors were being held. She shuddered when she thought about what would have to happen once they had located the other survivors. It was something the former Ecologist had not signed up for, despite the obscene amount of money on offer.

"When will we hear back about the jet? Who was *really* on it?" Lisa dared to ask, pushing her shades back up onto the bridge of her nose. As far as she was concerned, the longer it took, the more chance they had of their orders changing.

Sam's rugged face hardened and his bright eyes flashed like steel. "The Indians are having trouble finding out – which is odd." Sam straightened and started pacing nervously. When he spoke again, his voice was guarded and hushed. "There are so many things that could go wrong on this one, Lisa. We are not supposed to even be here, let alone hunting! If they can't find out about the jet, how the hell are they going to be able to stop this from getting out?"

Lisa offered him a lame smile, that hid her own concerns. "We are not being paid to worry about that, captain," she reminded him. "That is for them and their consciences – though what they are allowing us to do tells me they don't have any. We are only here for one thing. If we can retrieve the tiger without any of the locals knowing, then we will be gone before they realise we are here. By the end of the week, we will be rich and sunning ourselves in Hawaii."

Sam ran a slow hand through his beard and nodded.

A broad smile lit up his face. "You're right, as always." He reached for the radio and fixed his attention back on the map.

Cutting off the static, he spoke into the radio. "Status

report, Alpha?"

Lisa Myers wandered away to her tent in search of some solace, not hearing the response. She had asked to go with Alpha team this time, wanting to be there when it happened, when she finally finished selling her soul.

Always keen for her company, Sam Brooks had ordered her to stay behind, to look after the survivors and to be his '*good cop*'. It was the preferable option, though she knew Sam well enough by now to know what he was capable of.

Entering her tent, she headed over to her belongings and grabbed her binoculars. She needed a distraction, to settle the worry stirring away in her stomach.

Whatever happened next, the team had better make it happen fast. Time was running out and the window was closing with each hour that passed.

There could not be any further complications now, not after this.

CHAPTER EIGHT

Complications

Jon was roused from his dreams by a gentle hand. Groaning, he fought to find his senses and forced open a wary eye, fixing the old man who knelt beside his bed with a look that suggested it had better be worth it.

His host, stitched together by leathery skin and wrapped up in what looked to be a large diaper, smiled broadly at him, and thrust a steel cup under his nose of what was probably tea. Jon propped himself up on one sore elbow, grimacing as his ribs played out a painful tune. He accepted the cup and nodded his appreciation.

"Thank you," Jon said, sipping at the black liquid which he hoped was coffee. He hid his disappointment.

The antique before him was naked apart from the white cloth that thankfully covered his decency; his frail body was dark and thin, and Jon studied the bright eyes that intently watched him, full of long life, filled only with concern. The man watched him sip at the tea and Jon actually had to admit it tasted lovely. If he couldn't enjoy tea in India, where could he?

Jon returned his host's scrutiny, marvelling at his white hair, astonished that it fell in a thick cascade below his back. The wizened head with a red spot, just between both eyebrows, bobbed in response to his thoughts and the long, bearded face spilt into that smile again.

Realising that he was still in agony and should be panicking, Jon's circumstances overcame him again.

Thrusting the half-empty cup into his host's hands, he attempted to rise from bed. The old man placed a strong hand on his chest, shaking his head firmly.

Too tired to fight, Jon fell back onto the cot, catching his breath. Sunlight spilled into the hut through a window that had no glass and he could feel the fury of the day outside. Luckily there were no monkeys nearby, but the birds chattered away happily and a large insect hummed a tune as it buzzed by. He turned his head slowly.

"Where am I?" Jon asked. His host looked at him, cocking his head to one side. He juggled his thoughts for a moment, then smiled again.

Any initial hope Jon had at being found began to slip away. "Do you speak English?"

The man's eyes flashed in recognition. "English! English, yes." He sounded very proud of the fact and pointed at Jon. "English, yes?" He pretended to block an unseen delivery with an invisible cricket bat, then pointed at himself. "Sikh."

Jon groaned. Gathering his composure, he shook his head. "No!" he paused, as he was about to say he was Italian. Sighing, he thumped his chest. "American."

The man stared at him for a time and then smiled broadly. "Ah, Mickey Mouse. Elvis. JFK."

Jon laughed and his host joined in, not detecting the madness in his guest's sob.

Typical, Jon thought, too tired to even cuss. Here he was, plucked from the sky in India, and he had been saved by a mad hermit who couldn't speak English…

Jon looked up at the rafters. "I hope you are enjoying this?"

The old Sikh followed his gaze and then looked at him as if he was the deranged one.

Jon guessed that a mad hermit living alone in a jungle,

had chosen the location to be at one with himself and nature, to be alone with his spiritualism. As he looked about the hut, stared at the humble belongings; the cooking utensils, the burning incense, the fire pit and the old rocking chair, he doubted that the hermit would have a phone.

"You don't have a phone, do you?" Jon asked, turning to the old Sikh. He made an L-shape with his thumb and little finger, holding them to his mouth and right ear. "Phone?" Jon asked again, a little louder, as if that would somehow help.

The old man understood, clearly. He nodded rapidly, then shook his head.

Jon cursed under his breath, letting out his disappointment in a long sigh. "No internet, then?"

Smiling, the old man rose up on cracking knees and stared down at him for a time. Jon eyed him back, uncomfortable under the scrutiny.

"Rashim," the old Sikh said, patting his bony chest proudly.

"Jon," Galnia responded, dutifully. *Well that was some progress…*

His host rolled his lips over his guest's name and then, with that warming smile, he nodded and headed outside. Jon watched him leave, shading his eyes against the golden fire of the day.

If he was going to get back on his feet and out of there soon, he needed to rest, recover his strength and then try and find someone who had a brain and a phone.

The patrol stopped as the large man on point raised a clenched fist. Turning, he watched quietly as two of his team put down the cage they had been carrying and doubled over to catch their breaths.

Andersson watched them for a time, his own breath hard to find in his broad chest as he shouldered his rifle. He took a long pull from his canteen, relishing the taste of the cool water inside.

They were four hours from the *FOB*, the Forward Operations Base, now, and he had set a heavy pace, tabbing more than six miles over the challenging terrain in the blistering haze of the heat, each man carrying well over forty kilos of kit. Putting his canteen away, Mikael Andersson surveyed their surroundings, shielding his eyes against the high sun filling the gorge, wishing he was on a beach somewhere, sipping tequila.

That would come, Andersson knew, once they had the package and were slipping away towards their pay cheques and the jet that would spirit them from the country before they were noticed. He watched a bright-coloured parrot with a huge long tail slip across the gorge before him, and he tracked it through the scope of his rifle for a time as it hopped about the branches of a huge tree, before flashing away from view.

Wiping the sweat from his eyes with his neck scarf, Andersson felt himself wilt under the sun again, and he barked out a command for them to move on. The hand he ran through his beard came away sodden.

"How far, skip?" Raz asked, coming up slowly alongside him. They both stared up through the gorge, following the shimmering twist of the creek as it slipped from view.

Andersson checked his PDA. "Another hour in this heat," he surmised, feeling his own hopes wane. He was still amazed that the signal was so strong.

Hassan Ben Raz muttered, watching as the other two

hauled the steel cage up between them. Hopefully it wouldn't take that long as he didn't fancy another turn lugging that accursed cage through the jungle. His shoulders and back ached in remembrance.

Andersson waved them on, and they began following the creek northwards, picking the easiest path across the broken ground, loose stone and jagged boulders. Hassan hurried to catch up with him, resting the long, slim rifle on his left shoulder.

"I can't believe we actually found one alive," Raz admitted, not for the first time. He shook his head free of his wonder. "We heard the rumours when they put us on stand-by, but I doubted they were more than just that."

Andersson eyed the Moroccan. The jovial one of the team usually, his glistening face was clouded with worry. "Well, the footage we pulled from the remote camera before it stopped working confirms it for us. My only hope is that it's alive and we can get the helicopter to airlift it back to camp. She's no use to us dead, so we had better cross everything we can"

"*Inshallah*," Hassan said, looking heavenwards.

Andersson looked up at the clear sky overhead, searching the terrain and the conditions, rather than for any divine help. He doubted that Sam, despite his years of service, would be able to fly the helicopter anywhere near the narrow gorge, so they were going to be stuck in this shithole for longer than anticipated.

He growled at his own doubts. *One thing at a time, Mike*. In his experience, a problem only arose if you went looking for it.

An hour later, he found several of them.

Jon woke with a start. For a time, he lay where he was, listening to the drum of his heart, fighting with his instinct to move. Sunlight still spilled into the hut, its rays glistening on his sweating skin. Hearing his stomach growl for attention, Jon finally steeled himself for the pain that was to follow and propped himself up on shaking elbows.

He was alone. His host, Rash-whatever, was nowhere to be seen, though above the noise of the afternoon outside, Jon was sure he could hear droning prayers. Looking up, Jon blessed himself and drew strength from the fact that he was never truly alone, as he swung his legs to the earthen floor, scattered with fresh grass and older straw.

Kneading the pain from his temples with grubby palms, he buried his face in his hands and allowed his thoughts to wander for a time. If the hermit could not help him, Jon knew that he would have to find the nearest village soon, find someone who could understand what he was saying and call for the cavalry.

His positivity soon gave way to his paranoia and the worry that the jet's sabotage had somehow gone unnoticed. Surely the skies should have been filled with search parties by now? *Where the hell were they?*

Williams's earlier concern that they had been compromised – that the jet could not be tracked, left a gaping pit of worry in Jon's cramping stomach. Snarling, he focussed on his hunger and rose from the creaking bed.

The floor rushed to his head and Jon stumbled forward, knocking into the table and scattering one of the old chairs across the floor. Outside, the prayers died and the wattled door swung open, a slim shadow filling the sun.

The old Sikh came scurrying to his side, his concern and reprimands lost to Jon, as he was helped onto the recovered seat.

Rashim stood watching him, his thin hands knotted to his hips, his annoyance as sharp as his elbows. He said something that could not be understood again, but Jon felt like he was back in 5th Grade, getting a roasting from Mr. Wilson after being caught lifting up Mary Pope's dress to look at her panties.

Despite the Sikh's attention, Jon snorted at the memory and raised a hand in apology.

"I have to get home to my family," Jon sighed, dropping his hand into his lap. "Me, home?"

Rashim looked at Jon, shaking his head, trying not to smile. Talking like an infant would not make him understand any better. Bobbing his head, the Sikh studied the injured, yet determined man before him.

Slim and tall, his guest hunched over the table, his strong face covered in beads of sweat, his short, dark hair matted and plastered to his pale skin. His nose was proud, straight and flaring, as he dragged in the close air, trying to fill his lungs with the strength he would need, hoping to rediscover the strength that he had lost.

Fascinated by the handsome, yet angry face before him, Rashim watched Jon's thin lips, as they chewed on his discontent. He could detect the man's hidden fury as his dark brown eyes flashed in his direction.

Rashim offered a prayer to *Onkar* and clasped his hands together. This man, the man he had found and most surely saved, was a dangerous man. He could sense it – a man who readily embraced the *Five Thieves*. The very type of man he had hoped to never meet again.

Calming the old doubts in his heart, the hermit smiled, singing a mantra from the *Guru Granth Sahib*, the sacred scripture. Having dedicated his life, many decades ago, to his faith and duty to others, Rashim cast aside any judgement, placing one hand on the American's shoulder.

A smile creased the man's bitter features for a moment and Rashim nodded happily.

"Rest!" the Sikh ordered, motioning for Jon to remain where he was. He motioned several times to his mouth with his right hand and laughed when his guest's stomach growled in response.

Jon chuckled, watching as the old Sikh gathered up a wicker basket and a knife, before shuffling out on scraping sandals into the sun. As the door swung back into a frame it didn't really fit, he caught himself smiling broadly.

"Damned if I don't like you, old man," Jon said aloud. He sat back in his seat, blinking in surprise at his own admonition. In his forty-five years, he could count on one hand the people he could say that about.

And that was including the old Sikh.

Rashim gave Jon some time alone with his thoughts and for a while, Jon absently listened to the Sikh, as he busied himself outside then wandered away, jabbering to what sounded like chickens and the distant jingle of a bell.

Sighing, Jon touched the back of his head, tenderly probing the dried blood and thankful that his hand came away dry. The rest of him felt like shit, and trying not to sit in it, he closed his eyes, drifting away to peaceful serenity.

Well, for about three seconds...

Despite the tranquillity and the fact that it was the only time in his life where he could honestly say he had a bit of time to think clearly without any distraction, his predicament left him with even more space to think about what had happened and what would be going on, back home.

Jon cussed, then frowned. Not one to usually care about other people's feelings, it felt wrong somehow, to spoil the calm resonance of his host's house with his anger and selfishness. Sure, he had a good reason to feel pissed... annoyed, only one of several times that he could recall when he had valid cause to be so – but getting angry and throwing a grenade out of the pram wasn't going to help him focus.

You need to keep calm, Jonny.

Jon winced, as his brother's voice rasped from the shadows of the past. Shaking his head sadly, swallowing his disgust, Jon closed his eyes and groaned.

He then thought about Maria and Gio, could taste how his wife must be feeling at this moment. *Had she told Gio?* Probably not, what good would it do until there was some certainty?

Coughing up his guilt, Jon cleared his mind of any self-pity with a few more of his calming breaths. Maria would be beside herself with worry, helpless to do anything *but* worry. Jon however, could do something about it. He had been given a chance by the man upstairs and by Williams's piloting expertise. He owed them both to at least try.

The incense drifting lazily about the hut and clogging his nose was actually starting to help, and Jon made a mental note that his pilot, and Sara, if they were still alive, would never need to work again after this.

Tasting fresh worry on his lips, Jon thought about his empire, of what his absence would mean for those who waited in the shadows, watching patiently for the moment when the Galnia luck finally ran out.

Paolo Romano Jnr, his *Consigliere*, his right-hand, was as loyal as a dog and twice as dangerous. He would see that the Family business did not suffer, would ensure that any of his *Capos*, his captains, who may harbour designs to be the head of the family, did not try to wet their ambitions. Paolo had grown up with him; they had taken the Oath and bloodied their hands together. Often mistaken for brothers, Jon knew in his heart that Paolo did not want to be head of the Family, was happy to run the daily operations from the right side of the table.

Jon cocked his head to the other side, considering who actually might. Numerous faces of those who had tried, those who may yet, filled his mind. For a moment, he had a brief image of them all, lined up by his coffin, paying their respects at his wake and wiping away their tears of joy, not grief.

Make no mistakes, Jon thought, there were still many in the Family who had grown up with his father, those who still followed the old ways, who did not want to realise that the word on the street, the law that was laid down these days was done via WhatsApp and email, not over a Cafe Corretto and a game of cards.

Jon smiled. They saw him as a young inheritor, a man who did not follow the code, did not respect what it meant to be head of the Family. How wrong they were. Jon lived by the Oath he had taken, respected his father's legacy and all who had come before him, no matter what side of the knife they were on. He just understood that to survive, to maintain and to develop the business in this modern world, these rapidly changing times, you had to get with the picture.

Jon puffed out his cheeks. *And that was just his family...*

There were other Families like the *Calvantes*, those

who had tried and those who might still, but they were a problem for when he got out of this blasted jungle. Another obstacle for another day, that he would trip over when the time came.

No! You do need to keep calm, Jonny. For now, he had to get to a phone, then he had to find an ATM and get some clean clothes, before flying home to start looking into who had orchestrated this elaborate hit on him.

Ignoring his prior frustrations, Jon clenched his fists tight about his worry and swore.

How the fuck was he going to get out of this shit-hole, if he didn't have his passport? Jon screwed his face up, muttering as he realised he was going to have to rely on the U.S. Government to save his arse.

Oh, how the Feds will love this one. He was going to have to bend over and take a few from them for the next couple of years, if he wanted to carry on his empire, keep it safe to pass on to his son... if that was what he *truly* wanted to do.

Jon sat back in his chair, clutching at his tight chest. Sweat rolled down his left cheek as he stared at the question, hanging in the smoky air before him.

There had been times, recently, when the Feds were at his door, when the problems of treading the fine line between conquest and prison, had sent him fleeing to his study to break a few glasses and drift away with his music for a few hours as he tussled with his desire to walk away from it all – to truly enjoy his life with Maria and Gio.

Jon laughed wryly. He could never walk away from it. He had taken the Oath, had embraced the path before him. There could be no turning his back on the *Cosa Nostra* – the only way to be free of it was to be carried to the cemetery, like his father, his mother... like his brother. It was his curse, and his honour.

And his honour was the reason he was in Russia in the first damn place.

A shadow fell across the window as Rashim shuffled by, waving at him, and before Jon could raise a weak arm in return, the old man had gone. Jon sighed, dropping his hand into his lap. Even now, despite everything that happened, Jon could summon a vivid image of Anna into his mind, and his guilt did little to ease his torment.

Thinking of the Russians and the meeting that began this fiasco soured his mood further. Maria had roasted him before he flew out in person to Moscow, warning him of the danger of putting himself in the spotlight – but Jon was a man of his word, a man of respect, and still believed that his reputation counted for something.

The head of the Solntsevskaya Brotherhood, known only as Sergey, had not returned this respect. Jon was set to meet him in a neutral third-floor suite of the Tverskaya Hotel, near Red Square,

Taking one of his father's former hands Aleksi Cardov with him for protection, Jon had waited for two hours for the meeting, wondering if he should have listened to his wife and stayed away, despite the extra money it would have cost him, and the reputation he could have lost.

She was right, of course.

The woman Sergey sent to him, his right-hand 'man' Sokolova, was dressed more for evening dinner, than a meeting with a rival, a trick obviously designed to pull Jon's guard down. Wearing a single black number that was low on her milky white shoulders and high above the knees of her slender, stocking-clad legs, the confident blonde had swept into the room, flanked by two inked goons, assuring Jon of how pleased her employer was, and of how much he appreciated the respect Jon had shown to his family by coming in person.

Despite his anger at the affront, Jon had played the diplomacy game well, responding that he was equally pleased they could have this meeting, and of how he hoped that they could come to an agreement that would be acceptable and *beneficial* to both families.

Outwardly, Jon had remained calm as he poured her a whisky. Inwardly, he had known he was handing her a signed, blank cheque to save his Russian deal.

As she took up his offer of a seat, the woman had crossed her left leg over her right knee slowly, *Sharon Stone*-style. With blue eyes flashing from behind thick lashes, she had met Jon's appraisal boldly, her full lips parting in a red, glistening lip-stick smile that had lit up her pale, yet attractive face.

"It pleases him," Sokolova had nodded, her tongue licking slowly at her lips, "as it would please me if you were to call me Anna, Mr. Galnia."

Jon had agreed. Regaining his composure, he had set about the distasteful task of negotiating the fee he would have to pay for having a successful operation in a foreign, inhospitable and cut-throat country…

Anna had been good at her job. Really good, and it was why her superiors had sent her in the first place. She played her role perfectly, using her looks and powers of seduction to broker a deal that she already knew would have to be accepted.

After three hours of foreplay with terms and numbers, they had finally agreed on a figure of twenty percent of all of Volston's profits from the drugs, racketeering and money-laundering: paid up quarterly, without contest and without fail. Jon had hated, no detested, giving away his money, but he was clever enough to realise that day that it was the only way for his interests to continue to keep growing in the country, without bringing down the fire of the Solntsevskaya Brotherhood upon him. It had meant that he would end up several million U.S. dollars light a year, but it was a small price to pay in the long run, and in a perverse way, he had actually enjoyed it!

As she left, Anna had leant up to kiss him gently on one cheek, and Jon, even now, could still feel her light breath on his neck and smell her scented hair and expensive perfume.

Bloody expensive indeed!

"I *do* hope we shall meet again, Jon!" They had long-since dispensed with any formalities by that time, and Jon had sensed, if somewhat wistfully, that she actually meant it. He had felt her body, ever-so-slightly brushing against his as she had rested a gentle, warm hand upon his chest.

"As do I, Anna," he had said quietly, as she left with her entourage…

Jon rapped his fingers on the rough surface of the worm-ridden table, as he felt his desires and ambitions return to overwhelm his sadness, flooding through him like an orgasm. He was down, yes, but he was not out. He was ready for the next round, wherever that might take him, and if he found out that he had to bloody some soviet noses, had to start a war with them, then so be it. There was a debt to pay now and it was covered in someone else's blood.

Before Jon's anger could get the better of him, Rashim shuffled back into the hut, bringing a silent dose of calm and bright smiles with him.

Jon looked up from his recriminations and could not

help but smile. The old Sikh was carrying a wicker basket, full of vegetables.

"Eat, yes?" Rashim asked, nodding his head furtively.

It was one of the sweetest sounding things he had been asked in years and Jon responded to the question with a broad, rakish grin as he rose stiffly from his chair to help his host.

For a time, at least, Jon forgot about his predicament, forgot about his revenge and the woman who, despite his prior misgivings, he was beginning to suspect had set in motion the events that had plucked him from the sky.

The high, afternoon sun was unbearable, Andersson thought, as he shadowed the creek on the east shore, the only accessible terrain for his team. Pausing to look over one shoulder, he could see that the others were carrying the cage between them now, as the furious day drained their stamina and their canteens with each stumbling, heavy step.

Returning his gaze to the north, Andersson watched as a cloud of insects swirled in spirals over the crystal-clear waters of the creek in a silent dance that was illuminated by the golden heat. Shielding his eyes, the mercenary surveyed the gorge that rose up steeply on either side of them. A large bird of prey hung in the clear, high-definition sky above him for a time, and Andersson could see the Raptor's head turn to watch him as it glided on, the only thing that could give them away at the moment. Checking their location on his PDA, he confirmed to the others that they were almost there.

Ignoring the complaints and his desire to remind them that they were about to become rich, Mikael Andersson led Alpha team on, picking a safe route over the rocky shore to follow the creek to the north east. They were forced to wade through the water for a hundred yards or so, until the creek turned through a narrow pass into more hospitable terrain.

His heart was pounding as he stumbled on a loose stone and made his way across the open ground towards the jungle to the east. He couldn't grasp onto a thought as he checked his PDA, and called Hassan Raz forward.

The former pathfinder joined him at the shoulder, leaving Taylor and Parker to struggle with the cage.

"Is this it?" Raz asked, barely above a breath.

Andersson frowned, moving forward, double, then treble-checking their position. He looked back, his face pinched.

"It is," he admitted, jabbing his head at the thicket, towards the grass that was clearly flattened.

There was nothing there.

Their two companions decided they had had enough and dropped the cage, uncaring of the noise it made, unflinching under the furious stares that came their way.

Taylor, the shorter of the two men, stalked forward.

"What's the matter?" he asked, his anger painted on his pale features.

Andersson regarded the man with a cocked eyebrow, feeling some sympathy for the ginger-haired Ranger. It was bad enough for him, someone who was used to tropical conditions, but for a pale-skinned red-head, it must be hell on earth.

Andersson shook his head. "It should be here!"

Parker joined them, and as the patrol un-slung their rifles, they spread out in a silent line, moving towards the jungle. All was silent, except for the melodic passing water, and as Andersson ordered Taylor forward to check the terrain, Raz raised his cylindrical rifle, aiming it towards the shadows.

"Bollocks!" Taylor cursed, as he knelt down by the flattened grass, then looked about his surroundings.

The three onlookers waited patiently as their tracker surveyed the evidence before him, then rose up and moved deeper into the thicket. Andersson tensed, expecting to hear screams, then let out his worry when Taylor reappeared, holding both ends of the wire snare.

"What the hell is going on?" Taylor asked, though it wasn't really a question. "Someone let it go!"

He held up the Carabiner for them to see.

Parker threw a look at their leader. Andersson was scowling at his PDA, as if that would help him now. He watched patiently as the big man chewed his moustache and shouldered his M4A1 rifle. When the Swede finally put his thoughts and device away, he looked to Parker, as he knew he would.

"Jim," Andersson said softly. "Find the camera and see what you can pull from it."

Parker nodded as he shouldered his own weapon and moved off into the line of trees.

Andersson resisted the urge to call in what they had found as his team searched for answers. Keeping his worries to himself, the large mercenary studied their surroundings, eyeing the ground for any signs. He couldn't read anything, which was why the others had been sent with him, and he prayed that they would get a lucky break. There was far too much money at stake here.

Taylor returned first, pulling the hat from his head. His cropped hair was dripping and his pale features were flushed. They had worked many times together but this was the first time Andersson had seen him lose his cool.

"The tiger went north, up the creek," Taylor reported, fighting for a clean breath, "and it didn't eat whoever let it go, either."

The Swede scratched his bearded chin. "You are sure it was let go? It didn't escape?"

"No chance!" Taylor spat. "Well, not unless it figured out how to unscrew the carabiner. No, skip, *somebody* let it go. There are confused tracks leading away from here to the east. I also found a few drops of dried blood."

"Confused?"

Taylor nodded. "My best guess is that there were two people – perhaps one was injured, as I found drag marks."

"Fuck it!" Andersson raged. He paced away from his fury, then swung back towards it. "Well, we had better find something we can work with, or else we are all in the shit."

They turned towards Parker's cry, as he rose back up and carried his portable laptop towards them. His youthful, clean-shaven face flared with a mixture of hope and curious confusion.

"Luckily, the infra-red camera was still working, and I was able to download all the images from the last five days," Parker reported, as they crowded about him. He turned the screen towards the shade so they could see.

"Take a look at these shots from about six hours ago," he said, passing the computer into Andersson's large hands.

As they flicked through the last six photos from the camera, they shared incredulous looks as they viewed the five pictures of the huge tiger, sat trapped by the snare and almost filling the screen. In awed silence they choked on their disbelief as they came to the final image – an image of a dishevelled man dressed more for an office than a jungle, carrying a rock and heading towards the magnificent beast.

Andersson blinked free of his shock. "Get that sent over to Sam, pronto," he ordered, reaching for the radio clipped to his vest with a shaking hand.

"I want to know who the fuck that is, and I want to know now," he growled as he raised the radio and his anger to his lips to call it in.

CHAPTER NINE

Suspicious Minds

First Secretary Rana sipped at his cold coffee, sighed and put the cup back on his desk. Making a mental note to have a word with Samira about her inability to make a decent cup of anything, he stared at the folder on the desk before him and shook his head. It was the draft of the proposal for the statue, a weighty document that needed his attention before it was taken before the Lok Sabah in three days' time. Dragging the spectacles from his face, Rana tossed the frames onto the green folder and closed his eyes. There were so many things that cried for his attention, so many matters that needed sorting out... and yet he had no desire to think about any of them, except the one burning problem that could, if allowed to get out of hand, bring them all crashing down.

Aasim listened to the air conditioning for a time, its unbalanced blades rattling away like the Shatabdi Express. Outside, he could hear the distant breath of the city coming to life again, as the heat of the day became more bearable. For the briefest of moments, he wished he could return to his old life as a banker, with little or nothing to worry himself over, other than the happiness of his wife and family.

The meeting with Prime Minister Nehru had not gone well. With their thoughts already looking ahead to the 2024 elections, and the hue and cry of scandal and corruption ever loud in the media's throats, Chandra

Nehru and his party's supporters were facing the possibility that their tumultuous, unprecedented rise to power would end abruptly in a fall from grace and a lengthy stay in prison.

Measures were in place, naturally, to ensure another five years in power, but with events unfolding in Madhya Pradesh and the Americans demanding answers, they were walking a tightrope into the darkness of uncertainty.

Rana realised he had held onto his breath as he mulled over their options and let it out with a sigh. Scandal and corruption were never far from Chandra Nehru's side – in fact, if anything, he seemed to embrace it. Since 2014 and the elections that saw the Bharatiya Janata Party and its candidate Narendra Modi obtain the first overall majority in the Lok Sabha since 1984, Nehru had become a focus for the media to sharpen their knives upon.

Already tainted by the countless scandals that followed his early career, Chandra Nehru had somehow endured and very publicly announced his decision to leave the *Indian Congress Party* a week before the 2019 April elections. In a deal done with Modi behind closed doors, Nehru, the last ember in his party's dying political fire, consigned the coalition to years in the wilderness, whilst ensuring his own star continued to rise and his offshore accounts swelled by millions of Dollars. By swapping his allegiance to the BJP, Nehru, a very popular figure with the centre-left, working man, brought millions of lower caste votes with him as he began to eye up the position of Prime Minister in the 2024 elections.

Loved by the people, when Narendra Modi was forced to retire suddenly due to ill health earlier this year, two years after his resounding victory in the 2019 elections, Chandra Nehru was appointed acting Prime Minister a lot sooner than he had planned – a position he was determined to hang on to, no matter the cost to his reputation and bank balance.

The media were still in a frenzy over the appointment, labelling it '*The shame of our time.*'

Modi and Nehru were only related by the shadow of corruption that had dogged their early careers, and the press called it 'nepotistic', the swapping of one beloved politician for the tarnished side of the same coin. Both the out-going Modi and incoming Nehru had forged their early careers in Gujarat, and were still members of *Rashtriya Swayamsevak Sangh* – the Rivalist Conservative movement also known as the National Volunteer Movement. Nehru, in particular, was still unable to shake off the accusations of his complicity in the sectarian slaughter of Muslims that took place in the region, in 2002. Aasim Rana knew the stories, had heard the rumours, and knowing Nehru well, he could not discount the accusations.

Chandra Nehru, though the main focus of the oppositions' hatred, was not alone, and it was a fact that the Prime Minister constantly reminded the media when they hounded him at press conferences. In the 2014 elections, he pointed out, more than twenty percent of candidates had criminal charges raised against them, and that figure from the *ADR*, the Association for Democratic Reforms, was based solely upon the ones they knew about.

"Perhaps," Nehru had said pointedly in one interview, "it would be better for you to kill the problem at the root, instead of always trying to trim it from the top."

Twitter had melted over that response.

Rana blinked away his rising exhaustion and thought

back to the meeting in Nehru's offices. Alone, they had sat in the majestic wood-panelled room, sharing their quiet concerns over the news of the American's jet.

Not satisfied by the evidence so far, the Prime Minister had sat reclined in his high-backed, ornate leather chair, and fixed his ally with a murderous stare.

"We will not go down with this jet, Aasim," he had spat, draining his glass of brandy in one pull. "The Americans must be placated! We cannot have them at our backs this week, not when everything is at stake. Our survival depends on the success of the operation in Madhya Pradesh, and if the tiger is not captured alive, before news of the crash gets out, we will all be finished."

Aasim winced as he looked about his own office, pathetic in comparison to Nehru's grandeur. He had left the Prime Minister with promises to find out more about the mysterious jet, and as to why it could not be traced.

"Our mutual *friend* will join you this evening," Nehru had promised him. "He will ensure that we have the answers to our questions."

Aasim shuddered as he thought about the man in question, and he jumped as the internal com flared to life. With a shaking hand, he leant across the desk and pushed the flashing red button.

"What is it?" he barked, more annoyed at his own lack of self-control.

Samira's voice soothed him momentarily. "*Forgive me, First Secretary*," she pleaded. "*I know you were not to be disturbed, but I have Thomas Miller from the American Embassy on the line for you again – he insisted he speak to you.*"

"No, it should be I who asks for forgiveness, Samira," Aasim said, sighing heavily. "I did not mean to snap.

Please, put him through, but no further calls today."

"*Yes, First Secretary.*" As she put the call through, Rana gathered his composure, attempting to calm his nerves and clear his mind for what was to come.

"Mr. Miller," Aasim said, smiling into the receiver, "forgive the delay. How may I help you?"

There was a pause, one that was just long enough to convey silent annoyance. When he spoke, however, the American's voice was professionally even. "*I was hoping, First Secretary, that you would have some news for me? I have not heard anything for some hours, and Washington are keen for news. Do you have anything new you can tell me, sir?*"

Rana swallowed, tapping the overly-long nails of his free hand across the green folder on his desk.

"I must offer my apologies, ambassador," Rana began, attempting to sound earnest. "As you can appreciate, it has been a day full of shock and concern. I have been busy collating any evidence we can find, before coming back to you."

"*And do you have anything?*" Miller asked, his voice soft and barely heard above the air-conditioning.

"Very little, I am afraid," Rana replied, pushing on swiftly. "It is most puzzling to us, as once this jet approached Indian airspace, it could not be tracked. There is no record of the jet, no evidence, other than the message the woman received on her phone, that it even crossed India. I can tell you are shocked, and I can only join you in your surprise. As you know, we have enforced strict no-fly zones over much of the country and any aircraft breaking such conditions would have surely been detected, immediately."

Rana licked his lips. He could almost hear Miller's thoughts on the other end of the line, as he digested what he was hearing.

"Rest assured, that we are dedicating all of our resources to the matter," Rana pushed on. "I am currently awaiting satellite imagery of the area in question and am liaising closely with the local Governors of all central Indian states. We have the most diligent eyes in the air and on the ground for you, sir."

All lies, of course. Rana's heart was in his mouth. He could feel an imaginary noose tighten about his own neck.

The American's soft voice broke across his anxiety. "*Thank you, Secretary Rana. I must apologise for any abruptness. As you can imagine, we are extremely concerned for the safety of our citizens. In these situations, the first few hours are critical, and it has been almost twenty-four now without further development*."

"I understand fully, ambassador," Rana agreed, nodding his head. He felt a chill creep up his back suddenly and he flicked a nervous glance to the closed door. *Had he heard voices in the room beyond?* "If I may ask, do you have any information for us? We have no details on the jet, nor how many people we are looking for, their names, for instance? It would be most helpful if we had the information to hand."

"*Of course, sir*," Thomas Miller said, and Rana could hear him shuffling papers. "*I will forward the details of the jet, its itinerary and passenger data to your office as soon as we finish here. I can tell you now, sir, that there were four civilians on board, three U.S. nationals and one British citizen. The owner is a man called Jon Galnia; it was his wife who received the voicemail and alerted the authorities*."

Rana felt some of the burden slip from his thin shoulders. Clenching a fist, he sank back into the chair and the arms of his relief.

"That is most helpful, Mr. Miller, thank you," Rana offered, and meant it. "As soon as I have any further information..."

"*Please do,*" Miller interjected. "*We are keeping it from our media for now, and have assurances from the families of all concerned that we won't report the crash until we have firm evidence. I would ask you, sir, for the sake of their privacy, that this matter is kept from the public eye for now.*"

Rana smiled. "Of course, ambassador, I fully understand." He leant forward, ready to hang up.

"*I am available tomorrow, First Secretary,*" Miller continued, halting Rana's hand. "*I think it would be beneficial if we could meet up, so that we might share all the evidence we have to date and discuss this further.*"

"Of course," Rana said through gritted teeth. "My secretary will confirm a time for us to meet in the morning. Perhaps it would be better for you to come to Raisina Hill, if that is suitable to you?"

"*It would be, sir,*" the American replied. "*I shall wait to hear from you, First Secretary. In the meantime, should we find out anything ourselves, I will be in touch. Good evening, sir.*"

The line went dead and Rana listened to the static for a few moments, before hanging up. Moaning, he buried his face in his hands and tried to massage away his fears.

If the Americans started digging around themselves...

Shaking his head, Aasim picked up his fountain pen and wrote down the name the American had given to him on the cover of the green folder.

Jon Galnia.

Samira Jethwani looked up from her computer screen as

the door to the office opened without a knock and a tall man dressed in a pin-striped grey suit swept into the room. He did not look at her as he headed for the First Secretary's office, did not even register that she was there.

"Excuse me, sir," Samira called, her surprise dragging her from her seat. "You cannot just walk in – you must have an appointment."

The man took three more steps towards the closed door then stopped, turning slowly.

Samira hesitated as she stepped from behind her desk, her chair spinning behind her, and stared nervously at the man. He fixed her with a cold glare, offset by the warm smile that flashed broadly across his face.

"The First Secretary is expecting me," the man stated, offering his hands wide. "That will be all for this evening, Samira. We won't be requiring your services again today."

Samira blinked, staring in disbelief at the stranger. *Who in the heavens was this man to tell her what she was to do?*

The man was lean and tall, dressed impeccably in his finery. His short, greying hair confirmed that he was into the autumn of his life, and his dark, hollowed face radiated a handsome charm that could captivate a room. But his eyes, those piercing eyes of the deepest brown, fixed her with a stare that hinted at the real man, lurking behind a surface that Samira dared not scratch.

"My services are required until the First Secretary tells me otherwise," Samira bristled defiantly, placing her shaking hands on her hips.

She was not about to be bullied, even if this impeccable man was from a higher caste and was, she suspected, someone she should not make an enemy of.

"It is okay, please," the man soothed her, holding his hands higher in submission. "I am expected, though your diary will disagree."

For the first time, Samira detected the Kashmiri accent underneath the man's neutral tone. He carried no briefcase, nothing, and did not even wear an identification badge.

Before Samira could say anything else, the man turned away and headed for the closed door. He paused as his long, thin hand hovered over the handle. When Samira could not find her voice to protest further, he nodded his head in satisfaction and slipped inside the room beyond without knocking.

Gasping for breath, Samira stumbled back to her chair, collapsing into it as the door was pulled quietly closed. Her heart raced as she struggled with what had just happened. She had never seen that man before. In the months since she had started her position in the Secretariat, she had never felt such fear.

As a young woman, working amongst so many power-hungry egos, she had felt unease on Raisina Hill, of course, but only chauvinism – never, never anything that came close to the fright she had just received.

The only other time in her life she had experienced such fear, was on the day she had witnessed a terrible crash, whilst driving home to visit her mother in Chandu. Samira had been visiting for the weekend, last September, after having just graduated and moved into her apartment in New Delhi. A Tata truck had lost a wheel and swerved across the Basai Road into bystanders, who were waiting for a bus outside a pharmacy. Three cars behind, Samira had stopped to help, had witnessed the carnage and dramatic loss of life...

Shuddering at the memory, Samira tried to shut out the images of that terrible day, attempting to focus on the man. Although he looked like any other minister, Samira was certain he was anything but. He carried himself about his business with a surety that bordered on arrogance. What was about to take place behind the closed door? What was that man doing here?

What was the First Secretary up to?

Reaching for her bag and coat, Samira waited patiently; listening to the warning in her heart and for the internal call that she was sure was soon to follow.

The last light of the day seemingly failed as the tall man pushed his way into the office and closed the door gently behind him.

"Dismiss that girl," the newcomer hissed, as he stalked towards Rana's desk. "If you do not, *I* will."

Aasim glared at him, though, judging by the man's expression, it did little to unsettle him. "You are to leave her alone," Rana warned, waving a finger. "She is not involved in any of this, nor shall she be."

Smiling, the man waited patiently, his arms folded across his chest. When the First Secretary had dismissed his aide, when they heard her leave, he unfurled his arms and leant across the desk, palms pressed deep into the wood.

"Well?" the man demanded. "What news?"

Rana licked his lips. "Things progress."

The newcomer raised an eyebrow over his mocking smile. "Yes, they do, don't they? However, it seems, as always, it is I who know more than you. Must I always have to clear up other people's incompetence?"

"It has been a trying day," Rana riled. "Spare me the insults! I have no time to cross swords with you."

The tall man dragged a seat back as he unbuttoned his jacket and sat down fluidly. Leaning back, he crossed his left leg over his right knee and threaded patient fingers together.

"Then sheath your anger and tell me the facts of the situation," the man purred. "Enlighten me!"

"The Americans grow impatient," Rana admitted, swallowing his cold coffee. For once he didn't mind the taste. "This mysterious jet has raised many problems for us – the Gods surely do not favour what we are doing."

The man waved a dismissive hand, then returned it to his lap. "You worry about the Americans; I'll worry about the Gods. We have a small window of opportunity, which we must grasp with both hands."

"And just how do we do that?" Rana snarled, his composure shredding between them. "The Americans seek a jet that we cannot find – they demand answers I cannot give. We have our men in the military and Aviation Authority masking what is happening in the reserve, but we have nothing else of substance."

The man across from the First Secretary flashed him a confident grin. "Ah, but we do. Only a few hours ago, I received word that the team have located the crashed jet, but several miles from where the tiger is. They have secured two survivors and one corpse, and are currently seeking any other passengers."

Rana leant forward. "I have word from the Americans that there were four people on board. The U.S. embassy is sending me the details of the jet, the passenger list and itinerary. But I do have to hand the name of the missing husband, the owner of the jet, a Jon Galnia."

For once the man's smile was genuine. "Excellent work, Aasim. That will be all I need from you tonight."

Rana blinked. "Excuse me?"

The man rose up and smoothed away the creases in his suit. "You have laboured long and hard enough for one day. I shall look into this *Jon Galnia*. I am curious as to why his jet did not want to be found."

Rana was frozen in the grip of his shock. *I am being dismissed from my own office.*

"But this is my office," Rana said, his voice hollow and lame.

The man moved around the table. Looming over Rana, he placed gentle hands on his taught shoulders.

"Go home, rest," he soothed, massaging the knotted muscles beneath his fingers. "I will need access to both you and your aide's computers for my night's work. Insha-allah, I will have matters in hand before dawn."

Rana rose on heavy legs from his chair and leant forward to enter his log-in details on the screen.

"Very well," he sighed, feeling his weariness and desire to be away from this man wash over him. "You can access Samira's workstation from here."

The man ignored him, as Rana stumbled over to his hat stand to retrieve his coat. Fixing his attention on the workstation, the man did not register as the First Secretary gathered up his phone and briefcase, bade his farewells for the night ahead and moved towards the door.

"What about the mission?" Rana could not help but ask. "What are we to do with the survivors of the crash?"

"All is proceeding to plan," the man responded, looking up over the screen at him. "In the coming hours they will have the tiger and we shall have secured our next five years, no matter the cost. As far as the rest of the world is concerned, there was no jet, there are no survivors – do you understand?"

Rana nodded. Sickened at the implications, at the

thought of what would have to happen next, he hurried from his office on legs he could not feel.

The cold, confident smile of his usurper chased him to his car, and swiftly across to the east side of the city and the sanctuary that was, for now, still waiting for him.

Never a beast to sleep for long, the city was alive again now as people headed home from work, made their way out into the evening to stroll, to socialise, to sell their wares.

Having decided to leave her car at home that day, Samira Jethwani waited patiently in line for her bus, listening to the chatter around her, watching the faces of those she shared the evening with. Raisina Hill was emptying for the day, and for those who did not own their own transport home, were not highly positioned enough to have their own driver to worry about the roads, there was only the bus and the pavement. After a busy, stressful afternoon, Samira did not relish the thought of an hour-long walk across the city, dodging the traffic and the crowds. She needed to rest, to lose herself to normality for a time, to be amongst those who would not judge her, would probably not even take notice of her.

The would-be passengers consisted of a swathe of suits, all free from another day at the Secretariat, mingling with several waiting families who were a splash of welcome joy and vibrancy amidst the dour, weary code of politics.

A small, beautiful bright-eyed child watched Samira, tugging at her mother's hand as she pointed at the '*Lady's clothes*'. Samira flashed a smile and the child hid her face in the bright blue cloth of her mother's traditional dress. It wouldn't be the first time, it wouldn't be the last. Seeing her colleagues from the Hill afresh, she realised that she was the only woman amidst the suited men.

Turning from the family to eye the road for the bus, Samira looked back towards Raisina Hill. She blinked at the sight; the two striking domed buildings of the north and south Secretariat flanked each other warily and were framed by a cloudless sky of the most magnificent amber. The sun was setting now, fingers of defiance stretching forth one last time as the traffic swarmed by and their horns of caution rang out.

Samira could not believe she was working on the Hill, was still unsure of the fortuitous turn in her path that had blessed her with this chance. Shaking her head, Samira made a note to offer her thanks to Lord Ganesha before she ate that evening, to thank him for continuing to grant her this wonderful opportunity.

For however long that may be...

Her phone had been hot all afternoon, her ear even hotter when she had cancelled the First Secretary's interview with the press. Journalist Narinda Singh from *NDTV* had been so annoyed that she had even hung up the phone on Samira, leaving the First Secretary's aide staring in open-mouthed shock as she listened to the angry, dismissive spit of static.

Samira knew that the press was out to get the Prime Minister, and by default, First Secretary Rana. She also knew that she, too, would be thrust into the turbulence – but she had not anticipated the stress and exhaustion she would be feeling so early into her role. The pressure upon the office was a heavy burden, weighing down upon them all... and it was already taking a heavy toll, she could tell.

After being in an air-conditioned office all day she

was already sweating from the heat, and Samira felt a chill work its way slowly up the sweat that was running down her back. Before she could stop herself, Samira thought about the man who had forced his way into the office, had dismissed her without so much as a care for her feelings.

Who was this man to command me so?

The family began to chatter in excitement as the bus rounded the corner and several passengers stuck their hands or briefcases out to command it to stop. As the driver expertly forced his way through the weaving artery of traffic, clogged by car, scooter, cart and pedestrian, to screech to a halt before them, Samira was jostled from behind.

Sending her own apology graciously over her shoulder, she turned back to wait for her turn to find a seat. As she stepped up onto the bus and presented her ticket to a driver she did not know, Samira stopped. Casting a fretful look through the dusty windows of the bus, she suddenly wondered how, in Ganesha's name, the mysterious man knew who she was?

CHAPTER TEN

Reflections

The man did not keep his promises that day. He kept Sara Gonzales waiting long into the evening, preparing herself for his questions and worrying about Robert's health, and she did not realise how hungry she was until their other captor, the woman, returned with food for them both.

Putting the tray down on the table, the woman wordlessly moved to Robert's side, taking him by a limp wrist to check his pulse. With her heart in her throat, Sara watched on silently, one eye on her captor, the other flicking hungrily towards the tray and the two steel canteens of food that steamed enticingly there.

"He's a strong one," her captor observed, dropping Robert's wrist to his lap. She tenderly checked his head wounds over and removed his gag, before rising sluggishly to her feet. Planting curious hands on her slender hips, she turned to Sara.

"He should recover," she offered, eyeing her captive. Sensing the defiance brimming there, she added, "I'm sorry he hit him so hard. Men tend to act before they think."

Sara sank deeper into her bed and watched the woman wordlessly. Shrugging, the woman turned towards the food and Sara caught a scent of insect repellent on the mournful breeze that filled the tent.

It was dark outside now and Sara could hear the

distant thrum of a generator as it joined the insects in their nocturnal symphony. The noise was over-powering, and for the briefest of moments Sara thought of similar hot nights, sat out on the veranda with her mother back home, drinking Modelo and listening to Valentin Elizalde.

Despite her desire to get away from Cananea, from the life she did not want to live, she would have given anything to be back there now, listening to the local gossip and suffocating from the mundane.

The woman turned, her plaited hair swinging up and over one shoulder like Lara Croft. As she came close, Sara could see the pistol, holstered at her right hip.

"I'm going to have to feed you, I am afraid," the woman said, smiling in apology.

Sara nodded her head. "Who are you people? Why are you keeping us here like this?"

Lisa stared down into the woman's bright eyes and could see she was on a precipice, teetering on the slopes of defiance and capitulation.

"It is best you don't ask," Lisa stated, fighting against her own instinct for compassion. "My companion will not see you until the morning now. You must be truthful with him; you *must* answer his questions."

Sara did her best to hide her anger, but failed miserably.

"You must," the woman reiterated. "He is not a man to lie to!"

Sara nodded her head again and watched as the woman filled a spoon with the stew she had brought for them. With a steady hand, the woman fed Sara the bland tasting meal, one spoonful at a time, but could not meet her defiant eyes. When she was finished, the woman rose from the bedside and took the empty canteen to the tray.

She returned with a bottle of water, unscrewing the cap as she came.

"I will come back at first light," she promised, allowing Sara to drink. "You will need the bathroom by then, I am sure."

Sara nodded her thanks as the woman rose up. "What is your name?"

Lisa stared down at the dishevelled, dusky beauty before her. "It's best you don't know," she said, shaking her head sadly. Turning, the woman strode out into the night, leaving her captive to stare at the canvas door as it flapped in her wake.

Growling, Sara tugged madly at her restraints. Something was coming, she could tell, and when it came, she wanted to be as far away from these people as she could be. She needed to escape, she was even more certain of that now, or she would never leave this tent.

Moaning, Sara looked over at Robert and willed the pilot to come back to her.

Jon Galnia woke to the sounds of the cold dawn's chorus and lay where he was for a time, listening to the long, piercing call of some bird that wanted to be heard above everything else. Yawning into the back of his left hand, Jon was surprised that he was not angry at the noise; if anything, he welcomed it. Back home, if he had been dragged from his sleep like this, he would have been furious, tempted to shoot the damned thing, and it would have ruined his day and everybody else's around him.

He shook his head ruefully. After last night he was, perhaps for the first time in his life, able to look back at himself, to dissect and truthfully analyse the person he was, the man other people either respected, or generally hated. He hadn't liked what he had found.

Jesus, what a dick.

Selfishness is something the selfish do not see by their very nature, and had he not been dropped from the sky, here, to this place, Jon was certain he would never have been able to realise that.

He looked about the hut for the source of his apparent renaissance, but the hermit was nowhere to be seen. Jon grinned. Rashan, or whatever his name was, had cooked a fabulous meal for them over his fire pit, some kind of dhal. Generally, Jon stayed clear of Indian food as it gave his guts and his wife something to complain about, but here, in the middle of nowhere, in the depths of his starvation, it was the best thing, apart from Italian food, of course, that he had ever tasted.

"You could sell this stuff in a top Beverly Hills restaurant for $60 a dish," Jon had said – and meant it – as they sat on the straw-strewn floor around the fire.

The old Sikh had just smiled broadly at him, nodding his ancient head enthusiastically as his guest had picked up some more of his supper with his right hand and, rather clumsily, put it into his mouth.

Jon stretched out his aching legs, wincing at how stiff his joints were. Sitting by the waning fire for hours last night, chatting to each other in a language neither understood, had left him barely able to rise. The old Sikh had helped him out into the darkness, leaving him to attend to nature, as he stared up at the breath-taking tapestry of stars above him. After he had finished relieving his discomfort, Jon had stumbled back into the hut and fell onto his bed, whilst his host had curled up on the ground.

Jon whistled and shook his head. Up in Beverley

Hills, he had seen some sights, but *nothing* like that; the light pollution back home, even up there, could draw away the darkness, leaving the Californian night sky filled with an orange glow.

Well it is the new black...

He went to move but his aching frame protested, and for a time Jon actually listened to his body. *When I get home*, he thought, puffing out his cheeks, *I am going to have to start going with Maria to Pilates – I'm not getting any younger!*

Smiling to himself, Jon sat up again, fighting against his injuries. He felt stronger today, his agony fading to pain, and it was something he felt that he could deal with. After all, what choice did he have? He had to find civilisation today, had to leave this sanctuary and head back out into the real world... even if he felt he needed a few more days of contemplation.

Last night, about the fire, Jon had shared his love of his family with the old man, showing him a photo he had in his wallet, taken the previous year on the Staten Island Ferry once the Lockdown had been lifted. The old Sikh had beamed, smiling broadly as Jon pointed to his wife and son and named them. Tears glistened in Rashim's eyes, when Jon said he could keep the picture. Jon swallowed hard. He had said some things to the Sikh that he had never said to anyone else before, not even to Maria. Here, in this remote, silent confessional, Jon had given his host enough dirt to put him in the chair.

Best I get going, Jon thought, fighting against the dark thoughts surfacing. He didn't want to still be here when his Cosa Nostra code and paranoia got the better of him. He knew who he was, knew what he was capable of, and he didn't want to be around the Sikh when the old Jon Galnia returned...

Rashim shuffled into the hut sometime later, the early morning sun spilling in behind him, though nowhere near as bright as his welcoming smile.

Rising from the bed, Jon threw his host a similarly warm greeting and went to help him with the heavy wicker basket of vegetables.

Bobbing his head in thanks, the old man directed his helper to the rickety table and began preparing breakfast. As Jon prattled away about nothing and watched on in awe, the Sikh expertly peeled and diced vegetables with a sharp knife, displaying skills that even a Michelin-starred chef would be envious of.

Rashim then proceeded to make *Chapattis* and Jon marvelled at the old man's skills. A lover of food himself, Jon could conjure up a few Italian dishes, but beyond that, or a slice of toast, he preferred to let somebody else cook for him.

Licking his lips, Jon eventually sat down to the best breakfast he could recall; a medley of spiced vegetables and breads, that filled his stomach with gentle fire and cleansed the woolly sleep from his mouth.

Slow to finish, Jon watched the old Sikh as he wrapped some more food in giant leaves and began piling them into a worn, cloth sack.

"You kicking me out?" Jon enquired, smiling.

Of course, Rashim did not understand, but he nodded enthusiastically, waiting patiently for his guest to finish off his food. When Jon rose stiffly, arching his back to stretch the cramp from his lean frame, Rashim motioned for him to follow him outside.

"Holy shi–" Jon breathed. Lost for words, he shielded his eyes against the rising sun. Having only been out during the night, Jon could only stare in wonderment at his surroundings.

Nestled on the steep slopes of a hillside, Rashim's retreat was surrounded by the jungle, hidden from the world and those who might spoil the serenity of his sanctuary. Rashim had been busy, it seemed. He had, Jon suspected, worked the hillside himself over many years, terracing the steep incline so that he could plant crops and live off the land.

Jon whistled in admiration, flicking an impressed look to his host. Rashim nodded, smiling, and they turned their attention back to sight before them. Tall trees spilled about Rashim's home, sweeping down the hillside to cradle the Sikh's boundary in their wooded embrace.

Jon could not tell how much of the hillside Rashim had tilled, as an early morning mist sat sullenly below them, filling the valley with its discontent. Hearing the jingle of a bell, Jon swept his gaze towards the right and noticed the old goat that wandered about a ramshackle enclosure, peering curiously in their direction.

That would explain the milk, Jon thought, somewhat relieved. He turned to speak to the old Sikh, pausing as a chicken wandered by, pecking at the bare ground in search of seed.

"What now?" Jon asked himself. He could see the worn trail that snaked down the hillside from terrace to terrace, and the Italian-American suddenly wondered how in Hell's name the old Sikh had got him up here?

Rashim put a thin hand on the left shoulder of Jon's ruined shirt, steering him gently to a table under the straw eaves of the hut, towards the wooden bowl resting there. The old man touched his face, smiling, before gesturing to Jon's sullen cheeks, and moving the bowl closer to his guest.

123

Jon grinned and moved to the bowl, catching a brief reflection of his haggard face in the water, before he splashed himself fully awake. Sighing with relief, Jon finally stumbled back, running a hand over his stubbled jaw-line.

He preferred a clean face and his skin itched in complaint, souring his calm demeanour momentarily. When Jon eventually turned back from his displeasure, Rashim handed him the cloth sack and a small water skin.

Jon accepted the gifts silently, hiding his eyes away for a time as he struggled against the unexpected emotion welling up inside of him. This man, this complete stranger, had shown him nothing but care and compassion. There was no end-game, no ulterior motive behind his kindness – he was just one human being showing love for his fellow man.

Jon's stomach churned, his own bile reprimanding him. He never did anything for anyone else unless there was something to be gained from it – some favour he could call in when needed, some angle he could work and use at a later date for his own personal gain and advancement.

Rashim could sense his guest's discomfort and reached out to touch Jon's head. When the westerner looked up, his eyes full of emotion, the old Sikh smiled broadly and pointed to a trail that ran along the ridgeline, away from the hut through the jungle to the north.

"Ranchha," Rashim said, pointing north vigorously, "Ranchha!"

Jon followed the sharp-nailed finger to the tree line. "Phone?" he flicked his hope about the Sikh's dark face, feeling his heart race when Rashim nodded.

The old man dropped to his leathery knees and began

drawing in the dirt with his finger. Jon hunkered down beside him, watching as Rashim drew a small house, then pointed to the hut. He then proceeded to draw a trail, stopping to point to the north along the path, then, some distance from the hut, he drew another trail, heading south from the main path, towards a collection of squares.

"Ranchha," he beamed, prodding the dirt.

On his own knees now, Jon placed a thankful hand on Rashim's shoulder, squeezing it happily.

"Thank you, Rashim," he whispered, his throat catching. "I can never repay you for your kindness, but on my blood, I promise that if I can, one day I will."

They helped each other up and Jon held out his free hand towards the old Sikh. It hung between them, shaking in the crisp morning air.

Rashim stared at it, then smiled. He clasped his palms together and bowed low, before reaching out to grip Jon's hand.

Jon grinned. "Look after yourself, old man," he said. He released the old Sikh's hand, and Rashim produced the family photo Jon had given to him the night before.

"Keep it," Jon said, his throat constricting. "Whenever you look at it, know that they will be thinking fondly of you as well."

Rashim had probably not understood a word of what was said, but he sensed their meaning and held the photo to his chest, smiling. Realising he was getting too emotional, Jon gathered up his meagre possessions and headed quickly towards the jungle to the north.

As he reached the tall trees he paused, however, turning slowly to look back towards the hut. Rashim watched him, one hand raised in farewell, his smile and eyes brighter than the rising sun, warmer than the grey sky overhead.

Clasping his hands together in farewell, Jon bowed. It felt strange to offer such humble thanks and respect to someone, as he was only used to receiving it.

Smiling one last time, Jon waved, and then hurried into the jungle towards his freedom.

Robert Williams awoke to the sound of his heart, raging unchecked in his pounding head. As he tried to grab a firm hold on his senses, he heard the gasp of relief, somewhere away to his left.

"Oh, Robert," Sara cried happily.

The confused pilot went to shield his eyes from the bright sun that split the shadows of the tent he found himself in, then panicked when he could not move his arms.

"It's okay, it's okay," Sara soothed him, as Robert began to struggle against the bonds that secured him to a pole in the centre of the tent. "Just calm down a moment, take a breath."

Robert's face swung towards the Mexican and he smiled at the blurred vision before him. Blinking the fog from his eyes, a thankful smile stole across his battered and burnt features, before being chased away by crisp, fresh pain.

"What happened?" he asked, his eyes clouded with confusion. He looked about their surroundings again, his mind trying to catch up with what he was seeing. "Where are we?"

Sara watched as Robert began to tug furiously at his restraints again and calmed him down with hushed whispers.

"I was hoping you could tell me?" she said, flicking a guarded look towards the sun. "All I can tell you is that we are being held against our wishes... and that we are in trouble."

Whispers of what had happened began to stir in Robert's mind, and screwing his eyes shut he tried to grasp hold of them as his head began to pound furiously. His throat was dry, raw to the point of hoarseness and his face and body were still stiff from pain. He went to sniff in some fresh air, but suddenly realised that his nose was broken and clogged with thick, dried blood.

Fragmented images of their rescue came to the fore. Robert winced as he relived the moment he had been struck by their would-be rescuers, and felt renewed grief as he recalled the loss of his co-pilot, Steven Gaines.

Robert turned slowly, fighting against his pain and studied Sara. She looked desperate; her bright, captivating eyes filled with wild worry. Battered and bruised, her clothes were ruined and her tousled hair was charred from the explosion. As she struggled with her tied wrists and tried, despite her bandaged leg, to drag her bed closer to him, Robert thought again that she looked a lot like his own daughter, had never looked more beautiful.

"Well, whoever they are," Robert coughed, realising he may have been staring, "they are dangerous! There were at least six of them, as far as I can recall, all of them carrying weapons."

Close enough to him now, Sara leant in close, eyeing the sun-filled entrance as she whispered in Robert's ear. "They do not know who we are."

The pilot frowned. "But, I thought... I just presumed they were here for Jon. If that's not the case, then what are they doing here?"

"I don't know. But why would they ask for our names? Surely–"

Sara stiffened, as she heard the approach of booted feet. Dragging her bed back hurriedly to where she hoped it had been, they settled down into their own disconsolation, trying their best not to look guilty.

Thrown wide, the tent flap was held back by the redhead as the tall man with the tattoos stalked purposefully into the room, followed dutifully by his companion. Sara felt her heart race as he came forward, her need for the bathroom forgotten as she saw that he carried a large smartphone in his left hand, raised protectively to his chest. His right hand gripped a pistol.

The man's bearded features flared to life as he noticed that Robert was conscious. With only a brief hesitation, he moved towards Sara, his eyes narrowing angrily.

"Tell me everything you know about this man, *Sara Gonzales*," he hissed, spitting out her name and holding the phone around for her to see the grainy image of her employer. "Where is Jon Galnia?"

Before she could respond, before Sara could hide away from her shock, the man moved towards Robert and smashed him in the face with the handle of the pistol. As Robert's head snapped back from the force of the blow and blood began to swell in the vicious cut to his cheek, the man put the barrel of the pistol to the pilot's forehead.

He looked back towards her, the picture still held out for her to see.

"5... 4... 3..."

CHAPTER ELEVEN

"Don't Look Back in Anger..."

The man slipped through the mist and jungle, heading silently along the worn trail, a rifle cradled in his arms. Stopping, he shielded his eyes and stared up the steep slopes of the hillside, hesitating as he saw the terracing before him, heavy with crop. The path that had been getting more worn as the miles slipped away, creased up the slopes towards the hut and the wraith-like tendrils of smoke that curled up into the dour morning sky.

Fighting to remain calm, the man turned, watching as his comrades appeared like ghosts behind him. Spreading out on either side of their leader, as one, they looked up the unforgiving incline.

Mikael Andersson was angry, angry enough to allow his professionalism a little vacation. They had spent most of the night tracking the tiger, following its trail deeper into the dark jungle along the gorge until it was impossible for them to track it any further.

Fresh orders had come through on the radio a few hours from dawn, as they strung up their makeshift camp and hoped to steal a few hours of sleep. What remained of the night proved a restless one, and they dragged themselves from their hammocks early the next morning, eager to make their own tracks back to where they had found evidence of the man who had set free their prize.

Brooks had not been apologetic over the radio, would not listen to Andersson's complaints that they were so close to capturing it – that once they had it and were away, nothing else would matter.

'This doesn't come from me and it is not a debate,' Brooks had snarled into his ear. *'Find the third survivor. Find him fast, before he gets to safety and alerts people to our presence here and tells the world we've got a fucking living tiger.'*

Andersson scowled. *What a waste of fucking time!* Yes, the bastard had caused them some grief by setting it free, and they owed him for that – but if they lost the tiger, the Indians wouldn't get their dirty money and nobody would get paid. So what if the man got to safety? Who cared if he did? If they didn't mess about, they would be out of here by then, far away, spending vast amounts of money, so it wouldn't matter.

Let the Indians worry about it. Whoever had set this up clearly didn't want the world to know about the tiger, and were more concerned about the proceeds than the survival of a species, already thought to be extinct. Andersson expected there was an obscene amount of money on the offering table to capture the tiger, and he was getting paid enough not to worry about what would happen to the beast when they caught her.

Sighing, Andersson gave in and listened to some sense for a few moments. If they messed up this one, Brooks and his team would never work for their employers again – would never get *any* private contracts. Reputation was everything in this game. He would be back chasing pirates off the Horn of Africa, or if his reputation was completely screwed (and his employer certainly had the power to do that), he would be stacking shelves in IKEA before he could write up his résumé.

No! he decided, shaking his head. *Some lucky bastard was not going to do that to him.*

"We are wasting time," Taylor hissed at his shoulder and Andersson threw the tracker a dark, warning look. "The longer wc follow the survivor, the less chance I will have of finding the tiger. Isn't that why they hired us?"

Taylor had a point. Without the tiger, none of it would matter, none of them would matter.

"If he is not here, then screw Brooks, Galnia can wait," the Swede spat. "I am not going to jeopardise the mission and our money because Sam hasn't got any hair left on his balls."

"That makes two of you then," Taylor grinned, splitting the tension.

Andersson dealt him a murderous glare, then chuckled, giving him the middle finger. "Better to be bald than have ginger pubes."

Hassan Raz moved past them all, shaking his head. "Come on *Habibis*, let's find this fucker and get back on target."

The Moroccan, not one to usually demean himself with infantile profanities, headed for the trail. The cylindrical rifle was shouldered now, and he carried an MP5 in his assured, gloved hands.

Andersson waved the others forward with a guarded look about their surroundings. Flicking the safety off his rifle, he followed his team up the trail into the hopeful day.

The old Sikh stepped out into the rising sun, his smile brightening the day as the four men came silently up the trail towards him. The short, dark-skinned man in the lead carried a weapon and came forward, one gloved hand raised in greeting.

"*Ssalamū 'lekum*," he said, though did not smile.

"*Sat Sri Akal Ji*," Rashim responded, placing his shaking hands together in greeting.

Behind the Moroccan, the westerners spread out, their eyes sweeping the surroundings. Silence filled the cool morning air and even the birds fell silent. In between the two groups, a chicken wandered about their feet, ignorant to the rising tension.

Andersson studied the old man before them, watching him for a time as he remained with his palms together, his head bowed respectfully. Flicking a look to Taylor and Parker, he jerked his head to towards the hut. They swept past the owner, who tensed at their approach, and as they kicked down the thin door the Swede turned his attention to the Moroccan.

"Find out what he knows, quickly," Andersson growled.

Nodding, Raz moved forward, grabbing the old man by his impressive beard. Jerking his head up, he stared deep into the Sikh's bright eyes and said something that Andersson could not understand.

As the Moroccan dragged the Sikh away by his long hair towards the rear of the hut, the Swede began searching the area outside the shack then stopped, staring down at something drawn in the dust. Frowning, he stubbed it with the toe of one boot and knelt down, waving a curious chicken away with a firm hand.

Rising up moments later, he looked towards the rising screams and headed in search of his own answers.

Jon Galnia had a spring in his step as he followed the twisting trail through the jungle along the ridgeline. Whereas once he would have scowled at the terrain, found anger in every root, vine and damned monkey that got in his way, he now observed only the beauty of his surroundings, thanks only to the real prospect of finding a phone and getting home.

Hope was usually a promise unfulfilled; a journey more enjoyable than the actual destination, but it was amazing what a little *genuine* hope could do for you. Jon was slipping into his old mindset now, ready for the storm that would follow him back over the Atlantic to America and unleash its fury upon whoever had ditched him here.

Jon hesitated, only briefly, a small part of him happy for the solace, happy to be away from all that scrutiny, power-playing, fawning and foreplay – the constant dance with the authorities, the merry-go-round of his daily life.

A wild pig crossed his trail and Jon stopped, watching, waiting to see if it would charge him down and gore him to death. The large pig was feeling charitable and snuffled around the ground and thicket for a time before slipping away from view.

Smiling wryly, Jon shouldered his sack and cast a final look back through the jungle, picturing the sanctuary that he had left behind. Even now, it seemed that it had happened to somebody else, and as Jon continued on his way, deep down he knew that he would never keep his promise to the old Sikh.

Jon discarded his doubts on a sigh. He knew who he was – what he was, and one night wasn't going to change that. But he would learn from it.... he owed Rashim that much, at the very least.

As lost to his thoughts as he was, Jon did not register the shot at first. He blinked, listening as the tranquillity was broken and wondered if he had even really heard it. A second shot cracked, scattering several birds and a lone monkey away through the jungle about him, and he felt his skin crawl after them.

He had heard enough gunshots in his time...

Jon looked back through the jungle, fighting against his rising paranoia. Trying to tread lightly through his concern, he listened to the following silence for some time.

There was no doubting it, he *had* heard gunshots; two stark, chilling reports of what had happened. The thing that really scared the shit out of him was that deep down he knew where it had come from, too.

Hesitating, Jon fought back against a tide of questions, all shouting out for attention in his throbbing temple at the same time.

What has happened? One demanded.

You know what has just happened, another countered, ominously.

Turning back to the north trail, Jon hurried on for three strides, slowed for another two, and then stopped.

Closing his eyes, he drew in a steadying breath and then slowly let it out.

His body, already soaked in a cold sweat, chilled him to the bone.

If I carry on, I will be free.

He took another step forward, and then stopped again. He would never truly be free of the path he had chosen, the curse that haunted his bloodline.

Jon Galnia was not destined for a quiet life, enjoying his Sundays, sat reading the LA Times and deciding whether or not to go to church. He had not been born to a normal life – that was something he could never have, despite how much he would wish it some days.

Cursing, Jon turned and headed back the way he had just come. After several hundred metres he began jogging, despite the lack of breath in his lungs. Some moments later, as he listened to the deathly silence of his surroundings and searched for his courage, he began to run.

By the time Jon Galnia reached the vicinity of his former sanctuary, he knew something was seriously wrong. All about him the jungle was silent – no chatter, no cacophony of life, only the telling silence of a remorseful day. Slowing, Jon dragged a wet hand through even wetter hair and tried to flick it dry in the rising heat. Searching for a breath he could not find, he noticed a family of monkeys in the trees, away to his right.

Jon shuddered. There were no curious stares, no interested heads bobbing his way. They sat silently, huddled together on their branches, heads bowed.

Swallowing his fear, Jon paced about, staring ahead along the trail through the shards of knifing sunlight. Overhead, the clearing blue sky deepened in colour as the sun regained control of the day. Steeling himself, he took tentative steps forward on his ruined shoes.

Something was clearly wrong, Jon could tell. There was no serenity to be found here now, just a hollow void filling with foreboding.

The only other time he had sensed such a warning was on the day he had walked into a warehouse; into the trap he knew had been set, but one he was powerless to walk away from. Closing his eyes to the part of his past he had tried to forget most, Jon drew in a faltering breath, held it close and then threw it away. Nodding his head at the memory that would never leave him, he crept forward on legs he could no longer feel.

Despite the rising heat, the air was still cold in the

shadows and on the distant cusp of the steep hillside, from where Jon could just make out Rashim's hut. Having not yet given in to the sun's warming touch, a wistful breath of air caressed Jon's face as the trees began to thin and he approached the quiet sanctuary ahead.

Searching about, Jon picked up a fallen stick, nothing to rival his previous trusty weapon, but one he could use, nonetheless. The jungle was still quiet, worryingly so, and there was little trace left of the calming ambience to the area.

Usually a city boy, preferring busy concrete sidewalks to a granite mountainside, he could tell that the land and its inhabitants were trying to warn him with their unnatural silence. Carefully putting down the sack he was carrying, Jon gripped the broad stick tightly in clammy hands and padded quietly ahead towards the perimeter of the clearing. The land was quiet.

Across from where Jon hid behind a tall, sharp-barked tree, Rashim's hut was dark. No candle's light flickered from within, and the curl of black wispy smoke from the fire pit was absent. The tall trees that protected the terracing and glade stood by silently as the Italian-American loitered. The grim, silent sentinels watched on, struggling to tell him of what had happened here.

Breathing heavily, Jon made his mind up and stalked slowly towards the hut, his ears and eyes scanning the surroundings for danger. The door to the hut, once rickety, was now broken, hanging off one fragile hinge and urging him to come closer, still. In his chest, Jon's heart was beating out another message, however, his selfishness warning him to move away.

Resisting the urge to call out to Rashim and warn any unwanted visitors of his arrival, Jon sent a quick look down the terracing. The early morning mist had cleared now and the land was silent, the crops unattended. Stepping closer, he fixed his eyes upon the broken doorway. The blood was rushing in his head, drowning out everything as he stepped up to the opening.

Holding his nerves in check, Jon unceremoniously asked the door to open up with a designer foot, revealing the horrors within.

A whirlwind had seemingly visited the hut, picking up everything inside and scattering them about without regard. The rickety bed, the old bookcase and their tenants, the worm-infested table and chairs; all carelessly thrown about the room, chaos replacing harmony. The fire pit was cold now, the bowls and basket from the glorious breakfast they had shared earlier, broken, like the memory of the time Jon had hoped to carry fondly with him to safety.

The old Sikh was nowhere to be seen, and Jon jumped back in fright as a chicken wandered from amidst the chaos and regarded him with what might have been relief. Reining in his fears, Jon turned back to the morning outside.

"Rashim?" he hissed, as loud as he dared. There was no reply, no answer. Stick in hand, Jon moved back out, shielding his eyes against the brightness.

As he moved from under the shade of the porch, Jon could see that the goat was still in its pen. It peered at him over the fencing, bleating a welcome that he ignored. Peering down the slope for something he might have missed, Jon was certain whoever had fired the shots was no longer here. Banishing his thoughts, the questions of who they were and why they were here, Jon searched to the side and rear of the hut.

Any resolve and hope that Rashim may have fled

deserted Jon, however, as he found the old man, laying face down in the long grass that bordered a patch of fruit bushes behind his home.

"No!"

Crying out, Jon threw his stick to one side and rushed to the Sikh's aid. Dropping to his battered and bruised knees, he reached out a shaking hand and gently turned Rashim over.

Jon fell back, his revulsion catching in his throat.

The old man's face was unrecognisable; no more than a bloodied pulp of flesh and ruined teeth. His eyes were swollen, though not closed, dark blood congealing about their lids. Had it not been for his torn beard, twisted and clotted by blood, Jon would not have recognised him.

Rashim was dead. The single gunshot to the temple would have killed him instantly, but Jon had seen enough brutality in his time to know the old Sikh had not died well. He had been beaten and tortured before the end, and they had been in a hurry. Whoever did this to Rashim, had not taken their time. When they had what they had come for, or perhaps frustrated that they didn't, they had cut off his magnificent mane of hair and shot him twice – once in the head, and then again through the heart for good measure.

Before he realised it, Jon was crying. As he stared up at the sky, searching for answers, he gave in to his emotions.

For some time, he rocked back and forth, juggling his distress with his anger. This kind, peaceful man had gone out of his way to help him, had done nothing to warrant such an end, except perhaps, to have met Jon Galnia.

Jon's fury turned his thoughts fully to the question of Rashim's murderers. There was no coincidence with what had happened here, just a terrible tragedy visited upon an innocent man. Whoever had done this to the Sikh had been searching for him, they had to have been. *But who were they?*

His Cosa Nostra paranoia kicked in, full throttle. It had to be the bastards who had sabotaged his jet. They must have sent someone to check, to confirm that he was toast and out of the picture. When they realised he was not amongst the wreckage and the dead, they had come looking for him.

An hour sooner, and they would have found me…

Calming down momentarily, he looked towards the old man. Any thoughts about his own predicament seemed lame, compared to what had happened to Rashim.

Shaking his sorrow free, Jon crawled over to the Sikh, staring down at the ruined face and trying to remember the kindness and life that had once radiated there.

"I am so sorry," Jon whispered, closing the old man's sightless, staring eyes.

Jon stayed beside Rashim for a while longer, clutching the Sikh's frail, broken hands in his own. When he finally rose up, he stretched the sorrow from his taught muscles. With a final nod of thanks, he turned away. Leaving his saviour to nature, Jon moved back inside the hut, searching amongst the chaos. After a time, he found Rashim's slender, curved knife, and slipped the blade back into its ornate sheath.

I am going to need you, Jon thought. He went to turn away, and then spied the black and white photos, scattered in the shadows. Clearing the carnage aside, he picked them up, flicking through several old pictures that showed a young boy, sat on an ornate wooden chair. Dressed in fine silks and wearing a jewel encrusted headdress that was crowned by a feathered plume, the striking little boy smiled towards someone, watching from the wings of history, beside the photographer.

Jon breathed in awe. It was a striking photo, but it was far too old to be Rashim. *But who was it?* More photos showed similarly formal shots of a regal looking family, sat together on a large divan, all elegantly dressed, all showered in jewels that spoke loudly from an age, long past, of the family's wealth and status.

"No wonder you liked me," Jon said aloud, trying to find a smile. Rashim had kept these photos, when he had given up everything else to come and be at one with himself. They must have meant something to him...

Jon paused, feeling the bile catch in his throat. He had not found the photo he had given to Rashim, and after a frantic look about the carnage, he knew that they had taken it.

Rising up, Jon folded the pictures and placed them in a torn pocket. Moving to the broken door, he hesitated and then turned back, imagining a happier time, sat around the fire pit, sharing unintelligible stories.

"You will not be forgotten, my friend," Jon whispered. "*Grazie mille.*" Smiling sadly, he stalked from the hut and went to retrieve his sack of provisions.

In the shade of the tall trees, he stared back along the path. The day was still silent, though with the thoughts raging away in his head, he couldn't really tell.

Gripping his stick in his hand, Jon turned away from his path home and walked back out into the sun.

Staring down the hillside, Jon's eyes narrowed.

"I don't know who sent you," he hissed, spittle flying from his lips. "But whoever you fucking are, you are going to regret it."

Despite his promise, despite his broiling hatred, as

Jon Galnia headed down the snaking path, he still remembered to free the goat from its pen as he passed.

CHAPTER TWELVE

Subtle Ripostes

United States Federal Aviation Attaché Thomas Miller stared across the carpeted corridor at the magnificent photograph hanging from the wood-panelled wall. It was quiet at the moment, much quieter than the bustling city surrounding Raisina Hill, and a respectful silence was being observed by the workers at the South Secretariat building, as they came and went about their business. Many dealt him curious looks as they passed by, but all were accompanied by broad smiles of greeting.

Despite his initial irritation of having been left out in a hallway with what was probably the worst cup of tea he had ever tasted, Miller crossed one leg over the other and rested his cup and saucer in his lap as he returned his attentions to the photograph of Mahatma Gandhi. Since his time in India, the attaché had seen many photos of India's most beloved son, but none so striking as the one he had seen here; a young Gandhi, dressed in a splendid woollen suit, sporting an impressive dark moustache and full head of raven-black hair.

Thomas smiled in wonderment. Even an ambitious young man from Somerset, in Maryland, drawn to D.C. in search of a political career, had heard of Mahatma Gandhi – who could not recognise his image, even if they knew nothing of the man?

Since his arrival in India in the July of 2016, after his transfer from Washington's Executive Secretariat to the

American Embassy in New Delhi, Miller had done all he could with the personal time he had available to understand why so many people fell in love with India. Away from his family and friends, he had hated the country at first, the smells, the poverty, the assault to his senses and his stomach. After several weeks on the toilet, unable to control his gut, he wished he had never heard of the place, had never desired anything more than to work on his family's farm, instead.

But slowly, surely, without realising it, his stomach began to settle and he began to embrace the country and its people, falling steadily in love with the new life he had sought to escape for the first three months. From its bustling, choked streets full of vibrancy, colour and adventure, to the sweeping, turbulent history of the country, India began to claim him, and the American began to explore, immersing himself in the food, the culture, the way of life. He began to study and visit as much as he could, when he was able.

Turning his thoughts back to the photograph, Miller thought about his recent visit to *Rajghat*, to the National Gandhi museum. There, amidst curious stares and photo requests from several Indian families, he had followed, literally, in Gandhi's footsteps; taking the same the path the Father of the Nation had on his fateful walk through the grounds, on the evening of January 30th, 1948. It was the most humbling experience, one of many since his time in India, and the attaché knew that when he was eventually recalled back Stateside, he would be reluctant to leave.

His thoughts distracted, Thomas instinctively sipped at his cold tea and regretted it. Sighing, he closed his eyes. There were still no hard facts about the crash, no evidence that it had actually even happened. As the demands from Washington growled louder in his ears and the pressure at *Chanakyapuri*, where the New Delhi's U.S. Embassy was located, became more uncomfortable, Miller battled against the image of being shipped home to a desk job, in a basement somewhere out of the way, his burgeoning career over before it had even truly begun.

Any premonitions he may have had scattered as the First Secretary's charming aide returned, filling his dark thoughts with the brightest smile. As she came confidently towards him and flicked a surreptitious look at his tea, he rose to his feet and lost himself deep within her wide, dark eyes.

"First Secretary Rana will see you now, Mr. Miller," the woman announced. Smiling shyly, she would not meet his eyes for longer than was deemed acceptable. As she took the cup and saucer from his hands, their fingers brushed over one another briefly, and he caught the faint scent of her perfume on the fan-conditioned breeze.

Clearing his throat for his thanks, Thomas fumbled about for his briefcase and followed the woman towards the open door at the end of the hallway. Cursing himself for bumbling about like a teenager, Miller followed the young woman silently, trying to clear his mind for the game of political chess he was about to play.

Hiding his frustration at this necessary distraction, First Secretary Rana slipped his smile into place and adjusted the loose spectacles on his nose as Samira showed the American into his office and made the formal announcements to both men.

Dismissing his aide and joining the younger man in their rejection of her offer for more tea, Rana smiled and slipped around his desk to offer the American his hand.

"Mr. Miller," Rana said, gripping the soft, yet stronger hand that was presented to him. "Forgive the delay. I know you must be busy."

As they dropped each other's handshake, the First Secretary studied his guest; putting a firm face to the man he had made sure he found out as much about as he could before the meeting.

Impeccably dressed in a dark, plain suit and blue tie, Thomas Miller carried himself to the offered chair with a purpose that only the young and ambitious possessed. Rana waited for him to be seated, before returning to his own chair, remembering a day when he had been that young, though not harbouring the same desire.

The attaché was of fair height, a good head above Rana, and had short, dark hair; combed to one side and held in place by too much Brylcreem. A strong jaw line defined the handsome, youthful face that met the First Secretary's scrutiny with a smile that instantly brightened his demeanour. Thick brows arched over his focussed, hazel eyes, and his lips parted in greeting under a small, straight nose, framing his bright teeth.

"I appreciate the time, First Secretary," Miller responded. "It is a pleasure to meet you in person, sir, and I hope that we can both gain much from our meeting."

Rana smiled, guarding his thoughts carefully. "Of course, of course. It is a matter of continuing concern for both our nations, and rest assured, we are doing everything possible under these peculiar circumstances to find out what has happened to the jet."

There was no attempt to hide the way he said *peculiar* as Rana moved his first attacking piece across the imaginary chess board. Thomas Miller studied the small, thin suit across from him. Of course, he had found out everything he could about the First Secretary; his aides working on it for the last two days, since they had first spoken on the telephone.

Rana continued to smile across at him. A perfect face for a man of, until the last few years, very little, if any political ambition, other than to represent his district, Vasant Vihar, as he had done for the last ten years. Popular, yet not popular enough, Aasim Rana had been happy to fight for local issues, but little else, until Chandra Nehru had made him an offer that he apparently could not refuse.

Aware of the silence filling between them and the strain at the corners of the First Secretary's smile, Miller remembered his manners. Grasping hold of the facts, he let go of his speculative imagination.

Dragging his briefcase on to his lap, Thomas Miller thumbed the code into the lock and opened it, drawing forth a manila folder with the United States Eagle on the front cover and 'Confidential' stamped across it in warning red.

"I have hard copies of the information I forwarded to you yesterday, First Secretary," Miller said, handing the folder across with a smile. "The itinerary and destination for the jet are within, with direct contact details for myself and the colleagues who are assisting me and the White House with this matter."

Rana accepted the folder, nodding his thanks. He held up his other hand, hoping that it was not shaking too clearly. "Please, Mr. Miller, call me Aasim."

Thomas tilted his head in accord, dutifully offering the same courtesy in return.

"Now, I know our time is precious," Rana began, ignoring the contents of the folder and threading his thin hands together on top of it. "So, let me bring you up to date with everything we have been able to ascertain for our close, American friends."

Rana paused, ordering his thoughts, before continuing. "Thanks to your information and our own diligence, we have liaised with both the Indian Civil Aviation Authority and the Military to discover that, as far as we can positively tell, the aircraft did not in fact enter Indian Airspace."

Miller digested what he was hearing and blinked in surprise. "But we were led to believe that there was evidence to say that the jet had crossed central Indian Airspace; our own data would suggest the same thing. Are you now telling me this is not the case?"

Rana nodded his head, hearing his own heart above the attaché's words. "Detailed reports from the military and Civil authorities had both concluded that the jet did not cross India – there is no record of it, I am afraid, despite initial suggestions to the contrary. Our own satellite images and intense searches of the central regions from both the air and on the ground have given us nothing, absolutely nothing. If there had been a crash, if there was a jet in trouble, people would have raised the alarm – there would have been sightings, most certainly."

This meeting is not going the way I had anticipated, Miller thought, sensing the threat to his King on the board.

"This does not make any sense, sir!" Miller exclaimed, shaking his head in disbelief.

Aasim Rana shared his agreement, his eyes full of sympathy. "We are totally perplexed by this mystery, and naturally, you have our utmost assurances that we will continue to dedicate our efforts and considerable resources to the matter. But I am afraid, little short of that and sharing the data on what we have discovered, there is not much more we can do at this time, Thomas, except to offer the Prime Minister's deepest regrets."

The First Secretary watched the young American, sensing his turmoil as he realised he would not get anything to share with his superiors today, nothing of substance that would satisfy the U.S. authorities and the families of the missing.

Naturally, all of the data and documents that Rana's office would collate and hand over to the Americans were falsified, all trace of the jet removed, hidden by those in place, loyal to the Prime Minister – they had taken a great many precautions to ensure the operation in Madhya Pradesh was not discovered, a fortuitous decision that could never have foreseen such unexpected complications. The one sighting of the jet, reported to the local state police in Madhya Pradesh, had already been silenced by those on the ground and in the pocket of the Prime Minister.

"I will have Samira deliver the documents personally to you this afternoon, Mr. Miller," Rana announced over his sympathy. "But, before we return to our investigations, I must share some concerns of my own with you."

Miller closed his briefcase, forgotten on his lap, and placed it back beside his chair. He felt his skin prickle in warning as the fan above his head rattled loudly, increasing the headache building in his temples.

"Concerns?" Miller asked, frowning.

Rana nodded. "After you very kindly shared all your data with us, I thought it prudent to find out more about the people we were searching for – it seems to me, though naturally any U.S. citizen in danger would warrant such attention, there is more to this than we were first led to believe."

Miller licked his lips. He had feared this moment, and although he had gone over his response in his mind many times, he could tell that the First Secretary was already waiting to strike home his advantage.

"I presume, sir, you are referring to the owner of the jet, Mister Galnia?"

"Indeed I am," Rana responded, far too quickly. "It would seem to me that a man such as this Jon Galnia, already investigated by the police and your Federal Bureau of Investigation, a man who has strong ties to the American and Russian Mafia, with countless fingers of suspicion pointing his way, may well not *want* to be found. Have you considered the possibility that this message was intended to create a diversion for some reason? Perhaps he wanted the U.S. authorities to think that he had crashed, was even dead?"

Miller stiffened. Of course, the FBI had already contacted him with their concerns, had alerted the CIA of that very possibility. But, first and foremost, the welfare of the U.S. and British citizens was paramount to him. All other eventualities and speculation would have to wait.

"We have, of course, sir, considered that possibility," Miller said softly, his voice scattered across his fraying composure. "But their welfare is our first priority. I, and Washington, can only thank you for your ongoing cooperation in this matter, a clear sign that the friendship our two great nations share is stronger than ever. We will, of course, continue to share our findings and update you on any tangible progress."

Rana rose first, watching impassively as Miller dragged himself up with his briefcase in hand. Crossing to his side, the First Secretary reaffirmed his dedication to the problem, of how it would be for the betterment of all involved to get to the bottom of this challenging mystery.

With a firmer handshake this time, Rana guided the young Ambassador to the door with a consolatory hand on his tense left shoulder, delivering him into Samira's care.

Once they were gone and he was alone with his thoughts, Aasim Rana closed the door to his office and sank back into the embrace of the wood. Offering a prayer of thanks for the timely investigation into this Jon Galnia, the First Secretary hurried for his desk and for the hidden burner phone.

Samira Jethwani escorted the American back to the entrance hall, asking the staff at the reception for Mr. Miller's driver to be summoned. A shadow of the charming man that had arrived on the Hill, Samira politely excused herself from his side and left him alone to his thoughts, assuring him of her attendance later that day with the information entrusted into her care.

Stopping in the doorway, with one heeled shoe on the first marble step, Samira sent a look back toward the American. Framed in sunshine, he sat waiting for his car, his eyes staring far away, searching deep through his concerns. Whatever had happened in the First Secretary's office had clearly not taken the direction he would have wished for.

Hoping she would have a better, more pleasant reunion with the handsome American later that afternoon, Samira headed back to her office to deal with the work that was piling up far too quickly on her desk.

Back in her office, before she unlocked the screen on her

laptop, Samira headed to the First Secretary's door, to enquire if he needed anything after the intense meeting. As she neared, she could hear Aasim Rana talking quietly to someone. Aasim had always told her to knock before entering, though he never minded her intrusions when he was on the phone.

She was about to knock and push her way into the office when she stopped, her hand hovering over the polished oak. Something in the First Secretary's tone stayed her hand. Frowning, the young aide was about to walk discreetly away when she hesitated. He was not scheduled for any meetings today – he had cleared his diary (again) after the telephone call from the American, the previous day. This, in itself, was causing her terrible headaches, as the journalist from NDTV had called several times to vent her frustrations at what she saw as the First Secretary's consistent derogation of his duties and obligations.

"...the American went even better than we could have hoped for. We have more time now, time that we must use well."

Samira could not help but listen, her youthful curiosity outweighing her conscience and duty to her employer.

"Yes, yes," Rana responded quietly to an unheard voice, forcing Samira to press her ear against the cold wood. She flicked a look to her phone console, frowning when she could not see any solid light to indicate that he was using his office phone.

"I have distracted his investigation with our facts. He has gone home now with, how would they say it? '*His tail between his legs*'." Rana paused to chuckle at his own apparent joke. "I do not think he will bother us again for some time – we have hidden ourselves quite well from him for now. This Miller may be young and inexperienced, but we should not do him the discourtesy of underestimating him."

Samira backed away; the rest of the conversation lost as she stumbled to her desk.

Her hands were shaking as she gripped the corner of her desk. She should not have been listening, prayed that she had not. But as Samira slumped down on her chair and stared at the black screen that reflected her fears back at her, she knew that whatever was happening, whatever the American had been hoping to find, there was no doubt in her mind that Aasim Rana was trying to thwart his efforts.

Shuddering, Samira knew that whether she liked it or not, she was now complicit in his lies, and in the coming days she was going to have to decide what she was going to do about it.

CHAPTER THIRTEEN

Deliberations

The pilot ran a hand across his haggard face, wincing as the pain from the fresh cut, his burns and broken nose reminded him that time was running out. He shuddered as he sank down onto the bed he had now been cuffed to, following the ordeal they had suffered earlier that morning.

Shuddering, Robert attempted to banish the memories of what had happened, and thought he could still feel the kiss of the pistol pressed to his head. He had been terrified, trapped in his confusion and unable to stop staring up the barrel of impending doom as the man with the gun counted down, his anger directed at Sara.

As the seconds ran out, Sara had screamed for him to stop, and thankfully the bastard had pulled the pistol away from Robert's forehead, training it on the Mexican flight attendant. As Sara stammered and sobbed her way through a detailed account of what had happened, where they had been and where they were bound for, Robert had studied the woman standing behind the man who threatened them, watching the events unfolding before her.

Robert was sure, just for a moment, that he had seen something on her pale features, a look of disgust for how her companion was going about his business. It had been there, he was sure of it, but it was stolen away in an instant, as she flicked her eyes to him and slipped her unreadable mask back in place.

Before they left, the man cuffed them both about the head with a warning of what would happen if they were not compliant, and for the briefest of moments, Robert feared the man would make an example of him, as he turned angrily on him, raising the pistol. Before he could do anything else, the woman had put a calming hand on his shoulder, coaxing him out into the bright day.

Thinking of Sara, he looked to the enticing day outside, but his strength and hopes were fading with each moment that dragged past.

Sara was right! Whoever these people were, they had not, initially, been here for them. They had probably not even realised the jet had crashed, before they entered the region.

The woman had returned, an hour after the man had forced the information from Sara's lips, to take her off for her bathroom break. Feeling suddenly very alone, selfishly, the pilot yearned for her return. Resting his raging mind, Robert closed his eyes and waited for their red-haired captor to bring Sara back.

The flight attendant was forced back into the tent moments later at an arm's and pistol's length, and this time Sara was ordered to bind herself to the bed again with a pair of handcuffs.

"I'll bring you some food later," the woman said, fixing them both with an even look. "You can use the bathroom then, Williams."

Robert nodded, trying to remain humble, and waited until she had departed again, before snapping his head to Sara.

"Well?"

Sara sighed and shook her tresses about her filthy features in despair. "I do not know what we have stumbled into here, Rob. All I know is that as soon as they find Jon, we are going to die."

Robert swallowed his fear as he felt his skin stiffen. "What did you see?" he dared to ask.

"There are several tents out there, and we are camped near to the shores of a huge lake. I can see hills, or a peak in the distance," she paused to shake her head again. "They have crates of supplies, weapons and a radio, which I presume is to keep in touch with the rest of their team. There are six tents – so that matches up to what you said earlier."

Robert's hopes of escape were dashed as he tugged at his raw wrist and restraint. Somehow, they had to get free, past their armed captors and to safety. *Easy!*

"So, what are we going to do?"

Sara sat up on her bed and leant as close as she could for her whispers to be heard. "They are focussed on Jon at the moment, but they are here for something else. I saw what looked to be an animal cage of some description in the back of the helicopter..."

Robert frowned. "They are hunters?" he shook his head, was about to say something, then stopped, his mind working away madly.

Sara could see the look that crossed Robert's likeable face and left him to deliberate for a few moments. He looked wild now, his clothes blackened and torn, the lines of his advancing years deepened by smoke and blood, but he must have been a handsome man, she thought suddenly, back in his youth, the kind of man she liked to get into trouble with, probably still did…

Puffing out her cheeks to hide her thoughts, she lay back down on the bed, relieved from the pressure on her bladder and the earlier threat to her decency. Closing her eyes, Sara shut out images of the pistol pressed to

155

Robert's head and of her shame at saving her own life, perhaps at the cost of another.

The Beverly Hills sunshine warmed Maria Galnia as she sat on her veranda, listening to the American official on the other end of the line. It was early morning, and the birds were lively in the grounds of the estate, lifting her spirits above her anger, momentarily.

Crossing her legs, she pulled her nightgown back in place to hide her decency and nodded to, though did not really register, what the U.S. official was saying to her.

"Thank you for letting me know this personally, Mr. Miller," Maria said automatically, as she ended the call.

Throwing the phone onto the table, she picked up her coffee and sipped at it, glad for the rush the specialty blend always gave her in the morning. Resting it in her lap, she buried her head in her free hand and massaged away her concerns.

In the last day, she had been on the phone constantly, had been visited by the FBI, who had quizzed her at length about Jon's trip to Moscow, of his plans from there. They had taken her phone away to analyse the voicemail Jon had left her, and she was thankful, in a way, that Jon was hopeless at keeping in contact – who knows what they would have found, if he had left it on her *business* cell.

Dragging her ragged locks back up over her head with a slim hand, Maria chewed her top lip. It was the only time the Feds had been allowed into their home without a warrant and it must have really pissed them off.

Smiling, Maria sank back into her seat and stared out across the grounds of Villa de Valdez. Another lonely day in paradise...

The sprinklers were already saluting the heat and the gardeners were in attendance, tending to the plants, shipped from around the world to create a little piece of everywhere. Over the last year, much to Jon's annoyance, she had spent a private fortune on shipments from Kew Gardens in London.

Shaking her head, she smoothed out the creases in the silk covering her legs and shuddered. It had been two days, and there was still no word about the crash. From what the ambassador had just fed back to her, it seemed like it might be some time before there was.

It just didn't make any sense. If Jon had something planned, he would have shared it with her. They shared everything, after all. She scowled. There was no faking that voicemail. Despite Jon's apparent calm, there was chaos all about, and it really did sound like he was in a jet about to crash.

The thought that she might not see Jon again stole the warmth from her day and Maria sighed heavily. Gio was already asking about his papa, as Jon was never away from home for more than a night usually – well, not these days, and she had placated their son with promises that his papa would be back soon.

What am I going to tell him if his father never comes home?

Maria growled. She was not some emotionally challenged soccer mom, she was of the blood, and it was like red steel in her veins. As soon as she had alerted the U.S. embassy in Delhi about her husband's message, she contacted their men on the ground in Moscow.

Maksim Lebedev had been just as shocked at the news, genuine shock that no amount of acting could have portrayed. One of Jon's father's old guard, Maksim was as loyal as the day was long and had served the young inheritor well, since Jon took other his father's empire.

Running operations from behind the scenes, both Maksim, and Aleksi Cardov ran the reputable shell companies that were fronts for their more sinister activities; protection rackets for smaller businesses and the distribution of narcotics shipped in from Pakistani-controlled Kashmir. The nameless drugs were then distributed to the dealers on the streets, who sold it to the needy low-life and high-life that were drawn to the Ramenki district they controlled, one of the more thriving areas of Moscow.

Maksim had promised to look into it from his end, and had updated her on his findings more than the U.S. authorities had so far.

Sipping her coffee, Maria thought about what she would have to deal with before her husband came home, and of how much coffee she would need to see her through it. There was no doubt in her mind that Jon was going to walk in through the front door soon, his rakish smile broad. Before long, she would be pulling her hair out again, wishing that she had some peace and quiet, that he were someplace else.

"Oh, I miss you, Jon," she said softly, feeling her chest tighten with both longing and loathing.

Later that morning, following the much-needed distraction of a shower, pilates, and a trip to look at the new Aston Martin she had her eye on, Maria came home to find Jon's consigliere waiting for her in the reading room.

"Still no news, Maria?" Paolo Romano Jnr asked, rising from the leather sofa to greet her. From the back of the huge Italian recliner, Capone opened one feline eye sullenly, then returned to chase after his fading dreams.

"Nothing at all," Maria sighed, tip-toeing as they kissed each other on both cheeks. Paolo held her hands gently in his huge slabs of meat, his dark eyes full of concern.

Maria held on for longer than she should have then pulled away. Offering a seat back to the man known on the street as *Il Lupo* – the Wolf – on account that he was the last person you wanted knocking on your door, Maria sat in Jon's favourite reading chair, an old Italian Fruit Wood, dating back from the 17th century. Crossing her legs, she rested her elbows on her bare knees and leant forward.

"It appears that the line of investigation has turned from one of concern to suspicion – they think Jon was up to no good and this is all his doing," Maria snarled, her eyes flashing angrily.

"That's bull," Paolo agreed. The large Italian shook his head, picking his irritation from the threads of his designer suit. Immaculately dressed in a grey pinstripe, fashioned in the style of the 1920s, Romano Jnr was a typical old-school gangster. Whilst everyone else these days did things by phone and *face-time*, he still gave personal visits, carried a flick-knife, told the time by a pocket watch and used a payphone.

Impossibly handsome, his square, broad face looked as if it was chiselled from marble, like his ancestors. A hawked nose added gravitas to his already imposing countenance, and the long scar that traced down his left cheek and neck to his collared shoulder, underlined everything with a stark warning.

Paolo Romano Jnr was a man to respect on the street, but, more importantly, he was *the* man to fear.

His eyes, twin orbs of green and blue, swirled as he mulled over the problem. As he licked his thin lips, Maria could tell he was trying to hide his concern – that for now, he was in charge.

And they both knew he was not a man to lead...

"So, what do we do next, Mari?" Paolo asked. He was like a brother to them both, and apart from Jon, only he was allowed to address her like that. "The whispers have already started, and the *Avvoltoi* are beginning to circle."

"We have to keep this between us," Maria began, reiterating the obvious. "If the other families hear about this, they will think us weak. We cannot let anyone beyond this room know what is happening... and we must act fast, *you* must act, Paolo."

"What do you need me to do?" There was no hesitation, no hint of wariness in his voice.

Playing with the hem of her pale blue summer dress, Maria sat back in her chair, running a red fingernail over the antique wood.

"I need you to charter a private jet to Bahrain," she said, holding his eyes intently. "Question anyone who was working as ground crew that day. Find out what you can from them."

Paolo frowned, his worry creasing across his broad brow like an earthquake. "But I will be needed here, Mari. I have to run things downtown for Jon, whilst he is away. If I up and leave, well, you know what will happen."

Maria nodded. "I do. But I cannot trust anyone else with this, Jon wouldn't, either. I've already been in touch with Aleksi and Maksim. They are discreetly looking into the possibility that the Russians were involved. They are the obvious suspects, but we would have to be more than certain of the facts before we start pointing our finger their way."

Paolo bobbed his head in agreement, his wonderment at the vision of beauty before him evident on his face. Jon may have been the head of the family, but his wife was most certainly the brains. She had quickly deduced that if the Russians had made a peace with Jon, a statement like this would do more damage than good. Furthermore, the jet's safe arrival in Bahrain could suggest that Jon's other enemies, and there were plenty of them, had taken steps to bring him down from there.

"Take three days and find out what you can, Paolo," Maria continued. "We can decide what to do next, once you are on the ground. I will run things from here in your absence – no, don't argue. I have done it before, and I will think of something to keep the others in check."

Paolo reined in his anger. There was no point arguing with her, she would not change her mind. As he rose up and took her gently by each shoulder to kiss her pale cheeks, he could tell that she was already in charge.

"If there is anything to find out, I will find it, Mari," he promised her. Turning, he headed for the door to hide his worry.

His hand was on the handle when Maria spoke again.

"Listen at the doors, Wolf," she said firmly, "don't knock on them."

"Si, signora," he responded dutifully.

Paolo cleared his mind of all the things he had to do before he left, and it wasn't until he was in his Cadillac Coupe and speeding south back down Coldwater Canyon Drive that he smiled.

Maria had not said anything about kicking down the doors.

CHAPTER FOURTEEN

Preparations

By the time Samira Jethwani made her way across the city to the U.S. Embassy in the diplomatic enclave of Chanakyapuri, it was deep into the afternoon. The rest of her morning had been like the heat of the day, a swirling haze that offered her no respite from her problems and discomfort.

Toiling with her workload and the needs of the First Secretary, Samira had dutifully gone about her business with dedication and diligence. On the two occasions she had been summoned to his office, Aasim Rana had seemed in high spirits. He had even told her that once she had delivered the documents to the embassy, she could go home for the day.

That did little to ease her fears. She had never been allowed home early. Aasim Rana claimed every single second of time from your day and expected more if he asked for it.

Paying the driver of the *tuk-tuk,* the auto-rickshaw, Samira stepped out onto the broad, bone-white pavement that lined the *Shantipath*, the main road through the enclave, and walked the remaining distance through the crowds towards the security of the U.S. Embassy. Designed by architect Edward Durrell Stone in the 1950s, she had never been here before, and for a time she stood outside the entrance, marvelling at the beautiful buildings within the heavily guarded compound.

Clutching her delivery to her chest, she waited patiently in line, absently listening to the chatter about her, the noise of the world swirling all around. When her turn came, she provided her credentials and was thankful that she was already expected. Her legs were heavy and her feet sore, as she followed the directions that took her around the beautiful pool and fountain, towards the chancery.

Samira stood listening to the fountain as she stared towards the chancery, lost to the quiet serenity of her surroundings. People swept by her, minding their own business as they headed up the broad marble steps towards the rectangular white building, its architecture a marvellous collaboration of Indian and American craftsmanship.

Birds sang from the woodland nearby that framed the north-eastern end of the embassy complex, and Samira was thankful, for a time at least, that she could forget about her troubles and relax for a moment.

Finally, aware that some guards were watching her, she headed up the stairs and stepped through the glass doors into the cool calm of the embassy, joining another queue and patiently awaiting her turn. It was soon clear to her, though, that she would not get to see Thomas Miller again today, and she hid her disappointment well as she signed over her documents to the helpful, polite young woman.

Disappointed, she asked the clerk to pass on her regards to the attaché and without releasing why, asked that her own business card would reach him as well. The woman accepted the card with a smile and assured her that she would pass it on. Feeling the warmth on her cheeks, Samira headed back into the sun, to hide her embarrassment in the heat.

As she hurried back towards the Shantipath, the Peace Road, to search for a rickshaw home, a tall, elegant woman dressed in a striking orange Salwar suit and carrying a shoulder bag, slipped from underneath the shade of a nearby tree, and made her way purposefully along the pavement towards her.

"Excuse me," the woman called out, her tone urgent, her accent from the Punjab, perhaps.

"Can I help you?" Samira enquired. The woman was in her late thirties, maybe older, but, when she smiled, her youth returned to her dark cheeks and lit up her emerald eyes.

"I think you can," the newcomer admitted, stepping in front of her to block Samira's path to a waiting line of tuk-tuks. "You are Samira Jethwani, yes?"

Samira stopped, any heat draining from her body. "How did you know that? Who are you? I do not believe we have met before."

"We have spoken," the woman replied, fishing through her western-styled shoulder bag. Her loose, long dark hair fell about her face as she searched and when she finally looked up, she presented a white business card to Samira, holding it up for her to see.

Samira's heart sank as she read the name on the stark card. Narinda Singh, Journalist and *NDTV* News correspondent.

Her guard up, Samira met the woman's knowing look and offered a terse smile. "Namaste, Miss Singh," she began, easing the rising tension with a gentle laugh. "What a coincidence, I was just thinking about you earlier. I am pleased to have the opportunity to apologise in person for not coming back to you today."

Narinda was the embodiment of humility, as she tossed Samira's apology aside with a shake of her head.

"There is no need, Miss Jethwani," she said, pressing her card into Samira's hand. "I just happened to be here, writing an article in preparation for the 60th celebrations of the Embassy next year, when I saw you leaving the compound."

"How fortuitous," Samira replied. She did not believe for one moment that journalists had *that* much time on their hands to prepare so far ahead. She looked back towards the embassy. "It is a truly marvellous building."

"Yes, it is," the journalist began, pausing long enough to draw Samira's attention back. "Might I enquire as to why you are here today, Miss Jethwani?"

"You may," the First Secretary's aide answered, "I was delivering some documents on my way home."

Miss Singh nodded her head. "How very kind of you, and in this heat," she paused, waving her hand dramatically. "Perhaps we could find some shade, take in some tea?"

Samira felt her pulse quicken, and as she faltered, searching for an excuse, the journalist reached out to take her hand.

"Please, I am not after anything. I understand you would not say anything to me, anyhow. I just wanted to know a couple of things... strictly off the record." She held Samira's furtive gaze for a time, smiling reassuringly.

Say nothing.

Forgetting to respond, Samira allowed the journalist to step through the silent opening.

"Why would Federal Attaché Thomas Miller have a meeting with First Secretary Rana this morning?"

Silence.

"And why now, suddenly, would his office be sharing information with the U.S. Embassy, here in New Delhi?"

Samira hid her face, her cheeks burning as the rest of her body shook in a cold sweat. "I cannot answer that, you must know this?" She began to step around the journalist, but Narinda Singh was not about to let her prey escape so easily.

"Ok, just one more question, Miss Jethwani," she took hold of Samira's arm. "What is going on with Aasim Rana? Why will he not speak to me? This will not be good for him, the longer this goes on."

Samira glared at the woman. "I am not at liberty to say. I do not know why – but I will try to get you the meeting you cherish so much."

Narinda Singh removed her hand and stepped aside. "Thank you, Miss Jethwani. You have my card. If you ever want to talk, would like that cup of tea, you know how to reach me."

Nodding, Samira hurried to the line of rickshaws, her heels cracking like her nerves. As the tuk-tuk driver spirited her away back down the Shantipath, Samira stole a look back across the traffic towards the reporter.

Narinda Singh was already on her phone, watching her departure with a smile on her face.

Robert Williams had always wanted to visit India, had hoped one day to see a tiger in its natural habitat, to experience that breathless awe that several of his friends had had back in the sixties, during what was now termed their '*gap year.*' Robert had never had that luxury and had been regretting it ever since – but then, you chose your own path through life and things, in his humble opinion, always happened for a reason and were meant to be, no matter what. Regret only dragged you away from what was before you.

He had toyed, again, with a trip to see the tigers in Ranthambore after Covid-19, but then the Feline Flu had decimated their numbers, threatened all the cats, both great and small, around the world. All access to the national parks where the great cats lived were withdrawn, and had remained so, ever since. Even now, it seemed to him that it was straight from the pages of some thriller, or a film with famous actors posing as scientists, fighting budget constraints and each other, racing against a ticking clock to save the plagued species around the globe.

A lover of history and an anorak of science and nature, too, Robert had studied every detail of the outbreak, and ultimately, as many others had, donated a fortune towards the early cures, hoping to save their beloved pets and the declining population in the wild. Sadly, the vaccine labelled with the hashtag on the internet as *Phoenix*, had not come in time to save his own cat. Lilly had died in agony from failing kidneys and heart failure, wasting away before her family over a period of six weeks and thousands of pounds.

Robert sighed. As the World Wildlife Fund and all the other organisations worked together to save the big and domestic cats from extinction, the television channels, the papers and the ether were choked with the unfolding catastrophe and old documentaries, that only served to underline the unfolding tragedy. Robert had seen many of them before the outbreak, had been inspired by the efforts of those who gave up so much to protect, in particular, the tiger.

It had all started when he had watched a program on the *BBC* some years before, about a group of scientists and TV personalities who were trying to get the countries along the southern Himalayan boundaries to create a Tiger Corridor, a place in these fragmented states where tigers lived. Garnering political and environmental assurances to ensure that all great cats living in each of these countries would have a collaboration of protection against hunting, poaching and persecution by locals whose livestock were being threatened, TV naturalist and adventurer Steve Backshall headed the team that spent three programmes on expedition in the secretive Himalayan Kingdom of Bhutan, filming and recording what they found.

It had been so inspiring to Robert and his wife, Janine, that they had hoped that when he retired, they would volunteer in India, to help the WWF's Project Tiger in their remaining years. Regime change in Bhutan, followed by the human pandemic and shortly after that, the Feline Flu outbreak, had shattered any hope that Robert would get to do his small part towards preserving and protecting those magnificent beasts.

Well, that was until Sara mentioned about the animal cage. From that moment on, he couldn't help but get swept up in some far-fetched conspiracy, imagining that these mercenaries, and as far as he could tell that's exactly what they were, had come to India seeking a living tiger.

All the evidence from the experts, the governments, and charities around the world had suggested for the last few months that the tiger was now extinct, and after no sightings for months, that, perhaps, so too was the beautiful, elusive snow leopard.

Robert smiled, despite his predicament and morosity, thinking of the John le Carré thrillers he enjoyed reading.

Had they stumbled into, or rather landed upon something here?

He laughed, loud and hard, and Sara snapped awake, fixing him with a look that suggested the blow to his head had done some lasting damage.

Frankly, Robert was inclined to agree with her. He had definitely read too many books, watched too many films. He would never see a tiger in the wild, would from now on only be able to see the emaciated, stuffed creatures that over-filled every museum across the globe. Robert knew, despite everything else going on around the world, united for one moment during the Covid-19 pandemic and Feline Flu outbreak, but at each other's throats again now, it was the modern millennium's tragedy for mankind.

But if there was a tiger alive... it would be worth a fortune to the right people! How had it survived, when all others had perished?

Stop it! Robert berated himself, pouring ash on the watered seeds of his imagination. He had to get serious. He and Sara had to decide what they were going to do, how they were going to escape before they were, most likely, going to die.

The tent flap was hauled aside, and like every other time, his heart stopped as he watched forlornly, expecting Jon Galnia to be thrown into their canvas prison, battered and bruised, his eyes blazing. His relief slipped out on a smile that halted the red-haired woman in the entrance.

Narrowing her eyes at the unexpected welcome, she came towards him, ignoring the defiant look Sara dealt her.

"Do you need the bathroom?" she asked the pilot, as she handed him a plate of sandwiches.

Robert eyed the offering, listening to the growl of his stomach. It was probably the worst attempt at a sandwich he had ever seen – two thin slices of white bread that hid something in between... somewhere.

"Not at the moment," he muttered, not wanting to meet his captor's gaze. He looked up eventually. "There is *something* I need."

The woman put the plate down on the bed beside him, ignoring his question as she handed Sara her lunch. Robert watched her closely, his eyes drawn to the pistol in the holster at her side, searching her figure vainly for sign of the key to his freedom.

As Sara began devouring her bread surprise, failing to hide her hunger, and then several chews later, her disgust, the woman turned back to Robert, taking several steps back towards the tent's entrance.

"What is it?" she asked, her face flushed from the heat outside. She placed her hands on her hips. "I cannot tell you anything, so save your breath."

Robert felt his frustrations rise, swelling and raging away inside of him. Shaking, his eyes blazed away angrily. "I demand to know why we are being held against our will. After all we have been through, we should be in a hospital – not being threatened with guns. I am a British Citizen and you are in breach of... well, God knows how many laws and conventions by incarcerating us like this!"

Sara nearly choked on her hunger. She dealt Robert a horrified look, flicking her fears to the woman, as she folded her hands together and looked nervously towards the day outside.

Two steps took her to Robert's side and she struck him across the face, snapping his head back.

"Shut up, you old fool," she hissed in his ear, spittle flying from her lips. She was shaking uncontrollably now and Sara was not sure whether it was from anger, or from worry. "If you carry on like this, you won't leave here at all."

Robert blinked the tears from his eyes and found his breath. "Come now miss, we both know that we are not going anywhere. Have the decency to be straight with us – as soon as our employer has been found, you will, well your companions will, do whatever is necessary to hide what it is you are *actually* doing here."

Emboldened by the pilot's courage, Sara dragged the woman's attention her way.

"Just tell us your name," the Mexican pleaded. "It's obvious we are only alive because you haven't found Jon yet – and until you do, you might need us to force him to give himself up. Quid pro quo miss," Sara said sarcastically. "Come on! What harm can it do to show us a little compassion?"

Ignoring the sinking feeling in her heart that Jon Galnia did not give a damn about them, would leave them to rot if it meant he could get home to his wife and son, Sara fashioned her anger into desperation, pleading with their captor for something, anything to hold on to. Inwardly, though, she wanted to punch her.

The red-head chewed her bottom lip for a time, wringing her hands together nervously. Finally, she shrugged and went to leave without a word. She hesitated as she held open the canvas door, then turned to look back over her left shoulder.

"I'm Lisa," she blurted and then was gone.

Robert looked across at Sara and forced a smile. His heart was raging, his face was stinging. They shared a nod, as she found her own smile.

It was a victory, a small victory, but one nevertheless. Every one they could get would help them to win the battle – history had taught him that, constantly. As they settled down to formulate their escape, Robert knew that they would only get one chance.

An attempt to fly, or the chance to die.

What could possibly go wrong...?

CHAPTER FIFTEEN

Prey

Andersson called Alpha Team to a halt as Taylor bent low and ran a hand over the ground. For a time, the Swede watched on with his other companions, their weariness compounded by the long tab along the river bed, carrying the empty cage that became heavier with each breath and step.

Dabbing at his brow with his neck scarf, Andersson looked behind. The canyon twisted away towards the high sun, blinding their way back. He forced out his cheeks and shook his head.

Galnia had been at the hut, but all they had to show for their hunt was a picture of the bastard and a trail, as enticing as it was, that would lead them even further away from the real reason they were there.

And they had already wasted too much time chasing after shadows. They had taken their eyes from the prize for too long. True to his word and the mission, Andersson cut Galnia loose and gave the order to move out.

After descending from the shack, Taylor had tracked the tiger north, following it through the gorge and sometimes into the jungle. Their tracker was certain that the tiger, possibly a female because of the length of the stride and size of the paw prints, lived in this part of the reserve. It was close to a water source, had the protection of the gorge and dense jungle to hunt in. The region was alive and abundant with prey, making it the perfect territory for a tiger... apparently.

Andersson was happy to let the tracker take the lead, and listened on with interest as he pointed out the signs of *her* passing; the deep, broad prints in the low riverbanks, the high scratch marks, old and fresh, raked into the trunks of tall trees, the pungent aroma of a freshly scented territory.

It was just a shame that they had to hunt her down.

Andersson scowled and folded his irritation across his chest. Dress it up how he may, but why should he let a species' survival get in the way of a small fortune? Mankind had perfected destruction over thousands of years, always for power, forever about the profit, never much about anything else, and if they didn't grab this opportunity, some other willing party would.

Brooks had said something to him before they set out from Germany and it had stuck with him.

'*The tiger has had its day. Mother Nature has decided that. We just need to make sure we finish the job for her.*'

Brooks was a bastard. He didn't care about anything if it wasn't green and didn't allow him to pay off his gambling debts. If it wasn't a tiger, it would have been something, or someone else they'd be hunting.

The Swede sighed. *When will it be our turn?* He wondered.

Taylor rose up and dragged Andersson's thoughts back to the hunt with a wide smile. He came back slowly, choosing his steps carefully, quietly.

"The tracks are *very* fresh," he whispered, as the team gathered about. He looked back over his shoulder. "There is a tributary up ahead that feeds into a small pool. It's shaded there, the perfect place to cool down."

"Sounds good to me," Parker grinned.

"Not for us, you knob," Taylor sighed, punching him on one arm. "The tiger. She has hunted, I can tell that, as I have seen blood and entrails. She will feed again, and then sleep. When she wakes up, she will want water, will need a bath."

"A bit like my wife," Raz chuckled.

Andersson fixed them with an irritated look. "So, we hunker down? Wait for her to come out?"

Taylor nodded, masking his concern. "Exactly!"

"How long before I get my shot?" Raz asked, patting his cylindrical rifle.

"As long as it takes," Andersson growled. He looked back towards the cage. "Hide that bloody thing."

Raz and Parker groaned, then slunk off back along the gorge towards it. Andersson watched them for a moment, checked his watch, then turned back to Taylor.

"Brooks will want a status soon," he said, "let's hope we have something to tell him."

It could take days, Taylor thought. He nodded, instead. "I'm sure we will."

Satisfied, Andersson started moving ahead, taking the same care the tracker had. As he knelt down to inspect the tracks for himself, Taylor swallowed his doubts.

Brooks was going to lose it when he found out they had given up on Galnia.

Somehow, though he was not entirely sure how, Jon Galnia found his way back through the jungle to the gorge and creek. For a time, he stood with his hands on his hips, fighting for breath, struggling with his emotions.

All about him, the land was filled with sounds of life,

his ears full of their joy, his eyes dazzled by the bright sun that drenched the gorge. Turning his head away, he stared through a hue of purple blotches at the wire snare that had trapped the tiger. Shaking his head at the memory, Jon fell back into his despair as he thought about Rashim.

When the outbreak had swept across the globe and the frenzied response and race was in full stride, there were those, naturally, who had complained that mankind had never responded as quickly to human tragedy around the globe in quite the same way they had to save the felines.

#whataboutus?

There was a time when Jon would have agreed, but not now, not today after he had witnessed what a human was capable of doing to his fellow man.

Jon clenched his fists, feeling his cracked side tighten painfully.

The world would be better off without us, Jon thought. He soon pulled himself down from his self-righteous perch, as he thought about the day he had killed his own brother…

Snarling, Jon moved across the ground towards the creek, his dark memories scattering as he noticed the boot marks in the silt, spied the deep imprint of what appeared to be a large crate.

Swatting a cloud of curious insects away, Jon looked up the creek, seeing the boot marks that headed along the gorge in the same direction the tiger had fled. Blinking away his shock, Jon was hit by a strange, uncomfortable revelation – the knowledge that whoever these bastards were, they were not here for him, he was not that important. They had actually come for the tiger...

Jon laughed, a little too loud, and looked warily about his surroundings. He had probably pissed them off by freeing the beast and they had tracked him to Rashim's hut, thinking that the old Sikh had freed it. To do *that* to someone suggested a great deal to the Don. These people were determined and not to be messed with.

The Italian-American spat his distaste towards the creek. *But by my blood, they are going to be messed with.*

Ignoring the deep pit of concern about the path he was about to take, Jon banished the thoughts of his wife and son, their faces silently pleading him to stay safe, to come home to them. Filling his vision with images of the Sikh lying behind his hut, instead, Jon closed his eyes and cleared his mind with a few calming breaths.

Moments later, his eyes snapped open and they were filled with a clear, bright clarity of purpose. Eyeing the steep slope he had tumbled down, and searching vainly for his trusty stick, Jon turned northwards and followed his prey along the creek.

Parker hunkered down against the rough tree, his eyes fixed through the lifting shadows on the pool. For many hours they had hidden within sight of the water, listening to each other's guarded breaths, watching and waiting for millions of their dollars to turn up.

Contrary to Taylor's assurances and Andersson's gullibility, the tiger did not come for a drink and dip in the inviting, clear waters of the pool. A couple of birds and deer had, but no great cat. At one point, before the cold, clear night had gathered in close, they had been stirred from their vigilance by the distant cough and cries of warning. All of them had stirred in excitement, finding one another's anticipation in the thicket and silence of the misty gloom.

After an hour of shallow breaths and little else, the

jungle had rallied as the unseen threat passed on. Taylor had cursed quietly, shrugging nonchalantly.

Parker flicked his tired gaze to his right, just managing to find Andersson, hidden well amongst some dense foliage. The Swede met his gaze and did not even try to hide his worry and impatience.

Parker winced. They had all heard Brooks' fury in their earpieces, when he had been told that they had given up on this Jon Galnia to go after the tiger. After he had ranted himself hoarse and signed off with the warning about '*No loose ends*', they had stood quietly together, sharing their shame at what had happened to the old man and that they had not told their leader.

The young tech sighed and closed his eyes. He had worked several times with Brooks and was starting to wish that he had stayed with Andersson, chasing pirates across the southern hemisphere. Things had been a lot easier, less complicated back then.

Thinking of his home, Parker dreamt that he was back in Yorkshire, back in the Dales. He'd left there, years ago, dreaming that he could make a difference, hoping that he could find himself amidst the unjustified angst and bitterness his youth had ingrained in him.

For a time he had, but he soon became disillusioned with the Army life, fed up of seeing his comrades fall in the arse-end of nowhere for a cause that they did not fully understand, or believe in. When he took a round in the chest in Afghanistan, in a small hamlet just east of Marjah, in the Nad Ali District of Helmand Province, he had been sent home and had left the army due to his injuries. Parker had suffered for quite some time after that with his health and civilian life. His hometown seemed smaller, as did all the problems he had incurred there during his youth, and it wasn't long before he was yearning for that which he despised the most.

Looking for a way back, to experience the camaraderie he couldn't find in the shadows and cobwebs of the Green Dragon Inn, Parker used his skills and experience to get a job protecting merchant ships in the Suez. It was there that he first met Andersson, and later, Taylor; it was there that he had found himself again and started to earn some real money.

Blinking his past away, Parker stared about his tranquil surroundings. The dark blanket of the previous night was slipping away now, lifted at the edges by the grey hands of the coming dawn. Glad to be free of his night vision device, the Yorkshireman longed for the warmth of the day. Before that, however, the cold insisted that he needed to take a leak.

Signalling to Andersson that he was bursting, he slipped from his position across the ground on elbows and knees, as far from the pool and as downwind as he could. When he was safely away, he rose up, choosing his footing with care as he crept towards the privacy of a suitable tree and checked the area for spiders and snakes.

Flicking a look around for the tiger, to make sure that he wasn't about to be torn to pieces, Parker reached for his discomfort and inadvertently let out a long, deep sigh.

Jon stifled a yawn to hide his breath, nestling deeper into the warmth of the base of the tall tree he had spent the cold night behind. Without any of Rashim's supplies left now, he fought against his rising hunger and thirst and almost didn't hear one of them, as they crawled from their concealment. Jon wasn't sure of where he was until the man sighed.

Buoyed by the adrenaline of the chase and his need to

discover who they were, what they were doing and why they had felt it necessary to murder the Sikh, Jon had been watching them ever since he had found the cage that was thankfully empty, hidden underneath some dense foliage, downstream from their position.

He had very nearly missed it and inadvertently walked into an ambush, but thanks to a couple of monkeys who were climbing over the steel frame, he had slipped towards it and away from the danger. After the find, Jon's caution had taken him deep into the jungle and, by sheer blind luck, behind their location. Again, his faith had kept him alive as he crept forward on his designer shoes, cover to cover and behind his tree. From there, he had observed the four men over the coming hours, picking out where each of them hid, listening to their subtle movements and low whispers as he finished off his food supply.

Hoping his own hunger and cooling body did not force him to give up on his revenge and send him back to the hut for warmth and shelter, Jon watched on, waiting for the inevitable opportunity he sensed he would get.

He watched them deep into the night, well beyond the time he could actually see them, finally falling asleep from exhaustion in the early hours of his third day in India. When Jon awoke with a start, some time later, his body was tight with cramp, his cold skin sweaty and feverish.

Scowling, Jon hugged himself, wishing that he had taken his second option and made his way to the village to find help. There was still a chance that Robert and Sara had survived the explosion, though he had not even given them a second thought as he chased his own skin to safety.

What's done is done, his father used to say, and Jon nodded his head. He had made his decision, for better or for worse, and, by the Lord's grace, he would see it through – he always did.

Rich beyond any real need, Jon had more money than he could ever spend, had never wanted for anything. It was his thirst for something more that drove him on, a tangible need to challenge himself and everything that he was, to court new danger, to stick two fingers up at the authorities who chased him, or the enemies who wanted him dead.

Jon was not a fool, however. He knew that Lady Luck was a fickle bitch, and he had used his fair share of her generosity up in the last few days, alone. If he was to scratch his itch, feed the habit of his curiosity, he had to be careful, and more importantly, he had to be quick, as he couldn't last another night out in the cold, dressed as he was.

Before his mind could react, he was on his feet, creeping slowly, carefully towards the man who was taking a leak. As he stepped over each twig and leaf as if it were a mountain, Jon could not hear a thing as his head was pounding fearfully. Closer now, he could see the back of the man's cropped head, could see that he wore military fatigues and equipment, his high-end weaponry slung over a shoulder and holstered at one hip.

The man sighed quietly as steam rose into the air, and he leant back into the arms of his relief.

Jon's hand went into his left pocket and returned with fingers clenched tightly about the hilt of the Sikh's curved knife.

Five steps away... the man began to shake himself dry.
Three steps away... he zipped himself up.
Two steps away now... Jon raised his knife, drew in a

slow, cautious breath.

The man tensed, his head turned.

In the lifting gloom, shadows turned to flame, subtly at first, and then quickly, as the huge tiger slipped into view. Testing the air with a curious nose, the great cat's whiskers twitched as it came forward on silent paws, down to the side of the pool to drink.

Trapped by their breathless awe, none of the men watching could react as they surveyed nature's miracle and balanced their consciences against their mission.

It was Andersson who finally broke the spell. His whisper echoed in each man's earpiece, barely heard, but powerful enough to shake them free.

"Take her down."

Slowly pulling back the bolt, the mercenary reached for the small case, open on the ground before him. Carefully, Hassan Raz picked up one of the darts and slid it into the breach. With his eyes locked on the great cat, the Moroccan inched the chamber shut, his breath failing as the tiger paused. Looking around, her great ears twitching, the tiger stared towards them for a time, before returning her thoughts to her thirst.

Raz raised the rifle, swallowing as his cold, shaking thumb slid the safety off. Nestling the weapon into his shoulder, he squinted down its shaking length at the magnificent beast. He had seen tigers before. Who hadn't? But here, in the context of the circumstances of the species' survival, in these uncertain times, he was suddenly not sure they should be doing this.

Well, for at least three heartbeats...

The tiger lapped at the still waters of the pool, her huge tongue still thirsty, her broad flanks full of yesterday's hunt. Letting out his held breath, the

Moroccan slipped the end of the barrel past a large leaf and sighted one last time on the tiger.

Air blasted his sweating, round face, as the feathered dart flashed across the clearing and took the tiger high in her neck. Roaring, the great cat sprang away through a shower of leaves, the undergrowth and jungle gathering in close behind her.

The jungle came alive as the three men were up on their feet and after the tiger. As they plunged into the unknown, Raz reached for another dart as they raced after their retirement fund.

Andersson yelled into his radio as they ran.

"*Get your arse back here, Parker.*"

In the ensuing chaos, Parker was just about to head off after his comrades when the jungle reached out and grabbed hold of him. As he struggled against the hand clamped over his mouth and tried to throw his weight behind him, he felt the cold kiss of a blade against his exposed throat, heard the rasping hiss of warning in his ear.

"Oh, no you don't," Jon Galnia snarled, piercing the man's throat with the tip of the blade. He dragged his prey away from the trunk and stench, pulling him back towards the privacy of another tree, a centimetre of the antique steel still embedded in the side of his neck.

The man went limp, allowing himself to be pulled back across the ground. When they were behind the next tree, Jon forced his prisoner onto his knees. Looking over a shaking shoulder, he ripped the earpiece from the man's ear.

"That's better," Jon said, reaffirming his grip on the man. "It's just you and me now."

"What do you want?" his captive asked, voice

trembling. The man had a strange accent, heavy and thick from a British county.

Jon bent close, his breath hissing in his captive's left ear. "I want to know who the fuck you are and why you killed the old man?"

Parker tensed under Jon's grip, and the Don twisted his blade, drawing more blood and a grimace from the mercenary.

"Well?" Jon snarled, when the man failed to respond.

Shuddering, the younger man nodded his head subtly. "Okay, okay. I had nothing to do with the old man, you have to believe me! It was terrible what they did to him."

Jon twisted the blade again. "Who did it to him?"

"You'll have to ask the Moroccan about that," Parker shuddered, picturing the old man's last moments.

"I intend to," Jon growled, feeling his hatred broil away. "Who are you people?"

"If I tell you, they will kill me," the man stammered, his body shaking. "You don't know who you are dealing with! You should walk away, while you still can."

It was a tempting offer, Jon had to admit. "As much as I'd like to, I will have to decline. Start talking, sonny, I'm starting to get pissed off, and that's not where you want me to be."

Parker would have nodded his head if he could, but if the blade went any deeper he would be staring at his own blood. His throat was on fire and he could feel the warmth running down his neck.

"You must be Galnia," Parker said, snorting. "Brooks said we should have gone after you. For once, the fucker was right."

Jon frowned, feeling his body react to the revelation. *They know who I am.*

"How the... how do you know my name?" He was too

shocked to swear.

"The crash, of course," Parker replied, failing to hide his sarcasm. "We hadn't expected that, it really threw a spanner in the works."

Jon's mind reeled. "How do you know my name?"

"One of the survivors told us, the woman," Parker blurted, spurred on by the anger rising in Galnia's question.

Jon almost let go of his captive, his shock running rife through his body. *Sara was alive!* If she was, that meant that Robert had rescued her. He must be alive, too.

"Where are they?" Jon demanded, regaining control.

"We have them at base camp," Parker sighed, "about two clicks south of the crash site. If you give yourself up, they will be fine..."

Kept alive for leverage.

Jon nodded, his mind already starting to plan ahead. Reining himself in, he stared down at the man, trembling away in his grip.

"Last question – what are you doing here?"

Parker chuckled. "You know why we are here, mate. You freed the bloody thing, didn't you?"

Jon felt his anger rise at the man's defiance. "Who do you work for? Who sent you?"

"I can't tell you that, Galnia," Parker pleaded, shaking. "I've told you too much, already. All I will say is that we are both in the shit now."

Jon chewed his top lip. He'd been there many times before, and one more swim wouldn't hurt.

"Now then," Jon whispered, returning his attention to Rashim's blade. "What shall I do with you?"

Jon felt the mercenary collapse in his arms. When Parker spoke, his sigh was louder than his response.

"You might as well kill me. I'm a dead man,

anyhow."

"Fair enough!"

Without hesitation, Jon dragged Rashim's wrath deep across the man's throat.

CHAPTER SIXTEEN

Tiger, tiger...

Andersson threw himself after Hassan Raz, the jungle whipping past him in a blur as they chased after the tiger that bounded away from them and was quickly lost from view. Taylor laboured at his side as the terrain began to rise steeply, and they were soon lagging seriously behind the squat shadow that was the Moroccan, who powered up the rugged slope into the gloom, despite the weight of his Bergen.

Aware of their apparent recklessness, Andersson knew that there were enough drugs in the dart to drop an elephant, and it was only a matter of time before he could get on the horn and give Brooks the good news.

Ahead of them, Raz could see the tiger, all flame and fury, as she slipped effortlessly through the jungle ahead of him. The land held its breath, watching on as the chase unfolded.

After some distance, and just before he lost sight of her behind some rocks, he could see that the dart was still in her neck and that she was beginning to slow down. He had been lucky with the shot, he knew that. It had almost missed, as he was aiming for her broad flank. Finding his breath, the Moroccan came to a halt. Doubling over, he fought to calm the fire in his chest and lungs and shrugged his heavy pack from his shoulders.

Overhead, the virgin dawn blushed with promise and Hassan knew that it was going to be an absolute bitch to airlift the cat from here. Not relishing the implication of that thought, he listened to his heart and surroundings, waiting for the others to catch up.

When they finally arrived, they were red-faced and exhausted, and the Moroccan scoffed inwardly. *Too much time sat wandering about on decks, firing warning shots at pirates...*

"Well?" Andersson managed to ask, as he flicked his bright eyes about their surroundings.

Raz tossed his head over his left shoulder, nodding towards the rocks. "I think she is having a rest." He looked back, an infectious grin flashing across his face.

Nodding, Andersson raised his weapon, jabbing two fingers to their left. Taylor and Raz slipped across the rough ground on careful boots and the Swede peeled off to the right.

With his breath in his throat, Andersson crept forward, the boulders looming large as he stepped over a rotting branch and raised his rifle. The landscape lit up as he trained his weapon's scope on the tiger slipping into view, and Taylor and Raz flanked it from the other side.

Lowering his weapon, Andersson dealt his companions a rare, broad smile.

The tiger was theirs.

Nestled down behind the rocks, the beautiful creature's head lolled to one side. Sensing the threat gathering close, she curled her mouth in a warning full of teeth, but could do little else.

Taylor watched on, as they stood silently, marvelling at the beautiful, unique creature before them, struggling with his conscience as he watched the erratic rise and fall of her flanks. As she panted away, the three of them reflecting in her huge eyes, they shared a look, a look worth millions of dollars. Grinning, Taylor put away his guilt and waited for the tiger's breath to calm down and even out. He didn't have to wait long.

When Andersson had his confirmation that the tiger was unconscious, he let out a whistle of relief that was long and piercing. Smiling, he crept closer and knelt down reverently on one knee, reaching out a tentative hand. He could feel her heart, pounding away beneath his hand as he ran it over her thick, soft fur, and felt the muscles spasm in her powerful flanks.

Soon, the three of them were gathered close, touching and feeling this miraculous payday beneath their hands. Taylor drew them back to the present, as he inspected the injury to her back leg.

"She must have fought hard to get free," the tracker observed, as he fished in his pack for his first aid kit. The tiger had cleansed her wound, but he wanted to be sure there was no infection – there was too much at stake here.

"Where's Parker?" Raz asked, scattering their awe.

Andersson rose up stiffly, his eyes still on their prize. "Where are you, Parker? Are you still taking a shit? You missed all the fun! We have her, repeat, we have her," he said into his comms, failing to hide his triumphant smile.

The silence in their earpieces was broken, moments later. "On my way."

With their elation ringing in their ears, they did not notice the strange tone in Parker's voice, did not detect the hesitancy.

Andersson shook his head. "Copy that!" he said, unable to take his eyes off the striped tapestry beneath him. If that tiger had caught one of them, there would be nothing left to extract.

"What do we do next?" Raz enquired. They had to act fast now. They needed to get the tiger in the cage before she woke again.

Andersson chewed his bottom lip. "Hass, you stay here and keep her sedated. Taylor and I will go and get the cage – we'll grab Parker and be back before you know it."

The Moroccan nodded, watching silently as they shouldered packs and weapons and made off back down the incline. As they slipped from view, he heard Andersson's voice in his earpiece.

"Eagle, this is Alpha, do you copy?"

Jon Galnia's heart was in his lap as he sat by the body, waiting to hear if his bluff had worked.

"Copy that," the voice echoed in his ear after a long, heart-stopping moment, and Jon grinned like a demented cat.

Shaking his head free of his relief, Jon turned his attention back to the mercenary he had killed, watching for a time as the blood continued its spread across the ground. Blinking, Jon turned the man over, ignoring the macabre double smile the empty eyes and face gave him.

It had been quite some time since Jon had bloodied his hands and he wasn't sure how he felt about this one. Usually, historically, it had been because of a dispute, a score that needed to be settled with old enemies, a warning that had to be given. The last one had been one of his own soldiers, a *Pentito*, a rat, who was trying to sell them out to the Feds. But this one...?

By association, this man had Rashim's blood on his hands, and he had paid for it, like the others would. They had killed the Sikh and they had, as potential leverage no doubt, captured Sara and Robert to make sure that there were no loose ends. If he didn't get to them soon, they would be dead, and that was not the kind of blood he wanted on his hands.

Wishing that he had taken Paolo with him, and knowing that things would have been a lot simpler if he had, Jon cast aside his doubts and stripped the corpse of its weapons. As he pulled off the man's body armour and belt pouches, Jon was not surprised, though he still swore, that the man did not have any I.D on him, nothing that would reveal who he was, where he came from and who had sent him.

As if any self-respecting mercenary would.

There was no doubt in Jon's mind now that these bastards were here illegally. The Indian authorities would never allow this kind of thing to take place on their soil, especially with the way things were; the international attention that was still focussed on them following the devastation that the outbreak had caused.

Casting aside thoughts of things he could not control, Jon breathed in deeply, hoping to calm himself down. Focussing on his ruined shoes, he slipped one off and unlaced the dead man's boots.

"Fuck it," he spat, after several minutes of trying to force his feet into them. "Looks like it is still you and me then, Roberto," he chuckled, as he slipped his Cavalli back on.

Clipping the communicator to his body armour and slotting the earpiece into his left ear, Jon rose on unsteady feet.

Crossing himself with his free hand, Jon dealt the heavens an apologetic look, flicked the safety off his assault rifle and slipped silently through the mist towards the distant pool.

It didn't take him long to reach the water, and with one eye fixed on the jungle around him, he knelt by the discarded pack, hidden underneath what could have been a Triffid. Rifling hurriedly through the pack, Jon pulled out a small laptop; a Roughbook, whatever the hell that was... Opening the screen, Jon's breath caught in his throat, as he tapped the touchpad and woke the device from its hibernation.

"*Figlio di puttana*," Jon swore, when he discovered he needed to enter an encryption code.

What was it with technology? Maria's phone used her finger-print to unlock it and that was fine if she was about – but in an emergency? How could anyone contact anyone if you couldn't access their bloody devices?

Jon chuckled, a little too loudly. *Perish the thought you might need to call someone after you had crashed in a jungle somewhere...*

Did he really expect mercenaries on a covert mission to have free access for him to the outside world – of course not, so why was he beating himself up over it?

Dragging his distracted thoughts away from Maria and back to the pack, Jon proceeded to throw anything that he didn't need, well, didn't want to carry, into the pool. By the time he shouldered the lighter pack, he had kept four spare clips for the rifle, two for the pistol, the rations, a mess kit, a canteen of water, medical supplies to stock up his dwindling cupboard, a pair of scissors, two knives, the notepad and a mobile phone that, surprise, surprise, needed a key code to access it and didn't unlock when he headed back to try the mercenary's fingerprint.

Taking a long pull from the water canteen, Jon dealt his surroundings a quick look. The sun knifed the grey dawn now with furious intent and several curious birds flitted about through the trees overhead to watch what he was doing.

"What now, Galnia?" he asked himself aloud.

There were two obvious options open to him, he thought.

One, he could make his way back to the crash site and try to find out where Sara and Robert were being kept.

Jon hesitated, swallowing down the thought that it would have been a lot easier if they had died in the crash. He had enough to worry about without their lives hanging in the balance before him like some guilty carrot.

Two, he just stayed where he was, kept to the shadows and killed every last one of the fuckers when they came back for their cage.

Jon snorted. This wasn't some Bruce Willis film; it wasn't Christmas in some high-rise. He would have to be careful, play it a lot smarter than he felt like he wanted to. These men were professionals, and although he had caught the young man with his trousers almost down, he wouldn't be so lucky next time.

Cursing, Jon reached down and picked up his rifle. Whatever was about to happen, he knew for certain that it was going to be a very long day.

Andersson frowned as he and Taylor came to a halt before the pool. There was no sign of Parker, but some of his gear was scattered in the water. He flicked a worried look at his comrade as his skin riled.

"Parker? Are you there?" Andersson hissed into his comms. They heard only silence in response.

"What the hell is going on?" Taylor said, moving around the left side of the pool. His rifle was raised, as he swept the jungle for an answer.

Andersson spoke into his communicator again. "Hassan, watch yourself. We may have company here.

Stay sharp and we'll be back soon."

"*Copy that*," came the reply, and Andersson could hear the worry in the Moroccan's voice.

The Swede scanned the jungle before them, the landscape magnified through his scope. Moving to the right side of the pool, he searched to the south, coming back in an arc to meet up with Taylor. Both men shook their heads at one another.

"What next?" Taylor asked quietly.

Andersson looked to the east, his gaze flicking over their nearby surroundings and past the spot where Jon had hidden Parker's body.

"Our share of the prize has just gone up considerably," he replied, though it was not a happy one. Shaking his head, Andersson nodded to the south-west.

"We get the cage and secure the package. That's our main priority. We'll call it in then that Parker's gone AWOL. Brooks is going to lose his shit, but we don't want them sending in Bravo at this point, we're too close now." Andersson looked back. "Any chance another animal did this? A bear? A leopard?"

Taylor spread his hands wide, shrugging. "No obvious signs by the pool. A bear may have gone through his pack, but there are no tracks. What about the American?"

Andersson frowned. "It could be any number of fuckers. There may be more at stake here than we thought. If the Indians have offered someone else the chance to take the tiger…"

Taylor nodded his head, swallowing his rising grief. He and Parker had spent some great nights together and he was going to miss the little bastard.

"Whoever did this is going to pay," Taylor promised.

Andersson clapped him on one shoulder and moved

past him towards the south-west.

Insects buzzed and birds sang as the two mercenaries closed in upon the location where they had hidden the cage. With a screech of warning that made both men grit their teeth, the two monkeys that had been playing on the bars of the steel frame leapt for safety through the trees above them.

Curtains of leaves fell to the floor in a silent shower, and despite the warning chill biting deep into the nape of his neck, Andersson relaxed a little. Any immediate threat in the vicinity would have sent the monkeys and their trailing long tails away already. Firing a look at Taylor, he could see that the Englishman was thinking the same thing.

"Let's grab this and get back," Andersson whispered, switching his attention to the jungle about them.

Taylor scowled as he nodded, but was wise enough to know that whoever had did whatever to Parker, they were waiting for a chance, a chance he was sure he was not going to give them.

Rifles raised, the two men covered the rough ground to the cage quickly, scoping the area for any immediate danger. After a time, when the jungle returned to its own business, they shouldered their rifles and positioned themselves at either end of the cage.

With a nod, they silently counted down from three and hauled the cage up. Grunting, Taylor led the way, as they bore the tiger's new home swiftly away to the north through the jungle.

Jon Galnia watched the men leave from the cover of the dense thicket to the south of their position. Letting out a held breath, he relaxed his trigger finger and buried his head in the grass. He had passed up a good chance for revenge, to ambush them before they knew what had hit them, but his patience, amazingly, had held out.

I have to be smarter than that, Jon thought, though he found little consolation. The two men looked like professionals, ex-military no doubt, trying to earn now what they hadn't done in service to their country.

If Jon was going to get the drop on them, he would have to wait, wait for them to have the tiger, wait for the three of them to be together again before he struck. They could not carry the cage and the beast for miles through the jungle, which meant that they would need help, help that would probably airlift them out of there – the kind of help that would give him a way home.

Rising up onto his sore knees, Jon did not even feel the pain in his side any more. With a look through the jungle and rising sun to the east, he swept up his weapon and belongings and slipped quietly away to find the spot he would kill them from.

CHAPTER SEVENTEEN

...shining bright

First Secretary Rana faced the phalanx of media from the shaded steps of the Parliament House, the Sansad Bhavan. Standing in what was hopefully just enough shadow behind the Prime Minister to retain some obscurity, Aasim listened to the questions thrown at Chandra Nehru and was thankful that it was not him having to face them.

The announcement for the plans to erect the statue of Mahatma Gandhi had been met with such euphoria, that it had swept from the chambers of the Lok Sabha, the House of the People, and filled the news channels and air waves before parliament's business had concluded for lunch.

Scanning the sea of smiling faces, it was not difficult to pick out those in the press who still sharpened their knives, however; who were not fooled by the smoke and the mirrors that resonated in the ears and from the screens of the nation, and would fill her pages in the morning. The scandals may be forgotten for a time, but they most certainly would not go away.

Narinda Singh was standing, as her status always afforded her, in prime position in the front ranks of the media, a pen pressed to pad. Aasim caught the knowing look she sent towards him and returned it with a gracious nod of his head. Samira had organised a timely interview with Miss Singh, and he would have to have his thoughts in order before he crossed swords with her later that afternoon.

Drifting away and not really listening to the barrage of questions from those who wilted in the noon sun, Rana knew that the day was not won yet. Chandra Nehru may be basking in their success and taking credit for the idea, but the Lok Sabha still had to vote. Whilst Aasim suspected the entire house would accede to the proposal, now that the nation and press were aware, he knew that if the operation in Madhya Pradesh was not resolved soon, their legacy could turn out to be something entirely different.

Clenching his hands tightly together to stop them shaking, Aasim Rana smiled into the snapping glare of the cameras and wished he was someplace else.

Samira Jethwani waited patiently, well away from the glare of the media, unimportant and unnoticed in the entrance to the Sansad Bhavan. It was only her second time in official capacity in the House of the People, and she was overcome with the knowledge that she was taking part in history. Dressed impeccably, she waited amongst the throng of aides and security, listening to the resonant voice of Chandra Nehru as he soaked up the plaudits and fended off any questions that would unsettle the moment, with a natural ease that had seen him safely through his political rise, so far.

Having spent several months working for the First Secretary now, Samira could tell that Aasim Rana was keen to get away. The pressure of the last few days was taking a telling toll on him, and she tussled with her emotions as she watched him fidget and squirm under the spotlight.

Playing nervously with the strap of her handbag,

Samira struggled with her own troubles. Since that fateful day, when the man had swept into her office, the worry and mystery of what Aasim Rana was up to had kept her awake at night, listening to the traffic outside her apartment, and the arguments of the Misras from the room above her. In the mirror that morning, before she had hidden away her troubles, Samira struggled to recognise the face that looked back at her.

Sighing, Samira remembered to slip her smile back into place and did her best to edge away from the suited man beside her. He had applied his old aftershave far too heavily that morning, and in the summer heat it was overpowering. She did not recognise the man, could not tell who he worked for and did not want to risk any unwanted attention by trying to see what the name said on his identification pass.

Without realising it, Samira thought of the American, Thomas Miller, and did her best to ignore the flutter in her breast as she thought of her joy at having a personal response by email from him, after leaving her business card. Silently thanking the lady at the embassy for passing it on, Samira's imagination ran wild as she thought about the westerner, his strong face and the honeyed softness to his kind voice.

Chiding herself for her fancifulness, Samira drifted away, thinking of her own life and the reclusive bubble that was her two-room apartment. It had all felt like such an adventure when she graduated from Aryabhatta College, on the South Campus of the University of Delhi, and had permanently moved to the city with her mother's blessing, to enhance her prospects and chase the dreams that would further her ambitions. And to a degree, her adventures so far, had.

With her high qualifications in Commerce and

Political Science, she had used her smile and looks to get her the job as Aasim Rana's secretary; a jewel of a position for one so young on her path. Even now she could recall the pride of her mother, the pure joy at her only child's success.

But that joy was short-lived, when the reality of being away from her mother and home had drowned in the realisation of how lonely the city life could be for a reserved, shy girl from the country.

Samira was not a selfish woman, however. In contrast to her own sickness to be home, and despite the amounts of money she could send back, it was the loneliness of her mother that weighed heaviest.

Her father, a diplomat for the Indian Embassy in London, had died over seven years ago now, and because of his radical views on arranged marriage, forged into determination by his studies at Oxford and his time in England, he had left a daughter and loving wife behind who had no immediate family or friends they could rely upon.

Breaking from traditional Hindi beliefs, Amar Jethwani had stated that when Samira was old enough to be considered for marriage, he would not hand his daughter to a man who '*did not have her heart*'. He himself had loved his wife Neelam for many years before they were blessed enough to have been chosen together.

He fervently declared to his friends and family, who pleaded with him to change his mind, that he would allow his *Sitaara*, his star, his daughter, to follow her own heart to find whomever was worthy enough to claim it. This defiant break from tradition had pulled their families apart, leaving him ostracised from his relatives at the cost of his daughter's own free will.

'*I would pay that price a thousand times again*,'

Samira's father had told her, on the day she had headed to university to further her college education.

Tilting her head to listen to her thoughts, Samira smiled. He had been such a strong, proud and kind man, taken far too soon by a disease the scientists could not cure.

I wonder what you would think of me now, papa? Samira thought, sadly.

Before Samira realised it, the press conference came to an abrupt end as the Prime Minister called a halt to proceedings with a wave of his hand and a broad smile on his face. With the calls of the press chasing after them, Samira was swept along by a tide of suits, all struggling to keep up with their respective charges. As the crowd began to thin out and peel off in different directions, Aasim Rana's secretary hung back, hiding in some shade as her employer and Chandra Nehru came to a halt, their heads pressed close as they whispered privately, away from the media and the spotlight.

To distract herself, Samira turned her head respectfully away, listening and watching some sparrows bicker and chase each other about in a nearby hedgerow. Absorbed by their antics and the din of the city around her, Samira almost missed that the impromptu meeting had ended and that Aasim Rana was beckoning for her to follow him. As she adjusted the bag on her shoulder and made to hurry after him, Chandra Nehru's retinue scurried past and it was then that she spotted the mystery man from the other day, as he fell in dutifully beside the Prime Minister.

Passing near to where she stood rooted in shock, her face cold in the sun, the tall man caught Samira's startled stare and tilted his head in greeting, a warm, yet frosted smile slipping across his dark features.

Staggering back into the arms of her fear, Samira fought against her panic and failed miserably. With her mind racing, she did her best to gather up the remnants of her scattered composure and hurried after Aasim Rana. There was a great deal of the day still left to contend with and as the sparrows came to a peaceful accord, Samira suspected that her troubles were only just beginning.

It was several hours later when Narinda Singh finally sat down to interview the man she had been chasing for weeks. In the privacy of an office suite, they sat down across a beautiful antique coffee table, exquisitely crafted, yet a clear western reminder from the days of the British Raj. In silence, they waited patiently for the First Secretary's aide to pour them each a cup of tea.

"Will there be anything else, First Secretary?" Samira asked when she had finished, aware of, yet pointedly ignoring, the tension in the room.

"No, thank you," Rana said, not taking his eyes from the pad the journalist was already scribbling on.

As Samira made for the door, Narinda Singh looked up, a broad smile on her face. "Thank you, Miss Jethwani. You have been wonderful to facilitate this meeting for me, and I shall not forget it."

With her heels rattling out a hasty retreat and a shy smile staining her features, Samira excused herself. Closing the door gently behind her, she let out a deep sigh of relief and went in search of the strong coffee that would hopefully keep her going for the next few hours.

Smiling at her host, the journalist leaned forward to pick up her cup and saucer. Aasim returned her warmth graciously, guarding his fears with a smile of anticipation.

The taste of the tea registered on Miss Singh's face and Aasim sat back in his chair, crossing his left leg over his right knee as she put the tea gently back down on the table.

"A wonderful member of my staff," Aasim offered, waving a hand.

"Yes," Narinda responded to the unsaid apology. Focussing her attention back to why she was there, the journalist reached again for her tools, ready for the coming battle.

Gripping her pen like a sword, Narinda Singh fixed her bright eyes on Aasim Rana.

"First Secretary, I thank you for your time on this most historic and warming day for our nation. It has been a long while coming and this glad news, as passed unanimously today in the Lok Sabha, will surely give joy to our nation."

Aasim bowed his head in thanks. "It has been something we have worked towards for some time, and with the shadows of the last two years for our nation, it is a joyous relief, a wonderful day to finally be able to have our Father watching over our fallen. A decision, I am certain, that will gladden the hearts of the people."

Scribble, scratch. Narinda jotted down her quotes for the news, a spidery scrawl of shorthand that Aasim could not read.

"Indeed," Narinda responded dutifully. She fixed the First Secretary with a knowing look. "I must also congratulate you personally on this success. The Prime Minister, as we all know, thinks only of himself, and such a thoughtful, wonderful gesture could only have come from this office, I am certain."

The temperature in the room dropped, as cold as the forgotten tea, and Aasim licked his lips delicately.

"I could not possibly comment on that, and I would have expected you to have waited for at least a few questions before attacking the Prime Minister."

Narinda Singh laughed, adding heavily to the tension. "I have waited for many weeks for this meeting, Aasim – did you expect me to simply address my notepad with hundreds of platitudes, platitudes which I am sure will already be filling the column inches in the press? I know you respect me more than that, First Secretary."

Despite what she might think he thought about her, Aasim was always impressed with her directness, her bluntness, her honesty, and he had to stop himself from falling into any traps she was laying for him.

"I have always admired you, Narinda, you know this," Aasim admitted, nodding. "But for at least one day this year, I was hoping that we could celebrate some good news for a change, and not search the shadows for the cobwebs of a story."

Miss Singh began scribbling away and Aasim winced. When she looked up over the glasses that had slipped down her nose, she smiled, hungry for more.

"The shadows are always there, First Secretary, especially in our political climate, with our political history. But there can be no hiding place for corruption, no shadow so dark that the light of truth cannot shine," Narinda said, holding her host's gaze. "The Prime Minister may have thrust a cold iron into the flames today, but it will not stop the fire of suspicion from burning."

Aasim felt himself tremble, his mind awash with his own fears, sick from what he had become embroiled in. He had been seduced by Chandra Nehru, as had so many others, won over by his ready charm and promises. Despite everything Aasim risked, these promises *had* been kept, allowing him to obtain much station and power.

Momentarily forgetting about the woman across from him, Aasim sighed. He felt like the fly, caught up in a spider's web, lured to the light like a moth to a flame, but ultimately destined for oblivion.

He sensed, with everything happening in Miss Singh's shadows, that he would, one day soon, pay a very heavy price for the cost of his success.

Narinda Singh had stopped writing and she watched the cracks appear in the First Secretary's outwardly calm demeanour. She almost pitied him then – *almost!* For many years she had searched for the truth behind the rumours, sought for the telling evidence that would prove the stories of Chandra Nehru's corruption, coercion, bribery and worse. She had become obsessed by the hunt, as she chased the evidence to prove that the rumours, no matter how unbelievable, were in fact actually true.

The police may have turned a blind eye these last years, filling their pockets, rather than their reports, but she had sources, sources too scared to come forward, but betrayed and wounded enough to want to help someone else with the courage to expose the truth.

Nobody had been more surprised than she, when the generally unnoticed and insignificant political figure of Aasim Rana had stepped into the limelight. But then, nobody more than she had been both gladdened and saddened by the huge step up he took into the political arena. Chandra Nehru destroyed the careers of anyone around him, and though she sensed she may be able to use the First Secretary to further her own agenda, she could not escape her guilt at being just another person that would use him at the same time.

"It must have been a long, trying and exhausting day for you, First Secretary," Narinda said, hoping to ease the tension in the room. "Can you give me any further details as to whom the artist is, and when the statue of Mahatma Gandhi Ji will be unveiled to the world?"

Aasim forced a smile and reached for his cold tea, hoping the taste would bring him back to his senses. It certainly worked, and he forced it down, offering his thanks.

"Of course, Miss Singh," he responded, resting the saucer on one knee. "You may exclusively announce to your readers and viewers that the statue will be crafted by the most skilled hands of Leela Chand Saini, daughter of the famous Nek Chand Saini. We will announce the details of the ceremony in the coming weeks."

Placing his tea down on the table, Aasim sat back in his chair, trying to find comfort in his words, but desperate to be away. Threading his hands together in his lap, he watched the joy on Narinda Singh's face, and was pleased that she evidently approved of the choice.

"That is most wonderful news," the journalist said, looking up from her pad. "I am sure the nation will applaud *your* choice."

Aasim swallowed his discomfort. "Now, is there anything else?" Seeing the light that flashed in the woman's eyes, he quickly wished he had not asked.

"Just one last question, First Secretary," Narinda purred. Forgetting, in her eagerness, where she was, she chewed upon her pen. "Can you tell me why you had a meeting with Thomas Miller from the American Embassy yesterday?"

"No, I cannot, on or off the record," Aasim bristled,

far too quickly. "Daily matters of state between India and America are none of your concern, and frankly, Miss Singh, I wonder why such an insignificant meeting should even be of importance for you to ask. Now, if we are done here, I have many matters I need to attend to. I appreciate your time and kind words and I can only apologise again that it has taken so long."

Narinda choked on her anger, rising to accept the abrupt hand that was thrust across the table towards her. Adding her own thanks into the frosty airspace between them, the journalist watched the First Secretary leave and sat back down into the comfort of her chair.

As she waited for Miss Jethwani to come and fetch her, Narinda Singh was very certain that she had only just begun to shine her torch into the darkness.

CHAPTER EIGHTEEN

Intervention

Jon watched the three men as they slipped from the cover of the tree line and picked their way down the gorge, struggling with the weight of the cage and the burden within. Eventually deciding he needed open space for his ambush, Galnia had chosen what he thought was a decent spot, a hundred or so metres south of where the cage had originally been left.

Taking up position behind some rugged ground and thicket, Jon was fairly certain that they could not airlift the tiger from within the dense jungle and had guessed, rather smugly now, that they would return to the gorge.

With his heart tapping out a warning, Jon watched on as they cautiously made their way towards the creek, setting the cage down to catch lost breaths. The two men he had seen before knelt down to eagerly splash their flushed faces with the cool waters of the creek, whilst the third man, the Moroccan, Jon guessed, stood guard by the cage, one eye on the still form of the great cat, his other sweeping their surroundings for danger.

They are on to me now, Jon thought, raising his weapon. Through his scope, he could see the detail of each man and committed their worried faces to memory. Wanting to save the Moroccan for last, Jon fixed his revenge upon the big one. As the large, bald-headed man rose up from his sore knees and massaged his back, Jon licked his lips nervously. The rifle felt heavy in his hands, the stock sharp in his shoulder. Drumming his right forefinger over the side of the rifle, he waited for them to take another few steps away from the cage, before he moved his shaking finger to the trigger.

The air hissed in warning as gunfire echoed through the gorge and Andersson felt the burn in his left shoulder and the bruising impact to his chest. Ignoring the agony and forgetting about their prize, the Swede, the Moroccan and the Englishman sprinted for cover, diving into the scrub as the jungle shredded all about them.

Taylor was at his side immediately, checking his shoulder and body armour over, but Andersson pushed him away angrily as leaves flicked and the air popped about them.

"*Helvete*," Andersson snarled, flicking his annoyance towards Hassan Raz. From the ground, he peered through the undergrowth, trying to find the shooter.

The low sun was in his eyes now and the Swede knew that whoever was ambushing them had chosen their spot well.

Reaching into his pouch, Andersson pulled out the sat phone and tossed it to the Moroccan. "Call it in, Hass."

As Raz caught the phone, Taylor frowned. "We don't know who we're – fuck it," he spat, as the ground before him puffed up with a stray round. "We don't know who, or how many we are up against."

"There's only one firing!" Raz pointed out.

"One suppressing – there could be dozens waiting for us to burn through our ammo. Calling it in now will only *complicate* things."

Andersson had to admit that Taylor was probably right. Brooks was probably in the air already, and he wouldn't want to screw up the operation this close to completion. Sure, he would have to let their employers know about the ambush, but if they sent in *Bravo*, their share of the spoils would start dwindling rapidly. They had to be certain. Scowling, he sucked in a breath, and then raised his head, going with his hunch.

"If that's you, Galnia," Andersson called out, "you should have stayed out of this."

Taylor pulled him back down by his injured shoulder. "What are you doing?"

Andersson met his glare with steel of his own. "Buying *you* some time. See if you can flank whoever's out there, get a head count if you can."

Taylor bit his lip, listening to the settling silence as the gunfire ceased. If it was Galnia, which he had to admit would make sense, then he would not have as much ammunition as they did – he certainly didn't have the training. The odds weren't that bad.

"Good luck," the Moroccan whispered, as he slipped the barrel of his rifle past some branches of the bush he was hiding underneath and trained it towards the south. Sunlight flashed in his brown eyes, narrowed by concern and anger.

Nodding, Taylor ditched his Bergen and started crawling away slowly to the east as Hassan's covering fire spat its angry response.

Jon's heart was uncontrollable as the adrenaline coursed through his body. He barely heard what they called out to him as he slipped from his cover, deeper into the jungle and away from the rasp of rounds that tore through where he had been hiding, moments before.

If they thought he was going to have a little chat with them, they were seriously mistaken. Jon was not, despite some people's opinion of him, an idiot. If he acknowledged who he was they would drag Sara and Robert out before him as leverage, and, God forbid, take steps for decisive action with his family back home... if they hadn't already.

No! No matter what, he had to stay calm, patient and in control. Jon grinned. Well, two out of three from his new life mantra wasn't so bad.

He was sure he had hit the big man, and in his surprise at making such a shot at that distance, had allowed them to sprint for safe cover. After half a volley of blind shots into the undergrowth, Jon had decided he had better save his bullets for what he could see, especially as he was not entirely sure how many rounds each clip held.

He was usually a pistol kind of a guy... a leftover fetish from all of those Sergio Leone westerns he had watched as a child.

Crossing himself, Jon found a large tree and hunkered down behind it. Stealing a look around the smooth trunk, he watched, waited and listened for their inevitable riposte.

He had more food and water now, he had protection, and for once Jon Galnia had no desire to be anywhere else.

Taylor scanned the jungle before him as he crouched and crept forward on his aching haunches, away from his comrades and the cage. The monkeys that had been playing in the area had already scattered into the shadows, and their distant, screeching departure still cut through his temple. Scowling, he licked the tension from his lips.

"Where are you, you bastard?" he asked his surroundings softly.

Taylor had spent the last few years with Parker and

Andersson, working the shipping lanes off Africa, deterring and taking down as many pirates as they could; filling their bank accounts with more bonuses than they could spend.

Well, Parker and Andersson couldn't spend it all, but then they didn't have two ex-wives clamouring for maintenance for the four seeds he had sown with them. Never one to resist a short skirt and sparkle of interest, Rick's trouser snake had caused more trouble for more families than any IED ever could. He had broken up now, how many was it? At least five relationships in the barracks with his infidelity, and that had brought down a whole world of hurt upon him.

By the time he had been *encouraged* to leave the Army and the Allenbrooke Barracks in Germany in 2013, he was already knee deep in debt and had even fewer friends than he had money.

Blinking back his past, Rick cursed himself for his stupidity, thinking of the women whose lives he had ruined along the way. He knew he was a dick and that was the trouble, he always thought with it, too.

His old staff-sergeant, Pap Wilkins, had said to him years ago that during combat, during times of crisis, it was amazing what your mind could drag up for you.

"Focus on the fight, not the shite," he had always said.

Taylor grinned. He had liked that old bastard. It was just a shame he had taken one in Helmand, three days before he was due to leave for the last time.

Focussing on the fight, Taylor scanned the jungle ahead of him. Their antagonist had gone to ground and was waiting for them to make the next move. *Smart, very smart*, although he probably had no idea how little time Alpha had. Every minute that slipped away inched their window of opportunity a little more closed. And he was so close now, did he want to risk everything by getting killed at the end? They had the tiger, so why risk it? Let him try it, let him come to them…

Turning his attention away from his orders, Taylor crawled back to Andersson and Raz, finally reaching them after what felt like another hour wasted, but was probably only minutes. The Swede had patched himself up, the shirt underneath his vest stained dark and padded out with bandages. The Moroccan, his impatience beginning to show in his gritted teeth, mopped the sweat from his brow with the sleeve of one arm as he fixed a worried look towards the still form of the tiger.

"It's quiet out there," Taylor whispered, noting the sweat also beading on Andersson's brow. "It's definitely Galnia, and he's keeping his distance for now. I marked a print that looked nothing like a combat boot, and I saw no signs of another unit. It's three against one."

Mike nodded, wincing. The morphine was helping, but the bullet was still in there and he would need Lisa to dig it out.

Taylor took up his position, facing east. "We should just grab the cage and get the hell out of here."

"A bad idea, my friend," Raz warned.

"That's what he is waiting for," Andersson grimaced.

Taylor cursed, looking back behind him. The jungle was silent, mocking their dilemma, and they were all aware of the sunlight slowly beginning to cook them.

"Well," the Brit said, reaching out a beckoning hand for the sat-phone in the Moroccan's pocket. "We can't sit here all day. We might as well give him the *good* news…"

After a moment's hesitation, Andersson nodded his consent, listening on with a sense of foreboding as Raz passed the Englishman the phone and Taylor started to tell Brooks what the hell was going on.

Left alone for the rest of the night, and the early hours of the morning, Robert Williams had to contend with a full bladder and the cold reality of their predicament that left any hope they held spinning on a fraying thread.

For many hours, since the woman they now knew to be Lisa had left them, Sara and Robert had deliberated over numerous plans, both of them desperate to come up with the idea that would see them to safety. Unfortunately, after dismissing various, dangerous and foolhardy plans, they only ended up tying themselves up further in their thread, and the strain was now clearly painted on both of their faces.

"I just don't see a way out of this," Sara said, breaking the silence. She turned her head from the pilot to hide her tears in a veil of tangled tresses.

Swallowing his fears, Robert looked on forlornly and crossed his legs, hoping to assuage his bladder's insistency. The pressure did little to ease his discomfort and he felt himself sliding into the chasm of despair that was beginning to fill their canvas prison. Sara had been the strong one, keeping him going. If she was losing faith…

"We have to hold on to hope," Robert whispered, his voice cracking. "We are still alive! They still need us, Sara, or we wouldn't be here now, would we?"

It took a while for his words to find their mark, but eventually Sara sniffed back her tears and wiped her eyes. When she turned round stiffly on her bed to look at him, they blazed with angry determination again. She nodded her head several times, but remained silent.

Offering her a faint smile, Robert turned his attention to the tent's entrance, as he heard the sound of distant approach. It was getting brighter in the tent now, the day outside still fighting for life, trying to find its temper for the day ahead. Sunlight cut through the lifting gloom as Lisa entered again, flicking her gaze from Sara, to him, and then back again.

When she spoke, her eyes searched Sara's grubby face. Seeing the defiance still alive there, she looked over to Robert. "Time for that bathroom break," she announced. Drawing her pistol, she tossed him the key to his freedom with her left hand.

Fumbling with the lock, Robert unlocked his cuffs and massaged his raw wrists. Nodding his thanks, he rose up stiffly and passed her back the key before she could ask.

"After you," Lisa said, motioning him out with a flick of her handgun.

Finding a breath, Robert stumbled on weak legs towards the canvas opening and daren't look at his friend. With Sara's eyes fixed hopefully upon him, the pilot stepped out into the world for the first time in two days.

Robert hesitated for a moment, shielding his eyes against the dawn, drinking in the welcome freshness of the air. The staleness of the tent was overbearing and for as long as he could, he would try to use this moment of freedom to regain some of his lost strength.

"To your left," Lisa ordered him, and he stumbled obediently towards the tall, narrow tent that he guessed must be their field lavatory.

As he walked on, using his age and weariness as an excuse to dally, he surveyed their surroundings. It was beautiful, beyond words.

The sun was rising slowly now, climbing the shadowy ridge of the hills beyond the lake, carpeted in creeping mist and filled by thousands of water birds who had gathered together for the previous night. Their squawks and debate filled the silence of the dawn and Robert was thankful for their company.

As he came closer to the tent, the pilot stole a glance towards the helicopter and tents behind him and felt his hopes rise. If he could just get free, if he could...

"Nothing there for you, Williams," Lisa said, gesturing for him to fix his focus ahead. Unlike the movies, she did not walk close to him, offering him a chance to take her by surprise. When he hesitated, certain that he could overpower her, given the opportunity, his captor raised her pistol a little higher, aiming it at his throat.

Turning back, Robert moved inside the lavatory to claim his first victory of the day.

As he was finishing, sometime later, Robert could hear the roar of excitement from somewhere beyond his throne room. The man's voice called out excitedly and Lisa responded with what sounded more like relief than glee.

"About time," she said, her voice trailing off as she moved away from the tent.

Peering out the flap, Robert could see the big man, still dressed in his army fatigues, his bared arms raised high. With a radio clutched triumphantly in one hand, he hurried to Lisa and swept her into a huge embrace. As he spun her about and set her down, Robert choked on his fears.

If their comrades had achieved what they came here for, then their chances of escape were rapidly starting to reduce – they needed to act now, before it was too late.

As the pair began whispering quietly to one another, Robert fixed his attention on the helicopter. He was not an expert on them, but judging by its size, it was probably a single-engine, light utility helicopter. If his memory served him well, the Indian military used the Hindustan Aeronautics company for their aircraft and these mercenaries, if that is what they were, had probably seconded it from a private seller in the country.

It had been a few years since he had flown helicopters, but Robert was fairly certain he could fly them out of here to safety. His breath caught in his throat as he steeled his nerves and, for the briefest of moments, thought about making a mad dash for freedom. As his muscles bunched, rising to the challenge, his guilt pulled him back, and the pilot became very aware of the small machine gun hanging from the man's shoulder.

Searching the camp, he looked for a weapon, left unattended that he could take, a knife, something he could use to defend himself with. There were plenty of ammunition boxes and supply crates stacked around the makeshift canteen, but beyond that, he could see little of use that he could steal.

Before his thoughts could catch up fully, Lisa turned her attention in his direction, nodded to her companion and began hurrying towards the tent.

"Finish off, Williams," she called out, and he stepped into the fresh air, before she reached him.

"What is happening?" Robert demanded, planting his hands on his hips. The man had already turned away and was hurrying over to one of the other tents on the far side of the camp.

The woman's face hardened, her pale skin flushed with what was either excitement, or anger. She stayed several arms lengths from him, her pistol raised towards him, her eyes blazing.

"None of your bloody business," she snarled.

Okay, Robert thought, she is angry.

"Back to your tent," Lisa ordered him. She stepped back as her prisoner dutifully obeyed, and then fell in behind him as he passed.

Fighting to regain some of her composure, Lisa Myers marched the pilot back to his incarceration. It wasn't until he was secure again and she was watching Brooks prepare the helicopter, that she found an easy breath.

This was it; this was the moment they had planned for. All those weeks of build-up, all the problems, the pressure and tension as they slipped illegally into the country via a remote airstrip in Vadodara, Gujarat – all the planning, nearly undone by fate, had come together at last! If the tiger *was* theirs, they could be out of the country by nightfall, off to deliver it to their employer, off to collect their dirty retirement fund.

Lisa shook her head. Life was never that easy. Before now, before the realisation of what they were doing had sunk in, she would have been delighted at the prospect, but now? Why, when she was on the cusp of being able to afford and do whatever she wanted for the rest of her life, did she feel so hollow? So damned empty inside?

Standing on the shore, with the waters lapping at her boots, Lisa stared at the mountain in the distance and knew, deep down in her heart, that she was about to pay a price she would never be able to recover from.

Cramp bit into Jon's calves, as he remained crouched low. Although it was still early, in the next few hours he would have to try and figure out how the Night Vision

Goggles actually worked, or he was screwed.

For what felt like a lifetime, he remained where he was, listening to the calm that was returning to his surroundings, relieved, somewhat, that they had not come after him. The chatter in his earpiece had also gone quiet, and Jon expected that they had switched to a different frequency now they knew they had an eavesdropper.

In the movies, the hero had it all figured out in his head by now, knew exactly what to do, reacted to trouble, got in to trouble, and then, ultimately, saved the day. Jon shook his head, the sweat running down his neck and flicking from his sodden hair.

Despite his attempts at going Rambo, he didn't have the upper hand and the silver-screen-given ability to dodge bullets... he didn't even have a needle and thread. He was in trouble, and he was starting to realise it.

No, he knew it!

Jon's code and his blood debt to Rashim had gotten him into some serious shit and he wasn't sure how he was going to get out of this one.

Snorting free of his doubt, Jon searched the lifting gloom for the three mercenaries and could see that they had remained where they were, close to their prize, watching, waiting.

Hunkering down, Jon sipped at his water, aware of how drained he was, how tired he felt. He was beginning to think that this was all some screwed up dream, that he was actually someplace else, watching someone else's film. He was still sifting through his options when he detected the first faint rumbles of discontent, the distant thudding in his head.

Fighting against his imagined headache, Jon listened again, feeling his hackles rise as he realised he was fine, that it was the mechanical thunder of an approaching helicopter. Dropping forward onto a sore knee, Jon peered through the dense undergrowth and could see that the three men were falling back to the cage now, ringing it protectively.

Jon could hear the roar of the rotors as the helicopter neared, and its sound filled the gorge with its fury. His ride was here, but there was no way today that he was going to be able to hitch a lift.

Cursing, Jon grabbed his rifle. Rising up stiffly he headed towards the noise.

"I see you, Alpha," Brooks acknowledged, as he hovered over the gorge. His heart was in mouth as he saw the cage and thought of all that money waiting down there for him.

"Secure LZ," Brooks said into his comm. "I'll get into position and lower the winch for you – we won't have long, so let's get this done quickly."

"*Copy that*," Andersson's voice acknowledged. Their eyes met, even at that distance, and Brooks expertly dropped lower into the gorge, feeling the bird protest as he stirred up trouble. Below him, the water began to fan out and the jungle swayed to a turbulent rhythm.

Holding his height steadily, reacting to each shift in the air, Brooks flicked the winch on and could hear it click into action. Below him, Taylor and Raz scanned the jungle for danger as Andersson reached out a gloved hand.

"*Got it*," the Swede said. Brooks could hear the relief in the voice in his ear and he kept things as steady as he could.

It was then that he heard the familiar report of gunfire and the sparks began to fly.

The helicopter lit up as Jon emptied his finger into it and the steel bird zinged in protest. He barely had time to enjoy his triumph as the jungle exploded all about him. Turning, Jon sent the last of his clip towards the men on the ground, and then plunged away from the bird as it rocked and bucked in the ravine, its furious agony punctuated by the trail of smoke coming from beneath the rotors.

As the jungle snapped and spat with bullets, Jon weaved his way through the trees, hoping they would shield him. Leaping over a low bush, he lost his footing and crashed to the ground heavily. As the air ripped from his lungs and his ribs protested, he released the empty clip and fumbled into his belt pouches for a fresh one.

Above him, the air roared with chaos, on the ground, it shook with anger as the footsteps of pursuit grew louder.

Andersson and Raz raced after the fleeing figure that was a blur amongst the trees, a hundred metres away from them. Their anger and bullets had calmed now, as their training returned and they waited for the shot that would end this.

"*Get that fucker*," Brooks' voice screamed in their ears. "*I can't hold her here. I have to get out and fix this before we can airlift her safely.*"

Andersson scowled, annoyed at himself for not finding the time to hook up the cage. With Galnia running amok, it wouldn't happen today, not now. This was getting ridiculous. They had to kill him, and kill him fast.

Hassan Raz was not in control of his emotions as they chased after their ambusher. Whilst the damage to the bird was superficial, could probably be repaired by dusk, the stray bullet that had taken Taylor in the neck meant that their fighting numbers were dwindling rapidly. Leaving the Englishman to save his own life, they had set off after Galnia before he could wreak more havoc.

"In pursuit, over," Andersson hissed into his comm. "Once we kill this bastard, we will make our way along the gorge as far as we can to the FOB."

"*Copy that*!" Brooks responded. Behind them, the thunder began to subside as the helicopter rose and banked away over the jungle towards the south-west.

The Swede shook his head. With Taylor down, but hopefully able to protect the tiger, and the extraction compromised, Brooks would have to call this in – they would have to send in Bravo.

Hearing the dollars drain from his bank account, Andersson focussed his attention back to the hunt. Survive first, worry about the money later. Slowing his charge, the Swede reined in the Moroccan, grabbing him by the shoulder.

"Ease down," Andersson hissed. His shoulder burned from the effort.

Eyes bright with frustration, Raz dragged in a calming breath and was about to say something when a shadow rose up away to his left, flitting away through the gathering gloom.

"Contact!" he roared, and his calm was lost once again.

Once seen as his enemy, the jungle was now Jon's friend as he raced through the trees, dodging the snap, crackle and pop of the gunfire all around him. With his head low and his heart hammering madly, he picked an erratic path and could have sworn that one of the bullets whispered its manufacturer's name as is sped past him and shattered the bark of a tree.

Muttering a forlorn prayer, not sure if it was heard over the spit of gunfire, Jon fled deeper into the jungle. Ahead of him, the day warmed up.

Behind him, Jon's pursuers started to gain.

CHAPTER NINETEEN

"...I heard you say"

The day had stretched on for what felt like more than twenty-four hours, and for as long as Samira Jethwani had worked at the Secretariat on Raisina Hill, she could not recall a more draining, turbulent day. With no sunshine or sunset to guide the passing hours, she had only the rattling fan and the silent hands of the wall clock for company. After Samira had shown the journalist safely from the hill, the First Secretary had been hiding away in his office.

'*No more calls today*,' he had sighed, ordering some tea and the pills that would calm the tension in his forehead. Since that time, in the middle of the afternoon, Aasim Rana had not emerged from behind his closed door, but he had been constantly on the telephone.

Samira opened the drawer to the left of her stocking-clad knee and stole a bite from the remnants of her lunch. Moaning in delight, she savoured the flavour of the *Golgappa* she had purchased from her favourite stall in the Tilak Nagar market earlier that morning, before she had caught her bus to work. Becoming somewhat addicted to the *Pani Puri* sold there since moving to the city, she had hoped to resist the temptations in recent weeks as her hips were starting to swell in protest.

Samira dabbed her lips with a paper towel and closed her eyes, losing herself to the taste and the cavernous hunger in her stomach. Time never seemed to allow a moment's respite on the Hill – she had been constantly on the phone, taking calls from Aasim's fellow members, all wishing him well, all wanting to line up privately to shake his hand and find a seat aboard the seemingly runaway train of success he was, in their minds, now clearly upon.

Sighing, the secretary stared down at her notepad, full of names and possible dates for future meetings. Transferring her weary eyes to the bright, flickering screen before her, she stared at the First Secretary's diary and wondered how in Lord Shiva's name she was ever going to be able to accommodate them all. And that was not even taking into account the number of journalists that wanted to find their own angle on the announcement that was already the biggest news story of the year.

Narinda Singh had swept from the Hill in silence, stopping only briefly to thank Samira for her help and reiterating that should she ever feel the need, she was *always* there for her. Standing in the shade, Samira had watched the journalist hurry away towards a nearby road where she had probably left her car and wondered why, with such a huge story on her pad, Narinda Singh did not seem happy.

Wistfully thinking of the last time she had seen daylight, a time check revealing that it was over five hours ago now, Samira fixed her eyes on his closed door and willed Aasim Rana to allow her home for the day.

Moments later, Samira jumped in her seat, hurriedly closing the drawer to hide away her emergency stash as the other door to the office opened. She had almost expected him, and as the tall, thin man strode into the room and closed the door softly behind him, Samira's smile of welcome slipped from her face.

The rattle of the fan hid the thunder in her breast and

225

Samira felt her skin crawl as the temperature in the room plummeted. Licking her lips, she stared at the man as he crossed to stand before her, his dark eyes bright with a smile that had not found his lips.

"Can I help you again, mister...?" she dared to ask, her wide eyes flicking to the breast pocket of his suit. Again, he wore no badge of identification.

With palms flat, he rested his hands upon Samira's desk, leaning subtly towards her.

"I think you have done more than enough for us for one day, Miss Jethwani," the man said, his hawkish face smoothing into a smile. "Why don't you go home for the day? You have worked incredibly hard these last few weeks for the First Secretary, and it has not gone unnoticed."

Shuddering, Samira fought for the words that would not come and she lost herself in his eyes, those bright eyes that lacked any warmth, but held so much more. Straightening, the man folded his arms across his chest, watching her, waiting for her to answer.

"It is for my employer to decide, sir," Samira blurted, amazed at her own inner strength. "I do not even know who you are, and if you are going to continue to come into my office and tell me what to do, I would hope that you would at least have the courtesy to tell me your name."

For the briefest of moments the man's demeanour changed, hardened by fury and then it was gone, replaced by a wide, broad smile and a chuckle that echoed about the room.

"Ah, Miss Jethwani," the man chortled, clapping his hands together to remind her he knew her name. "I can see why Aasim likes you so much. Forgive my manner, sweet child."

The man offered her a low bow, a gesture which, during the time of the British Raj, would have been counted chivalrous, but only came across today as mocking.

"I am Hamid," the man said softly, straightening. "And as I am now your new friend, you may go home for the evening."

Samira blinked. "I will check on the First Secretary before–"

"Please, go home," Hamid chuckled, holding up his hands again. It was then that Samira noted the pale crease of the ragged scar on his left palm for the first time. "I will let him know that you have gone, you have my word on this."

A cool silence settled between them as she dared to hold his gaze for a few seconds more. Turning her head away, she searched for her bag. Rising up, she shut down her computer for the day and accepted the coat he had already retrieved for her.

"Good evening, sir," Samira mustered, as she walked on unsteady heels towards the door.

Hamid watched her leave without a word, his smile still fixed upon his features. When she was gone, when the sound of her heels had faded away, he turned, striding towards Aasim Rana's office with a broader grin on his face.

At the end of the wood-panelled hallway, the same hall Thomas Miller had sat patiently in but two days before, Samira regained control of her composure. Smarting from the man's audacity, she slowed, coming to a stop. Calming herself further, she fought to steady her wild heart, and when she had, she turned, looking back along the carpeted hall towards the offices.

This man was dangerous, she could tell. His visits, unannounced and without clearance, hinted at deeper shadows, dark corners that people like Narinda Singh wanted, no, dared to expose.

Since the American's visit, Samira's daily routine had been turned upside down and she knew, deep in her heart, that this mysterious man, known only as Hamid, was involved or in charge of whatever was going on.

But her duty and loyalty was to the First Secretary. Despite his coolness, his indifference to her own needs and his infuriating ability to snap at the slightest of things, she knew he had been kind to her. He had given her the chance to follow her path, to rise above her aspirations and seek a career beyond anything her expectations could have ever conjured.

Was she going to jeopardise all of this by spying on him, by betraying him?

As she slipped off her heels and crept back down the hallway, Samira Jethwani knew that she was not doing it to betray him, she was doing it to save him.

Aasim Rana sighed as the man stepped into his office without any courtesy, bringing only his smile and shadows with him. Nodding his aching head, the First Secretary motioned for his guest to be seated and reached into a side drawer to pull forth a second glass.

"A drink?" Aasim asked, without looking up.

Hamid smiled, seeing the half-empty bottle of *Old Monk* on the desk. "Why not!" he chuckled, reaching for the glass the First Secretary passed to him.

"To a successful day," Aasim toasted, barely able to muster a smile as they crashed their glasses together.

Hardly touching his rum, the newcomer licked his lips and set the glass gently down on the desk. With a smile, he reclined in his chair and crossed one leg over the other, resting his hands together in his lap.

"A day to remember," Hamid said, holding the weary man's gaze. He could see all the stress, the pressure, burning away there, and noted the shadows darkening the corners of his eyes. "You have proven, yet again to the Prime Minister, that his faith in you was well placed."

Aasim nodded his head, his mind swimming from the rum. The lights in the room were hurting his eyes now, a room that was starting to swirl.

"It has been a triumph, for us all. I wonder though, I fear, if it has all been for nothing."

"You doubt what this day has achieved, Aasim?" Hamid asked, frowning. "You have the Lok Sabha, the public and the press behind you. In the days to come, when the date for the unveiling is announced, the Prime Minister will have the entire country in his hand... even the President. And soon, very soon, you will have all the money you need to buy it with."

Aasim reached for the desk, clumsily putting down his glass. "There has been news?" he asked, lost for breath.

Hamid smiled, his eyes glittering. "They have her, Aasim. By my blood, they have her!"

The First Secretary blinked. "And they are free? They are gone?"

"In time, in time," Nehru's man responded, holding a hand up to pre-empt any worry. If the room had not been dancing before his eyes, Rana may well have noticed the hesitancy in the man's words. It was there for but a heartbeat, then gone before it revealed he was hiding something from him.

"My team are ready to go in and secure the area. I am just waiting for confirmation that they have left the country and that the money we will need has been deposited. Once this is so, I shall accompany them to the crash site to oversee the operation."

"This is, this is wonderful news, my friend." Aasim could not believe how blessed the day was turning out to be. However, as he drained the rest of his glass, he felt the cold hand of reality grip his shoulder and he flinched with worry. "We should remain cautious, though. We still have to placate the Americans. They will want answers, answers that we must provide quickly for them."

"Do not worry yourself with this, my friend," Hamid said quietly. "The Americans will have the crash site and the bodies they desire – I will make certain of that. All you need to focus on now is dealing with their embassy, maintaining a dialogue with them and the momentum of our success. We will soon have the money from this deal, the money that will secure this party's power for many years to come."

Hamid was stick-straight in his chair now, his face flooded by excitement, his eyes bright with hunger. Aasim sat back in his chair, hearing the cold whisper of warning in his ear.

The man he knew only as Mister Hamid did far too much for Chandra Nehru, and the First Secretary feared what more he was capable of.

"Corruption comes at a heavy cost," Aasim responded wearily.

Hamid smiled. "It is a price we must all pay for the power we wield. Our country is founded upon struggle, it is something we relish. We have only just begun, you and I. Nehru has great things planned for us, for us all."

Aasim nodded his head, not truly hearing the man's words. His temple throbbed with worry and his hands were shaking. He had always thought that he could keep his office free from the heavy stain of corruption, could keep his integrity when all about him others were seduced by it, swept along by the greed and desires of the man that led them.

'*This is the way of things, the way of our politics*,' Nehru had said to him once, as they began negotiations with those seeking the tiger. '*Man has thirsted for power, for dominance, since he could walk on two legs. We are not so different from our forefathers as much as we may wish to be. The Gods watch over us, I am certain of it. Had they not, we would not be sat where we are today.*'

Stifling a sob, the First Secretary stared down at his hands, searching them vainly for the remnants of the honour he no longer held.

Samira Jethwani's horrified breath escaped her lips as she remained where she was, her left ear pressed to the door, her trembling fingertips touching the cold wood.

Her thoughts swirled like a tornado as she attempted to make sense of what she was hearing. In Aasim Rana's office, the two men continued to discuss the business of the late day, but above her screaming veins, she could not hear what they were saying.

Aasim Rana has lied to the Americans...

The international implication of what she was hearing was too much to cope with and her already tired mind began to scatter before her. Barely able to check her own thoughts, she was rooted to the spot by her shock and did not fully register that the men were rising from their seats.

What was going on? What had the First Secretary become involved in? Not even able to comprehend the meaning as to who these *people* had, who they were referring to, Samira stepped quietly back from the door. As she found a breath, she suddenly heard the man she now knew to be Hamid, rise from his seat with promises of further news as soon as he had it.

Clutching her breast to stop her heart escaping, Samira crept swiftly across the office. Her hand had the door open and she was thankful that it remained silent as she slipped through it and closed the old wood quietly behind her. Unknowingly, Hamid stepped into the room she had just vacated and bade his farewell to his conspirator.

Hurrying on shaking legs, Samira swept up her shoes and bag, stealing across the hall to an office, trying the handle. It was locked!

Scampering to the next, she tried that one and almost cried out to Lord Shiva as it opened. As Samira hurried inside and hid underneath the window, its blind thankfully down, she could hear the sound of footfall coming down the hall towards her hiding place.

Closer, closer he came. Close enough for her to hear his breath as he drew it in between the tune he was humming.

Samira held her own breath as his shadow slipped across the silent office and he stopped, close to the door. Above her raging heart, she could not tell where he was, whether she was about to be discovered.

"It is done," the man said quietly. There was silence, and then, moments later, Hamid spoke again. "Yes, we can proceed. I will leave later today, under the cover of night. I will be with you by morning."

The man continued on his way and Samira waited for many, many minutes for her legs and mind to start working again. Slowly, she rolled onto her knees and away from the window, reaching for a desk to help her rise. Splitting the blinds, she peered as far as she could down both lengths of the hallway.

All was quiet now, and gathering up her wits, Samira slipped quietly from the office and back into her shoes. As she stumbled away down the hallway, she wished she had just gone home, wished that she had not heard what she did.

Sometime later, as she stood alone, waiting for her bus home, Samira knew that despite the danger she would place herself in, she had to do something with the knowledge she held. Something terrible was going to happen, and if she wanted to reveal the truth of what she had just overheard, she would need more proof of what was going on. Samira shook her head.

Was she listening to herself? She was a glorified receptionist, the personal assistant to the First Secretary of India. What could she do, that others had not?

The bus swept hurriedly down the road towards her, and reaching out in greeting, Samira waited for her means of escape to stop before her. As the doors hissed open and she stepped up to greet the driver, Samira looked back towards the Secretariat and knew that she had to act fast.

And she was going to need help doing it.

CHAPTER TWENTY

Yippie-Ki-Yay

The distant, thudding approach of the helicopter cut through Lisa's thoughts, dragging her away from the spectacle of the sunlight glistening off the water before her. The sky was full of fire now, a magnificent canvas of deep orange and red, streaked by gently darkening brush-stroked clouds. Across the vast lake, the peak of Vulture's Point was silhouetted against the burning sky, and as she turned away to search the western skyline for the helicopter, Lisa wrapped her arms about her body to ward off the rising chill of worry in the air.

Sam Brooks' acidic voice cut through that worry, and she could tell he was furious as she spied the dark shape of the helicopter as it skimmed the treetops, a faint plume of smoke trailing in its wake. As it roared over her and Brooks swept about in an ungraceful arc across the shoreline to begin his descent, Lisa stole a look towards the captives' tent and could see faint movement within.

They would be fearing the worst, she surmised, and they would be right to. When they had the tiger, with or without Galnia's corpse, they would be left in the jungle, burned out like the wreckage of their jet.

Lisa shook her head, her hair, now loose and free, snapping about her shoulders in the turbulence. Gonzales and Williams' only crime had been one borne from bad luck, one which had seen them survive a plane crash only to be plunged into even greater peril... it just wasn't right.

Brooks cut the power to the engines, and as she waited for him to reach her, she was drawn to the rotor blades. Lost to their spin, a slow, resigned sigh of defeat escaped her lips.

They would not be going home today.

Brooks stalked up to her, his face full of thunder. "Fuck it," he swore, grinding his teeth in frustration. He threw a look back to the steel bird. "I am going to need to work through the day and night, but I should have her ready by dawn." He looked back, his face suddenly very tired.

"What about Galnia?" Myers asked, stepping close to put a comforting hand on one of his shaking shoulders.

"He should be dead by now," Brooks replied, his eyes bright with menace. "He had better be, or else..." He had not told her about Parker yet.

Lisa nodded, her mind scattered to a thousand possibilities. They had to be away, and soon, or the Indians would come calling. Word had already been received that they were on standby, waiting for the call that they could come in and clean up their mess.

No pressure there, then!

"What about those two?" Lisa dared to ask. She looked back towards the tent briefly and returned her gaze to Brooks. His eyes were hooded, but she could tell he was not happy.

"I don't know, Lees," Sam sighed. He shook his thoughts about his head. "We can't leave anyone alive, any thread that could unravel us."

"But we can't just murder them," Lisa protested, her eyes blazing. "They have done nothing wrong. Should they be punished for what we do?"

Brooks fell silent and looked back at the fading sunset. He stood with his back to her for quite some time, before turning back.

"I know, it's not right," he sighed, and Lisa was startled to see that he still had some of the man he once was left in him. "But if we don't do something, *they* will."

Lisa shuddered, watching the water as a huge flock of dark birds took to the wing and flapped silently, majestically away to the south, taking any of her hopes away with them.

Jon Galnia's chest was tight and on fire by the time he reached the dusty road. He had been running for hours, drawing his pursuers further away from their prize, not sure what he was going to do, but fairly sure the more he pissed them off, the better he would feel. Amidst his confusion and relief, he was too tired to register the thinning jungle at first, before slowing to a halt in the middle of the broad track.

Sweeping a hurried gaze to the left and right, he fought for a breath that would not come, imagining a convoy of police cars swarming towards him over the rough, undulating road.

It was empty.

Sighing, Jon threw a look back to the jungle, relieved that there was no sign or sight of pursuit, no longer the spit of death chasing after his flesh. Turning his attention back to the track and wondering, even now, where the hell he was, he looked across towards the dense jungle ahead of him and shook his head.

If he carried on running, he would get lost, would never be able to find his way back...

What I am trying to get back to?

Jon paused, frowning. He had been so swept up in his desire to avenge Rashim that he had not been thinking clearly – something that he had always been able to do.

"Perhaps I am still in shock?" he asked himself. His mind throbbed for an answer and all he could think of was that he was becoming delirious in the heat.

He had an empire, a legacy to protect, a wife and child who loved him and a score to settle with those who had tried to kill him. That should have been more than enough to send him running. But no, here he was throwing himself into even more danger for a man he barely knew, two captured employees and a tiger that was stupid enough to keep getting caught.

Jon sucked in a breath, blinking in shock. *Was it for the tiger...?*

You couldn't write this stuff. Selfish man puts himself in jeopardy to save the last known living tiger... well what self-respecting human being wouldn't?

Jon smarted at his own question. He wasn't self-respecting, he wasn't a man who cared about others, he was a selfish, ruthless bastard and that was the problem. So why was he here? Why hadn't he just kept walking away when he heard the gunshots?

Snorting, Jon looked down at his ruined shoes, seeing the laces undone on his left foot. He was going to need a hundred sessions of therapy if he actually survived this.

Grunting from the effort, Jon knelt down to tie his laces up.

It saved his life.

The silence of the fading day overhead exploded about him as the air popped angrily. Heart in mouth, he swept up his rifle and launched himself across the road into the jungle beyond, not noticing the thorns that tore the skin from his left cheek, and not hearing the chatter in his earpiece as he crashed to the ground, rolled into a tree and dragged himself behind it. Amazingly, the laptop in his pack was living up to its name and was still in one piece.

As Jon found his breath, he checked his weapon for damage and finally heard a voice, seeping through the noise of his pulse, pounding furiously away in his head.

"Give yourself up, Galnia," the voice hissed in his ear. "You cannot outrun us, but you can still survive this."

"Yeah, right," Jon responded. He peered around the tree, scanning the road and tree line beyond for danger.

This really was starting to feel like a *Die Hard* moment. He suddenly thought of his son, and prayed that he got the chance to watch it with him one day. Resisting the urge to use any quotes, Jon nestled the rifle into his shoulder.

"I am many things, but I am not a fucking idiot."

"No," came the reply, a while later. "You are not. We know all about you, Jon. We know where your family lives, we know about the dirt and blood that stains your hands."

Jon felt himself shake. "Then you also know what I am capable of. You do not want to start this with me. Threaten my family again and I'll rip your head from your shoulders with my bare hands."

The mocking laughter that echoed in his ear did little to calm him down, and Jon pounded the ground with his left fist.

"Believe me, Jon, you are nothing compared to those I work for, nothing. I am nothing!" the man sighed in his earpiece. "This can all end now. Just let us have the tiger; walk away from this whilst you still can. You have a family to think about, Jon, and judging by the photo I have, you wouldn't want us to pay your lovely wife a visit. Just give this madness up! If you do, your family and the prisoners will be left alone. Just leave us be to finish what we started."

Jon flexed his stinging hand free of its pain and smiled, ignoring the pathetic attempt to unsettle him.

"If you claim to know so much about me, then you know I will not. You killed that innocent man for no reason. All he did wrong was to show a stranger a little compassion. So, you listen to me now, fuckwit. I am going to kill you, kill all of you for what you did. It's a Karma kind of thing."

Jon winced. *That one wouldn't go down in movie history.*

Sensing they were talking to him to try and distract him, Jon flattened himself on the ground and began crawling away into the jungle, the shadows starting to close in all around him.

Andersson shook his head, scanning the road for signs of their prey. This Galnia was a piece of work. All the Intel they had received about him suggested he would have tried to cut a deal by now and use the situation to get a nice slice of the pie. But no! He was going against all he was supposed to be and had gotten himself involved in something he would not be able to walk away from now.

Jon Galnia had picked a fine time to find a conscience.

Switching frequency, Andersson checked in with Hassan Raz. "Are you in place, over?"

"*I am*," Raz replied immediately, his low voice underlining his words.

"I'll make my move across the road and flush him north," Andersson whispered. "We have to finish this now, but if we can, we take him alive."

Silence.

"Hassan?" Andersson growled.

"*Received, over*," Raz sulked.

"If not," the Swede said, rising up, one finger pressed to his ear to keep the comms in place, "we get this done and give the Indians his corpse."

Raising the rifle to scan the jungle ahead, Andersson stalked forward into nature's wall of silence.

Jon crouched low, flattened on his stomach. He had managed to lose the merc following him and kept moving for as long as he could, slipping deeper into the jungle and resting in a spot where he thought he would not be found. It was starting to get dark now, and if they had those night goggles with them, they would soon find him.

The smell of the cold, damp ground filled his nostrils as he listened to every sound the land had to offer, every shift in the leaves, every echo from the distant drill of a woodpecker. Closing his eyes, Jon fought against his exhaustion and the pain seeping through his body. He was aware of the torn flesh on his face now and it was stiff with agony.

Opening his eyes, Jon could not see anything in the thickening gloom apart from a solitary monkey, scratching its arse in a tree as it settled down for the night. As Galnia continued to search for tell of danger, he could see the huge ants away to his right, crawling over a rotted, fallen trunk, scurrying about their business in orderly hordes. Marvelling at them, he watched the leaves that were passed down the lines of marching ants, carried from one part of the jungle to their nest. As Jon watched on, he began to see the tracks in the earth, the channels that marked their passing.

Oh, how I would love to trade places with you, right

now, Jon thought, but he knew the ants were a lot smarter than that.

He shook his head in wonderment.

The slow approach of danger dragged him from his reverie, and flattening himself even lower into the ground, Jon watched on through the dense thicket as he spied the thick soles of combat boots, padding ever closer in a sweeping arc to where he was hiding. Leaving his rifle on the ground beside him, Jon slipped the knife free from his belt.

He needed to be quiet about this. By his reckoning, he still faced three hunters, and if he went in all guns blazing, he would bring them all down upon him.

Closer the boots came, nestling into the jungle floor, with each slow, careful searching step. As Jon was about to rise up, he heard the sudden, ominous click of a safety being released before him.

"Don't even think about it," Andersson said. He trained his rifle on the prone form trying to hide before him with one arm and pulled his Night Goggles off his face with the other.

"Drop your weapon, Jon. That's enough mischief for one day."

Swallowing down the fear choking his throat, Jon threw his knife aside and pushed himself up onto his knees. Grimacing, he rose up on weakening legs and put his hands on his head as the big man, the one he had shot earlier, ordered him from his hiding place with a meaningful flick of his rifle.

Scowling, Jon stumbled forward, throwing a look at the rotting tree trunk.

Fucking ants, he swore under his breath.

Andersson watched Galnia rise from his hiding place and

stumble out into clearer terrain. It was hard for the Swede to imagine that this dishevelled mess before him was a multi-billionaire, a ruthless, dangerous man and a high-ranking member of the American Mafia. Dressed in a piecemeal suit of ruined designer clothes and a combat vest, the lean, hawk-faced man came to stand before him, his face cut and bruised, his hair matted with blood.

"That's far enough," Andersson warned, as his prisoner tried to take a few steps closer.

Galnia stopped obediently, though his eyes were bright with anger. "So, here we are," he smiled, flicking his gaze about for opportunity. "What happens now?"

Andersson ignored him, thumbing his comm. "I've got him. Heading to you now, over."

Jon watched the tall mercenary as the man listened to the response in his ear, studying his broad shoulders, his square face and the gear that he carried. Jon definitely recognised him now as the man he had shot earlier, and was amazed that he was still on his feet and in the hunt.

"So, what now?" Jon asked again, seeing the impatience in his words mirrored in the big man's eyes. "We can't stand here all night. I am guessing you have places you need to be, so let's just cut to the chase. I wouldn't want *you* to get caught with your pants down."

"Stop talking," the big man growled. There was an accent there somewhere, hidden amongst the drawl of too many years in the mess. "I am taking you back. If you come quietly, this can still go well for you, despite everything you've done."

Jon snorted. "If you let me go, *you* can still walk away from this."

Before Jon could say anything else, the mercenary came forward, slamming the butt of his rifle into his face. With his vision spinning and pain ripping through his nose, Galnia stumbled to his knees.

As the man towered over him, Jon looked up, his eyes full of murder. "Damn it! Do you know how much these teeth cost me?" He spat thousands of loose dollars from his bloodied mouth onto the big man's boots.

"Shut up, get up, and move," the mercenary ordered, stepping back. He was smart enough to keep a sensible distance from his captive and watched on dispassionately as Galnia dragged himself up from the ground and put his hands back upon his head.

Jon dealt the man a wide, bloody smile. "Ok, you win. We are clearly not going to share a beer after all this, so I'll come quietly."

Andersson flicked his rifle to the north, calming himself down. If he lost it now, he lost control, and that would give Galnia the chance he was clearly probing for.

"I am disappointed though," Jon began as soon as Andersson finished talking. Before he could continue, the Swede was upon him again, the rifle slamming into his stomach, forcing him back onto his knees.

"Last chance," Andersson snarled, aiming his weapon at Jon's head. "Come quietly, or this is where you stay."

Jon grimaced, fighting against his body to keep on going. In his anger, the mercenary had not stepped back, was within a few tantalising metres of him now.

"Is this the part where you tell me all of your plans? How I will not be able to stop you?" Jon snarled back, spitting more blood from his mouth as he rose up. Another round of this and he would be out for the count.

Andersson shrugged away his impatience. "It doesn't matter now. This is not personal, Jon, this is just business. This time the money wins and the hero loses."

The Swede raised his rifle again, suddenly hearing movement behind him.

To the left of the mercenary, the monkey leapt from its branch to the next tree, keen to be away from all the commotion. For a moment only, it distracted Jon's captor.

"Not today," Jon spat.

Launching himself forward, he slammed into Andersson, feeling the rifle recoil as he slipped past the barrel and the weapon went off. With their breath exploding from their chests, both men crashed to the ground, the jungle spinning about them as they rolled and wrestled furiously for advantage.

With his strength waning, Jon quickly realised he was in trouble, as Andersson crashed his forearm into his face. Jon's nose snapped, and he was thrown aside by the force of the blow, allowing his opponent to rise to his knees. Both men scrambled up, the jungle silent about them as their ragged breaths drained away all sound. Flicking a sluggish look to where the rifle lay, Jon barely reacted as Andersson went for it. As the Swede swept the weapon up and tried to bring it to bear, Jon hammered a Roberto Cavalli into his wrist and watched in satisfaction as the rifle spun from his hand into a nearby bush.

Andersson roared as Jon followed up his kick with a furious fist to his injured shoulder, forcing him back. The mercenary lashed out with a wild, swinging arm that missed the mark and before he could recover, Galnia had landed another blow to the side of his head.

"I underestimated you," the Swede panted, grimacing. He slipped one hand slowly behind his back for the combat knife sheathed there.

"Everybody does," Galnia sighed.

Reaching underneath his body armour, Jon pulled out the pistol he had strapped there as Andersson pulled his knife free.

Their eyes met knowingly. Time slowed as the mercenary leapt forward.

Four gunshots broke the silence.

Rick Taylor sat with his back against a tree, no longer feeling the legs stretched out before him. There was little sun now, the shadows of the day lengthening and deepening ominously about him.

And it was cold now, so bloody cold.

Taylor coughed up more blood, pain seeping through the veil of morphine that masked his slow tab towards death, and he clamped a slickened hand over the soaked swab covering his neck wound.

No longer listening to the chatter on the comms, barely able to focus on each slow, rattling breath, Taylor tried to keep his lolling head still, sending a look towards the cage and the tiger.

She was awake now, had been for hours! Her wide, luminous eyes fixed accusingly on him, though she had not attempted to break free. It was as if, she too, had now accepted what was to follow.

Resisting the urge to shake his head, Taylor snorted. It was not how he had planned going out. If anything, he had seen himself in a huge penthouse, blowing his money from the mission on a night of whores, drugs and gambling. If he had chosen the way to go, it would have been drowning in a mountain of heroin and deep cleavage.

For once, Taylor thought about someone else other than himself, of the two wives he had never appreciated until he had lost them, and for once he chose to ignore Pap Wilkins advice to focus on the fight. Taylor shook his head sadly, despite the agony it caused him.

He had been far too young to marry the first time, and at eighteen, he was barely old enough to look after himself, let alone Mary. His mother had hoped that she would calm him down, that the young girl from Brighton with the university degree and the bright smile would keep him on the straight and narrow, and if the truth be told, she had – well, for at least six months.

It wasn't long before he was up to his old tricks again.

Three months after the birth of their second child, their second girl, Rick had been thrown out by his wife after the MPs had dragged him away one night, in a drunken rage and stupor. He had nearly been chucked out of the military then, too, but had somehow managed to stay in the forces. With Mary back in Brighton with the kids, he forgot about his failed marriage, of the years wasted, and threw himself back into his career and the beds of any women or prostitutes that would have him, or he could afford.

It turned out there were still quite a few women who liked a bad-boy, and he enjoyed himself over the next few years, being posted to Germany in 2009. After he came back from a tour in Afghanistan in 2011 it all went wrong, it went down the crapper when he fell in love with Katie. She was the one who should have calmed him down, she was the woman who every man in the regiment wanted – but he had ruined that, like he ruined everything else…

A shadow detached itself from the jungle, away to his right, down near to where the creek twisted away south through the gorge and from sight. As the figure came closer, Taylor broke into a chesty laugh, wincing as fire tore through his throat.

Jon Galnia limped cautiously close, his rifle trained

on him, and Taylor had to admire the balls on the man.

"You really are–" Taylor coughed, wheezing, "–the luckiest son of a bitch."

Seeing that he was no longer a threat, Jon hunkered down on aching haunches, throwing a look to the tiger, who watched on curiously.

"Like the cat, I think I have used all mine up," Jon muttered ruefully, as he tossed aside the man's forgotten weapon. Looking back, he held out a hand.

"Give me the keys."

Taylor nodded, too tired to fight. "In my right breast pocket." He fell silent as Galnia fished for his prize. When he had found it, the mercenary dragged up a breath. "Where are the others?"

Jon rose up, staring down at the dying man. There was blood everywhere and he was doomed to die this day.

"Your big friend waits for you," Jon hesitated, scowling. "The Moroccan? He will be back soon, I am sure."

Turning away, not seeing the anguish on Taylor's face, Jon approached the cage. The tiger watched his careful approach, a warning curl on her lips as she bared her fangs.

"This is becoming a habit, Tony," Jon soothed. He didn't have time to mess around, but he couldn't afford not to take care. His hand shook as the key rattled its way into the lock.

Turning the key, Jon opened the cage, keeping the door's bars between him and the big cat. For a time, she sniffed at the air, sensing, but unsure of her freedom. Slow seconds stretched into what felt like minutes as Jon slid his rifle from his shoulder into his left hand.

That would be typical, after all this trouble, if he had to kill the last tiger as he was trying to save it.

The tiger rose up to her full, magnificent height, almost up to Jon's chest, and padded cautiously from her captivity. Smelling blood, she swung her head to Taylor, fixing him with hungry eyes.

Time slowed, as the creek's melodic passing was lost to faltering hearts. As the big cat put one giant paw towards the mercenary, Jon rattled his rifle against the cage, breaking the moment.

"Go on now, go," Jon yelled, and the tiger stiffened to his command. Turning from her hunger, she leapt away into the jungle to the northeast, her orange flanks the last colour of a dying day as the thicket flicked in farewell.

Jon puffed out his cheeks, throwing a look at the mercenary. "I guess we are even, now."

Stalking back to Taylor, Jon knelt before him again. "Just let the tiger go. I am done – we are done, do you understand? I just want to get back home."

Taylor nodded, his head rolling dreamily on his shoulders. "Me too! There's a map in my pack, you'll be needing it more than me now." He raised a shaking arm, pointing down the creek towards the spot where Jon had tumbled down the gorge.

Finding what he wanted, Jon rose up, taking the man's phone with him as well. "What's the code?"

Taylor nearly choked on his laughter. "I-I'm not going to make it that easy for you. Go fuck yourself, Galnia."

Jon raised his rifle, then lowered it. He was a bastard, but he wasn't in the killing mood now, and the man had that look in his eyes, watching the past as his life flashed before him. Muttering in Italian, Jon fished through his own pack.

"Here, take this," Jon scowled, handing the dying man the last of his water and his phone back.

"If you have anyone you need to call..."

Taylor took them in his bloodied hands, his shock flaring in his eyes. Nodding his farewell, Jon turned.

Hurrying away to the south, he went in search of his stick.

CHAPTER TWENTY-ONE

The Greater Good

Narinda Singh checked her phone for the sixth time as she sat watching the morning stir to life outside the cafe. Whilst the new day moved on quickly, the clock had not, and as the allotted hour for her early meeting drew ever closer, each slow, agonising minute felt like days.

Distracting herself with her favourite Masala Chai, she flicked her attention to the newspaper on the table, her eyes narrowing as she read the daily batch of superlatives lauded upon the Prime Minister for his '*Humility*' and '*Benevolence*' to the nation. Even the President of India himself was praising Chandra Nehru, and scanning through the pages of dross, she found little mention, despite her previous day's efforts, to praise the First Secretary for his part in the story.

Narinda sipped at her tea, sighing. Already Aasim Rana was being brushed aside.

Customers were starting to file into the cafe now, wearing a mixture of the traditional Indian dress and the cancerous westernisation that was starting to sweep across the country. Suits, skirts, saris, blouses and jeans, a collage of the old and new, the bright warning of the direction the country was unwittingly taking. Already western shops were forcing local businesses off street corners and business parks; golden signs and expensive designer shops were stamping their heavy mark upon her beautiful city.

Looking at her phone, at the clothes she wore, Narinda suppressed a scowl. *Where did we lose our identity?* she wondered. *Where did I lose mine?*

She had been coming to the Oxford Bookstore *Cha Bar* in Connaught Place for several years now, and had become a regular there; so much so, that she had her own special seat by the window, a prime seat where she could watch the world outside, read a book or paper and escape her busy schedule for a time.

Resisting the urge to check the hour again, she stared out at the Barakhamba Road, across the hustle and bustle of the morning rush for work, towards the Fire Station. She had been there for some time already and, much to her relief, they had not been needed so far today.

Six years ago, when Narinda was filling her veins with coffee for the busy day ahead, the story that would change her life had happened right before her very eyes. Even now, she could recall the terrible crash outside the fire station, of the lives that were lost in the desperate attempt to avoid the sacred cow ambling across the lanes of traffic – of how she had been on hand to drag several survivors from the mangled wreckage of the car that had gone up in flames, so quickly, that even the fire crews could not reach them in time.

Narinda was always reminded of that fateful day, every time she came here. Staring at the old scars from the flames that had licked hungrily at her hands, she winced in remembrance, could still, even now, hear the screams of the two family members who had not been so fortunate.

Her first-hand account and the reports from bystanders, too shocked to react, had earned the then young reporter much press herself, dragging her through the ranks and into the higher echelons of the Indian Press in one terrible day. It had even won her two Ramnath Goenka awards that year.

Had she felt bad about her success following the misfortune of others? Despite the attention and the numerous articles that had been penned about her for many weeks to follow, had Narinda wished that she had been somewhere else on that fateful day?

Not for one second...

Putting down her teacup Narinda spied Samira Jethwani, as she crossed the road from behind the bus she had just arrived on. Forced to run the last few metres to safety, the First Secretary's aide hurried from view to enter the bookstore.

Licking her lips, Narinda tried to calm herself down. First and foremost, she had to remain focussed on the reason for their meeting, to actually listen to what the woman had to say before she tried to recruit her to her cause. It would be hard though, when all of her journalistic instinct told her that this could be the break she needed after all these years, after all the anonymous threats she had received, and all the hardships she had endured. But why was Samira suddenly so keen to meet when she had clearly imparted her dislike for her?

Try as she might, the journalist could not help but listen to the feeling in her gut.

This *was* the break she needed.

"Please, have a seat," Narinda smiled broadly, trying to settle Samira as the young woman looked around the cafe and flicked a nervous look to the world outside.

Offering her thanks, Miss Jethwani sat down and they shared the formalities of the morning weather as Narinda ordered a pot of tea for them both from the waitress.

Once the tea arrived and they were alone again,

Narinda sat forward, resting her folded hands on the table.

"I must admit to my surprise at hearing from you, Miss Jethwani," the journalist remarked, watching as Samira sipped at her tea and closed her eyes to better savour the excellent taste.

When she opened them again, they shone with worry, flicking to the road outside once more. "No more than I, Miss Singh," the aide admitted, when she glanced back.

"Please, just Narinda. We are friends here, nothing more."

Samira struggled to offer a smile, her makeup doing little to disguise the sleepless night she must have endured.

"So, as one friend to another, how can I help you, Samira?" the journalist asked, barely hearing her own words above her excited heart.

Dressed for work, Samira hid herself beneath a curtain of long, lustrous hair. "You once said to me if I needed to talk, you were here for me... I need to talk, but I fear for what I have to say."

Narinda licked her lips. Picking up her cup, she distracted her eagerness with a mouthful of tea. Her silence encouraged Samira to continue before she lost her nerve.

"If I tell you my troubles, they will become yours, and I worry for what that could mean for us both," Samira whispered and the journalist was forced to lean close to hear her words.

"I am used to trouble," Narinda replied quietly. "The shadows I search have offered me much concern, but know that I do not fear to tread there."

"You should do," Samira said. She panicked, nearly fleeing from her seat when a man stopped outside their window to check a text message on his phone. He looked up, spying his audience, and offered them a wide smile and a wave, before hurrying on his way.

"Please, relax," Narinda said, reaching to take Samira's shaking hands in her own. "You are amongst friends here, just take some tea first, find some breaths and then tell me your burdens."

Samira nodded her head, clutching the journalist's hands tightly. Drawing in some courage, she let her breath out slowly.

"Very well, Miss Singh," she said. "But I must warn you, what I am about to tell you will put us both in great danger."

With thirteen minutes to go before half time, Ahmed Fraja was on the edge of his seat, his hands clutching at the bowl of snacks he had not touched for the last ten minutes. An end-to-end game, much to the surprise of the commentators and pundits, Al Hala were giving a great show against the league leaders, Riffa SC, denied the lead only moments before by a shuddering crossbar.

Tucked away in his fifth-floor apartment, off road 1208, Ahmed could hear that all around him his neighbours were also watching the match, and he felt the pang of regret that they did not all come together to watch the game. The pace of life these days was forcing people into their own shells, away from their friends and the identity of a nation, founded upon comradeship and unity.

People just did not take the time anymore to be pleasant to one another, sometimes not even able to find a hello. Heads down, people channelled their lives through their phones, preferring to speak to virtual friends over the ones right before them.

The match was so loud on the TV in the apartment above him that Ahmed was tempted to turn his own down, but soon forgot about it as he perched on the edge of his chair to watch the corner that his favourite player Yakubu was about to take.

Ahmed's fortunes had changed recently, and for once, they had changed for the better. As soon as he received his money, as soon as the dust had settled and he was able to spend it without worry of suspicion, he would find himself someplace quiet, somewhere he didn't have to listen to the shouting kids next door, or the screaming wife below, never satisfied with her husband's wage or efforts around the house.

His bowl nearly flew across the room as the whole apartment block roared out, thinking the header had found the back of the net, but he clapped his hands to his head as he and several million people around the country realised that the score had remained 0-0.

In his excitement, Ahmed had not heard the knock at his door, and did not hear it again until his caller began to lose patience.

Scowling at the silhouette behind the frosted glass, he dragged himself away from the match to go and find out who in Allah's name would be calling during the biggest match of the season. The few friends he had were all working their shifts at the airport that evening, and Ahmed knew that he had been the lucky one this time.

Dragging open the door, he felt the full force of the heat outside and heard the blaring horns as drivers on the road below lost their patience under the fierce sun. Even at seven o'clock in the evening, the temperature caressed eighty degrees, and the slow, uneven fan on his ceiling did little to ease the discomfort.

"What do you want?" Ahmed barked in Arabic, swallowing any further words as he stared, wide-eyed, at the huge man stood before him. He was tall, so very tall, and dressed, even in this heat, in a dark western suit.

"Sorry to trouble you," the man apologised, removing his mirrored shades to fix the Bahraini with dark eyes. "It sounds like there is a game on, so I won't keep you long."

Ahmed swallowed. The man did not even attempt to talk to him in Arabic, and his accented English, scarred skin and clothes clearly showed that he was not a local. Despite the summer heat, Ahmed felt a chill sweep through his body and he did not even realise, despite the shouts of anger that rose throughout the tenement block, that his beloved team had just gone behind in the game.

"How can I help you?" Ahmed managed to ask. His throat was dry and his hands were shaking as he ran his left one over the sweat beading on his broad forehead.

"I come on behalf of our *mutual* friends," the man with the strange accent replied. He looked along the landing cautiously, then rubbed his gloved hands together. "It is probably best if we speak inside, where we cannot be heard."

Why was he wearing gloves in this heat?

Nodding his head, not sure he had a choice, Ahmed beckoned his guest inside and checked to see that nobody had seen the stranger arrive. If he was trying to blend in with the locals, he was not very good at it.

Shutting the door, he turned to his guest, fidgeting nervously as the man looked about his meagre apartment.

"Can I offer you some tea?" Ahmed enquired, as he flicked a look to the match and groaned. "It's always better, I find, to have a hot drink to cool you down in these conditions."

The man cocked his head to one side, then shook it gently. "No. Thank you, though." He looked about the apartment again. "Are you alone? What I have to say should not be for other ears."

"I live alone, these days," Ahmed stammered, wringing his hands together. "Since my wife, well, since she moved out–"

The huge man held up a gloved hand to silence his explanation. "Very good! I won't keep you long from your game."

Ahmed offered his guest a seat, but the man refused. "You speak of our mutual friends? I presume they are satisfied with my work?"

The man nodded. "They are, as should you be. You did your work diligently, and the Russians will pay you soon, very soon."

"I know not of whom you speak," the Bahraini said quietly. "I received the job through an intermediary; I was, as they have been, most careful in concealing our business *arrangement*."

"As well they might," the man agreed. He paused, the smile slipping from his face. "However, it is in all our interests that there can be no trail that leads others to your door, no evidence that would reveal who planted the device on the jet."

Before Ahmed could reply with his own assurances, the man took one lengthy step forward and grabbed him about the throat.

"It took me one day, a fistful of money and some gentle persuasion to gain access to the rota and security footage at the airport," the man hissed, pressing his mouth close to Ahmed's ear. "My small test, for very little money, revealed that on the night you sabotaged the jet there were five members of the ground crew logged in for work – the security footage, however, shows six working that night."

Ahmed baulked, his eyes white with fear. "I-I did not realise, I did not think–"

"No," the stranger growled, "You did not." He released his grip, allowing the Bahraini to find his breath and smooth down his ruffled soccer shirt. "Fortunately for you, I am a diligent man, far more so than our *friends* would have others believe. This is the kind of mistake that could have brought us all down, tied us to the sabotage which, I have to report, was a success and is the only reason why we are still talking."

The large man in the suit turned away and began heading for the door. If he heard Ahmed's sigh of relief, he chose to ignore it, and when his huge hand was on the handle, he paused, turning back.

"You should get that footage erased when you are in work tomorrow," Il Lupo suggested. Turning, he hauled the door open and stepped out into the evening heat.

Outside the apartment, Paolo leaned upon the railing, staring northeast across the glimmering city of Bahrain towards the airport on the island, Muharraq. A large jet was taking off from one of the runways, and the white and red plane's engines were lost to the din of the city below as it shimmered in the sky and banked towards the east across the Persian Gulf.

Putting his shades back on, Paolo whetted his lips and wished that he had accepted the man's offer for some tea. It was so hot here! Beneath his suit, his shirt was soaking, every pore weeping in protest at the intense dry heat. When he had stalked from the airport the morning before, irritated at the delay in getting his entry visa, Paolo had nearly turned around and took the next flight home.

Coming originally from Napoli, Paolo was used to the heat – but nothing like this. If it hadn't been for Maria's insistence, he would have let the dice lie where they had been cast.

The Italian shook his head as he fished into his breast pocket for his phone. Everyone had a price these days, it seemed, and nobody had the decency to hold out for a better offer anymore.

Through his contacts, contacts he had thought never to have to deal with again, Paolo had managed to easily gain access to the airport. After flashing some angry teeth and money around, he had tracked down Ahmed's colleagues – two of them who had been working on the ground the day Jon's jet had landed for refuelling. With little money, he had gained access to the security footage and flight logs, had seen for himself Jon's jet on the tarmac of the small, private runway.

Paolo sighed, massaging the building tension from the bridge of his nose. Ahmed's friends had sold him out for little more than the price of a few crates of beer...

As he flipped open his old phone, the Italian thought back to a time when he and Jon had robbed a liquor store near Staten Island Zoo, beating the owner near to death for a few bottles of cola and a packet of Oreos.

What price would he put on their friendship now?

Not mindful of the hour back home, Paolo listened as his call connected and started to ring. Several seconds later, he heard Maria's tired, yet rich voice. He suddenly felt a chill stir in the air.

"*What have you found out, Paolo?*" No formalities, no greeting, straight to the point, as always.

"The jet was sabotaged," Paolo said quietly. In the apartment, Ahmed had found his throat and was screaming at the television. "I cannot tell you yet by whom, but from what I have found out, Jon's message *was* accurate."

There was a long silence, before Maria responded. "*What's our next move?*"

Looking about him, Paolo rolled his tongue across the back of his teeth. "I am going to catch the next flight to Delhi, to see what I can find out there."

"*Be careful, Paolo*," Maria ordered him. "*If you can't find Jon, I need you back here, safely.*"

"I'll find him," Paolo growled. "I am going to fix this mess, I promise you, Maria."

She hung up without saying goodbye and Paolo shook his head sadly, his mind racing, his love for the woman, as always, lost on his lips.

"To Delhi, then," Il Lupo declared. He was only a few metres away from the apartment when he stopped, turning slowly.

Shaking his head again, Paolo walked back to the door and rapped hard upon the glass.

Ahmed appeared more quickly this time, peering out into the brightness with wide eyes.

"Salam! Just one more thing," Paolo promised, smiling. Grabbing the Bahraini by the throat, he clamped his other huge hand over Ahmed's mouth and forced him back inside his apartment.

Moments later, Ahmed cried out, his dying screams blending in with the anger across the city as his beloved team went 2-0 down in the game.

Samira Jethwani flinched in her seat as First Secretary Rana opened the door to his office and strode out purposefully. His eyes glittered with urgency as he looked to his aide.

Samira shook as she rose up hastily. She had only been at her desk for an hour, but every time he looked at her, she feared the truth of her betrayal flashed in her eyes.

"I am running late," Aasim Rana barked, as she passed him a manila folder. Snatching it from her hand, the First Secretary headed for the door as he forced it into his full briefcase. "After my meeting with the Minister of Health, I will take some lunch, before the interview with the Hindustan Times."

"Yes, First Secretary," Samira said, buzzing attentively at his side as he made to leave. "I will come and fetch you fifteen minutes before the interview. Will you require anything else, beforehand?"

Aasim paused in the doorway, then turned, a weary smile stealing across his face. "I can manage my day from here, thank you. Use this time to catch up on all your paperwork, and then, when you feel like it, you can go home for the day."

"Why, thank you, sir," Samira replied, returning his smile.

"You have been a great help to me," Aasim stated. Turning, he hurried away down the hallway, leaving his aide to watch after him.

Wincing, Samira closed the door and stumbled back to her desk. For the next hour, she toiled through her mounting workload, her mind wandering, her diligence and efficiency compromised by her meeting with Narinda Singh.

They had shared a long, guarded conversation,

Samira's revelations about the supposed plane crash and the attempt to hide it from the Americans, filling the journalist's eyes with hunger and desire. If she had expected, had hoped that Narinda would not want anything to do with the information, she was sorely mistaken.

Following their meeting, Samira could not recall getting to work, or the bus journey that had taken her there. She had stared out the window the entire journey, the city flashing by like a distant dream.

Narinda Singh had praised her for her bravery, the courage she had shown to bring her the information. Throughout history, the journalist had told her, it was selfless acts like her own that had changed the course of what was written down for those yet to be born.

Unsure of what else she could offer, Narinda had taken command of proceedings. The Americans, she surmised, must know about the jet, or at least suspect it was missing. Why else would they require such a meeting, and the information Samira had delivered to the embassy? Before she could get lost down a thousand different corridors of possibilities, Narinda had reined in her composure, thinking in black and white, like the reports in the newspapers.

'You must get a copy of the information you gave to Thomas Miller, for me' the journalist had said, her dark eyes wide with worry, but filled with hungry excitement. *'But, most importantly, you must find the First Secretary's phone, the one he uses to contact this Mister Hamid. If we have that, we can give it to the Americans, to prove the worth of the treachery you overheard. You are not alone in this anymore, Samira. I have my contacts also, and I will look into this mysterious man, Hamid, who has such free rein to come and do as he*

pleases. Together, you and I, we will find the truth, hidden beneath their lies.'

Shuddering, Samira returned to the present, staring towards Aasim Rana's office. The door was closed, daring her to continue down her path of betrayal.

It all still sounded so ridiculous, that a phone would be able to prove anything. If she gave Narinda what she wanted, if she took it to the Americans to expose what was going on, that Aasim Rana, no doubt at Prime Minister Nehru's behest, was trying to hide something terrible, they both would be committing treason – handing over restricted documents to a foreign power.

Was she prepared to dishonour herself and her family for a higher purpose?

As she stumbled over to the door, Samira knew that time was running out for them. If Aasim Rana was to be saved from his own fate, she had to act now, no matter the cost to her own safety.

As Samira reached a shaking hand out for the door handle, she sensed that now she had told Narinda Singh, she no longer even had a choice.

CHAPTER TWENTY-TWO

"This'll be the Day..."

Hassan Raz was sweating, despite the early hour. It was going to be another hot day, he could tell. Massaging the ache in the pit of his back, he rolled the cramp from his shoulders and neck and stepped away from the shallow grave, bowing his head in respectful prayer.

The previous night was like a distant dream now, and the Moroccan had managed to find a little sleep to keep himself going. Upon returning to Taylor, he had found him slipping into a coma, and before the Englishman had died, he had been able to tell him that Galnia had freed the tiger again, and was trying to make his way back home.

Distraught and angered beyond control, Hassan had not even noticed that Taylor had died, had passed on to a better place without a hand to guide him on his way. When he realised, the Moroccan's emotions overcame him, and switching off his radio he collapsed to the ground, staring at the empty cage.

It was over...

Hassan finally found Parker and buried him first, then went to find Andersson's body, laying him to rest where he had fallen. Too drained to bury a third friend that night, Hassan stumbled back through the darkness and collapsed beside the cage into the arms of his exhaustion. He slept, barely, and woke in the early hours before dawn, managing to eat some food, before setting about gathering up the remote cameras, trying to remove any trace of the fact that they were ever even there.

But what did it matter now? Hassan stepped out into the early morning light. He had no idea what the hour was, did not really care. Moving over to the creek, he washed his bloodied, earth-stained hands in the cool, crisp water, and rose up again, staring up at the blue sky.

Sighing, he tracked the dark shapes of some birds for a moment, before switching on his radio.

Almost immediately, Brooks' voice cut through the static, and he sounded like he was ready to explode.

"*Alpha, this is Eagle, do you copy me, over?*"

Sighing, Hassan swallowed his thoughts before answering. "Eagle, this is Alpha, over."

It took a few seconds for a response.

"*Where the fuck have you all been?*" Brooks was beyond simple anger now. His voice was stretched thinly across his nerves.

Hassan looked to where he had buried Taylor, then flicked his gaze back to the empty cage.

"Sam, Mike and Rick are dead. Galnia... escaped," he said, swallowing down his sadness.

There was silence, and Hassan could only imagine what Brooks was doing. After a long, uncomfortable moment which the Moroccan was too tired to fill, the Kiwi spoke, his voice thick with emotion.

"*Is the site secure, over?*"

Hassan nodded to himself. "Secure, over. I buried them in different locations, in unmarked graves..."

"*Status report?*"

"She is gone," Hassan said, wincing.

Once his ear had died down from all the cursing and cussing, the Moroccan stepped into the silence. "Galnia is probably making his way back to the crash site. I am going after him."

"*You have six hours,*" Brooks snarled in his ear. "*We will finish up here and come get you.*"

"Received," Hassan replied, dutifully.

"*Oh, and Raz,*" Brooks warned. "*Maintain radio contact this time.*"

The Moroccan licked his dry lips, shaking his head. Brooks was an idiot, and it seemed to him that the idiots were the ones always in charge. When they were out of the country, safely away from this, he would not have anything else to do with him.

After this fiasco, they would never get the chance to work together again, anyhow.

Stalking back to his belongings, Hassan picked up his gear and weapons. He dealt a last look through the trees towards the spot where he had buried Taylor and shook his head. Drawing in a breath, the Moroccan turned away.

Before he retired, there was one last thing he had to do.

Brooks walked away from Lisa before she could ask what had happened. The look on his face, the anger in his voice told her all she needed to know, and she hugged herself, watching his taut back as he strode to the shore to watch the wildlife on the lake's grey waters.

It had been a trying night, one filled with uncertainty and apprehension. Brooks had worked tirelessly to fix the helicopter, the darkness lit up by his lamps as he distracted his worry.

By the time the sun had started to rise in the east, Lisa had packed away most of the camp, stopping by their prisoners only the once with food, water and silence in response to their frightened questions.

Lisa grimaced. Today would not be a good day for anyone, no matter the outcome.

Eventually, Sam came back to her, his face clouded with their failure.

"Galnia freed the tiger and she is gone. It's over, Lisa," he said, barely able to hide his worry. "Raz is tracking Galnia now. I have given him six hours, then we are out of this shit-hole."

Lisa frowned, too confused to think. "But? But why bother with Galnia? We could still capture the tiger. Taylor is one of the best–"

Brooks swept up a silencing hand. "It's over, Lees. Raz is the only one left, t-the others are gone."

The Kiwi watched as Lisa stepped back in shocked silence. He reached for her then, but she pulled away, her eyes full of hurt and confusion.

"I-I don't understand," she managed.

"Neither do I," Brooks sighed, shaking his head. "We have to focus now. We have to tidy up things here and call it in. The Indians will be furious, and they will be here this evening – we had best be away before then."

Lisa fought for breath, hearing the edge to his words. Her mind raced, her heart tightened in grief and she could not find anything to say.

Their eyes met briefly and she knew exactly what that meant. She shook her head, her eyes pleadingly bright.

Brooks nodded his head firmly. "Once we are ready, I will deal with them. For now, we prep for extraction. When we get back, the first round is on me."

Brooks moved away for some privacy and as she saw him reach for his sat phone, she felt her skin crawl. *Forget the Indians*, they would have other chances to take the tiger, and there would be other unscrupulous billionaires hungry to claim her worth for whatever dark purpose. It was *their* employer who needed to be feared, who would be furious, beyond fury. There would be no coming back from this.

As Lisa heard Brooks start to report in, she closed her eyes, gathered up her tattered composure and went to carry out his orders. As she stumbled into her tent, Lisa thought, above everything else swirling about in her mind, that she would have loved, just once, to have seen a tiger in the wild.

Sara Gonzales was scared now. As the day slipped away for them, there was far too much going on outside their canvas cell to ease her concern. A long morning lengthened slowly into the afternoon, and as the hours crawled away from them, both survivors realised that their luck was continuing to elude them. There had been no opportunity to escape, no momentary lapse in concentration from their captors to give them a fighting chance, at the very least, for survival.

Straining to hear raised voices, both she and Robert had shared worried looks, though Sara could see the flash of hope in the pilot's face, as they heard Jon Galnia's name mentioned more than once.

With scant food and little water that day, both were now in need of the bathroom and further sustenance to fuel their hopes. As each hour slipped by, the sense of impending doom weighed down heavily upon them.

"It has gone very quiet out there," Robert whispered, breaking a lengthy silence. There wasn't much to say anymore. Unless a chance or rescue came to them, there was little hope left, it seemed...

Sara tugged at her raw wrists, firing the pilot an angry look. "That's not helping, Robert."

The tall pilot, his face still puffed up from bruises and raw with burns, offered her a wan smile.

"We have to hold on to hope, Sara," he responded. "We are not down yet. We must believe there will be a chance, and when it comes, we have to be alert enough to spot it."

He was right, she knew it, but it was pretty hard to remain positive when her anger had given way to despair. She had read a book once, where someone had said something about how fate was for people with no hope, destiny was for the ones who did something about it.

It sounded great on the page, but when you are faced with the reality of it...

The purposeful approach of heavy boots and the shadows stretching towards the tent dragged Sara from her thoughts. Sharing a startled look with Robert, they turned their wide eyes and hammering hearts towards the daylight streaming in through the opening.

The tall man strode through it first, a pistol in his right hand. He fixed them with an unreadable expression, stepping aside to allow the woman, Lisa, into the tent.

Without a word, barely able to meet their gazes, Lisa stumbled over to Robert first, the key to his freedom in one hand. With shaking hands, she unlocked the restraints on the pilot's wrists, and then turned, tossing a second key to her other prisoner.

"What are you going to do to us?" Sara demanded, her voice thick and dry as she struggled to unlock her handcuffs.

"Up!" the tall man growled, flicking his pistol meaningfully. When the Mexican refused to rise, her captor started towards her, his faced pinched by anger.

"He said *up*," Lisa snapped, dragging Sara roughly up

by her tangled hair. As they struggled against each other, Robert tensed to attack, then stepped back as the big Australian, Kiwi, whoever he was, turned his pistol on him.

Drawing her pistol with her free hand, Lisa jabbed it into Sara's side. "Please, just come with us."

Glancing down at the warning pressed into her ribs, Sara held the woman's eyes for a moment, before looking away from the source of her disgust.

"How can you people live with yourselves?" she snarled.

"Out, now," Brooks growled, waving his pistol towards the day outside.

Narinda Singh put the phone down and sat back in her chair, her hand shaking. Closing her eyes, she tried to clear her mind, attempted to focus on anything that wasn't related to intrigue, her hunger for justice and the danger she was placing herself in.

The din of the newsroom outside did little to distract her, and alone in her office, shut away from it all, she had never felt more vulnerable. Opening her eyes, she looked at the picture on her desk of the man she was going to marry in the spring, Anjay. They had met at Delhi University, had fallen in love instantly, and much to their joy, both families had approved of their agreeable match. Their careers, however, had delayed the marriage and pulled them apart; Anjay was currently halfway through a year's placement at the steel works his company Tata owned in the United Kingdom. They had spoken via the internet as often as possible, but in the last few days, she had been too busy, placating him with promises and kisses in her text messages.

There was so much to do, so much to fill her time, that she had not, until that phone call, realised how much she missed him, how much she wanted to confide in him and draw upon his strength. He would tell her, of course, that she had done enough, had set the ball of justice in motion and should walk away before it was too late and she was crushed by it. If Narinda told him what was happening now, her fiancée would be on the next flight home.

It was a tempting thought.

Narinda had heard from Samira, earlier that morning. The First Secretary's aide had managed to obtain copies of the files she had handed over to Thomas Miller, and, much more to the aide's shame, she had found the hidden phone.

Narinda picked up her pen and scribbled a note down on her pad, then circled it several times.

Cha Bar, 7pm.

Sighing, the journalist sipped her coffee. She had just managed to speak to Thomas Miller in person, and revealed her desire to share sensitive information with him, regarding the missing jet. Clearly not public knowledge, it had been more than enough to get him to clear his diary for a meeting with her the next day. Ignoring his demands for immediate satisfaction, and the warning that she was playing with peoples' lives, Narinda had told him only that she would have all the information he wanted, that evening. They were scheduled to meet at the American Embassy at 8am, the next morning.

She looked up as her editor tapped on her window. Mister Shukla bobbed his head meaningfully and waved sharply for her to follow him to his office. Sighing, Narinda nodded, staring about her own office. It was in disarray at the moment. She had lost focus on her workload, fixated on her desire to pursue the Prime Minister, and if she wasn't careful, she would lose her privacy as well.

Rising from her chair, Narinda went to face the wrath of her editor, consoled by the fact that in the coming days, if Samira's courage and fortune held, she would have a story for him that would win them all global recognition.

The afternoon sunlight cut through the canopy overhead like a golden blade, piercing the shadows and bringing several striking butterflies out to dance with one another. Had it not been for the fact they were being marched through the jungle towards their deaths, Robert Williams would have spent many minutes watching the beautiful display, marvelling at the miracle that was nature's craft.

Sweat dripped from his weary body, rivulets of heat that cooled on the fear sweeping through him. He had been so near to retirement, so close to keeping his promises to Janine that they would finally buy that Aston Martin and go travelling in the Highlands; their cares behind them and a picnic basket in the boot, as they had always promised each other they would, since University.

Robert could have started to rue the day he had said yes to Jon Galnia – but he did not. His wife, his children, their unborn grandchildren were set up for the rest of their lives now because of it, and he should not begrudge them that.

A tear ran down his battered face, mingling with his sweat. It would have been lovely to have been called *bampy*. He would have loved that...

Sara stumbled as her injured leg gave way, and he snatched out a hand to stop her from falling. The lovely woman at his side, still lovely, despite what had happened to her, smiled in thanks, and he saw a flash of the woman that was, fading back away behind a wall of despair.

"Keep moving," the man behind them growled, and not bothering to look back, Sara reached out a shaking hand, taking the pilot's left in her own.

Holding on to each other's comfort tightly, they continued up the rising ground into the streaming sun.

They travelled for some time, until the boots behind them stopped.

"That's far enough," the man commanded, bringing his prisoners to a halt on abrupt ankles, stiffened by terror. "Turn around."

Sara reached out to take Robert's hand again. They were in a small, quiet clearing, near to the largest tree she had ever seen, and they were alone, despite the sunshine. In the silence, even Mother Nature had deserted them now, it seemed.

She could not breathe, and her heart leapt in her breast as she searched the pilot's kind, yet ruined face. He held her gaze with gentle eyes, smiling sadly.

"It's okay," he said, though she read the words on his lips, did not hear them for the veins exploding in her head.

"I said *turn around*," the man snapped, his patience fraying with each passing second.

"If you are going to shoot us, it will have to be in the back," Sara said defiantly.

Brooks muttered under his breath, throwing a

sidelong glance at Lisa. She was watching them with eyes brimming with sadness. It still amazed him that she had signed up for this, and now, with her beside him, he wished that she had not.

Robert flinched as he heard the ominous click of a weapon behind him. Fighting for breath, he slowly turned around, pulling Sara with him to face their executioner.

He stood before them, a pistol in hand, Lisa a pace or two behind. Scowling, he raised his other hand, to show them a mobile phone.

"Whose is this?" he demanded.

Sara raised an arm she could not feel.

Shaking his head, the large man strode forward, handing Sara's hope back to her. "You have one call, in English," he hissed, "but you are only survivors, nothing more, do you understand? This never happened."

Sara nodded her head, her eyes blinking brightly. She dealt Robert an incredulous look, before dragging a ruined nail over the screen to unlock the phone.

The man grabbed her wrist momentarily with a gloved hand. "You never speak of us, you never met us. If anything is ever said, your families, your friends, they will all die. You do not mess with these people, is that clear?"

Sara nodded her understanding. Her heart was racing as she lifted the phone to her ear. Time seemed to slow as she looked to Robert, then back again to her captors. They had not lowered their weapons and were watching her intently.

The call was connecting and the line clicked as a voice she never thought she would ever hear again said hello in her ear.

"Mama," Sara sobbed, tears streaking down

blackened cheeks. "It's me, Sara. I don't have much time, so listen – I am fine, I really am – no, I didn't get your card. No, Mama, just listen..."

Brooks watched on, struggling with his emotions as the stewardess recounted their crash, that she had been knocked unconscious, and only now, able to use her phone. His mind was racing, his every thought focussed on the fact that each second that crawled by dragged them ever closer to a life behind bars, or worse. He could sense Lisa at his side, but dared not look at her. She had thought he was going to kill them, but once again, like everybody else, she had mistaken him.

Everything had gone to shit, so why take these poor bastards down with them? He was a selfish bastard, but he wasn't *that* much of a bastard.

He flicked his weapon urgently for Sara to finish the call and when she did, he strode forward, taking the phone from her hands.

"Get away and hide," Brooks warned them, holding both their startled gazes. He dropped the mobile phone to the ground and stamped the life from it with an angry boot. "They are coming, and you don't want to be here when they arrive."

Robert looked to Sara, then back to his captors. He could not believe what was happening.

"Th-thank you," he managed to say, his eyes wide with disbelief. Reaching out, Robert grabbed Sara by the hand and pulled her away through the jungle before they changed their minds.

"Good luck," Brooks called after them, and found he actually meant it.

Lisa Myers smiled as Brooks looked for her, and she put a hand on his shoulder. "That was a decent thing to do, Sam."

The tall Kiwi shrugged his indifference. "Come on, let's get back to the camp and get the hell out of here."

As he stalked away through the jungle, Lisa looked back through the trees, catching a glimpse of the survivors as they picked their way northwest up an incline towards safety.

"Safe journey," she whispered. Turning away, resisting the urge to go with them, Lisa followed Brooks back to the camp.

She would not see them again.

CHAPTER TWENTY-THREE

All Eventualities

Even with a map, Jon had somehow still managed to get lost. Not your typical Boy Scout growing up, and too busy causing chaos, Jon had never taken the time to learn orienteering, preferring the concrete pathways of Philadelphia as his playground. With the onset of technology and having everything on-demand, he, like everyone else in the world it seemed, was now happy to be told where to go and how to get there.

Without a phone and only his instincts to guide him, Galnia Junior had stumbled about the jungle the previous night with his reclaimed trusty stick in hand, hopefully heading in the right direction. Finding some shelter underneath a tree, but steering clear of any clefts in the rocky higher ground, Jon shared a cold, sleepless night with an owl, some insects and thankfully no spiders.

With limbs cramping and his mood darkening, Jon watched the dawn, using the coming day as his compass. With only a few early birds for company, he had set off again after a leak, his stolen food supply dwindling and his spirits and temper as low as the rising sun.

Jon hesitated on the trail, wiping the sweat from his brow as he spied the wild pigs snuffling happily through the brush ahead of him. There were seven of them, two large parents and their playful offspring. Looking from the stick in his left hand to the pistol stuffed into his belt, Jon decided he should give them a wide berth, despite the mouth-watering prospect of some roast pork, boar, whatever you wanted to call it.

He was thirsty now, having lost the morning behind him, though the terrain was becoming a little familiar, he hoped. One tree, one plant, one family of monkeys all looked the same after a while, however, and his head was spinning, despite his attempts at the leaf-drinking trick again.

Jon had only let the dying man have the water so that the Moroccan would have a distraction, someone to save and focus on – but in the rising heat, he wished that he had not. Through the long night, he had waited to be found, expected it, but nobody came, nowhere even close.

Heading higher up the rough, choking ground, Jon kept one eye on the jungle and the other warily on his route. The imminent danger from his pursuers may have abated, but the jungle still offered a hundred excuses for him to end his miserable existence. Gripping his stick and checking the map again, Jon promised himself that today would not be that day as he made his way to where he thought the jet had crashed.

He wasn't sure how long and far he had travelled, but finally Jon began to sense he was in the right area. As the ground became more even and the daylight found its mark on the jungle floor, he began to detect the unnatural smell in the air. Shielding his eyes, Jon scanned his surroundings, starting to pick out the scar that creased the land. As he hurried on, the damage his jet had caused became evident; blackened, charred leaves, the scattered remnants of fuselage and wing, the black spectre of the explosion that still, even three days later, hung in the air as testament to what had happened.

Stepping over a tangled, twisted piece of what might have once been the undercarriage; Jon covered his mouth and nose with a hand to fight off the kerosene that clogged his airways. Blinking his eyes clear of smoke, off to the south he could see faint tongues of fire, dancing lazily between the trees. Navigating a safe path, Jon was led on by the destruction of the crash, picking his way through mangled jet and blackened ground, burnt brush and uprooted trees. After a while, Jon could go no further, but from a safe distance he could see the remains of his million-dollar jet, and it amazed him that anyone had survived.

Jon blessed himself.

With his eyes stinging, Jon pulled out the map again, tracing what he thought was his route from where Rashim had lived to where the jet had crashed. Apparently, they had crashed in a Wildlife Reserve, a protected site called *Bandhavgarh National Park*; a vast place that, since the Feline Flu epidemic, would have been off-limits to everyone except the experts... and not forgetting the mercenaries, of course. There was an ancient fort, ruined temples and plenty of other places, most within walking distance, it transpired, that he could have sheltered in.

Sighing, Jon fished the folded photo from his shirt pocket and unfurled it, his heart racing as he briefly looked at the photo of his wife and son, the photo he had reclaimed from the big mercenary – the photo he had given to Rashim...

Chewing the grief from his dry lips, Jon followed the creek from its source on the map, high up in the hills, down to where it flowed out into a huge lake. He tapped the lake thoughtfully.

There was clear ground there, somewhere they could

have landed the helicopter, somewhere they might have taken Robert and Sara.

If you are still alive, Jon thought. He cleared his throat of any guilt and spat away the bad taste in his mouth. Either way, that was where he was headed. If they were there, he would rescue them, if not, well, then at least he would find some water.

As he went to put the map back in his pack, a sharp pain flared in his left hand as something struck him. Cursing, Jon flinched, leaping back as he slapped away the insect he had not heard.

Blinking in confusion, Jon stared down at the feathered dart embedded deep in the skin just between the thumb and forefinger. As he looked up and spun around, his eyes wide with realisation, he caught a glimpse of a figure, crouched on one knee at the side of a blackened dead tree. Time slowed as Jon's vision began to blur, it crawled as he slipped the rifle from his shoulder, and it almost stopped altogether as he tried to raise it. Another dart sprang from the end of a glinting rifle, leaping through the smoky air towards him.

As Jon tried to dodge, the dart took him in the left arm, just below the elbow, and as he squeezed off a few forlorn rounds towards his ambusher, he could already feel the tranquilisers seething through his veins.

"Ah, fu–" he slurred.

Before he could finish, the ground reached up and pulled him into its dark embrace.

Thanking Allah, Hassan Raz rose up. Shouldering his rifle, he walked over to Galnia as he twitched and thrashed about on the ground. Reaching the man who had ruined everything for them, the Moroccan put all his anger into the kick he drove into the man's ribs, and roared in satisfaction as he felt them crumple under his boot.

His hand shook as he towered over the comatose Jon Galnia and pulled the sidearm from its holster. Kicking the man onto his back, Hassan spat on the Italian-American's face and trained his pistol on him. Every inch of his flesh screamed at him for retribution, and for just a moment, he half-squeezed the trigger.

Holding back his anger, Hassan put the safety on and returned the weapon to its holster. Muttering a curse in his native tongue, he spoke English into his comm.

"Eagle, this is Alpha, over," he hissed. "I have Galnia, repeat, I have him."

Moments later, any jubilation was stolen from him as Brooks' maniacal laughter rang in his ear. "*You're an hour too late... bollocks, bollocks!*" There was a lengthy pause as the Kiwi attempted, and failed, to regain his composure. "*Sit tight for extraction, we'll come and get you.*"

Hassan shook his head, uncaring now, as he gave Brooks his location. Kneeling down by his prisoner, he gripped Jon's face in one hand, turning it to both sides to examine the man that had caused them so much trouble and had cost them so much money.

"My turn," Hassan snarled. "I won't be as quick with you as I was with your friend."

Samira Jethwani had stayed at her desk for most of the afternoon, chained to her work by her guilt and trapped by legs that would not allow her to escape. By the time her hunger and fear had wrested control of her thoughts, she was unknowingly late into her shift and far too deep under her pile of work.

Fortunately for her nerves, Aasim Rana did not return to his office again that day, stolen away, blessedly, by others far more deserving of his attention and favour. Rather perversely, however, it would have been better to have him there, as his absence left Samira alone to wallow in her treachery and cling on to her fraying composure.

The *185* bus rocked furiously as the driver crashed through a pothole, jolting the aide from her thoughts and bringing her back to the present. Yawning, Samira covered her mouth politely, so as not to start a wave of weariness with her fellow workers, all lost quietly to the efforts of their day. The city slipped by as her breath clouded the dirty window and Samira caught a glimpse of the Janpath Market, the food she so desperately needed slipping away from her. Light-headed now, after leaving the Secretariat, she had wandered down to India Gate and the Canopy. Sitting in the shade, she had stared at the empty platform and pictured the day when Mahatma Gandhi would watch over his people again.

Buying some water and a chocolate bar to keep her going from the cheery vendor nearby, Samira had sat for a long while, clutching her thoughts and her work bag close to her breast.

Her heart stirred in warning, as Samira knew she would soon be back at the Oxford Bookstore, and that Narinda Singh would be waiting for her again.

The First Secretary's aide had drafted a copy of her resignation before she left work that day, stating her lame excuses and reasons as to why she would wish to give up such a coveted position so early into her role. Samira had saved the letter to her desktop under a spurious file name, waiting for the day she would use it.

If Aasim Rana found out what she had done, how she had betrayed him, she would have no need of it.

On the phone, earlier that day, the journalist had cautioned her of such a move – if the First Secretary's phone hinted at his involvement in what was being covered up, he would suspect her betrayal immediately if she resigned. It was better, Narinda had cautioned, for her to remain in plain sight, so as not to draw attention her way.

Swallowing the lump of worry in her throat, Samira clutched at her bag, keenly aware of the phone and the manila folder within.

What am I doing? Samira thought, fighting back her tears.

You are doing your duty, her father's voice whispered in her mind.

Samira stifled a sob, as the memory of her father's kind voice faded away. Shuddering, she stared out of the window, watching as the choked streets and heavy traffic streamed by.

She chuckled, suddenly, ignoring the strange looks that came her way as she thought of something her father had once said to her, when she stated her determination to learn to drive.

"*There are three things you need if you wish to drive in India,*" he had chuckled. "*A good horn, good brakes – and good luck.*"

Samira wiped away her brimming tears, a deep breath misting the filthy glass.

She needed the latter now, more than ever...

The *185* screeched in protest as it pulled up at the stop across the busy road from the Oxford Bookstore. The young man beside Samira kindly vacated his seat as she rose unsteadily and offered him her thanks. As she walked on heels that felt like lead beneath her feet, Samira thanked the driver as he patiently waited for her to alight.

It was still bright, a hazy sky overhead cooling the anger of the day now. As Samira walked along the pavement to the rear of the bus, it pulled away in a cloud of protest, and as she went to step off the kerb to brave the traffic, a man crashed heavily into her.

"Oh!" Samira gasped, as the impact rippled through her body and stole away her breath.

"My apologies," the man offered, panting. He hurried away without a look towards her, stuffing his hands back into his pockets.

He must have been trying to avoid getting run down as he crossed the Barakhamba, Samira thought, and it wasn't until she turned to make the attempt herself that she registered the dull pain in her breast, and noticed the red bloom that was staining her blouse.

Narinda Singh watched the bus arrive from her favourite seat and pressed record on the Dictaphone, hiding it away in her hand bag. When she looked up, she saw Miss Jethwani for the first time that evening, as a man accidently crashed into her; thought nothing of it as he hurried away, until the aide staggered several paces forward, out into the busy road and sent a terrified, imploring look towards where she was sat.

As Samira dropped to her knees, one hand clutching at her bloodied breast, the other holding onto her work satchel, a car slammed into her with a screaming crunch that threw the young woman into the air with such force that she landed dozens of metres away.

Panicked screams began to rise up from startled bystanders, and several patrons inside the Cha Bar leapt up from their chairs into the arms of their shock.

Narinda cried out silently, her heart pounding, her skin stiffening as she rose up. Grabbing her belongings, she knocked over her drink and ran from the bookstore without paying. Standing on the pavement outside, she watched in horror as people rushed to offer the help that would not be needed, weaving amongst the traffic that had come to a shocked halt.

They killed her! A thousand conspiracies flooded Narinda's mind, and she could barely see Samira amongst those gathered close by. Her legs and neck were twisted unnaturally at grotesque angles, and her bright eyes were wide and unseeing, staring towards her through a matted tangle of hair and blood.

Narinda looked around helplessly, unable to comprehend what had happened, but knowing she had just been sent a telling warning. All about her, the road was in turmoil as some people stood silently, gripped by their shock, and others rushed to the scene – all, that was, except the man across the road from her, who stood near to the entrance of the fire station. He was not watching the crowd gathering around the dead woman, he watched on quietly, his dark eyes intently fixed upon the journalist.

The man smiled, shaking his head in disappointment.

As Narinda fled from the scene down a side road, her hopes scattered behind her as the papers from Samira's bag fluttered lazily about in the air and were carried away by a mournful breeze.

The two helicopters kept low as they thundered over the Satpura Range and circled the peak known to the locals as Vulture Point. In close formation, they slowly began to cross the huge lake towards the clear shores to the west, and from his seat in the back of the second steel bird, Mister Hamid watched his surroundings with a calm sense of awe and rising anticipation.

The sun was setting now, blushing its wistful farewell to a most telling day, and he knew, though his work was not yet done, that the Prime Minister would be extremely satisfied with the outcome.

In his left hand, his phone vibrated and the screen flared to life. Licking his lips and glad that he still had signal, the Kashmiri answered the unknown call.

"*It is done*," the voice reported. The line went dead.

Hamid sunk back in his chair, a thin smile slipping across his dark features. Closing his eyes, he let out a long, slow sigh.

He had liked the girl, he really had, but she had overheard too much, had discovered a courage that had proven far too bold to ignore. With the resources at his disposal, long before she had begun to suspect anything, Hamid had made sure her phones were tapped and that her computers and social media were being monitored.

'*A careless eye sees nothing*,' his father had said to him, many years before, '*a cautious eye sees all.*'

That piece of advice, offered to him as a parting warning from a dying father to an angry young son, had served him well on his path to success and retribution, and it continued to be the mantra he lived by, even now.

Hamid was well aware that there could be no oversights with what they were trying to achieve, no loose stones that would undermine the foundations they were laying for the future. As Aasim's aide's seemingly inane existence began to turn towards intrigue and treachery, Hamid knew that he would be forced to take action again.

As soon as she began to speak to the journalist, Samira Jethwani had become too much of a problem to ignore.

Shaking his head sadly, Hamid turned his attention out of the window and opened his eyes. The far shore and clear ground loomed close now, and he could feel the pilot bringing the helicopter to a slow stop.

Hamid had worked for Chandra Nehru for many years, had done more dark deeds than he could care to recall, but here, today, he knew it had all been worth it. His employer's rise to power had been carefully orchestrated over many decades, and although the eye of suspicion was never far from his shoulder, Chandra Nehru had been able to use his money, his power, his friends and their influence to shield him from the law courts. After today, he would have enough money to buy the law courts.

When the call had come through that *they* had finished their mission in the reserve and had left the country, Hamid and his men had taken off from their holding location – a small, secluded airstrip near Bhopal – to head to Bandhavgarh and clean up the site in preparation of their announcement to the Americans that they had discovered the crashed jet.

A restricted National Park offered the perfect excuse for the delay, a delay that was testing the strength of the bonds that tied the two countries together. Had the seat of power in the U.S. not changed recently, Hamid suspected that the pressure coming from Washington would have been too loud, too vociferous to ignore.

The reserve was still inhabited, but any who knew of

the tiger's survival had been paid off, or silenced. The man who had initially discovered evidence that a tiger had survived the Feline Flu had been killed, buried beneath the fresh tracks he had discovered.

The worth of such a beast was immeasurable, and the billions of American Dollars that had been offered to be allowed to capture it had been more than enough to allow the mercenaries onto India's sovereign soil. A tiger that had survived such a terrible epidemic could offer all kinds of medical breakthroughs... if that was why their benefactor wanted it. Whatever the reason for its capture, the prospect of and permission to capture the tiger had already deeply lined the pockets of Chandra Nehru's ambitions.

Once confirmation was received that the buyer was satisfied, they would receive four times the sum already given.

"There is a cage on the shore," the pilot reported, drawing Hamid's thoughts and attention out of the right window.

Frowning, the Kashmiri nodded. Waving for the man to land, he waited patiently as the pilot set the helicopter gently down upon the shore.

The doors were thrown open into a roaring storm as the team of armed soldiers disembarked. Throwing off his own restraints, Mister Hamid jumped from the helicopter, his boots sinking into the sandy shore, the rotors thundering above his head. Fifty yards away, the lead helicopter had also set down, and its passengers were spilling out into the fading day.

Head low, Hamid joined his men, spreading out warily as they moved towards the cage, weapons raised. Hamid drew his Glock, flicking off the safety as he followed the soldiers. As they neared, he felt his skin prickle with caution.

With the foreigners gone, taking evidence of their presence, camp and precious cargo with them, why would they leave a cage behind?

The soldiers came to a halt, stepping aside for Hamid as he joined them before the cage. Hamid met the confused glances of the two men nearest to him. There was an unconscious man in the cage, a badly battered and beaten man, who was chained to the bars at the rear of his steel cell.

Hamid blinked in surprise as he stepped close and recognised the man, hidden beneath a mask of blood, cuts and bruises.

Holstering his pistol and taking off his sunglasses, the Kashmiri pulled off the note that was pinned to the bars of the cage door.

MISSION Failed. It read. *BLAME HIM!*

CHAPTER TWENTY-FOUR

No Matter the Cost

Narinda Singh's hands shook as she tried to hold on to her cup of coffee. Checking the clock on the wall again she could see it was now 10:15pm and put her cup down on the gleaming wood table for fear of spilling it everywhere. Stifling a sob, the reporter hid her face in her hands and tried to shut out the image of Samira Jethwani's last moments in this life.

She failed miserably, and as her stomach cramped and her heart began to race, Narinda tried to recall how she had arrived at the American Embassy. Her recollection of the last few hours was hazy at best and, in her shock, she could only remember presenting herself to the security guard at the embassy, imploring that despite her unannounced visit, Federal Attaché Thomas Miller *would* want to see her.

Her credentials did little to impress the guard, though finally, after she all but got down on her hands and knees to beg him, the burly man sighed and went to make a call.

It took an indeterminable amount of time, time in which Narinda spent watching the road behind her, searching the gathering shadows for tell of danger, for those she could feel were watching her, even now. Eventually, the guard returned, his stern face slipping into an apologetic smile.

"Someone will come for you now, Miss Singh," the man said, handing back her identity card.

Shown into a small room by a polite young woman with the fairest of hair and eyes the colour of the bluest sky, Narinda had only the picture of The White House on the wall and a drinks machine to keep her company.

That had been over two hours ago, and in that time she could hear a lot of comings and goings outside the room. Each time she thought her solace would be broken, the footsteps and conversation hurried away from her.

Finally, when Narinda was about to give in to her better judgement and use her mobile to call her fiancé, the door snapped open and a tall, striking man in his late twenties hurried into the room.

"Forgive the delay, Miss Singh," the man said over a smile, and Narinda recognised the soft voice long before she could see the name on his security badge.

"Mr. Miller," Narinda blurted hastily, rising up to take his offered hand in her own. He motioned for his guest to sit, waiting patiently for her to reclaim her seat before he took one for himself and dragged it around the table to sit closer to her.

"Is everything alright?" he asked softly, his eyes flashing with concern. "I had not expected you until the morning..."

Gathering up what little composure she had left, Narinda shook her head. "Mr. Miller, you must understand that by coming here tonight I am placing myself in great danger, and putting my life in your hands."

Thomas Miller sat back in his chair, studying the woman before him. He had seen her before at some of the Embassy's press conferences from time to time, and the strong-willed, assured woman he had known then no longer sat before him.

He drew in a breath for what was about to happen. It

had already been a night of surprises, and as he unbuttoned his suit jacket, he suspected that it was going to be a long time before he found his bed.

"In your own time, please, Miss Singh, tell me what I can do for you."

Narinda shook her head, trying to free the dark images from her mind. "I will try my best, Mr. Miller, but I am not sure where to start."

Miller spread his hands out on the table. "Where do you fit into this?"

Narinda sighed, attempting to find the right words. "For some time, I have been delving into the corruption of the current Prime Minister, hoping to shine a light on all he would hide from the world. It has been a hard path, with many obstacles, and until today I have never feared so much for my life."

"Your life is in danger?" Miller asked, his eyebrows arched in surprise.

"It is now," Narinda replied. "As you know, I was to meet you tomorrow with evidence that may well prove my government is trying to hide that your jet did indeed crash on Indian soil. I was hoping that this information might also shed some much-needed light as to why this would be so, and for what purpose."

As she paused to gather her thoughts, Miller fidgeted nervously.

"I sense this is not the case any longer?"

Narinda looked up, her eyes glistening, her hands shaking. Before he could stop himself, the American reached out to comfort her.

Blinking back her tears, the reporter puffed out her fears and politely, gently withdrew her hands from his touch.

"Thank you," she smiled, clearing her throat behind a

hand. When she was able to continue, Miller could hear the grief in her words. "A young, brave woman, who sought only to help me uncover the truth about this deception was killed before me this... this evening, w-when she was trying to give me the evidence I was to pass on to you."

"Killed?" Miller blurted, his handsome features paling.

"She was murdered," Narinda whispered, lowering her head. When she looked up, her eyes blazed. "As she stepped off the bus to meet me, she stumbled into a man. Moments after, she was clutching her chest. I could see the confusion in her eyes, there was blood on her shirt and as she searched for help, she fell into the road… she did not survive. I moved to help her, but another man, a man I have never seen before, made it perfectly clear that I should walk away while I still could."

Thomas Miller shook his head and drummed a nervous beat out on the table with long fingers.

"Who was this woman?" Miller asked. Since events had started changing earlier that day, he had been keeping one eye on the news... there had been no mention of a murder in the city.

"It was Aasim Rana's aide, Samira Jethwani," Narinda replied, sobbing.

Thomas felt his skin stiffen as he thought back to the only time he had met the young woman, remembered how shy she had been – how lovely she had seemed. Clenching his drumming fingers into a fist, he waited for the journalist to regain her composure before speaking, and could not hide his anger.

"She was a very nice lady, I met her once," he growled. "She was also incredibly brave. Do you have the information she gave her life for?"

Narinda shook her head sadly, her unkempt hair hiding her sorrow. "I could not get to her bag as the man was watching me. Fearing for my life, I came straight here to see you. I do not know what happened to it – I do not know what to do, sir."

Miller rose from his seat. "Be reassured that we can offer you protection, Miss Singh. You are safe in the embassy, here on American soil. Those that would seek you harm, cannot reach you here."

Narinda crumpled under the weight of the burden she carried. She had persuaded Samira to help her, knowing how dangerous the people were that she was betraying, without, if she was truly honest with herself, any more than a passing thought to the aide's own safety, so obsessed as she was with bringing down the Prime Minister.

What am I going to do? She had shamed her family, brought dishonour to her future husband by wanting to help the Americans, just to further her own ambitions. *What will become of me now?*

There was no vision into her future where she could see that her life would ever be the same again.

"I thank you," Narinda said dutifully.

"Don't thank me yet, ma'am," Miller said, motioning for her to rise. "There has been a further development this afternoon; one that I fear will confirm your suspicions."

As the American moved to the door and opened it, Narinda rose, feeling her hopes lift. "Developments?" she dared to ask.

Despite the anger radiating in his strong face, Thomas Miller managed a faint smile as he held the door open for her.

"If I might ask you to follow me, Miss Singh, there is

someone I would like you to meet." He paused, licking his lips delicately. "But before you do, I must ask you to surrender all of your communication devices."

Maria Galnia slid her Corvette through the open wrought iron gates and up the sweeping drive, bringing the sports car to a slow halt outside Villa De Valdez. Squeezed into the back of the car, Gio was too busy playing on his Nintendo Switch to realise that he had arrived home from school.

"We are home, honey," Maria said, as she peered between the headrests to fix him with a look of reproach. Already his answers to questions about his day at school were a select collection of grunts, silent shrugs and the occasional, if she was lucky, 'Okay!'

Sighing, she cut him some slack as she picked up her handbag from the passenger seat and opened the driver's door. Gio had been asking about where his papa was and when he was coming home again, and to divert her own worry, Maria had allowed him some extra hours each day on his games.

As she pulled the keys from the ignition and swung a bare leg out into the sun, her phone began to ring. With one long leg touched to the drive, the other still in the foot-well, she pulled her mobile from her bag.

"I'm just going to take this outside, Gio," she told her son. He remained hidden in the back of the car and did not even notice she was gone.

Walking away for some privacy, Maria stood in the shade under the portico of the villa.

"Paolo," she greeted, tucking strands of wild hair behind an ear as she answered the call. "Where are you?"

"*Buona sera*," his strong voice responded. "*I have just landed in Delhi and cleared customs. Has there been any further news?*"

"No," Maria sighed. "I haven't heard anything of use from anyone, and my contact at the Embassy in Delhi is not returning my calls."

"*I could pay him a visit!*"

Maria laughed – a light sounding, yet weary chuckle that did little to ease her concerns. "I think it probably best that you don't."

"*What do you need from me, Maria?*" Paolo asked.

Flicking a distracted look to the car and spying the excited bob of a sandy mop, she smiled. "Just find yourself a hotel, sit tight and wait for some news. I cannot believe that the jet has vanished over India. Someone must have seen it come down, someone must know something."

She heard the negative thoughts down the line, all the way from Delhi.

"*Alright*," Il Lupo grunted, instead. "*But if we don't hear something soon, I am going to pay the Embassy a visit*."

"Fine," Maria relented. "Just stay close, and stay safe."

She hung up before he could respond.

Paolo Romano shook his huge head, marvelling. He had never met anyone like Maria, suspected he never would. Putting the phone back in his breast pocket, he stared about the arrivals lounge, searching for an exit sign. Off to his left, the stick of a man who had been trying to earn a few rupees by carrying his hand luggage was still hovering about, hopeful that he would change his mind.

Sighing, Paolo waved him over, and the man rushed

to his side, all smiles.

"Here," the Italian grinned, handing over his bag. "Find me a reliable taxi and a place to stay and it'll be worth your while."

Bobbing his head, the man led him on, warning bystanders out the way as he guided his charge through the crowds.

Paolo smiled. Already he felt more relaxed. At the last airport, the porters and hawkers did not take no as a viable answer – here, it seemed, 'no' and 'yes', worked in any language.

As Paolo was led towards the exit and the warm night outside, he began to suspect that if events continued to go the way they were playing out, he might still be able to avoid doing what needed to be done.

Thomas Miller led Narinda Singh through parts of the Embassy that journalists and the public were not normally allowed access to. As they walked down a bare hallway, several people hurried by, greeting the attaché with smiles and sending the reporter curious looks.

Feeling somewhat naked without her contact to the world outside, the journalist was happy for the American to take command of proceedings. As overloaded as her mind was, she doubted she could make any rational, sensible choices at the moment, anyhow.

He stopped outside a plain looking door, different only because it had a security scanner to the left of it.

"I have to remind you again that anything that is said or seen here during your stay is strictly off the record, Miss Singh," he stated, over his right shoulder.

Nodding obediently and offering him a further, reassuring nod, Narinda watched as he waved his pass over the scanner and the magnetic lock on the door released with a satisfying buzz.

"Follow me," Miller smiled. He opened the door, leading her into a medium sized air-conditioned room, full of activity.

The whole length of the wall across from them was lined with monitors, each showing static images of aerial surveillances, maps, and on one, NDTV's twenty-four-hour news channel. Two people sat at desks, hunched over computers, and a tall man in a dark suit stood behind them, arms folded across his chest as he surveyed the information before him.

Broad faced, the man was in his late forties, his jaw sporting a greying beard that complimented the youth of hair fading away on his head. Green eyes flicked towards the newcomers and he nodded brusquely in their direction, before turning his attention back to the bank of screens.

Narinda hung back respectfully as Thomas Miller walked forward and offered soft words in the ear that was bent towards him. Amidst all the noise, Narinda could not have heard what was said anyway, and she waited patiently for the introductions to be made.

Miller waved her over.

"Miss Narinda Singh, Ryan Weekes," he said, gesturing to the tall man.

"A pleasure," the man said, though he did not smile. He studied her with intense eyes, as he cordially shook her hand.

Without any explanation to Narinda as to what was going on, Miller relayed to Weekes what she had told him earlier. The tall man's eyebrows rose in shock, and he dealt her a startled look as he listened to the recount.

"This has been kept from the news, I suspect, for a

very good reason," Weekes said, grunting thoughtfully. He folded his arms across his chest and flicked a brief look to the Indian woman who worked one of the computers, before turning back to them.

"You have my sympathies for the loss of your asset," Weekes said, though there was no sympathy to be heard in his words. "The information she had would have been extremely useful."

"*She* was called Samira Jethwani." Narinda snapped, shamefully angered. "A young woman has lost her life, a–"

Ryan Weekes nodded, holding up an impatient hand.

"Miss Singh, I am sorry, but we must focus on unfolding events and save our grief for future days if we are to get to the truth of the matter. Earlier today, the Embassy here in Delhi, received a call from a woman in Mexico, one Ramona Gonzales. She claimed to have received a call from her daughter, Sara."

Without being asked, the Indian woman sat at the computer brought up a photo on the screen of a dark-haired woman's Driving Licence.

"Sara Gonzales," Weekes introduced, sweeping a hand towards the image. "Miss Gonzales was one of four people aboard a D-BUSY Bombardier Challenger 600 jet that took off from Bahrain Airport three days ago, destined for Hong Kong. Registered to a one Jon Galnia, a man known to the Federal Services of the United States, this jet was reported compromised and crashing over central India by the owner in a voicemail he left for his wife."

The identities of all on board were brought up on screens for Narinda to see. Two British nationals, apparently the pilot and co-pilot, and the owner of the jet, the man referenced to as Jon Galnia.

In the brief lull, Narinda's mind began to race. Despite her lack of evidence to present to them she had been invited into the fold, and as they continued to study the faces on the screens, she began to wonder why that was.

Ryan Weekes clearly worked for the American Government. He was probably a Field Operative for one of their organisations, the CIA, NSA, or something else. Whoever he was, Narinda doubted she would ever see him again after this meeting.

Weekes turned his thoughts back to her. "Sara Gonzales called her mother earlier this afternoon. She confirmed that the jet did indeed crash over central India, that she and the pilot, Robert Williams, and the owner, Jon Galnia survived – though the co-pilot Stephen Gaines, seen there on the right, did not."

Narinda Singh gasped, not trying to hide her shock. She flicked horrified looks between the two men who were now watching her intently.

"Then this means that, I mean to say–" the journalist could not grasp hold of her tongue. "Then Samira was correct in what she overheard, that my government did indeed cover up the crash..."

Thomas Miller nodded his head. "I am sorry to say, Miss Singh, that it does appear to be the case. What we are trying to ascertain, what my government hopes you will be able to assist us with, is why this would be the case."

Narinda looked at both men, and then stared at the images of those on board the jet. She blinked, unable to comprehend why Aasim Rana, why Chandra Nehru, would wish to hide this tragedy.

And why they were willing to have people killed to do so...?

"We have been able to trace the origins of the call," Ryan Weekes continued. "Triangulating the signal to central India, as mentioned by Jon Galnia in his voicemail, we were fairly confident that the jet had gone down somewhere in Madhya Pradesh."

Narinda nodded, too overwhelmed by the day's events to retain everything she was hearing. The resources needed to do that, especially in a foreign country, without permission, had her starting to question the legality of what the Americans were doing here.

"Understandably," Thomas Miller interjected, seeing the worry on her face, "This is a delicate situation. Usually, we would be liaising with your government, however..."

Miller let the statement hang in the air.

"The real question arising from the phone call is why the Indian Government, and as it now transpires in particular, those so high up in the cabinet, would want to hide the crash from us?" Weekes asked the room, his eyes fixed upon Narinda Singh. "Satellite images and aerial surveillance received in the last few hours have now pin-pointed and confirmed, I am afraid to say, Miss Singh, that your asset – Miss Jethwani, had indeed stumbled upon something far greater than she could have ascertained."

Weekes nodded to the man sat to the left at a computer screen, who turned back, tapping out rapidly on his keyboard. Several images appeared on the monitors and Narinda took a step closer, her heart pounding.

"As you can see from these satellite photos, the jet did indeed crash over central India. In fact, as image four shows," Weekes said evenly, motioning to the screen in question, "we now know that it went down in the Bandhavgarh National Park."

Narinda's head was pounding, and she felt dizzy as Ryan Weekes proceeded to show her more images of the crash site. His voice sounded distant, as if spoken from afar and under water, and as the journalist swooned, Thomas Miller reached out a steadying hand.

"I am alright," Narinda lied, offering a faint smile of thanks. "I need to hear this."

Miller nodded, and Weekes continued. "The next image was received two hours ago from a long standoff reconnaissance aircraft."

Narinda calmed herself with a steadying breath and her eyes widened as she realised what she was seeing.

Two helicopters had landed on the shore of a lake, some five kilometres from the crash site; easily traceable from the deep scar it had carved into the land as it came down. She looked questioningly at Ryan Weekes.

"What are they doing there?" she dared to ask. "Why haven't they contacted you to say they have found the jet?"

"If we wait a few days, Miss Singh, I believe they will," Weekes admitted. "But it is our task to find out the truth before all evidence has been erased, or buried. Having analysed the images and footage received over the last few hours, we can see, as shown on the next image, that they were more concerned at first, about this item left on the shore."

More detailed imagery appeared on the screen and Narinda squinted as she studied the top of what appeared to be a cage. At least a dozen figures were gathered about the cage. She felt a cold fear sweep through her as her mind began to work.

"There are two helicopters," Weekes continued, when there were no questions forthcoming. "These pictures were retrieved an hour ago."

Narinda could see one helicopter had remained with the cage. The other was gone.

"Studying all the imagery received from satellites and reconnaissance aircraft, we have been able to piece together a fairly detailed picture of what has been happening," Weekes offered. "One helicopter took off soon after landing, heading north to sweep the immediate area for some ten kilometres. It returned, some time later, at approximately eighteen hundred hours. An hour later, the same helicopter departs, and only then does any attention turn towards the jet's crash site."

Narinda could not take anymore, and despite her thirst for answers she was too exhausted to process what was going on. Her stomach riled at the thought of how deep rooted the corruption in her government must go, of the numerous agencies, offices and people that must have been involved to keep the crash a secret. And before any of that could be investigated, there was still the main question of why they would go to so much trouble, and risk so much?

"At first, we thought that perhaps the impossible had happened," Thomas Miller said, his concern for their guest evident on his face. "That perhaps a tiger had been found, living in the wild. Its worth to the world would be immeasurable, and the cage would certainly suggest that possibility. But when the helicopter departed, it didn't take a tiger with them, it took a man."

Narinda looked towards the final image that would be shown to her that night. She could indeed see that a figure was being dragged from the cage and loaded onto the helicopter.

"We suspect that this could be one of the survivors, Miss Singh," Ryan Weekes offered, folding his arms across his chest again. "We will need to do some more investigation before we can confirm this, however." He looked towards Thomas Miller and they shared something unsaid.

"Miss Singh," Miller smiled warmly, drawing her gaze to him. "While we continue to look into matters, as I promised, you will be kept safe from harm, here at the embassy. In the coming days your testimony may well prove invaluable to us, should matters escalate and the international community become involved. I hope, for the sake of our two great nations, this does not prove to be so, but I must ask in the interim that you remain here, as much for your own safety as our own security, and that you refrain from any contact with the outside world."

Narinda nodded her agreement, too overwhelmed and too shocked to fight back. She needed to rest, to regain her strength for what was ahead of them.

"Thank you, Mr. Miller," she said, inclining her head in gratitude. She looked to the mysterious man, who nodded in her direction. "Mr. Weekes."

Miller opened the door and handed the journalist into the care of the blonde-haired woman Narinda had met earlier. As she was led away, the attaché stepped back into the makeshift operations centre and closed the door behind him.

"Right," Weekes said growling. "Now that we have got diplomatic relations out of the way, we can get on with the real business of finding out who was in that cage."

Miller moved to stand beside the CIA Field Director and nodded. He couldn't believe what had happened this afternoon. One moment, he was finalising the details of a fund-raiser with UNICEF to help street children in India, the next, the CIA were barging into his office.

With the Ambassador away in Brussels, Thomas Miller, as the Federal Aviation Attaché, was Ryan Weekes' first point of contact. The next few hours played out like an episode of *24*, and by the time Narinda Singh arrived at the embassy, the attaché was beginning to feel more like Jack Bauer than Thomas Miller. There was no doubt in his mind that Narinda Singh was only being kept around because of her investigations into Chandra Nehru's cabinet and the information she may have unearthed about them. Had Samira Jethwani not overheard the First Secretary talking, and been murdered, the journalist would not be here at all.

"We do not have much time," Weekes had said to him, as they commandeered an empty office. "What we are about to do is highly inappropriate, and in the eyes of the international community, highly illegal. But know that I come here with the full backing from Langley *and* Washington."

If he had any objections, it ended there for Miller, and he was under no illusions that the re-tasking of satellites at such short notice came with the full weight of the American Intelligence Agency behind it.

Weekes cocked an eyebrow towards him. "That girl's death may have just given us the leverage we need."

Miller grimaced. "Even without her evidence, without the phone?"

Ryan Weekes smiled. "We have the name Mister Hamid, now. We are looking into him, cross-checking his aliases, studying the few images we have of him when he has appeared in public. We don't have a lot to go on, but the name is a start. The man is a ghost, hiding in plain sight."

Feeling more like he worked at the *Bureau*, than the embassy, Miller was ashamed that he had been thinking about a TV show when the reality of what was happening was far more serious.

"The only people who can shed light upon what has been happening in Madhya Pradesh these last few days, are the survivors," Weekes stated, looking back towards the monitors. "Let's try to save them, shall we?"

CHAPTER TWENTY-FIVE

In This Proud Land

"Who else knows she is here?"

Without waiting for an answer, the speaker slammed his bloodied fist into the face of the battered man, tied up and lolling dreamily in the chair before him. The sound of the impact echoed about the garage area, bouncing gleefully off the shelved walls as it drowned out the distant sounds of passing traffic. Life carried on outside in the world, blissfully unaware or uncaring of what was occurring inside the garage.

The man in the chair's head snapped back from the force of the blow, his broken nose pummelled across his destroyed face. He would have toppled over backwards if a second man behind him hadn't caught him and shoved him forward like a reluctant fighter, forced to carry on with his beating.

"It's senseless to continue with this," the first man purred seductively in fluent English, his Kashmiri accent barely evident. "Why lose your life over her? You cannot stop the inevitable, you only delay it somewhat. My employer is a patient man, but there are people who have invested millions of dollars to find her; and although your intervention has actually impressed them, they *will* find her. Who would have ever thought that a man with your reputation could have done what you did!"

The seated man mumbled something through his ruined face, blood dribbling through the tangled mass of broken and twisted teeth. His eyes were sealed shut by the blood congealing around their lids and the wound on his head still bled profusely.

Leaning close, the man turned his head to try and hear the faint words spilling unintelligibly from his lips. "What is that you say *bhaaee*?"

"I said '*Go fuck yourself*!" the man spat defiantly, his voice suddenly clear and concise.

Sighing, the Kashmiri stepped back; wiping the bloodied spittle from his face as he shook his head.

"You Americans, you never know when to let go," he said, regret in his voice as he rolled his fingers and cracked his knuckles. "Unfortunately for you my friend, I am not as patient as my employers."

"I'm not American, cock-sucker. How many times do I have to tell you people?" the battered man said, snorting in contempt.

Ignoring him, the man stepped in close once again.

Jon braced himself for the next blow and when it came, he barely felt it. His body was a mess, feeling more like a rump steak than a human being now, and he took each blow, each cut like the dead cow, ready for the frying pan, ready for the final chew.

His head was flung back as another fist caught him on his right cheek, and despite the impact, he felt little more than dull agony. Jon lolled his head, buying himself some time as he heard the man panting for breath, saw the blood-spattered shoes step back to gather some much-needed strength.

He couldn't remember how he came to be here, had no idea where *here* was, or who these people were. All he knew was that the Moroccan's tranquilizers had helped him survive this far, but the pain was starting to seep through the veil of drugs in his system now. Soon, the broken fingers, the burns, bruises and cuts would take centre stage and the shock of what he had already endured would probably kill him.

Time was running out...

Jon lifted his head, barely seeing the older man before him. The sun outside wreathed him in shadows, and he could only see the man's eyes, as he regained his composure and wiped his bloodied hands on a cloth.

"I don't know what you want from me," Jon slurred. "What more can I say?"

Before the words were from his lips, the man was before him again, one hand wrapped tightly about his prisoner's throat.

"Who did you tell, who have you called?" the man hissed, his stale breath blasting beads of blood from Jon's face.

Jon snorted, glad that his nose was broken and he couldn't smell how bad his breath actually was.

"I didn't have my phone," Jon growled, fighting for air as his captor continued to strangle him. "Your goons' devices all had codes. For the hundredth and final time, fuckwit, *I did not call anyone*."

The man released his choking grip and if Jon's hands had been free, he would have rubbed his neck. Coughing, Jon spat blood onto the floor and groaned.

"She will be found," the man promised him. "But your actions have cost us a lot of money, your intervention has set us back many months."

"Oh," Jon said, scowling. "Sorry for crashing in the jungle and for trying to survive. I'm not sorry for trying to save a species, though."

Jon swallowed, seeing the anger flare in his captor's eyes. Behind him, he sensed the man holding his chair stiffen nervously.

The Kashmiri shook his head, then laughed.

"I like you Jon Galnia," the man smiled, shaking his head, "I truly do! You, most of all, are a man who will understand the concept of family, of honour, of a blood debt. You know why we do the things we must, and you will understand why I am about to do what your actions have forced me to do."

Ignoring the panic flaring in Jon's eyes, Hamid turned away from him and motioned for the second guard, stationed by the door, to fetch his leverage. When the armed man was gone, he turned back.

"Many years ago, my ancestors were driven from our homeland by the British, forced to scrape and survive in the mountains to the north. They were not to be defeated, they would not forget who they were and so they endured; they lived and passed on their tales, their desire to one day conquer those who had ruined our destiny. Sharing the knowledge of our ancestry, the strength of our blood, they knew that one day, those of the blood would reclaim the power that was lost."

Jon watched through blood-crusted, hooded eyes, as the man pulled a metre-length piece of yellow scarf from his left pocket. In his other hand, he produced Rashim's knife, and Jon snarled angrily, rocking in his chair.

The man caressed the scarf, wringing his hands and the blade lovingly through the cloth. He looked up, smiling.

"It is fitting, I feel, that my rise to power, the influence I now have will be enforced here this day, in this way."

Jon swallowed fearfully as they waited in silence, watching each other. The pain in Jon's body was barely controllable now, and he knew that long before they killed him, if he didn't fight back, he would pass out.

As he tried to tense his damaged hands, thought for one glorious moment he would rise up and take his captors by surprise, the door to the garage opened again and the guard returned, dragging a prisoner with him.

Jon's hopes slipped from his lips in a forlorn sob as the other prisoner was thrown into the chair, dragged into position across from him.

It was Robert Williams.

Thomas Miller had managed only a few hours rest that night, as events continued to play out like some ridiculous TV show. Stumbling into a room at the embassy, well into the early hours of a new week, he had fallen into a tormented sleep on a sofa, thrashing his way through to dawn with dreams he could not recall.

Whilst he slept, events had moved on quickly, and the number of staff enlisted by Weekes had doubled over night to ensure no stone was left unturned.

Following a large mug of coffee in the canteen and some buttered toast for breakfast, he had managed to avoid Narinda Singh, regrouping in the makeshift operations centre that had once been a spare meeting and training room.

That had been three hours ago, now.

"*Three minutes*," the voice in his earpiece echoed. Ryan Weekes dealt him a look and the attaché could tell that he was just as nervous. What was about to happen contravened endless international laws, and if it didn't succeed...

The breakthrough had come a few hours before dawn. One of the team managed to track the helicopter via footage from the surveillance aircraft, and from that moment on, with the resources and technology at their disposal, they had followed it across Madhya Pradesh to an airfield outside Bhopal. From there, further intelligence and images lifted locally from CCTV and traffic cameras, had allowed them to identify and then follow the three vehicles using drones, from the remote airfield, to an industrial area on the north-western side of the city. When he arrived in the morning with coffee and toast in hand, Miller had been brought up to speed with events, had been shown the aerial surveillance images of the industrial warehouses the man from the cage and two others had been taken to.

"We cannot be certain," Weekes had said, ordering the image to be enhanced, "but I would wager you a small country that one of these figures we see here on screen is our Mister Hamid. The other three, the prisoners, well, they are most likely, one, or all of the survivors from the crash."

It was clear that Weekes wanted to know more about this man from the way he clenched his hands every time he said his name. The fact he did not appear on any watch lists only served to heighten his desire and curiosity.

That had been two hours ago now, and after this day, Miller knew that he would be sworn to God only knows how many official secrets acts, and to sign Heaven knew how many papers to corroborate this.

"*Scorpion, this is Phoenix 1. In position, over*," his earpiece told him. Seconds later, *Phoenix 2* were also in place.

All eyes were drawn to the real-time footage from the drone, in position high over the target building.

Miller began chewing his fingernails, a habit he had not been able to shake from childhood. Taking his nerves out on his hands, he watched the two four-man teams, saw them running across open ground towards their stacking points, outside the compound.

Thermal imagery from the drone over the compound had revealed ten people inside, and with no access to Phoenix's body cameras to watch the unfolding action, they would have to rely on radio communications for updates. Whatever happened in the next few minutes would only ever be for the eyes of a select, privileged few.

Weekes looked to the Indian woman, still in position over her keyboard. "Mina?"

She looked back, one hand pressed to steady her headphones. "All is quiet, sir. No local chatter," she reported, turning away. The relief was evident in her tired, hazel eyes.

"*Awaiting the order, over*," the leader of Phoenix 1 reported in, as his team stacked up against one of the vehicles used to transport the prisoners.

Weekes was already on the phone, talking quietly to Langley, maybe even someone else, somewhere higher up the chain.

Miller was shaking uncontrollably now. Unable to watch anymore, he looked away. He could not believe how what had started out as a routine week, was now the most surreal, unbelievable one of his life.

Seconds slipped slowly away and as his human instincts got the better of him, the attaché stole another glance at the monitors. Weekes was nodding his head, as he listened to the unheard voice on the other end of his cell.

"Yes, sir," he said moments later. "Thank you, sir."

Weekes ended the call and spoke into his radio communicator.

"Authorisation given," Weekes said evenly. "You are

a go, Phoenix. Engage!"

The room held its breath.

"Robert!" Galnia spluttered, his joy, though short-lived, was obvious. As long as he could recall, Jon had never been happier to see anybody. It was his first connection to the real world, the life he thought he had lost.

This *was* really happening – he wasn't going mad.

"Sir," Robert replied. The Brit looked a mess, but Jon could hear the relief mixed in his voice, along with the fear. "I am okay. Sara is here, too. We almost got away..."

They smiled briefly at one another, giving each a moment of silent strength before their captor moved to stand beside the pilot. He looked thoughtfully from the scarf in his left hand, to the blade in his right, before turning to look back.

"The tiger was an end to justify our means, and now, thanks to you, we know she lives," the lean, sharp-faced man said, smiling. "She is not some myth, some wistful figment of our imagination. There will be others who will want to have her, and we will, eventually, give her to them."

Hamid moved behind the pilot, putting Rashim's ceremonial knife back in his pocket. He took the scarf firmly in both hands. "But you have caused us a great deal of pain and embarrassment, Jon Galnia. And for that, and by the blood of my ancestors, I repay you for your trouble."

"Don't," Jon pleaded, his blood-crusted eye-lids tearing apart angrily. "He has nothing to do with this!"

Before he could say anything else, their captor wrapped the scarf tightly about Robert's throat, pulling him back out of his seat.

Eyes bulging, the tall pilot kicked and thrashed, struggling against the life that was being choked from him.

Hamid watched Jon, smiling over the pilot's head, as he watched him try to fight against his constraints. The guard behind stepped close, punching the Italian-American in the side of the head.

"Sshh, sshhh," Hamid whispered in Robert's ear. "Don't fight against me. Give it to me, let it go."

Robert growled, pushing back with his fading strength. He felt his captor stumble slightly, but before he could make the most of his advantage, the guard who had fetched him from his makeshift cell, moved close and kicked the legs from beneath him.

The pilot's vision began to fade, filled by speckled stars.

It was then that they all heard the sounds of gunfire.

The room froze, paused like a scene from some macabre film. Robert was on his knees, the life being throttled from him by his captor as Jon looked up, hope flaring in his eyes.

Play resumed, and relaxing the scarf, Hamid looked towards the two guards, as they heard distant shouts and the reply of gunfire.

Jon watched on, fighting against false hope as Robert fell to his knees and coughed up some bile. Their captor and tormentor snapped something in his native tongue and the guards headed for the door, machine pistols raised. When they were gone, he turned, a rueful smile slipping across his dark features.

"It seems, Mister Galnia," he chuckled slowly, reverently folding up the scarf, "that the Gods truly favour you."

"Just the one," Jon replied, his hatred blazing in his eyes, fresh blood running down his face.

To the rear of the building, screams rose up, cut short by the dull snap of gunfire, and as Hamid looked towards the sound, distracted, Robert rose up, ramming his head back into his captor's face.

As the dull crunch of a shattered cheek echoed about the garage, Jon stood up on heavy legs, still strapped to the chair. Time slowed, as Hamid recovered his senses and fell back from the pilot's attempts to knock him over. As the Indian, Kashmiri, whoever he was, reached for the pistol holstered at his ribs, Jon threw his weight behind him, slamming the chair down onto the concrete.

The chair cracked, but did not break and, rather foolishly, Jon was left looking up at a strip-light that winked mockingly at him.

This was not the way I imagined checking out, Jon thought bitterly. It was certainly not the light, he thought, that would one day guide him.

There was a sound, a dull thud, as Robert crashed to the floor and Jon, despite the thunder of panic in his head, heard two gunshots, followed by the footsteps, walking slowly towards him.

A shadow slipped across him and a face appeared, blocking out the light.

"A valiant effort," Hamid said, smiling down at his prisoner. "It is a shame we could not become better acquainted, but I fear we shall not meet again in this life."

Jon tensed as the man raised his pistol.

"Good bye, Jon Galnia," Hamid said.

Jon closed his eyes, waiting for the end. He tried to picture his wife and son, but he could not find them amongst his fear.

Moments later he heard the door open and close. The

garage fell silent.

And Jon wept.

Sara Gonzales recoiled, trying to hide away deeper inside the cupboard that was her new prison. Shouts rose up then were cut short, as muffled gunfire filled the building they had been dragged into, blindfolded.

Booted feet rushed by the door and three shots echoed loudly. A moment later, the corridor outside was seething with bullets that opened up holes in the door and sent her ducking for cover. She heard cries of pain, followed seconds later by a clatter and two soft thumps.

Sobbing, Sara slid down the wall. Hugging her knees, she hid her face. They had so very nearly escaped the jungle, had travelled some distance before they had detected the distant approach of a helicopter. Fearing their captors had changed their minds and not trusting the air any more, both she and Robert had found some dense undergrowth to hide in.

It had not saved them, and within the hour they had been captured by heavily-armed soldiers, their faces and identity covered by dark scarves.

Gagged and bound once more, they had been bundled into a helicopter and flown back to the lake. It was there that they had been reunited, though she was not aware of it, with their employer, Jon Galnia.

"Put the weapon down," a voice barked suddenly, from the hallway outside. *An American voice!*

"On the ground – NOW!"

"I think not," a calm voice responded.

The hallway outside echoed with one swift shot, followed immediately by two muffled ones.

A body hit the ground.

CHAPTER TWENTY-SIX

The Truth of All Things

Jon Galnia woke with a start, fresh pain seething through his body. Barely seeing through his heavily lidded eyes, he ignored the glass of water beside his bed and fumbled for the button. He pressed it, satisfied by the beep and the dose of morphine it still allowed his veins to have.

Sweating, Jon fell back into the pillows, sighing in relief as the pain, for a while, began to ease. With a heavily bandaged hand and some effort, he dragged the thin sheet back up over his body.

For three days he had rested, safe in this bare room, God knows where, visited only by a doctor and his needs tended to by a young nurse. Too tired to be angry, Jon had probed his hosts with calm questions and was told, as he expected, very little other than *someone* would come to see him soon, and that he was *safe now*.

Thankful to be alive, Jon was happy for the rest and the medical care, not caring where and who was paying for it. Judging by his carers and rescuers accents, the nation that had been for so long trying to incarcerate him had been the very country that had just rescued him.

Still a distant dream at best, Jon could only recall the room exploding with his rescuers; armed Special Forces, Navy Seals, or perhaps even more mercenaries, their calm voices soothing him, telling him they were all safe now. Jon had been cut from his restraints and bundled out of the room as gently as time permitted. As they had freed him from his seat and lifted him up, Jon had dared to look towards Robert Williams.

Despite the pain in his broken ribs, Jon chuckled and shook his head. Robert was being helped up too, and with steadying arms, had even managed to walk towards the exit.

As he was carried from the room and away from his confusion, Jon spied the phone that a soldier was stooping down to recover.

It was smashed, and had two bullet holes in it...

Unable, even now, to fully comprehend why their torturer had allowed them both to live, Jon suspected that it was not a mercy. To allow someone to live with the knowledge you had their life in your hands and chose not to take it was a powerful tool – one that Jon had used to great effect himself several times, to instill fear in his enemies and underline his reputation.

Well, whatever the reason, Jon just offered up prayers of thanks that he had. It was funny, but in a strange way, Jon admired the man. He went about his bloody business calmly and coolly, and despite it all, his *Modus Operandi*, his code, was something that Jon could appreciate, could relate to.

In another time and place, Jon would have liked to have got to know him better. He would have been a man he could have worked with.

The door opened up and a fresh face walked into the room, well, not so fresh, but one he hadn't seen before. The female nurse hovered at the door for a time to see if she was needed, and then ignored, she slipped away, closing the door gently behind her.

Jon eyed the balding man, noting, through his haze of medication, that he had a beard a badger would have been proud of.

"Ryan Weekes," the man introduced himself as he sat on the edge of the bed.

"I guess you are the man I have to thank for my life," Jon surmised, the words souring on his lips. Thanking people was not something he found easy to do, though in the circumstances, he was glad to this time.

"Indirectly, yes," Ryan Weekes smiled. He flicked his eyes over his patient. "How are you feeling?"

"Like shit," Jon admitted, forcing a smile. "But alive!"

Weekes nodded, chewing his tongue thoughtfully. "Mr. Galnia, you are currently being kept at an undisclosed location for your own safety. There are many things happening that I cannot tell you about at this time, and because of the sensitivity of events surrounding your rescue, it will probably remain that way until we can get you back stateside."

They eyed each other for a time, and eventually Jon nodded, though it cost him a great deal of pain to do so. "That's fine by me. All I want to do is get out of this country and back home to my wife and son. If you can sort that out for me, I will be indebted to you."

Weekes smiled. "We are working on that, so just rest for now. I'll have a phone delivered to you presently, so that you can call your wife. Naturally, I would ask you not to disclose the events surrounding your time in India, until you are back in the U.S."

"Understood," Jon grinned. His heart was pounding at the prospect of hearing Maria's voice again.

Weekes nodded and rose up. He moved to pick up the chart at the end of the bed and read the notes, eyebrows rising.

"You are a lucky man," the American observed.

"No need to tell me that," Jon grimaced. Until the

doctor had told him what was wrong with him, he hadn't realised what a mess he actually was.

"We should be able to move you to the American Embassy in Delhi in a few days," Weeks said, moving to leave. He paused when his hand was on the door's handle and turned. "You can tell your wife that you should be home by the end of the week."

Jon thanked the man, falling back onto the bed. It sounded like the Indians were still trying to cover up the crash, hiding from the Americans and the world that it had ever even happened. From what Robert and Sara had been able to tell him, what they had been able to share as they were reunited in a dark SUV with blacked out windows – driven to a safe location away from the building they had all thought to die in – was that the tiger had been the prize, that somebody, somewhere high up the chain of power in the country had been trying to make a tidy profit from it, too.

What they hadn't planned on, however, was a jet crashing in the same region, its surviving passengers too bloody obstinate to die.

Jon snorted. He still couldn't believe how quickly the Americans had found them. It was nothing short of a miracle, and he was determined, when he could think straighter, that he would find out the truth of it, and that if he ever got the chance, those responsible for saving him would be rewarded. If not, well, he would light a few candles for them.

He had already promised Sara and Robert as much. No amount, no words were able to sum up how glad he was that they were alive, and how sorry he was for the mess he had involved them in.

Sara had promised they could talk about *that* on the flight home, and Robert had thanked him, before they were separated. His only wish, the pilot had stated, was that he was allowed to retire, talking of his desire to spend the rest of his days safely on the ground.

After all they had been through it was the least Jon could allow him to do.

They all knew they would be questioned at length, quizzed about all they had endured, all they had witnessed, and quietly, together, they had decided to heed the mercenary's warning, leaving all mention of them out of their stories. It would be far easier to blame it on the Indians for now, and Jon did not want to throw too much help the American's way.

For now, Jon thought, wincing as he thought about Rashim.

It was some time, and more morphine later, when Sara Gonzales entered Jon's room. Still battered and bruised from her ordeal, the Mexican dealt her employer a bright smile as she limped across to his bedside.

"It's good to see you," Jon said, surprised at how much he actually meant it.

Sara returned the compliment. "They asked me to give you this," she smiled again, passing him a burner phone. "I have already called home... they asked me to remind you to be careful of what you say."

Jon nodded. A man always on his guard, he was going to have to be extra cautious for quite some time. As Sara made to leave, he reached out with a damaged hand and stopped her.

"Thank you," he smiled, though slightly sick of this bad habit he was developing. When she was gone, Jon unlocked the phone with a sore, yet thankfully unbroken thumb. They hadn't started work properly on his right hand by the time the cavalry arrived.

He stared at the screen for a time and it felt strange. He had been away from civilisation for some time now and once he made this call, there would be no turning back from it.

Drawing in a deep breath, Jon tapped out the number.

The call took forever to connect, each cracking buzz accompanied by a huge drum beat in his chest. He had no idea what time it was back home, as his makeshift hospital room had no windows, no clock, and the phone's time had not been set.

"*Hello?*" the softest, sweetest thing he had ever heard filled his ear. Maria was cautious, he could tell, wary of the un-registered number that was calling her personal cell.

"*Hello?*" she asked again.

"Mari?" Jon croaked, his throat choked with emotion. "It's me, Jon."

Shock, silence, joy, happiness.

It was something in that order, and Jon would never be able to recall fully what they talked about that day. All he knew was that he blubbed like a baby as they sobbed down the line to one another.

Naturally, of course, Maria wanted to know what the fuck had happened, and despite the medication coursing through him, Jon felt himself stir. He always swore, cussed like a drunken trooper, but Maria? She rarely cursed, and when she did, it was all the more arousing from her lips.

"I can't tell you at the moment, honey," he winced. He wanted to, but the cell was probably being monitored. "I'll fill you in soon, I promise. It's not something we should talk about over the phone."

"*I'm just glad you're okay,*" Maria whispered. "*Gio*

has been asking where you are. He will be, we both *will be so pleased to have you home. I-I, I have been lost without you, Jon, thinking that I wouldn't see you again...*"

Jon swallowed hard, searching for something to say. He wiped away the tears that were blinding his eyes and tried to regain his composure. "They have said I should be home in a few days. There are some legal things to tie up before I can leave the country. I lost my passport in the crash..."

Even now it sounded strange to say '*the crash*' out loud. It made it feel real enough, although now it was starting to feel like a dream that had happened to somebody else.

"*Just stay safe and come home to us*," Maria ordered him. Though her voice was strained with emotion, she was gathering up her composure again, he could tell. "*I will text you Paolo's number, Jon. He is in Delhi. Call him.*"

Jon promised he would and after the call ended, once he had regained the remains of his own composure, he dialled the number Maria had texted him, along with the message '*We love you x x x*'.

As soon as Paolo answered the phone, Jon felt like he was back in the real world again and it touched him that Paolo had flown out all the way to India to find him.

"Ciao, Paolo," Jon greeted, as if everything was ok, as if it was just another day.

Eventually, Il Lupo recovered from the shock and managed to find his voice. "*Boss, where the fuck have you been? We have been so worried about you.*"

"It's a very long story," Jon replied, eyeing the door, "One for another day. Maria told me you are in Delhi. You came all this way to find me, Paolo? I am touched, brother. I mean it!"

"*Now, stop all that*," Paolo growled. "*Where are you? I'll come and get you.*"

Jon chuckled. "I have no fucking idea! I am going to have to rely on the CIA to get me home, or whoever the hell the people looking after me, are."

If he was disappointed, Paolo hid it well and roared with laughter in his ear. "*That must piss them off, no end! They've wanted to get their hands on you for years and now they finally do, they are being forced to help you – oh, the sweet irony.*"

"I am not home yet," Jon warned, laughing. "They might still decide to lock me up while they have the chance. Speaking of which, you should get back home – take care of things for me, until I am back. We have a lot to talk about."

"*We do,*" Paolo agreed and Jon could hear the concern in his voice. "*I have found out some things in Bahrain. You won't like it.*"

"I never do," Jon sighed, reaching for the button again. Already he was feeling the strain from the pace of the modern world, his world, the world he chose to live in. For a brief moment he wished he was back in the jungle, sat in the hut, having supper with Rashim.

"*All I will say, brother, is that you were right,*" Paolo confirmed. "*What we need to find out now, though, is why, and by whom.*"

Jon winced. It had been some time since he had thought about that, and it drove deeper than any of the wounds he was suffering from.

"That is not for today," Jon warned. "I have my suspicions, though we need proof before we go down *that* road."

Paolo grunted in his ear. "*Agreed! If* they *are behind*

it, as I suspect they might be, we need to talk to this 'Anna', in private. She would be a good place to start."

Jon nodded his head, licking his lips at the prospect.

"Enough business," Jon barked. "Get yourself home. We will talk again when I get back."

"*Right, boss,*" Il Lupo replied. "*Arrivederci, brother.*"

Jon hung up the call and tossed the phone onto his lap. For a time, he stared down the bed at his bare feet, wiggling his toes thoughtfully.

Sighing, Jon relaxed. There was plenty of fresh trouble ahead, he could sense that. But there were only so many scores you could settle in one day and for now he needed to rest, regain his strength and clear his mind for future strife.

Somehow, he had survived, astonishingly he had endured, and for now, first and foremost, he should count his blessings and get home safely to his wife and son. There would be other battles that needed to be fought, other wars that he would have to become embroiled in.

But next time, Jon promised himself, he would be the one who was ready, he would be the one in charge of his destiny, the one determining the fates of others.

Satisfied at his silent declaration, of his revengeful pact and the path he would set himself upon, Jon fell back into the arms of his medication.

It would be some hours before Jon sat up in bed, wondering just how the fuck Paolo knew Anna Sokolova's name...

The First Secretary of India Aasim Rana stared out over the heads of the sea of journalists, barely registering what Chandra Nehru was saying at his Press Conference, hardly aware that proceedings were drawing to a close.

For over an hour now, since the announcement to the country that Leela Chand Saini had been given the honour to sculpt the statue of Mahatma Gandhi that would proudly fill the void of The Canopy at India Gate, the journalists had taken their pictures, asked their questions of the Prime Minister and the artist, who stood together in unity, smiling into the media glare, safe in the knowledge that their faces were trending on Twitter and would grace the front covers the next day and the lead news articles that night.

Chandra Nehru was flying high, his smile broader than the steps they stood on outside the Sansad Bhavan, which was starting to become his favourite place to speak to the country from.

More photographers vied for the perfect shot at the front of the wall of journalists, and Aasim Rana flinched with each snapping whirr and flash from their cameras. The last few days had been hard to grasp hold of, as events, in his own view, spiralled dangerously out of control.

Shivering in the warmth of the day, Aasim watched on as Chandra Nehru airily articulated some answer away to his left, his free hand resting far too daringly away from public view on the small of Miss Chand Sani's back. She looked rather radiant in her mint green sari, her bare arms adorned by beautiful bands of silver and gold as she stood closer to the Prime Minister than was generally considered acceptable.

A deep chasm opened up in the First Secretary's stomach as he looked away. She looked and reminded him far too much of Samira.

Dazzled by the sun, Aasim sweated away in his suit, a cold sweat that had haunted him and his sleep ever since the news had reached him of his aide's death. Following his utter shock, the First Secretary had stormed into Chandra Nehru's office, slamming the door so hard behind him that the Prime Minister had actually raised one eyebrow.

"You have heard then, I take it?" Nehru had asked him, knowing full well that he had.

"I told your man that she was not to be harmed, she was not to be touched," Aasim had raged, silenced by a withering glare and raised hand from the man who was starting to lose sight of the small detail, the oversights that could trip them up and bring them all crashing down.

"And we would have," Chandra Nehru had admitted, trying to look sincere in his false sorrow. "But she was about to betray you, Aasim – betray *us*. I could not allow that to happen."

Aasim blinked back his rising tears, aware that he was still standing in the public spotlight. Even now, some five days since her death, Samira's shade still haunted him, the Gods mocking him for his neglect, seduced by his thirst and hunger for power. The thought that she would have turned so readily against him, when he thought she had been so meek, so loyal, was a deeper cut than the actual shock of her loss.

What have I become? Aasim Rana had asked himself, ever since her death.

His wife, his dear, loyal wife had sensed the change in her husband, and eager to avoid her interrogations, Aasim had not been home for three nights. He had taken spare clothes and some bedding from their house whilst she was out shopping, and had not been home since, had avoided her calls from that moment.

Chandra Nehru had told him to stay strong, to remain focussed on the task at hand, but the news that the tiger had not been captured, that the survivors of the crash had been the ones to thwart their plans, had brought his resolve crashing down about him.

There would be no further money to line and fill their political war chest; there was no way now that the Americans could be kept at bay.

Further news that Mister Hamid had been killed, and that the survivors of the crashed jet had been rescued by an undiscovered covert team, had meant heated meetings with the Prime Minister and the members of those he described as his *Inner Circle*, that included the Minister of Home affairs, the Finance Secretary and the Chief Election Commissioner.

Clearly, Chandra Nehru had told them, the Americans had taken matters into their own hands. Somehow, though the facts remained unclear, the survivors had escaped and had managed to get word out of their survival. The Gods, in their wisdom had decreed it so, and so they would all have to accept their wishes, would have to find a way to avoid their wrath and the storms that whispered menacingly at them from the darkening horizon.

"But what about the jet?" Aasim had asked, incredulous that the Prime Minister did not seem the least bit perturbed.

"What about it?" Nehru had sneered. "It will be hard for them to throw accusations at us, when they, too, have contravened international law by operating illegally on our beloved soil. We, too, would have a case to bring to any international tribunal."

"But, but?" the Finance Secretary Ajay Joshi had spluttered over his cold cup of tea, searching around the room for support.

The other members of the Inner Circle had looked to

their drinks, however, as Chandra Nehru scowled, his face twisting with anger. "We will start the dialogue with them and give them what they want. We will announce that the jet has been found and that we will allow them access to the wreckage to retrieve any bodies. We will give them *anything* that they need."

"And as for the survivors?" the Minister of Home Affairs, Rajiv Sharma had asked the Prime Minister.

"They will play their part, I am sure," Nehru had responded confidently, though he would not shine any further light on his assurances.

Aasim Rana snapped his thoughts back to the present. In two days' time the news would be leaked that the jet, which had been reported missing over a week ago but had been kept from the public because of where it had potentially crashed, had been found. The Americans, so far, were maintaining a dignified impasse, thankful of the cooperation and grateful of their *respected friends'* assistance with the matter.

Aasim licked his dry lips, disgusted at the taste of his own corruption. He was so lost in his own self-loathing, that he did not hear, at first, the hearty applause as the press conference came to a close.

"And now, as both myself and Miss Chand Sani adjourn inside for further questions, I would place you in the care of our most dutiful First Secretary, Aasim Rana, who I am afraid to say has some sad news to impart to you."

Hearing his own name, Aasim blinked and somehow found a smile, his eyes meeting briefly with Chandra Nehru.

It had been decided that the First Secretary would rightly be the one to confirm the rumours and report on the facts of the woman who had been murdered in the city recently.

Aasim thanked the Prime Minister, politely waiting for him and his guest to depart. When he turned back to address the crowd, he could already see that some of the journalists were putting away their pads and pens, that some of them were starting to leave. He did not have a reputation, he knew, for commanding attention, for courting the headlines.

Aasim cleared his throat.

"Thank you, Prime Minister Nehru," he said, his voice quiet. He stared out at the faces, his heart tight, gripped by his sadness. Studying the front line of reporters, he could not see Narinda Singh in their ranks, and her absence since Samira's murder, and the subsequent warning that she had been given, was of great concern. *Where was she?*

"It is with great regret on such a joyful day, and with much sorrow, that I can confirm to you that which many of you have already suspected," Aasim continued, his voice gaining some weight. "Five days ago, a young woman was murdered in the city, brutally attacked in view of many bystanders. It is, with even heavier sorrow, that I must tell you today that the woman killed was my own personal aide, Samira Jethwani."

The pads were coming back out, and those still loitering in their escape within earshot, turned back hastily.

"At this time, I would ask you that you give both her family and my office the privacy that we need in this troubling time. Be assured that investigations are ongoing and every effort is being made to find the culprit responsible for this hideous... for this most... this..."

Aasim Rana fell silent, looking at the sea of faces, noting the heads that turned questioningly to one another.

With his palms pressed angrily into the podium, the First Secretary stared down at his shaking hands, imagining the blood that was staining them.

He looked up, his thin face fixed into a stern mask. When he spoke, it was barely, at first, above a whisper.

"Greatness is a matter of perspective," he began, closing his eyes. "And when I came to office two years ago, I believed that I could make a difference. In my own heart, I truly thought that I could bring about change.

But I was wrong, as so many before me have also been, and my perspective was misguided. I now know that there cannot be change, there will never be any change until the cancerous corruption of our political system has been cut out. In my own, misguided quest, I have failed, and I have dishonoured the Gods and the people of Mother India by becoming seduced by the very thing I have striven to eradicate. And now, not only do I have the burden of my own actions to bear, I also have the blood of my colleague staining my hands."

Aasim swallowed, staring out at the wall of stunned silence that greeted him. Before the last of the power he would ever wield in his life waned, he continued.

"In a bid to cement the power we have, there are those within our government who have sought to strengthen that seat by filling the dark coffers of our office with the money we will need to bribe and keep a hold of it, no matter the cost. I may well not survive this path to see justice done, but I can, in my own shame, set aflame the cleansing torch you will need to burn out the corruption that stains our great nation. On this day of celebration, in honour of our Great Father's memory, let us, together, begin to right these wrongs."

Chandra Nehru and Leela Chand Sani were just settling down for their first television interview when the door to the reading room burst inwards and he was summoned hastily out into the hallway beyond.

"What is it?" Nehru hissed, irritated beyond irritation at the intrusion.

"Aasim," the Finance Minister gasped, his skin paling visibly. "We have to stop him, he is–"

With his eyes widening, the Prime Minister threw the man aside, racing for the entrance to the Sansad Bhavan. He could see the podium Aasim stood at, looming large as he addressed the tide of journalists, all surging towards him for a clearer view.

As he ran desperately towards the daylight outside, Chandra Nehru began to hear what his First Secretary was saying to the world and he came to an abrupt, terrified stop, barely registering the violent flashes of light that turned towards the shadows where he stood.

As the deadly sights of a hundred media rifles trained themselves upon him and his fear took control, the Prime Minister wondered how it had come to pass that the conviction of one man had just changed the fate of so many people and, perhaps, the course of history itself.

Epilogue – Part One

Jon Galnia closed his eyes, allowing the beautiful chords and strings of the music to sweep him away from his troubles. Sitting back in his favourite antique chair, he crossed one leg over the other and rested the half-drained glass of single malt on his knee.

Home! Losing himself to the music, Jon sighed, allowing his mind to relax for a time. Alone in the house now, except for the bodyguards stationed on the gate outside, he had found some time to himself, the first real time in the two weeks since his joyful return home. Maria and Gio were out for a few hours, shopping for Jon's *secret* birthday present. Well, secret in the fact that Gio had already told his father what he was going to buy him, but had kept it from his mother.

Jon grinned, drifting away happily for a time. The reunion with his wife and child still left him an emotional wreck, and he thanked God, every second he could, for his chance to see them again. He allowed Ludovico Einaudi's haunting music to fill his thoughts for a time, before the darker side of his nature took a hold again.

His homecoming had been one shrouded in secrecy. Flown from India under the tightest security, Jon and Sara had escaped the furore that was sweeping the country under the cover of night, arriving back on U.S. soil before anyone had even noticed they were gone.

The First Secretary's press conference was still trending just about everywhere, filling every channel and column inch across the globe. Since the high-profile arrests in the Indian government had started, Jon had been following events with keen interest, wondering how it would all play out, desperate to know if he would be able to stay out of the spotlight and avoid the Feds' scheduled questioning.

So far, he had. All of the survivors had. With the revelation about the crash, of the events that had happened in Central India made public, the internet was aflame with the news.

Even then, with the Prime Minister and half of his cabinet behind bars, the truth had been hidden by both the Americans and the Indians, each hoping that the silence of what had really occurred could be buried, despite the public testimony of Aasim Rana.

The shamed First Secretary of India was under constant protection, those trying to bring a case against Chandra Nehru fearful that Rana would not survive long enough to bring down the corrupt Prime Minister. Rumours were abound that Chandra Nehru was fighting back from his cell, even now, afforded all the luxuries of his station from prison, still trying to buy his way out of trouble.

When the news was leaked to the Indian Press four days after the high-profile arrests, that a tiger had been seen alive in Bandhavgarh National Park, and that Chandra Nehru had been trying to sell the great cat to the highest bidder, the internet exploded with conspiracy theories, as everyone, except the parties involved, did their best to fill in the blanks.

There was even the suggestion that Jon himself, now that he had been named as one of the survivors, had been trying to seize the tiger, that he had been the one working with the Indians to capture the beast. It was even being touted around that the crash had been faked, and that the information was scarce because of this.

Jon chuckled. *I wish I had thought of that...*

Shaking his head, Jon sipped his single malt. He hadn't said a word, and to the best of his knowledge, neither had the other survivors. With a smile, Jon raised his glass and toasted Robert, thinking fondly of his former pilot, who had stayed on in India for another week to wait for his co-pilot's body to be repatriated.

Jon's instincts told him that Robert had been the one to leak the news of the tiger. Either that or the press swarming around Delhi must have squeezed it out of him... If it was him who leaked the news, whilst still managing to keep the mercenaries involvement out of the tale, it had far-reaching consequences. Since the revelation about the tiger, almost all of the conservation and wildlife organisations around the world had become involved in the race to protect the 'Last Tiger'.

Thousands of individuals had even flown across the globe to form a human barrier around the National Park, keeping a watchful eye on those who would seek greed over a species' survival. Jon's tiger was even trending on Twitter.

#Saveher

Before he had left Delhi, Jon had also met with Thomas Miller at the U.S. Embassy. From their discussions, it soon became clear that the truth was being swept aside, that both nations could not point fingers at one another now that Aasim Rana had carried forth the torch of justice.

As a favour to Jon, Miller had arranged for him to meet with Narinda Singh before she left the embassy to sacrifice her own safety for the truth. Jon was silently grateful, as the meeting helped to shed more light on what the hell had been going on, and further muddy the waters of his involvement, pointing the journalist, strictly off the record, in the direction of the man he now knew to be called *Mister Hamid*.

"In my opinion," the journalist had told him, "Chandra Nehru recruited Aasim Rana because he was not a political force. Nobody would ever suspect his involvement. Before he faces justice, I believe Nehru will sacrifice Rana, and that, despite his courage, the First Secretary will be the one to take the blame for this. I sincerely believe the Prime Minister hired Rana for the eventuality that one day he might need him for this very purpose."

Probably true, Jon had thought at the time. If he were in Nehru's shoes, he would do the same.

Jon had been impressed with the woman's spirit, in fact, he was pretty glad she wasn't living in the U.S. and trying to expose him.

Two weeks later, and the feisty journalist was spearheading the charge for truth, brazenly back in the public arena, not afraid to wield her words of justice as she came to the aid of the disgraced First Secretary, championing his bravery and his selfless sacrifice.

She was, at this time, shouting loudly, but finding that she had very little support in her sympathy for Aasim Rana.

Opening his eyes, Jon looked about his study, sighing happily. It was his favourite part of the house, a place to think, to reflect, to escape what needed to be done.

Jon scowled as he thought of Paolo Romano, of the inadvertent slip that had led him to think his best friend knew more about the crash than he had let on. Upon their reunion, it was as if nothing had happened, that the crash was just a minor lump in the road. If Paolo thought for a moment that Jon harboured any suspicions, he didn't show it.

Jon picked up the pistol, resting on the arm of the chair and studied it. There was a great deal of work to do, and whilst he did it, he would need to watch his back. Knowing that from now on he only had three people in the world he could trust, left him on edge.

He had to be careful, and he had to keep his circle of trust tight if he was going to get to the bottom of why Paolo would want to betray him. Their blood was thicker than any hereditary bond and it scarred him deeply.

Jon thought of Maria and wondered suddenly if he already had the answer.

The antique phone on the stand across from him rang and Jon commanded Cortana to mute the music. Irritated at the interruption to his private time, Jon extricated himself from his chair and hobbled over to it. His wounds were healing, but his body hadn't been told about it yet.

If it's another reporter, I am going to lose it, Jon thought, as he picked up the receiver and snapped into it.

"*You have caused us a great deal of trouble, Mr. Galnia,*" a voice said evenly. "*Your continuing silence affords you our temporary grace, but you should know this, when the time is right, you will have to pay for your interference.*"

"I wasn't there, did you hear me?" Jon snarled. He couldn't place the accent, but it was familiar. Angered, but not concerned they had his number, Jon paced about the study.

"If you come near me, come near my family, the world will hear about what you were up to, what you did. You may have lost the battle, but I have kept my silence, so think on that before you start a war with me."

The line went dead.

Slamming the receiver down, Jon hobbled to the

window, staring out at the fading sun.

If he thought having survived the crash and what had followed was the end of his problems, he was seriously deluding himself. It was starting to feel like he had paid a heavy price for escaping the Reaper this time, and it would be a while before he came to realise the size of his debt.

Sighing, Jon went in search of his whisky. He took a few calming breaths and sips from his tumbler as he looked at the ornate knife he had on display. It was Rashim's knife, the old weapon he had pleaded he be allowed to keep.

Jon raised his glass, thinking sadly of his friend, before falling back onto his chair.

He had many battles to fight, but those were battles for another day. For now, he was alive, and he was home again with his wife and son.

And that was priceless, worth more than anything he would ever come to own.

Part Two
Three Months Later

The jungle was silent as the tiger slipped into the sunlight that knifed through the canopy overhead and warmed her memory of the bitterly cold night. It was quiet now, and the great cat sniffed the air, seeking tell of those who were still looking for her.

Sensing no danger, the tiger swung her huge head about. Her whiskers flickered in the sun as she curled her lips impatiently and growled. Turning, she padded away into the jungle.

Moments later, her three cubs bounded into the open, and hurried playfully after her.

The End

About the Author

Since reading The Lord of the Rings at an early age, and later, the works of his favourite author, David Gemmell, Anthony has been inspired to write his own stories.

When he is not forging tales and filling blank pages, Anthony spends his time working in his local library, reading, board gaming and enjoying adventures of his own.

Anthony lives in Wales with his wife, Amy, and their cat, Mertle.

He is currently working on 'Rise of Eagles,' his fifth novel.

You can keep up-to-date with his news here: -

Website: http://anthonylavisher.com

Twitter: @alavisher

Facebook: www.facebook.com/lavisherauthor

Printed in Great Britain
by Amazon